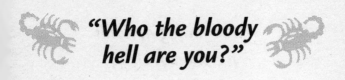

"Who the bloody hell are you?"

. . . Dowler asked.

Scorpion glanced at the remaining side mirror. There was only one truck still behind them on the road and it was at least a couple of hundred meters back. For the moment they were keeping their distance, possibly communicating to others to block the road somewhere up ahead.

. . . Even if they made the border, whatever he had come to Africa for, whatever he might have fantasized about with Sandrine, was over, Scorpion thought. CNN, al Jazeera, and the rest of the media would be over this like flies on garbage. He couldn't let them put him on television or even know he existed. He wouldn't even be able to say goodbye. He'd never see her again . . .

But he was wrong. Something that was happening at that very moment in a leafy neighborhood in a city on another continent was about to change everything, including his decision never to do another mission.

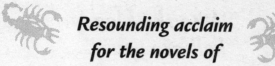

Resounding acclaim for the novels of

ANDREW KAPLAN

By Andrew Kaplan

SCORPION DECEPTION
SCORPION WINTER
SCORPION BETRAYAL
WAR OF THE RAVEN
DRAGONFIRE
SCORPION
HOUR OF THE ASSASSINS

ANDREW KAPLAN

SCORPION DECEPTION

HARPER

An Imprint of HarperCollins*Publishers*

HARPER

An Imprint of HarperCollins*Publishers*
10 East 53rd Street
New York, New York 10022-5299

Copyright © 2013 by Andrew Kaplan
ISBN 978-0-06-221965-7

First Harper premium printing: June 2013

10 9 8 7 6 5 4 3 2 1

For my late mother and father,
Rose and Joseph Kaplan.
May their memory be for a blessing.

"All war is deception."
—Sun Tzu

SCORPION
DECEPTION

 **PROLOGUE**

Khorramshahr, Iran
1986

The boy was next in line to be shot. He was thin, dark-haired, about seven, small for his age. He was younger than the other boys, most of them teen-age Basiji, volunteers for the front. They had been rounded up from schools and playgrounds across Iran to be *shahidan*. Martyrs. There weren't enough guns or ammunition for the Iranian forces fighting the Iraqis. The Basiji boys were sent unarmed to clear the minefields with their bodies ahead of the human wave attacks of Iranian Army and Pasdaran Revolutionary Guard soldiers. "Saddam Hussein has artillery; Iran has men," the ayatollahs said.

But the boys lined up were those who had pan-icked under enemy fire or ran when the first mine exploded. They had been brought to a warehouse parking lot near the port to be executed for cow-ardice. The warehouse's brick wall and the concrete pavement in front of it were stained red and pock-marked by bullets.

The executions had gone on for almost an hour

when it became the boy's turn. His small size caught the eye of the Pasdaran commander's wife, Zeeba. In her black chador she was a common figure at these executions. Among the Baradaran of the Revolutionary Guard in Khorramshahr, the woman Zeeba was called "Mother Death." It was said she had more steel for the Revolution in her than any man.

"What's that one doing there? He's too little for a *shahid*," she said.

Her husband checked his clipboard.

"He's a Yahud." A Jew. "From Isfahan."

There had been a recent execution of Jews, Zionist spies for Israel, in Isfahan. No doubt the boy's family had been caught up in it, she thought. What a pity. Such a good-looking little boy with beautiful brown eyes. Something in his eyes made her uncomfortable. They reminded her of her own son, Rahim. Two Pasdaran guards grabbed the boy and marched him toward the wall. There were some forty bodies stacked like wood. They were beginning to stink in the hot sun.

Just then, the sirens sounded, followed by the high-pitched sound of an incoming Iraqi shell.

"Incoming! Take cover!" someone screamed, immediately followed by an explosion in the street. Everyone started running.

There was a bomb shelter in the port, but there wasn't time to reach it. As Zeeba ran for cover next to the wall, she heard the whistle of a shell sounding like it was coming right down on top of her. *"Allahu akhbar!"* God is great! It was all she had time to think or pray before it exploded in the parking area, killing two of the prisoners and scattering the rest.

The force of the blast knocked her off her feet. She could smell the explosive and feel its hot wind on her skin. She got up and started toward the warehouse. As she did so, the little boy ran into her.

She held him. He didn't try to get away. Just looked up at her with those brown eyes. At that moment she did something she was never able to explain to herself. Perhaps because the shell had come so close and she'd almost just died. Or because before the Revolution, her best friend in school, Fareeza, had been Jewish. She grabbed the boy's arm and began running out of the parking area with him. Out of the corner of her eye she could see her husband looking strangely at her. She continued running.

In the street, people were lying on the pavement, some wounded, others with their arms over their heads. Still others ran to get inside the warehouse. A shell screamed overhead and exploded near a building on the street leading to the port. Pieces of the building rained down around them, peppering the street with shrapnel. Zeeba hit the ground, pulling the boy down with her. She could feel him trembling against her as fragments of the building splattered around them. They lay in the street waiting for the next shell to blast them into nothingness. Was what she was doing a sin? she wondered.

Another shell exploded down toward the Bulwar Road near the harbor. As a woman, she did not know the Quran as a good Muslim should, but she seemed to remember something about the Prophet of Allah, peace be upon him, saying that it was good to help orphans. She had heard about the executions in Isfahan. Two Jewish women had been raped over a hundred times before they were killed. The men, those Zionist *jasoosa*, had been chained between trucks and literally pulled to pieces. She looked at the boy. Was it possible he had witnessed such things?

O Allah, you demand much, she thought, wondering if she should just walk away. If she brought the boy back to the warehouse or left him here, he would surely die. A shell exploded far up the street. A second shell exploded louder and closer, less than a hundred meters away. The next one would come down right on top of them. She buried her head in her arms, certain she was about to die, the boy next to her on the pavement. She waited, every nerve screaming, unable to breathe.

Nothing happened.

The shelling had stopped. Zeeba looked up. People were starting to get off the ground. She stood and pulled the boy up with her. What should she do? She didn't even know why she had saved him. What had possessed her? What would she tell her husband? It was just that he looked so little standing there, not much bigger than Rahim.

She knew she had to do something. People were walking, running, some looking anxiously to the west, toward the Iraqi front. The shelling might start again any minute. She took the boy's hand and began walking, remembering that before the Revolution there had been a synagogue a few blocks from here. She walked quickly, pulling the boy with her.

"What is your name?" she asked him.

He looked at her but didn't answer. Was he dumb? she wondered. Traumatized? He wasn't retarded.

His eyes were too intelligent for that. Perhaps for Allah, his name didn't matter.

She turned the corner and saw the old synagogue. It looked battered, ruined. All the buildings in the city were scarred, but this one was barely standing, more a ruin than a building. There were holes in the facade and roof, and deep scars gouged by bullets and shrapnel during the fighting. Someone had painted *Marg bar Esra'il*, Death to Israel, on the door. She knocked and waited.

No one answered. She knocked again. And again.

A small door in the building next to the synagogue opened. It looked like a shop where they had stopped selling anything a long time ago. A gray-haired man stepped out. He wore a tattered suit jacket and a *kipa* on his head.

"*Salam*. May I help you, *khanoom*?" the man said.

"Here," she said, shoving the boy at him. "He's a Yahud, from Isfahan. If you don't take him, he'll be executed."

The man looked at her. The boy looked at neither of them. He said nothing. Zeeba turned and walked away. She kept waiting for the boy or the man to call after her, but there was only the scrape of her shoes on the pavement and the sun casting her shadow ahead of her as she walked. When she reached the corner, she looked back. The street was empty. The Jews, she thought. They take care of their own. Something we could learn from them.

She never saw the boy again.

It took the Jews two weeks to move the boy, whom they named Davood, from Khorramshahr to Tabriz.

With the help of Kurdish smugglers, they got him over the mountains to Mosul in Kurdish Iraq and from there to Turkey. In Diyarbakir, a local Jewish businessman provided the boy with false papers that got him on a flight from Istanbul to Tel Aviv.

The boy arrived alone at two in the morning at Ben Gurion Airport in Israel. He was the last one off the plane. By the time he walked out, the other passengers had left the gate area. The only one there to meet him was a heavyset middle-aged Iranian Jew, Shlomo, from the Sochnut, the Jewish Agency.

When Shlomo saw him standing all alone in the terminal, in shorts and a T-shirt, holding nothing but the papers they had given him, he knelt and put his hands on the boy's shoulders.

"You're in Israel," he said in Farsi. "You're safe now."

For the first time since he had watched his parents murdered in Isfahan, the boy spoke.

"I don't want to be safe," he said.

CHAPTER ONE

Lower Shabelle Region,
Somalia, The Present

"Kata'lahu." You kill him, Khalaf said to the American in Arabic.

Khalaf stood behind Dowler, his long razor-sharp *belawa* knife at the British aid worker's throat. Dowler, on his knees in the sand, hands tied behind him, face pockmarked with cigarette burns, had the dazed look—part fear, part sheer disbelief—that comes in the final seconds when a person realizes he is about to die.

You stupid twit, the American code-named Scorpion thought.

"No. You want him dead, do it yourself," Scorpion replied in Fusha; standard Arabic.

"Kill him or we kill you," Khalaf growled, motioning to one of his Al-Shabaab militiamen. The man put the muzzle of his AK-47 to Scorpion's head, his finger on the trigger.

"I thought we were having *shah hawaash*," Scorpion said, implying that they still had unfinished business. He gestured at the spread of tea, bread, and dates on the blanket under the shade of a plastic tarp a few feet away. "The tea is still hot," he added, reminding Khalaf of the Somali courtesy due a guest.

"Why not?" Khalaf said, kicking Dowler down to the sand.

Khalaf came over and sat on the ground beneath the tarp. Scorpion sat cross-legged at an angle to him, facing two of Khalaf's militiamen, their faces hidden behind red-checked keffiyeh scarves, fingers on the trigger guards of their AK-47s. Scorpion kept his hand on his leg near the Glock 28 he had in a tear-away ankle holster hidden under his jeans.

They sipped the cardamom and cinnamon flavored tea in thimble-sized metal cups. The day was hot, with only the faintest hint of a breeze stirring dust devils on the savannah; featureless but for the dry thorn scrub and, in the distance, a stunted acacia tree. It hadn't rained in this part of Somalia in six years.

As was the custom, Scorpion smacked his lips loudly in appreciation.

"You are taking the children to Dadaab?" Khalaf gestured at the Toyota pickup truck crammed with children stacked like cordwood, broiling in the hot African sun. Scorpion had bought the truck in Nairobi only a week earlier, from a dealer on South-B Road, next to the hospital. He had been bringing the children across the border to the refugee camp at Dadaab, in Kenya, when Khalaf's Al-Shabaab militiamen stopped him at a roadblock.

"*Inshallah*," Scorpion said. God willing. "If it is permitted." Reaching into his backpack, he pulled out a plastic bag bulging with *qat*. He gestured for them to take it. As soon as he did, he realized it was a mistake. The eyes of the three men stayed riveted on his backpack.

Khalaf looked up at the American, and for a moment the two men studied each other. Sheikh Mukhtar Ali Khalaf was a thin coffee-colored man in his fifties. He wore a *ma'awis*, a Somali-style sarong, and on his head a *koofiyud* cap, embroidered, Scorpion noted, with the colors and pattern of a sheikh of the powerful Dubil tribe. He was notorious. Across the Lower Shabelle there were stories of beheadings, torture with power drills, and mass graves. Those who had met Khalaf and lived to tell the tale considered him a homicidal maniac. No doubt Dowler, on his knees in the sand, might have something to say about that.

Khalaf nodded, and soon they were all chewing the mildly narcotic leaves that even more than tea was the Somali national habit. The two men with the AK-47s pulled down the scarves covering their faces and one of them almost smiled. We're bonding, old buddies, Scorpion thought, chewing the green-tasting leaves like a teenager with a wad of gum.

"The toll for the children is two hundred," Khalaf said.

"Shillings?" Scorpion asked. Two hundred Somali shillings was about twelve cents American. Not a real number, but a way to start the bargaining.

Khalaf laughed and the soldiers smiled, showing mouths with rotten yellow teeth caked green with chewed *qat*.

"Two hundred dollars American," Khalaf said. "Apiece."

"My elder brother makes a joke." Scorpion grimaced, doing the arithmetic in his head. Sixteen kids in the truck. All that were still alive out of the twenty-four at the school he had gone into Somalia to get; $3,200. "One hundred," he said.

"Two," Khalaf said, impatience in his voice. Scorpion wasn't sure if it was Khalaf's craziness, the *qat* making him more aggressive, or both. But he was right at the edge. "Plus a thousand for you and the truck."

"I'll need money to bribe the border guards," Scorpion said.

"Or I kill you now and take everything in your *klee'asa*," Khalaf said, indicating the backpack. Scorpion watched the two men finger the triggers of the AK-47s.

"*Maashi. Mafi mushkila.*" Okay. No problem, Scorpion agreed, smiling.

Khalaf stood up.

It was just rotten luck he had run into the roadblock on the way from Baidoa to the border, Scorpion thought, getting up. Worse still for Dowler, captured a few days earlier. Dowler had been fool enough to try to bring food supplies to Mogadishu without first bribing the tribal leaders. Now Dowler was a complication. If he tried to save the British aid worker, ten-to-one they'd kill them both. And Scorpion knew if he died, the children would die. Some of them were barely clinging to life as it was.

Time to decide. He took a deep breath, calculating. It would take him 2.5 seconds to pull up his jeans leg and fire the Glock from his calf holster. Plus at least two seconds to deal with Khalaf and one of the soldiers. No good. Even if the remaining soldier's reaction time was slow, it would take him at most two to three seconds to bring the AK-47 into line and shoot.

It wasn't going to work.

Still, accuracy wasn't the AK's long suit. Despite its small size, the Glock 28 fired a .380 auto bullet with low recoil characteristics. No problem there. He glanced toward the Toyota pickup. It was a good sixty meters away. A decent NCAA running back could do it in under eight seconds. It would take him at least ten or eleven. But what about Dowler? In his condition, how fast could he run? Khalaf had close to a hundred Al-Shabaab soldiers armed to the teeth all around the area.

Don't be stupid, he told himself. It was Dowler or the children. He couldn't save both.

If not for Sandrine, he wouldn't have gone into Somalia in the first place.

Two days earlier. The small boy lay on his side, barely breathing. They were in the hospital tent, crowded with patients, in the Ifo refugee camp in Dadaab, Kenya. The Frenchwoman, Dr. Sandrine Delange, checked the boy's breathing, heartbeat, and temperature, then adjusted the drip feeding into his tiny arm.

"It's no good. He'll die today," she said in English to Scorpion.

"Are you sure?" he asked.

"Look at his upper arm. Less than 115 millimeters circumference. Smaller than a golf ball. She got him here too late," indicating the child's mother, squatting beside the bed, looking up at the white woman doctor. "The child has pneumonia and gastroenteritis brought on by severe malnutrition. It affects the immune system like AIDS. His little body has nothing to fight the infection with."

She patted the mother's shoulder. Scorpion couldn't take his eyes off her. Slim, beautiful, straight chestnut-brown hair carelessly tied back, and almond-shaped eyes, like no one he had ever seen; multicolored, with gold around the pupils, surrounded by emerald green and an outer ring of pure blue. Lion's eyes, he thought of them, because of the gold.

"How do you do this?" he asked as they walked to the next bed.

"How not?" brushing a wisp of hair out of her eyes. "Besides, there are always others. Thousands. And you, David? What are you running away from?" she asked. Scorpion was using the cover name, David Cheyne, an American from Los Angeles.

"What makes you think I'm running away?" he said, thinking in an odd way that Shaefer, the CIA station chief in Bucharest and his closest friend in U.S. intelligence, had implied the same thing when he had called him from Rome before coming to Africa. He and Shaefer had history together; the only two survivors of a Taliban ambush at FOBE, Forward Operating Base Echo, in North Waziristan.

"Where are you?" Shaefer had asked.

"Not Herzliya," he said, naming the suburb north of Tel Aviv where the Israeli Mossad had its head-quarters, meaning he had decided not to take on the mission the Israelis and the CIA had wanted him to. As an independent operative, a gun for hire, he had the option. But he didn't want another mission. Not after Ukraine, he thought. "I'm done."

"It's not that simple. You can't just walk away," Shaefer had said.

"I know," he said.

"What will you do?"

"Get clean," he said, ending the call and imme-diately contacting a private arms dealer he knew in Luxembourg, to make sure he was equipped in case someone came after him in Africa.

"People think they come to Africa to do good. But," Sandrine, the French woman doctor said, slid-ing into French, "*tout le monde ici est aussi fuyant.*" Everyone here is also running away.

She had been surprised that this athletic-looking American with the strange gray eyes, a scar over one of them, spoke French. But then, everything about him was a mystery. He had just suddenly ap-peared at the camp. When asked, he wouldn't talk about himself. But the truck and the medicines he had brought with him had been a godsend.

"Including you?" he asked. It was impossible, he told himself. What you're feeling for her isn't real. It's too soon. A rebound after having to leave Iryna behind in Kiev. Except he knew better.

"Of course me. Why do you think I asked?"

A Somali woman in a vivid Van Gogh blue and yellow *direh* robe came by then and told them about the children trapped and starving in a school across the border in Baidoa.

Later, outside the MPLM tent, passing around what Cowell, the red-headed Scot, said was his last bottle of Glenlivet, Moreau, the handsome French surgeon, a craggy Louis Jourdan with a three-day stubble, had said: "It's *shonde* about those kids in Baidoa," using the Swahili word for shit.

"A few of us could go. Bring them here," Jennifer, the Canadian nurse, said.

"Don't be bloody daft," Cowell said. "There's fighting all over there. You'd have to go through two sets of front lines. Twice! Going and coming, plus tribal pirates, assorted bandits, and Al-Shabaab all over the fucking place. It'd be bloody suicide."

"So we do nothing," Sandrine said, her profile outlined in fire by the last rays of the setting sun.

"Too bloody true. They're buggered," Cowell said. "Poor little sods."

That's when Scorpion understood why he had come to Africa and what he was going to do. He had skills they didn't have. Skills honed in his youth in the Arabian desert, in the U.S. Army Rangers and Delta Force in Iraq and Afghanistan, and as a highly trained operative in the CIA. After an assassination operation, he had left the CIA to work as a freelance agent known only to certain top echelons within the intelligence community. With a little luck—no, be honest, a lot of luck—he might get through where they couldn't.

That night, Sandrine came to his tent in the CARE compound. He started to say something, but she put her finger to his lips. She pushed him back on the cot and got on top of him, kissing his face and lips, then working her way down his body, tugging at his undershorts, followed by the brief fumble to put on protection.

It's impossible, he thought, even as her lips grazed him. He had seen the way the men all looked at her. There was a rumor she had turned down a marriage proposal from one of the richest men in France. Earlier that day, Moreau had caught him looking at her and told him, "Don't even think about it. Many have tried. She is *d'un abord difficile*." Unapproachable.

The feel of her was unbelievable. Smoother than any silk. She was like a drug. The two of them moving together on the creaking cot like the rhythm of the sea.

Afterward, pulling on her clothes in the dark, she said, "Don't think this means anything, because it doesn't."

"Why me?"

"Who should it be? Moreau, who thinks he's so handsome, and because he doesn't wear a wedding ring thinks I don't know he has a wife and two kids in Neuilly-sur-Seine? Or Cowell, who'd fuck a monkey if it would let him? God, men are idiots."

"True," he said. "But why me?"

"I know how they look at me. A not-so-bad-looking white woman in Africa . . ." She shrugged. "It's not about me." Sitting on the edge of the cot, she brushed a lock of hair out of his eyes. "Maybe it's the scar over your eye. I don't know." She stood up. "Don't ask women to explain themselves. Half the time even we don't know why we do things."

"Don't," he said.

"Don't what?"

"Don't bullshit," he said. "It insults both of us. Just tell me the truth. Why me?"

She looked at him as if seeing him for the first time. She took in his lean, muscled torso, dark bed-tousled hair, the scars on his arms and ribs. His stillness.

"I don't want this talked about," she said. "You seem the type who can keep a secret."

He had to smile to himself. Given that barely six weeks earlier he'd been lying naked and tortured in a freezing cell in Ukraine waiting for them to put a bullet in the back of his head, there was more than a little truth to that.

She turned then stopped as she lifted the tent flap and peered out into the darkness.

"I'll see you in the morning?" she asked.

"I'll be gone. I have some things I have to do," making a mental checklist of what he would need to get through to Baidoa.

"I was right. You are running away," she said. For an instant her silhouette was framed against the stars, and then she was gone.

"No, walking away," he said aloud to himself.

But nothing prepared him for Baidoa. There was fighting around the city, which was held by Al-Shabaab of the Mirifle tribe, and he had to bribe his way through two front lines, African Union troops and Al-Shabaab's, to get into the city. The school was a one-story concrete building on a dirt street in the hilly Isha district, which, like most of the buildings in this part of the city, was shot full of holes, the concrete crumbling like moldy cheese.

Around the building were more than a dozen bodies, women, children, a barefoot soldier, bloated and discolored in the sun. The stench was indescribable. It looked like one of the women had been raped before she was killed, her *direh* pulled up around her neck, a dried bloodstain between her naked legs splayed wide. Scorpion took a moment and pulled the *direh* down to cover her.

Inside the school the smell was even worse. Boys from ages three to about ten or eleven lay on the concrete floor in a large room, some stirring, most still. They were pitifully thin, covered with fecal matter, some in pools of diarrhea and urine. Others were clearly dead. The walls were scarred by bullets and political slogans spray-painted in Arabic that read: "Death to the African Union!"

A boy in shorts and bare feet, about ten, came up to him, holding an empty plastic bowl.

"*Ma'a*," the boy said. Water.

"I'll bring some," Scorpion replied in Arabic. "What's your name?"

"Ghedi," the boy said, reaching out to touch the white man's hand as if to make sure he was real. Several of the other boys started to stir. One crawled toward Scorpion, who went to a hallway that led to a crude kitchen and to the sink. In it, a small lizard the size of his hand, with a flat multispiked tail, scuttled away as he approached. He turned the tap but nothing came out. He felt a tug on his sleeve. The boy, Ghedi, looked up at him.

"Where are the girls?" Scorpion asked.

The boy pointed to a doorway. Scorpion went

through the doorway to another room, lit by a ray of sunlight through a hole in the ceiling. It was filled with girls in bright blue *direhs*, some stretched out and covered in filth, others sitting on the floor. School uniforms, Scorpion thought as they began to crowd around him like chicks around a mother hen.

"Follow me," he told them, leading them through the boys' room and outside. Once there, he grabbed two handfuls of plastic water jugs from the truck.

"You mustn't overfeed starving children. Especially at first," Sandrine had cautioned him on his first day in the camp in the triage area. "Their metabolic system is broken. Too much protein will damage the liver even more, possibly irreparably. Just a moderate amount of water, preferably with electrolytes, and depending on the size of the child, a single Plumpy'nut bar. *Pas plus*." No more. "Just to hold them till we can take care of them."

He spent the next few hours feeding them and using some of the precious water in the plastic jugs to clean them up as best he could and get them settled on a blanket under a plastic tarp awning tied to four poles he rigged up at the corners of the Toyota truck bed. Out of the twenty-four orphan children, who were supposed to have been trapped in the school, only sixteen were still alive. The boy, Ghedi, helped him organize them, and one of the older girls, a pretty little thing with a shy smile named Nadifa, helped him clean up the girls.

The hell of it was he had almost pulled it off. Just another forty kilometers or so to the crossroads at Bilis Qooqaan and then a straight run on paved road of maybe ninety klicks to the Kenyan border. Except for the lousy luck of the roadblock and that idiot, Dowler, Scorpion thought as he looked into the madness-filled eyes of Sheikh Khalaf.

Khalaf pulled Dowler up by his hair to a kneeling position, the *belawa* gleaming in the sun. He tossed the knife at Scorpion's feet.

"*Yallah.* You do it. Cut his head off," Khalaf said.

"I'm sure there's someone who would pay a lot of money for the Eenglizi," Scorpion said, meaning Dowler. "Let me try."

"Look at his face. The cigarette marks. The Western media, al Jazeera, would say bad things about us." Khalaf made a hand gesture like tossing something away that in Somalia means no. "He has to die."

"Then do it yourself," Scorpion growled, thinking, Go to hell, you insane son of a bitch.

"No, you do it," Khalaf said, looking at him strangely. "Unless you want to join him." The two militiamen shifted their stance, weapons trained on Scorpion. "I take the children. Two of the boys are old enough to be soldiers. The rest . . ." He shrugged. "As for the girls, no reason for them to still be virgins before they die."

He's lying, Scorpion decided. He's not going to leave me alive as a witness, or the children, having noted one of the militiamen smiling behind his face scarf. This was just some sadistic game Khalaf was playing.

Scorpion picked the *belawa* off the ground and put it to Dowler's throat. He looked at the two militiamen. Which one was slower? The smaller one was working his *qat*, his cheek bulging like a chipmunk. He's thinking about something else, Scorpion thought, already moving.

He slashed sideways, whipping the *belawa* with his wrist, slashing Khalaf's throat from ear to ear, and without stopping, in a single motion, threw the *belawa* at the bigger militiaman, the knife embedding deep into his belly. The instant the *belawa* left his hand, Scorpion dived sideways, pulling at his jeans leg and ripping the Glock from the ankle holster.

The smaller militiaman swung the AK-47 around, but only got two rounds off, missing Scorpion, who fired from the ground, hitting him in the forehead. Scorpion started toward the bigger militiaman, who had pulled the *belawa* out of his body and was trying to stem the gush of blood with one hand while bringing his AK-47 into firing position with the other. Scorpion shot him in the throat and grabbed the gun.

Then he grabbed Dowler's arm and pulled him up.

"Run, dammit," he growled, scooping up his backpack as he yanked Dowler toward the truck, running hard.

Sixty meters.

Dowler stumbled as he tried to keep up. Scorpion spotted about a dozen Al-Shabaab militiamen not far from the truck. They were looking around to see where the shooting had come from.

Fifty meters.

One of the militiamen spotted the two white men

running toward the truck and pointed, shouting to the others.

Forty meters.

Dowler was panting heavily, almost falling then catching himself and staggering after Scorpion. Two then three of the militiamen near the road brought their AK-47s into firing position.

Thirty meters.

"I can't make it," Dowler panted.

"Fine. I'll leave you behind," Scorpion snapped, swinging his AK-47 into shooting position as he ran.

Twenty meters.

Bullets ripped into the sand around them. Scorpion dropped to his knee and fired a burst at the three militiamen, taking them down one-two-three and sending two others scrambling for cover. Pulling at Dowler's shirt, he ran on toward the Toyota, where one of the older boys peeked over the side of the truck bed, then seeing the running white men, ducked back down.

Ten meters.

A militiaman came around the front of the truck. At a dead run, Scorpion fired a burst from the AK, first missing him, then hitting him in the chest. He flung the cab door open and climbed in, bullets tearing into the metal side of the truck. As he turned the ignition, Dowler, panting heavily, pulled himself into the passenger seat, moving the boy, Ghedi, aside. Dowler pulled the child onto his lap as the truck skidded onto the road.

Scorpion shifted, gunning the accelerator hard as it could go, the noise of the engine drowned by a hail of bullets pinging around the truck or riddling the metal sides, one of them smashing a spiderwebbed hole in the windshield. The speedometer crept up till it hit 135 kilometers per hour; as fast as it would go. The truck rocked and bounced on the uneven road, and he could hear the high-pitched screams of the children as they ping-ponged around in the truck bed.

"*Tahrir kala!*" Scorpion shouted to them over his shoulder. Hang on! To Dowler: "Are you hit?"

Dowler looked down at his body as if it belonged to someone else. Behind them in the truck side mirrors, racing after them on the road and paralleling them across the dusty savannah, were half a dozen trucks filled with militiamen, all shooting in their direction.

"I'm all right. Who are you?" he said.

"American," Scorpion said, handing him the AK-47. "Ever use one of these?"

Dowler shook his head.

"Stick it out the window. Hold tight; it kicks. Aim a short burst at one of the trucks. For Chrissakes, try not to shoot one of the kids."

"I'll be lucky I don't shoot myself," Dowler said, staring at the weapon as if it were something from science fiction.

"Doesn't matter. It's just to let them know we're armed," Scorpion said, flooring the accelerator as if he could push it through the metal floor, while reaching back with one hand to the compartment behind his seat. Dowler fired a burst from the AK, the rifle rocking up so high from the recoil he nearly put a bullet through the roof. A spray of bullets from a truck racing nearly abreast of them spattered through the cab, one of them barely missing Scorpion's head. From the back of the truck, he heard a child scream.

Christ! One of them's been hit, he thought, pulling the FAD assault rifle from the compartment.

"Hold the wheel! Tight!" he shouted to Dowler as he racked the pump action to load a 40mm grenade into the launcher.

"Good Lord!" Dowler exclaimed. "Where'd you get that?"

"Peru," he said, leaning across Dowler to sight the weapon on the truck as they bounced on the uneven road. The other truck was nearly up to them and less than twenty meters away, militiamen blazing at them on full automatic. He aimed at the driver, squeezed the trigger and ducked back. The other truck exploded in a blast of fire, the hot wind of it knocking them sideways.

Scorpion fought the wheel to regain control. Grabbing Dowler's hand and slamming it back on the steering wheel, he heaved up as he pumped the grenade launcher and leaned out the driver's window, facing back. Bullets smashed around him, one of them shattering the side mirror. He fired the grenade at the windshield of the truck closest behind them, only twenty or so meters away, and watched it explode as his own truck swerved, nearly toppling him out. He fired an automatic burst at another truck farther back as it turned off the road to avoid the flames of the exploding truck in front of it.

Pulling himself back into the cab, Scorpion grabbed the wheel from Dowler, who just stared at him.

"Who the bloody hell are you?" he asked.

Scorpion glanced at the remaining side mirror. There was only one truck still behind them on the road and it was at least a couple of hundred meters back. For the moment they were keeping their distance, possibly communicating to others to block the road somewhere up ahead.

He checked the fuel gauge. Less than a quarter of a tank left. He tapped it to make sure it was working. It was a miracle the fuel tank hadn't been hit, he thought. They still had at least a hundred kilometers to the Kenyan border, maybe more. They hadn't hit the intersection to the main road at Bilis Qooqaan yet. He tried to calculate fuel. At the speed he was going, figure ten, twelve miles per gallon. It was going to be close. Too close.

The boy, Ghedi, looked wide-eyed at him. Scorpion, thinking he trusted the kid more than Dowler, touched his shoulder and handed him the FAD.

"Ara ko'daisa," he told the boy. Hold this. Dowler was staring at him too.

"I suppose I should thank you for saving my life," he said.

Even if they made the border, whatever he had come to Africa for, whatever he might have fantasized about with Sandrine, was over, Scorpion thought. CNN, al Jazeera, and the rest of the media would be over this like flies on garbage. He couldn't let them put him on television or even know he existed. As soon as he got the children to Dadaab, he'd have to disappear. He wouldn't even be able to say goodbye. He'd never see her again.

"Shut up," he told Dowler.

But he was wrong. Something that was happening at that very moment in a leafy neighborhood in a city on another continent was about to change everything, including his decision never to do another mission.

CHAPTER TWO

Bern,
Switzerland

The girl was the key. That and the timing. They would have at most nine minutes. Realistically, Scale thought, closer to seven, before the Kantonspolizei arrived in force and they'd be trapped. Even if his roadblocks and the explosives worked perfectly.

It had taken him weeks to study the target and come up with a plan that the Gardener would approve. The problem was, the place was a fortress. He knew going in that he would lose some, perhaps all, of the team. "The real question, *baradar*," brother, the Gardener had asked, "is not whether it can be done, but whether *you* can do it?" The Gardener looked at him then with those brown almost coal black eyes that for many were the last thing they ever saw, and even Scale felt a chill.

It was the Gardener himself who had given him his code name. Named for the saw-scaled viper, the most venomous snake in the Middle East. He liked it. He was a small man, thin, with little physical presence except for his oversize hands that looked like they belonged to a much larger man. Hands he had worked his entire life to strengthen, endlessly squeezing *lastik* balls till they could crush like a vise. A child that other children avoided or made fun of. He couldn't remember a single friend, not one true *dust*, from his childhood. But now his name made others fear him, even members of his own team, he thought, returning to the problem.

The American embassy in Bern was located at Sulgeneckstrasse 19, a tree-lined street in the Monbijou district. It was a white six-story structure on extensive grounds behind a high wrought-iron fence, with concrete driveway barriers to prevent a car-bomb attack. Outside the embassy, a Swiss security policeman with a SIG assault rifle stood guard twenty-four hours a day. The only way in was on foot past him. At the front gate, you had to pass a U.S. guard shack where visitors were asked to empty their pockets and were X-ray screened before being allowed to stand in line outside the building. No baggage, backpacks, purses, or packages of any kind were allowed.

Once past the guard shack, you went down a covered walkway to the building, where you had to go through two additional security checkpoints under the eye of a high-tech security post behind bulletproof glass. Surveillance cameras covered every possible approach as well as all interior areas and hallways. Security was provided 24/7 by armed United States Marines, six of them on duty at any given time.

Even assuming you could get past all that, eliminate the Marines and get in, you'd still have only seven minutes before the Kantonspolizei arrived in force, leaving no way out.

The girl's name was Liyan. She had to be attractive, Scale insisted. She had to hold their attention for at least two or three seconds. And they couldn't suspect her, so she had to wear Western clothes and look sexy. A twenty-two-year-old college student, she was trim, dark-eyed, and modern enough not to wear a *hejab*. Her family were Syrian Kurds from Aleppo, and Scale had false-flagged her by convincing her he was from the GSD, the Syrian internal security service. They had arrested her brother during the Arab Spring revolt, and he threatened that unless she cooperated, her brother would be shot.

Reasonable enough, since the Gardener's contacts within the GSD had confirmed that the brother was already dead.

Another lie was that she had been told her only job was to get the explosives—C-4 pressed flat and shaped to the curves of her body inside her undergarments—into the building. No ball bearings, no shrapnel, nothing added that would set off the metal detectors. She had been told to take it off in a restroom for them to use inside the embassy. In fact, she would not survive the attack, and if by some chance they were able to identify her body later, Scale thought, the blame would fall on the Syrians or the Kurds.

Now, coming from the blue parking zone on Rainmattstrasse, he took one final look at the embassy and gate that had been his obsession for weeks. He scanned the roof and sides of the building, spotting at least a dozen video cameras, knowing there were probably more that he couldn't see. His every move was being recorded that very second on videos that would later be scrutinized pixel by pixel for every last detail. His people were waiting in the SUV around the corner. The other two vehicles, a van truck and an old bus, were in position. Both were packed with C-4 and ammonium nitrate fertilizer and gasoline. They would act as roadblocks, one near Kapellenstrasse, the other at the Schwarztorstrasse intersection to slow the Kantonspolizei and isolate the embassy from either approach. The rest depended on timing and the girl, Liyan.

Seven minutes from now, *inshallah*, God willing, either he would have done it or he would be dead, he thought as he crossed the street, touching his false moustache, latex nose prosthesis and sunglasses, and pressing the button on his chronometer watch to start the countdown.

He smiled and nodded pleasantly at the Swiss policeman who barely glanced at him. As soon as he was behind the man, he pulled out his Beretta 92FS with the sound suppressor and killed him with a single shot to the back of the head. A half-dozen steps took him to the guard shack, where the Marine security guard had just turned from his computer screen. Scale slipped his hand with the gun under the bulletproof glass panel and shot him in the face. As he headed on the walkway toward the building, he could hear someone from the non–U.S. citizen queue scream and the sounds of his team coming up fast behind him. Then his cell phone vibrated.

Scale dived to the ground. The detonator was on a two-second delay, and as he hit the pavement, the front of the building exploded outward with unbelievable force, bits of debris and glass and human flesh flying past like shrapnel. His ears ringing, the air thick with dust and the smell of explosive, burning meat, and charred metal, he got to his feet. Turning around, he saw his team getting off the ground, their ski masks on, HK G36K assault rifles ready to go.

He pulled on his ski mask and checked his watch. Six minutes and twenty-eight seconds remaining.

"Come on!" he shouted in English—the only language they were to use till it was over—and ran at the gaping opening ripped in the side of the building where the door and checkpoint had been.

They went through the opening. The lobby was a shambles. It was filled with debris and blood and body parts, the security post utterly destroyed. There were two bodies by the far door, including a Marine guard struggling to move. A bloody foot in a high-heeled shoe lying on its side on the floor was all that was left of the girl, Liyan. Scale went over and shot the Marine in the head, then motioned to the others. They had six floors to cover and needed to move quickly. Before he left, Scale pulled a small IED from his jacket pocket and planted it next to the opening, where anyone coming would have to enter.

They headed for the stairs. Two for each floor. Scale motioned to Hadi, recognizing him by his blue ski mask. The two of them went down and out back to the second metal detector post. The door burst open and a Marine with an M4 carbine came out running. His eyes widened, but before he could react, Hadi fired a burst that cut him down. Scale went over and put a bullet in his head to make sure. Grabbing the M4 from the dead Marine, he racked the charging handle and switched to full automatic, safety off. Four Marines down, he counted; one at the guard shack, two at the security post, and now this one. That left two.

Coming into the main reception area, they spotted four civilians—three men and an older woman—who had been running for the door. He and Hadi fired simultaneously; two long automatic bursts that took down all of them. They could hear sounds of firing from the higher floors as the team went from office to office, killing everyone they found.

He motioned to Hadi to work his way down the hallway, glancing up at a security camera, secure behind the ski mask. *"Kir tu kunet,"* he cursed the camera under his breath, kicking the bodies. The woman was still breathing. He shot her again and started up the stairs, checking his watch.

Five minutes left.

There was a firefight on the third floor. The remaining Marines, he thought. He ignored the shooting and continued to the fourth floor, going door to door. There was no one in the first two offices, but in the third he found five people: three men standing, their hands raised, a young woman crouched behind a couch, and another woman hiding behind a desk. First he killed the men, then the woman behind the couch. The woman behind the desk made a run for it and he shot her in the back, and as she lay writhing on the floor, put another burst into her.

In the next office, he found an attractive blond woman feeding pages into a shredder. She froze the second he came in.

"Please, don't," she said, her lips trembling. "I'll do anything you want."

"I know," he said, motioning her closer. "Where are the CIA offices?"

"Sixth floor," she said, coming around the desk. She came closer. He could smell her perfume. Lilacs. She wore a white blouse and a neat gray skirt. She really was very pretty. They could hear screams and the sounds of shooting on the other floors. Then the sound of a grenade exploding on the floor below made the floor vibrate beneath them. F1 grenade, he thought. Hopefully, it took out the last two Marines.

The firing stopped. They got them, he decided.

"Which offices?"

"All of them. They have the whole floor," she said.

"Anything else?"

She shook her head, a tear forming in the corner of her eye.

"It's going to be all right," he said soothingly, and shot her with the M4.

He killed four more on that floor, then on the stairs ran into Hadi and Maziar, who wore the ski mask with the red stripe.

"Did we lose any?" Scale asked as they headed up.

"Three. Jalal, Mohsen, and Ashkan," Hadi said.

"Marines. *Madar sagan*," Maziar cursed them. Sons of bitches. "We killed them both."

"Speak only English," Scale hissed. He checked his watch. Less than a minute and a half left. "Take the next floor," he told them, and sprinted to the top floor.

As he reached the landing, he heard the sound of heavy gunfire on the floor below. Hadi and Maziar, he thought. Stepping into the hallway, he was nearly killed by a pistol shot. He pulled back and dropped to the floor.

Suddenly, an incredibly loud explosion shook the building, rattling and shattering windows. It came from the direction of Kapellenstrasse. The roadblock. He was running out of time. The question was, how long would the roadblock hold them?

The shot had come from the left side of the hallway. Someone taking cover in an office, firing from the doorway, he thought, pulling the pin on a Russian F1 grenade. About four meters, he estimated, tossing the grenade and counting. It was a 3.5 second fuse, and as soon as it exploded he ran at it firing the M4.

There were two dead men in white shirts turned red with blood lying in the doorway, one with an S&W .357 pistol—the one who had been shooting. Scale went through the offices methodically, rushing through the door first, then ducking in to check. There was only return fire from one office, near the end of the hallway, and another F1 grenade took care of the men inside. He killed fourteen on that floor, the last in a corner office with a name plate on the door that read: MICHAEL BRAND, CHIEF POLITICAL LIAISON OFFICER. Dead giveaway for CIA, he thought. Brand was a big man. He lay on the carpeted floor, clutching his chest where he'd been shot, staring venomously at Scale.

"Who are you?" Brand asked.

By way of an answer, Scale knelt, put the Beretta to his forehead and pulled the trigger. Brand's head flopped back, blood and bits of his skull seeping into the carpet.

Scale checked his watch. Eight minutes and forty-two seconds had elapsed. They had taken too long. The Swiss polizei would be past the roadblock any second now, unless they had gone around to approach the embassy from the other side. Even as he was thinking that, the building was rocked again by another powerful explosion coming from the direction of the Schwarztorstrasse intersection, glass flying from the few remaining windows. Got you, you stupid *seyyedan*, he thought. There was still a tiny bit of time.

He heard something behind him and whirled, ready to fire. Hadi and Maziar. He motioned them close.

"Quick. The flash drives. Start with the ambassador's office on the fourth floor and work down. I'll take this floor," he whispered, moving to the laptop on Brand's desk. Checking to make sure it was on, he plugged a flash drive into a USB port. It would automatically download every document and data file on the hard drive.

He didn't wait, but went to the next office. Stepping over the bodies of a man and a woman, he plugged in another flash drive and repeated the process, going from office to office. In the sixth office, he peeked out the window at the street and grounds below. Two polizei vans were pulling up. Men in body armor armed with SIG assault rifles began setting up a perimeter.

Time to go.

He pressed a contact number on his cell phone and sent a call. Hadi and Maziar would know what it meant, he thought as he raced down the hallway, popping into each office, pulling the flash drives and dropping them in his pocket.

He ran down the stairs, Hadi and Maziar just ahead of him. They heard the sound of polizei from outside. It was going to be close. As they reached the landing of the second floor, they heard men come into the building. Scale pulled out the cell phone, selected the contact number and pressed Send. The three of them hit the floor as the IED he had left at the opening went off, deafening them and shaking the floor.

They got up and ran down the remaining stairs, the area filled with smoke and the screams of the wounded polizei hit by the IED. The three men went out the back. The embassy grounds were green with trees and lawns and a vegetable garden. They ran through the garden toward the spiked wrought iron fence at the back of the property, knocking over the wooden stakes along the way.

They just reached it when shots rang out behind them. Hadi boosted Scale, who perched atop the fence. Thirty meters away he could see the black BMW SUV waiting for them on Bruckenstrasse. Hadi was hit as he started to boost Maziar. He sagged down, clinging to the fence bars, as Maziar scrambled up, over the top, and down the other side like a monkey. Still at the top of the fence, Scale fired a long burst back at the polizei. Hadi looked desperately up at him, his eyes wide behind the ski mask.

"Give me your flash drives," Scale said, reaching down, bullets ripping through the leaves of a nearby tree. Hadi managed to hand them up, then sank down again, collapsing on the grass. Scale could see a blood spot the size of his palm on Hadi's back. He kicked over and dropped to the other side. The polizei were charging, firing as they came. A bullet pinged on one of the iron bars next to him.

He looked back and fired a quick burst from the M4 at Hadi to make sure he was dead, then ran for the SUV. Danush was driving, and took off as soon as they were inside. They pulled off their ski masks, out of breath, their faces flushed. Scale took off his false nose and mustache. He would get rid of them later.

"Where are the others?" Danush asked.

Maziar shook his head. Scale checked the time. Nine minutes and forty-six seconds had elapsed. Danush drove across the bridge to the Kirchenfeld side of the river, his face grim.

"Give me your flash drives," Scale ordered. Maziar handed them to him. "Stay with the plan," he told them. "If you're stopped, you know what to do." The SUV had been rigged with C4. If stopped by the polizei, they would detonate. There would be no live witnesses for the FIS or the CIA to interrogate, and as little as possible left as evidence.

They drove around, slowing to let the white Kantonspolizei patrol cars, their sirens blasting, race by.

As soon as Scale got out in the Old City, Danush sped off. They would take the A1 autoroute, and if they made it, all of them would reconnect in Zurich.

He walked the cobblestoned Spitalgasse, stone-gray buildings around him and tram wires overhead. He took the tram near the Zytglogge—the city's landmark medieval clock tower, with its high pointed spire—to Gurtenbahn, where he caught the red funicular up the steep side of the Gurten, Bern's local mountain. He watched the scenery as they ascended, thick with trees, some still covered with snow.

It was cold at the top. Scale pulled up the zipper of his jacket and walked to the lookout. There were about twenty people, tourists and a few local families, enjoying the view. From there he could see across the city to the snow-covered Alps in the distance, though he couldn't see the American embassy. He took out the cell phone, the last time he would use this one, and called a number in Zurich. He was not surprised that no one answered, and waited for the beep for voice mail. It was a cutout. He had no idea who would pick up the message or how they would pass it along.

"*Gol ghermez*," he said in Farsi, and clicked off. Red rose; the signal for success.

He removed the SIM card from the phone, put on gloves, wiped both the phone and the SIM with a sterile wipe to remove any trace of fingerprints or DNA, then tossed the phone into a trash can. When he got down into the city, he would get rid of the SIM.

Scale took a deep breath then, enjoying the view.

A little blond boy, perhaps two or three years old, looked up at him. After a moment the boy smiled. He smiled back, and the boy shyly pressed his face against his mother's leg. He'd done it, he thought. The flash drives would be sent via DHL to a post office box in Madrid. There would be two days of watching TV in the apartment on Gutenbergstrasse till things eased up, then a train and the next mission.

The Gardener would be pleased.

CHAPTER THREE

*Nairobi,
Kenya*

"**W**hy here? Place stinks of curry," Soames said. He was a big man with a linebacker's shoulders and short fair hair that didn't disguise a bald spot. Harris's pit bull, Rabinowich called him. Scorpion didn't think much of Blake Soames, All-American Boy, and he trusted his boss, Bob Harris, deputy director of the CIA's National Clandestine Service, even less. "And flies," brushing one away. "I hate Indian food. We could've met at the Norfolk."

They were sitting in the back of a small shop in the Diamond Plaza mall in the Parklands district. Before connecting, Scorpion had watched from across the street to make sure Soames hadn't been followed. The shop sold pirated DVDs and video games, and Scorpion had bribed the owner to disappear for a half hour. A waiter from one of the chicken tikka restaurants—"Please welcome good sir, better than chowpatty," grabbing at Scorpion when he first entered the open-air food court—had brought them cold bottles of Tusker beer. He kept trying to get them to order till Scorpion shoved a hundred shilling *tipu* in his hand and he left.

"Why not post it on Facebook while you're at it?" Scorpion said. There was no way of going to the Norfolk, a luxury colonial hotel that went back to "Out of Africa" days, without attracting attention from every intelligence service and watcher in East Africa, from the Chinese Guoanbu to al Qaeda.

Soames leaned forward, beefy forearms on his knees, motioning Scorpion closer. That was his style. Fellow jocks in a football huddle. Scorpion almost smiled, remembering Rabinowich's poem about Soames that had gone viral inside the CIA.

> *My name is Soames,*
> *I've no use for combs,*
> *Or clever little poems;*
> *I am Bob Harris's bitchy-poo,*
> *Tell me fellow spook, whose bitch are you?*

"You heard about Switzerland?" Soames began.

Scorpion sat up straight. It was a mission pitch. Except every time he had gone on an operation for Harris, he'd lived to regret it.

"Tell Harris to go fuck himself."

Soames just smirked. Scorpion stared at him.

"What's so funny?"

"He said you'd say that," grinning widely. "He also said don't take no for an answer."

"I'll save you the trouble," Scorpion said, getting up to leave. "I won't even let you ask the question."

"Rabinowich said to tell you there's something you need to hear."

Dave Rabinowich was acknowledged even by his enemies to be the most brilliant intelligence analyst within the CIA. A graduate of MIT when he was only eighteen, Rabinowich was on a track to win a Fields when he decided to join the CIA because, he explained, "real world mathematics is more interesting because everyone is always lying." He was also one of only two people in the American intelligence community whose judgment Scorpion trusted.

Scorpion sat back down, his arms folded over his chest.

"I hope Rabinowich also told you that you better not be bullshitting me," he said.

Soames took a swig of the Tusker and wiped his mouth with the back of his hand.

"This isn't half bad," he said about the beer. "About Bern. You saw the TV?"

Scorpion nodded. It was on the drive to Nairobi, taking Sandrine to the airport.

Sandrine had been packing when he got back from Somalia with the children. She had to go to Paris. Something about funding for the nonprofit she worked for.

"I'm their show pony," she said. "They tart me up *à la dernière mode* for these big charity affairs, and if I don't do it, we can't keep these children alive."

She helped triage the children he'd brought in. Despite the way he'd mucked it up and the bullets hitting the truck, all sixteen were still alive. Before he left them in the hospital tent, the boy, Ghedi, took his hand and wouldn't let go.

"*Safa an'a weedu?*" he asked. Will you come back? Sandrine watched them, her lion's eyes unreadable.

"I will, *inshallah*," Scorpion said.

"Everyone says this, but they don't come," the boy said.

Scorpion knelt so he could look straight into Ghedi's dark brown eyes. He already knew with Sandrine it was a *coup de foudre*. A lightning bolt. And now the Somali boy's fingers clutching at his hand. He had never felt like this before. What was happening to him?

"I'll come back. I promise. *Eeven ana o'whyish*," he added. If I'm still alive. Ghedi looked at him with his big dark eyes and nodded. A promise.

Scorpion and Sandrine both had to leave for the airport. For him, there was no choice. He had to get away before the press got to Dowler. Already some of the aid workers were looking at him and talking among themselves. Just to make sure, under the excuse of treating Dowler for his burn wounds, Sandrine gave the Englishman a sedative that would knock him out for twenty-four hours.

Sandrine gave Scorpion a long look when she saw how shot up the Toyota pickup was. It was riddled with bullet holes. Before they left for Nairobi, Cowell volunteered to come along to bring the truck back to Dadaab.

"He just wants an excuse to go to Nairobi. Get at the whores on Koinange Street," Sandrine whispered to Scorpion, inclining her head at Cowell as they bounced on the rough dirt track to Garissa that passed for a road. Scorpion kept the FAD assault rifle ready. The area between Dadaab and Garissa was rife with pirates and Al-Shabaab. Cowell's and Sandrine's eyes widened when they saw the FAD.

"Is that for real?" Cowell asked.

"How do you think I got out of Somalia?" Scorpion replied.

For a long while, driving through an empty landscape, except for the occasional baobab tree in the distance, no one spoke. Crossing the bridge over the muddy Tana River, they passed a troop of baboons pawing through garbage from a *manyatta* slum on the outskirts of Garissa. Africa, Scorpion thought.

Garissa was a border town on the human trafficking route between Somalia and Nairobi. Somalis and Luo tradesmen shared the streets with refugees, aid workers, bandits, thugs, herds of camels, and Kenyan soldiers in fatigues and red berets with HK assault rifles.

They stopped for lunch at the Nomad Hotel, the local watering hole, where Scorpion saw the news about the Bern attack on the TV behind the bar. Nearly everyone at the embassy had been killed. Forty-eight dead. Three survived. A man and a young woman staffer who hid in a closet, and one of the Marines, in critical condition, were still alive.

Al Qaeda claimed responsibility, but the TV announcer said that Swiss and American authorities were skeptical. A short video from an embassy security camera beamed worldwide showed ski-masked gunmen moving through the corridors, methodically tossing grenades and firing into offices.

"Well, that'll bloody gee things up," Cowell said when they were back on a real road, the paved A3 to Nairobi.

But neither Scorpion nor Sandrine responded. We'll probably never see each other again, Scorpion thought, and wondered if she was thinking the same thing. They drove the long miles of low scrub and sand till the gridlock of Nairobi, under its endless haze of smog.

At Jomo Kenyatta Airport, they only had a few seconds together at the curb, Cowell watching them from the truck. Her eyes searched his face.

"I keep thinking you're running from the police, but that's not it, is it?" she asked. "And you're not going to tell me, are you?"

He didn't say anything. The less she knew, the safer she'd be, he thought.

"*Au revoir*, David," she said, and turned away.

"My name's not David. It's Nick," he blurted out, not knowing why he told her. He hadn't used his real name in so long, it didn't feel like it belonged to him. She whirled around.

"You bastard! Who the hell asked you to be honest?" Annoyed, frustrated, unbelievably beautiful.

"You can't tell anyone. It's dangerous," he said while slipping a strip of paper into her handbag without her noticing. On it he had written a Gmail address known to only two people in the world: Rabinowich and his closest friend in the CIA, Shaefer.

"*Alors quoi?* Is this supposed to make me interested, this mystery? Thank God I'm leaving." Shaking her head, her hair rippling like wheat.

"I didn't want to lie anymore," he said.

She looked at him with her lion's eyes.

"Then you're a fool." And as she turned to go: *"C'est impossible. Adieu."*

"Bon voyage," he muttered. She said *adieu*, he thought, watching her walk away into the terminal like a kick in the gut. Not *au revoir*. It really is good-bye.

After they left the airport, Cowell dropped him off downtown. Scorpion watched him drive away in the pickup, then caught a vividly-colored *matatu* minibus to an Internet café on Mama Ngina Street across from the Hilton. It only took a few minutes online for him to spot the "Flagstaff" e-mail from one of Rabinowich's cover Hotmail accounts. *Flagstaff* was the CIA's current emergency code. It meant Flash Critical, the highest level of operational urgency. It was only used when all hell had broken loose.

"So the Company's messed their diapers. What's that got to do with me?" Scorpion said to Soames, his eyes restlessly checking Diamond Plaza through the store window.

"If you mean are they shitting bricks in Washington, that's the understatement of the century," Soames said. "Congress is ready to bomb the hell out of somebody. They're just waiting for us to tell them who."

"And?"

Soames shifted uncomfortably. He leaned closer.

"This is coming from the top. The Director of Central Intelligence himself wants you in on this. So does the National Security Advisor. They asked for you personally. It's a mess."

Neither man spoke. From a radio somewhere came the sound of Kenyan hip hop; some song about "nothing to lose" heard over the street sounds and the calls of the Indian waiters to potential customers. Soames was wearing his sincere look like a merit badge.

"Look," Scorpion said. "I don't know what Harris is cooking up, but what I said before goes. I'm not interested." Soames put down his beer. He looked at Scorpion with pale unblinking eyes.

"You really think we're all bureaucratic assholes, don't you?" he said. "That we don't have a goddamn clue."

"The sad thing is, some of you do have a clue. But there's too much politics. Anyway, let's cut the foreplay, shall we?" Scorpion said. "You made your pitch and I'm not buying. What is it Rabinowich thinks I have to know?"

"They got everything," Soames growled.

"Who?"

"Those sons-a-bitches who attacked the embassy," pushing the Tusker bottle away. "They got everything from the computers, from the ambassador and station chief on down. Everything! Everyone's going nuts. State, DOD, NSA, the White House, us. Everyone!"

Scorpion heard horns honking out on Masari Road and the klaxon of a police car. Another Nairobi smash-up, he thought. Shouting, bribes, and local Mungiki youths sneaking off with whatever in either car wasn't locked down. It felt like a bad omen.

He studied Soames's posture. The man had a tell,

rubbing his little finger. He was holding something back.

"You don't have a clue who did it, do you?" he said.

Soames nodded. "AQAP," he said, meaning Al Qaeda in the Arabian Peninsula, "claims they did it, but no one believes them. They wore ski masks, spoke little. Security monitors only picked up a few words. English, with indeterminate accents. They hardly spoke. Not enough voice data to nail it down. We're dead in the water."

"What does Rabinowich think?"

"Uh-uh, amigo." Soames smirked. "You got to pay to play." He sat there, a big man dwarfing the small plastic chair he was sitting in like an American Buddha.

Scorpion picked up his bottle of Tusker by the neck. Something in the way he held it seemed to remind Soames that it could be used as a weapon.

"I meant it. I'm not interested," Scorpion said. "You jerks sent me a Flagstaff, so unless that doesn't mean anything anymore, just say what you came to say and we'll both get the hell out of here."

Soames shifted uncomfortably. "They got a list of all Company ops in Europe and the Middle East. Operations officers, Core collectors, joes, codes, the works," he said.

"Are you kidding?" Scorpion shook his head. "Somebody had all that on a computer in an embassy in Switzerland, where the only real business is visas and tax fraud, and you wonder why I think you clowns can't be trusted?"

"You still don't get it, asshole," Soames said,

a nasty smile playing on his lips. "That's not why I'm here. We're doing you a favor, courtesy of Bob Harris and Dave Rabinowich. They think you deserve it because of past service and because maybe, just maybe, you'll be of use again. But just between us girls, there's some of us who would be happy to leave a prima donna like you hanging out in the cold."

"Meaning?"

"They got your name too, Scorpion. You're on the list."

Christ, he thought, looking out the window at people at outside tables, talking and eating, everything smelling of Tandoori and curry, as though the world was a rational place.

"How bad?" he asked finally.

"Remember the Kilbane cover?" On the Ukraine operation, the Company had supplied Scorpion with cover ID as a journalist named Michael Kilbane working for Reuters out of London. He had jettisoned the cover during the mission, but now, because of an entry on a computer in Bern, it was coming back to haunt him.

"They got my picture? They know what I look like?" He felt a shiver go up his spine. When he was a child, the Bedouin said it meant someone was weeping over your grave.

Soames nodded. "Just the cover and the code name, 'Scorpion.' Nothing else, except . . . " He hesitated. "Langley checked the backup server. They got the Kilbane photo."

Scorpion stared coldly at him. Somebody who was good enough to take out a fortified U.S. embassy guarded by Marines and all the high tech in the world now had him on an enemies list, and they knew his code name and what he looked like. It was bad enough.

"Just answer me one question," he said through clenched teeth. "What the hell was it doing in an embassy file—*in Switzerland!*"

"The latest re-org. We're all supposed to share information. Hold hands and play nice. No more 9/11s. All very Kumbaya. Total crapola. Welcome to the new improved, better-than-ever Washington," raising his Tusker in a mock toast and taking a long swig. "Where the hell's that waiter? I want another of these—or . . ." He squinted suspiciously at the bottle. " . . . is it going to give me the Nairobi runs?"

Scorpion got ready to go. Soames looked at him.

"What do I tell Bob Harris?" he asked.

"Tell him to kiss off."

"The administration's going to take it to the U.N. Security Council, as if it matters what those jerk-offs do," Soames murmured, not looking at him. "There's gonna be a war."

"With whom?"

"We'll find out who did it. Trust me. And when we do . . ." Soames said, balling his fist.

"Go ahead. Knock yourselves out. It's got nothing to do with me."

"They're talking about going to Congress for a declaration of war. Nobody's done that since Roosevelt. Pentagon's gearing up, but it isn't just about finding out who did it. We need proof for the whole world. No more screw-ups. Bob really needs you on this one," Soames said, putting on his best *win one for the Gipper* expression.

"Tell Harris he's a big boy. He needs to learn how to cross the street by himself for a change," Scorpion said, getting up.

"What will you do?" Soames said, staring blankly at the floor as though he wasn't relishing reporting a wasted trip to Harris. "About Kilbane and all?"

"I'll take care of it."

"How?" Looking like a kid who had lost his lunch money. "They'll ask."

"Yeah," Scorpion said over his shoulder. "But I don't have to answer."

CHAPTER FOUR

Hamburg,
Germany

The ferry left the Finkenwender dock precisely at 9:00 P.M., heading upriver to the next stop on the Elbe River. The night was cool, drizzly, the outside deck wet and deserted except for a lone man wearing glasses and a newsie cap at the bow rail. Because of the weather, the other passengers stayed inside the cabin on the deck below. Scorpion turned up his collar against the rain, the lights along the shore shimmery reflections on the dark surface of the river.

Almost done, he thought. He had checked into The George, a boutique hotel in the St. Georg district that was like a private English men's club improbably dropped in the middle of Germany. On the TV, all the news was about the crisis in Switzerland. There were reports of a worldwide manhunt for information on the Bern attackers. The Americans had called an emergency NATO meeting. The media was speculating wildly. Al Jazeera had reported from an "unnamed" source in the Gulf region that an al Qaeda leader, Tamer al-Warafi, had provided a tape claiming responsibility for the attack. But al Jazeera had not yet released the tape.

In New Delhi, a government source implied that it had been an operation by Pakistan's covert ISI's SS division as a reprisal for U.S. drone attacks in northern Pakistan. Israel's foreign minister, Shalom Goldman, claimed it was the Iranians. Which the Iranian foreign minister, Hamid Gayeghrani, angrily denied, declaring that such a charge was just what one could expect from a "regime of devils spawned in hell."

Scorpion had spent the afternoon at an Internet café on Kleiner Schäferkamp across from a wooded park. He used a European singles chat room to contact Mendy69 in Vilnius, Lithuania. A little man in a wheelchair born with a child's twisted tiny legs that never grew, Aldis Slavickas aka Mendy69— after Mendeleev, the inventor of the Periodic Table, and the sex position—was a born criminal and the most brilliant computer hacker Scorpion knew. He had first used Slavickas to bulletproof his French cover ID, the identity he used for his home base in Sardinia. Slavickas had been able to penetrate the presumably impregnable firewalls and databases in the French Ministry of the Interior, as well as the DST and the DGSE, the French foreign intelligence service.

In the chat room, Mendy69 posed as Giedre, a sexy nineteen-year-old female blonde with a fetish for leather. Scorpion was an aging French businessman named Max, because no matter what cover name he used, Mendy69 insisted on calling him Max anyway. They corresponded in French.

The first part of the job Scorpion wanted was to change his photo in the Reuters personnel database at their Canary Wharf office in London for the Michael Kilbane journalist credentials he had used in Ukraine, so it no longer resembled his face.

Mendy69 typed: *pas de problème, mon chéri Max.* No problem, my darling Max. *I will make it so your own mother wouldn't know you.*

"*Bon. And the Ukrainian things, you naughty girl?* referring to the same photo that had been used for Kilbane's Ukrainian visa, now residing in Ukrainian Militsiya and SBU internal security databases in Kiev.

That's not so simple, my little wolf, Slavickas responded.

He would need something; an internal password, Mendy69 responded. He said he knew someone inside. The good thing about *ce pays primitif*—this primitive country, Ukraine—he said, was from the president on down, there was no one you couldn't bribe. Scorpion offered one thousand euros, and Mendy69 responded that it was too much for the Ukrainian piece of shit he would bribe. Two hundred would be plenty, and he, Mendy69, would keep the other eight hundred providing *cher* Max would spank him.

Almost laughing out loud at that one, Scorpion gave Mendy69 a dummy Gmail account to let him know when it was done and he would Paypal him the money. Before he left, he checked the BBC Internet news site. He was stunned by an article headlined: AMERICAN AID WORKER SAVES SOMALI CHILDREN. In it, they quoted aid workers in Dadaab, Kenya, about a mysterious American aid worker, David Cheyne, who had saved twenty-eight children—Scorpion had no idea how the number had grown from sixteen to twenty-eight or where they could have gotten that from—who were trapped by the war in Somalia. Apparently, the aid worker "had no comment about his heroic act, but stated that without the help of a British aid worker, Ian Dowler, he wouldn't have made it through." So at least he knew who the source of the article was. That little prick, Dowler, who was now claiming credit for the rescue. Even worse, someone had taken a cell phone photo of him that accompanied the article. It was a bit fuzzy from a distance and caught him from the side, holding one of the children and talking with Sandrine, identified in the caption as Dr. Sandrine Delange of MPLM, Médecins Pour Le Monde; Doctors for the World.

Bloody hell, he thought, glancing uneasily around the Internet café as if everyone might recognize him any second. The only good thing was that he didn't think someone could identify him just from the sideways photo or could easily match it to the Kilbane cover ID photo. As for the Cheyne cover ID, he'd gotten rid of it as soon as he had left Africa.

David Cheyne no longer existed, and outside the context of Africa, anyone would be hard-put to identify him as Cheyne. He was now using a Canadian passport in the name of Richard Cahill, an industrial engineer from Vaughan, north of Toronto.

That evening, having a drink at the bar at the hotel, he got the modified photo from Lithuania on his iPhone. Mendy69 was right. Tiny changes in facial distance vectors between features used by facial recognition software, a microscopic thickening of the nose, an imperceptible narrowing of the distance between the eyes, a change of eye color and a pattern modification, and no one would call them the same person. His own mother wouldn't know him.

Not that she would anyway, Scorpion reflected as he stood on the deck of the ferry. She'd died when he was a toddler; tensing as he felt someone come up beside him. A Middle Eastern man with a beard, his hair wet from the drizzle.

"Haben Sie einen Gletscher Eis Bonbon, bitte?" the man said, asking for a piece of a popular brand of candy.

"I still prefer the ice cream at the White Tower on Pasdaran Avenue," Scorpion replied in English, referencing the coffee shop in Tehran he had mentioned to establish his bona fides with the man next to him, Ahmad Harandi, the Mossad mole in the Hamburg Islamic Masjid, when they had first met during the Palestinian operation.

"Scorpion," Harandi said.

Scorpion nodded. "Who's your friend in the shadows at the back of the deck near the bridge?" he said.

"He's with me," Harandi said. "We need to keep it short. This is dangerous."

"More than you know. Whoever hit the American embassy in Bern got CIA computer files on the Palestinian operation. That means you too."

"Sheisse!" Shit! "How could such a thing happen?!" Harandi exclaimed.

"They got *sheisse* on me too. That's why this," Scorpion said, touching the three-day stubble on his face, then the rain-spattered glasses and the newsie cap to help change the image.

"So I'm blown?"

Scorpion nodded grimly.

"Almost certainly. That's why I had to see you personally. So you'd know it was real."

"*Sheisse*," Harandi said again. "I have to leave Germany." He looked sideways at Scorpion, his face wet from the rain. "This blows everything. Years down the drain. Herzliya will go crazy," referring to the Tel Aviv suburb where the Mossad's headquarters were located.

"The Americans are ready to go to war," Scorpion said. "They just haven't figured out with whom."

"I know. It's all anyone's talking about on the TV. Madness."

Scorpion felt the ferry shudder as it pulled up to the Neumühlen-Övelgönne landing. There was damn little time before things blew, he thought, watching crewmen secure the ferry to the quay. Two passengers got off and several more got on.

"What have you heard?" Scorpion asked. The Islamic Masjid in Hamburg's Uhlenhorst district was a hotbed of Iranian Twelvers and intelligence activities, which was why the Israelis had planted Harandi there as a mole in the first place. If the Iranians had something going in Europe, it was likely that Harandi had heard something.

"Nothing. Not a *verdammte* thing," Harandi muttered, looking around furtively. The ferry's engine throbbed as they pulled away from the landing. "It wasn't the MOIS,"—the Iranian foreign intelligence service, the equivalent of the Iranian CIA—"or Hezbollah."

"You're sure?"

Harandi shrugged. "One never knows. But if it were, I would've heard something."

"So either it's not the Iranians, or—" Scorpion stopped. "What about Niru-ye Quds?" The Quds Force, the Special Forces unit of the Revolutionary Guards; the Iranian equivalent of the U.S. Delta Force or Navy SEALs. "Or Kta'eb Hezbollah or Asaib al-Haq?" Factions within the Revolutionary Guards.

"I don't know. There's been nothing."

Harandi looked like he was about to say something more but had held back. They stared out at the darkness. There were other ships and boats on the river, lights reflecting on the water. The ferry's engine began to throb as it headed in toward the next river landing. The sign over the dock read: DOCKLAND FISCHEREIHAFEN. They were running out of time.

Scorpion glanced up toward the bridge. A man in a seaman's wool cap looked away as soon as he caught Scorpion looking up at him.

Shit, he thought.

"What else? This is me. What aren't you telling me?" Scorpion asked.

"Nothing. I've got to go as soon as we get to Sankt Pauli," Harandi said, grabbing the rail for balance as the ferry bumped against the landing. He took out a handkerchief to wipe the rain from his face as the ferry unloaded passengers and a half-dozen more boarded. He's holding something back, Scorpion thought, glancing at Harandi. Another couple of minutes and it would be too late.

He had to resist the urge to look up at the bridge. If the man with the seaman's cap worked there, how the hell could they have known about him meeting Harandi on the ferry? Unless the man had simply gone up to the bridge and either bribed or just requested that they let him stand there because of the rain. That could happen, he thought. Within a minute the ferry was again moving back out into the river. He couldn't wait any longer.

"C'mon, *dust*." Farsi for friend, Scorpion said. "What is it?"

Harandi shrugged. "Something someone said. An odd reference. It's nothing."

"So now we'll both know nothing. What was it?"

" 'Saw-scale viper,' something like that."

"You mean the *mar*?" The Farsi word for snake.

Harandi nodded.

"What's it mean? Some kind of code?" Scorpion asked.

"I don't know."

"Where'd you hear it?"

"That's what was so strange. A guest imam, an ayatollah from Qom, used it in a sermon at the Masjid the Friday before the attack in Switzerland. Something about doing evil and being bitten by a saw-scaled *tirmar*." Viper. "Some kind of metaphor." Harandi grimaced, as if to say he wasn't responsible for what some religious idiot said.

"He said 'saw-scaled viper'? He used those words exactly?"

"Possibly. I might have misheard."

"What was so strange about it?"

"I don't know. But it struck me as odd at the time. Not just saying 'snake,' but a specific type of very poisonous snake. It was too precise, if you know what I mean. Almost like he was sending a message. Probably nothing," he said again, and shrugged. "You get paranoid in this business."

"This ayatollah, what was his name?"

"Nihbakhti. Ayatollah Ali Nihbakhti," he said, and looked around. The ferry was slowing, shuddering as it approached the Landungsbrücken landing. "I have to go. Thank you for warning me. *Khoda hafez, dust.*" Goodbye, friend, he said in Farsi.

"Ahmad, don't go back to your house. Leave now," Scorpion said. "The needle's off the chart on this one."

"You too. We must both be careful, *dust. Viel glück.*" Good luck, Harandi said, heading for the ladder down to the main deck. The man from the shadows followed him down the ladder. The ferry had docked and the passengers began to crowd off.

Scorpion watched Harandi walk onto the covered walkway to the landing, followed by the bodyguard. He glanced up at the bridge. The man in the seaman's cap was watching the passengers debark, talking on a cell phone.

Scorpion went down to the main deck as if to debark, but stepped into the main cabin instead. A minute later the man in the seaman's cap came down to the main deck, carrying a satchel. Looking around once, he stepped onto the covered walkway to the shore.

Shit. Scorpion took out his latest disposable cell phone and called Harandi's cell. There was no answer; the call went to voice mail. Following protocol, Harandi had turned his cell phone off. Only now there was no way to warn him. If anyone got their hands on Harandi's cell phone, Scorpion thought, they'd get the number of his disposable cell phone too.

Making sure no one saw him, he took the SIM card out of his cell phone and dropped it over the side. He watched it sink into the dark water, then crossed to the other side, tossed the empty cell phone into the river, and followed the last passengers to the walkway.

Coming out on the street, he saw Harandi and his bodyguard get into a dark VW sedan. The man in the seaman's cap went over to a parked BMW motorcycle, pulled on a helmet and followed. Scorpion ran to the taxi stand and jumped into the first one in line. The driver looked like a Moroccan.

"Follow the motorbike," he said in bad German. The taxi driver started and turned on the meter. Taking a chance on Arabic, Scorpion added, *"Man aiyan ta'in ta?"* Where are you from?

"Algeria, *sayid*," the driver said, looking at him in the rearview mirror.

"Stay with the motorbike, but don't get too close," Scorpion added as they turned up Davidstrasse, its wet cobblestones glistening from the street lamps. They passed the wide Reeperbahn, with its Burger Kings, sex shops, and prostitutes, crowded this time of night despite the rain. The motorcycle maintained a constant distance from Harandi's VW, and

Scorpion's driver stayed back but kept the motorcycle in sight.

"Where are we going, *sayid*?" the taxi driver asked.

"Just follow," Scorpion said, checking the rearview mirror to make sure they were the caboose on this train. He wasn't sure where Harandi was headed or if he had spotted the motorcycle, and he cursed inwardly at not being able to warn him. He would have loved to make a move on the motorcycle, but he wasn't driving and there was no way to do it without getting the taxi driver killed.

The VW went up Hein-Hoyerstrasse, then turned at Paulinenplatz, a small tree-filled park; they appeared to be looking for a parking place. Harandi must've decided to go back to his apartment to clean things up, Scorpion reflected, knowing that once he left, Iranians from the Masjid would go over it with a fine-tooth comb. You idiot, he thought, feeling helpless to do anything. Whatever happened now, it was too late.

The VW stopped to pull into a parking space. The motorcycle came up beside the VW, slowed as the rider leaned over and attached something black to the car door, then suddenly revving the engine, sped off. The motorcycle raced down the street in a roar.

"*Bess! Waqif! Bombela!*" Stop! Stop! Bomb! Scorpion screamed to his driver. The driver just had time to slam on the brakes, the taxi screeching to a stop an instant before the VW exploded in an orange fireball that rocked the street. The powerful blast cast a fiery glare across the buildings, the shock wave buffeting the taxi like a toy shaken by a dog. Fragments from the VW peppered the taxi like hail as Scorpion dived flat onto the backseat.

When he looked up, the driver was staring wide-eyed through his windshield, chipped and cracked from the explosion. His face was bleeding from broken glass cuts but he didn't appear seriously hurt. The burning wreck of the chassis was all that remained of the VW. Scorpion jumped out into the street, where a man's severed hand lay next to an overturned café table. He couldn't tell if it was Harandi's. He felt sick, stumbled over to a tree to brace himself and looked up. The motorcycle was nowhere to be seen.

A hundred-to-one the motorcyclist had videoed his meeting with Harandi, he thought. Hopefully, all they got were his back and cap, with maybe a glimpse of his glasses, spotted with raindrops. Not enough to ID him, and he would immediately get rid of the glasses and cap to change the image. Whoever they were, it was clear they were already using the Bern data. That was the only way they could've gotten on to Harandi.

His regular iPhone vibrated and he answered. It was an e-mail from the Gmail account known only to Rabinowich and Schaefer. Only it wasn't either of them. It read:

Vendredi. la marée. 8è. 20h. Urgent.

Friday, the La Marée restaurant in the 8th Arrondissement in Paris at 8:00 P.M. Urgent.

It was Sandrine, he thought. It couldn't be anyone

else. She was the only other person who knew that e-mail account. She wanted to see him. And it didn't sound like she'd e-mailed because she actually wanted to see him. Something had happened. Hence the "urgent."

God, what insane timing, he thought as he stared at the smoldering frame of the VW and the wreckage-strewn street filling with people, windows opening in buildings around the park, spectators peering out. He had to get away, he thought, climbing back into the taxi and patting the stunned driver on the shoulder.

One thing was clear: his turn was coming.

And now he had put her in danger too.

CHAPTER FIVE

Paris,
France

"I wasn't sure you would come," she said. It was the first time he had seen her wearing makeup, and in a green sheath dress and bronze eye shadow that brought out the gold in her lion's eyes, she took his breath away. "I wasn't so nice the last time."

"You knew I'd come," Scorpion said. "You didn't dress like that for the chef de cuisine."

They were sitting at a table at La Marée, a clubby restaurant with Tudor-style leaded windows on the Right Bank not far from the Arc de Triomphe. They were the only ones speaking English in the crowded restaurant, sharing a superb Montrachet white wine along with the freshest *fines de claire* oysters he'd ever tasted. The restaurant was famous for its seafood.

"*Alors,*" she smiled. "There are two occasions when a woman must look absolutely fabulous. When she's going to see a man she's interested in and when she's getting rid of a man, so he can properly appreciate what he's lost."

"And which is this?"

"*Allez au diable*," she laughed, her laughter clear as a bell. Go to hell. "Impossible man."

The waiter came over and they ordered. Around them, well-dressed French couples were doing what the French did best, eating and talking. The evening sparkled, and looking at her, Africa and what had happened in Switzerland and Hamburg seemed far away. Except for the brown Peugeot 308 he had spotted following his taxi in from the airport.

Who could have made him at De Gaulle? he had wondered, watching as the Peugeot followed them in on the A1, past the Périphérique and into the city, making the turn from the Boulevard de la Chapelle onto Boulevard de Magenta. And then it hit him like the persistent beep-beep-beep of an alarm.

They didn't know who he was in Hamburg, and in any case, he had gotten rid of the glasses, cap, and shaved the stubble to change his image. It had to be either Bern, the photo ID from the Kilbane cover, or that stupid article from Africa. Or worse, something else. Something he didn't know about.

Except how had they gotten onto him in Paris? And so quickly? He'd watched the brown Peugeot in the taxi's rearview mirror, not relaxing even when it didn't follow their turn onto Rue Saint-Martin. Either he was being paranoid or they had switched off and someone else was following now.

"You said it was urgent," he began, as they sat in the restaurant.

She nodded. "I was at a charity *spectacle*, *très chic*, at the Grand Palais for *les MPLM*. This man came up to me. Said he was a journalist. He was asking about you."

"What did you tell him?"

"That you were an American. That I hardly knew you, which of course is true." The waiter brought them chilled langoustines for an appetizer and refilled their glasses. She waited till he left. "He wanted to know if I knew where you were."

"And?"

"I told him I had no idea, and if I did, I certainly wouldn't tell him." She smiled wryly.

"That doesn't sound terribly urgent," he said, sipping the wine.

"It was his manner," she said. "I had a bad feeling. There was something about him."

"Describe him."

"Middle Eastern. Arab or Iranian. Small man. His hands were very big, like they belonged to a much bigger man. And his journalist's *carte*. It looked cheap, phony. His clothes too. He gave me, in French we say, *la chair de poule?*"

"He gave you the creeps."

"Yes, he creeped me." She frowned. "But it wasn't just that."

"Something spooked you. What was it?" he said, looking up as the waiter brought his sole meunière and Sandrine her pike quenelles in shellfish sauce.

"For a journalist, he didn't seem interested in the story. Not the children, not the bravery or what happened in Somalia, nothing. It was all about you. He wanted to know where you were. He showed me a photo."

Scorpion put his fork down. His sole meunière stuck in his throat. It was unbelievably good and at the same time terrible because he knew it was all about to go to hell.

"Of me?" he said.

She nodded. "Not the one from the article. A different one and with a different name."

"Michael Kilbane?" he asked.

She nodded again. "He asked if it was you."

Christ, he thought, taking a deep breath. He was blown. Someone had put it together.

"What did you tell him?"

She shook her head, her hair swaying like a curtain.

"I said it didn't look like you to me." She looked at him sharply. "But it was you. And I don't think he believed me."

For a moment neither of them spoke. There was laughter from another table, a family. A thin man with a long nose shook his head and told them: "*Non, non. Mais c'est vrai.*" No, no, but it's true, and they laughed again.

"I don't know what to call you," Sandrine said softly. "I don't even know why I'm here."

"The food's good," he said, and in spite of herself, she sputtered, laughing.

"Damn you," she laughed. "So what is your name? Is it really Nick? Or is it Michael, or do you have one for every day of the week?"

He wiped his mouth with his napkin.

"I shouldn't have come. It was stupid. Self-indulgent. I'm so very sorry," he said, frowning. "We need to leave Paris. Both of us. Tonight."

"What are you talking about? I'm not leaving."

"Look, I know it sounds insane, but right now you'd be safer in Africa. I think you should go back to Dadaab. Now. Right away. I'm begging you."

She examined him with her lion's eyes.

"You know," she said, "the Canadian nurse, Jennifer. She e-mailed me. She said the boy, Ghedi, the one you saved from Somalia, all he talks about is you. That you're coming for him."

"I will," he said, his voice thick. He had to take a sip of wine to go on. "Have to clean this up first."

"I don't understand any of this. Why did you come tonight? Truly?"

He looked at her. Smooth golden skin, high cheekbones, and eyes like no one else's.

"You know why," he said, barely able to get it out. The effect she had on him was unbelievable.

"*Tiens!*" she whispered, mostly to herself. "Come on," she said, taking his hand for him to get up.

"Where are we going?" he said, following her up and motioning to the waiter for the bill.

"My place. I'm going to rip your clothes off and have sex with you."

As they headed for the door, the waiter, a Gallic half smile on his lips as if he knew exactly why they were leaving, handed him the bill, and Scorpion shoved a handful of euros at him.

"Why?" he asked as they nodded to the maître d' and stepped outside, the street dark and nearly empty except for the streetlights shining on the cobblestones and darkened shop windows.

"I don't care whether you're lying or telling the truth," she said. "That was the sexiest proposition I've ever heard in my life." They started walking toward the Place des Ternes when he stopped suddenly. He had spotted the brown Peugeot parked near the corner.

She looked at him, and he pulled her close as if to kiss her, his eyes quartering the Peugeot and the street. He put his lips to her ear.

"When we get to the Place des Ternes, don't ask questions. Run down the stairs to the Metro without me. Make sure you're not followed home. I'll come later if I can. What's the address?"

"What's going on?" she whispered back.

"We're being followed," he said, and kissed her so long and hard he almost forgot what he was doing.

"Mon dieu," she said, catching her breath. "Eight rue du Terrage, *au troisième étage*. It's in the 10th Arrondissement, near the Canal St. Martin."

"I know the canal," he said, taking her arm, the two walking together. He had spotted a glint of metal reflected from the shadows in a parked Renault Mégane half a block behind them. As they walked toward the lights of the Place des Ternes, he could feel her trembling beside him.

In the center of the square was the entrance to the Metro, and next to it a shuttered flower stall. Scorpion spotted a front tail behind a tree near the stall. He didn't have to turn around to sense the tail behind them. They were bracketed.

"Is this how it's going to be?" Sandrine whispered.

"Je ne sais pas comment il va être." I don't know how it is going to be. "Run!" he said abruptly, pushing her toward the Metro entrance. He had a sense

of her running down the stairs as he whirled and kneeled into a shooting position, pulling the Glock from the ankle holster under his trouser leg.

"*Ne bougez, trouduc!*" he shouted at the shadow. Don't move, asshole!

The shadow detached from the side of the flower stall and ran toward the Avenue de Wagram. A Middle Eastern–looking man in a windbreaker. Scorpion started after him. He needed him alive, he thought, running as hard as he could, wondering why the man hadn't fired first.

The man, wearing a windbreaker, hopped onto a motorbike parked vertically between cars. Dodging a passing red Citroen, Scorpion raced toward the curb. He needed to get out of traffic and get a clean shot. He had almost reached the curb when he got his answer about why the man in the windbreaker hadn't fired.

A bullet pinged off the cobblestones less than two inches from his foot. Scorpion dived between two parked cars and wriggled under one of them. He peered out from beneath the car. The shot had made no sound. Whoever fired must have been using a sound suppressor.

He quartered the area looking for the source of the shot. It hadn't come from behind, from rue du Faubourg St.-Honoré. Other than the man in the windbreaker, he had spotted no one and no one had followed Sandrine down the stairs to the Metro. So where the hell did the shot come from? he wondered, pulling off his jacket.

His thoughts were broken by the sound of an engine revving. Scorpion peeked out from under the car and saw the man on the motorbike cut into traffic. He flicked his jacket out toward the sidewalk while rolling the other way to the street, looking around wildly while snapping into a kneeling shooting position. He was about to fire when something moved, a shadow or a reflection; something out of the corner of his eye made him look up, and he just had time to roll back under the car as another bullet ricocheted off the cobblestones, barely missing his head. He heard a woman scream and saw another woman, crossing the street to the Metro with a small dog, look up. He watched her, the sound of the motorbike fading up the avenue.

The shot had come from a roof or upper floor apartment building on Avenue de Wagram near the little square. The middle-age woman with the dog shouted, *"Aidez-moi! Police!"*—Help! Police!— scooped up her dog and ran to the Metro stairs. A couple walking across the square ran back from where they'd come.

The shot had come from above on his side of the street, Scorpion realized. It had to be a rifle because even a marksman couldn't have come so close while shooting from above at that distance with a pistol. Also, he wouldn't have been in an apartment, because before he and Sandrine decided to take the Metro to her place, they hadn't known they would be walking to the Place des Ternes. The tails must have spotted them heading this way, figured out where they were going, and the sniper—part of the front tail team—went into the apartment building above the pharmacy. He would have gone up to the roof for what should have been an easy kill. It was the red Citroen that saved him, forcing him to step aside, spoiling the sniper's first shot.

Whoever they were, they were good. He wouldn't get lucky again.

It was about four meters from under the car to the front door of the apartment house. A ledge between the top floor and the roof would give him some protection from the sniper shooting vertically down. There would be no time to ring the bell for the concierge; it would take perhaps seven or eight seconds to bump the front door lock with his Peterson universal key. He would only be vulnerable during the two or three seconds on the open sidewalk.

It would all depend on how fast the sniper's reaction time was, he thought. Also, a pure vertical shot was difficult; the kind people almost never fired in their lives. The bullet would not have a curved trajectory. The sniper would have to adjust the sight lower than normal to hit the desired point of impact. Scorpion knew that moving fast, at night, he would present a minimal target from above, where all the sniper would see were his head and shoulders.

They'd set it up well, he realized. The man on the motorbike had been a decoy. Another few seconds, and if he hadn't shoved Sandrine to the Metro stairs, the sniper would have killed them both. He had told her that knowing him would be dangerous, and she'd probably wondered if he was being melodramatic. He hadn't expected it to be proven right so quickly.

Did the sniper know about the vertical trajectory? he wondered. One way to find out. Taking a deep breath, he rolled out from under the car and sprinted to the apartment house door, a bullet drilling into the sidewalk behind him as he slammed himself flat in the doorway.

He had been right. The sniper overshot the point of impact by a few critical centimeters.

Scorpion used the Peterson universal key to open the door and enter the building. The hallway was typically Parisian: a patterned tile floor, flowered wallpaper, a staircase and narrow elevator. Gun ready, he pressed the button for the timed hall light and looked up the staircase. Nothing moved.

He pushed the button for the elevator, and using the noise as it started down to cover his footsteps, climbed the stairs, whipping around at every turn and landing, ready to fire. The timed hall light went off. He crept up to the top floor, his eyes slowly adjusting to the dark. Reaching the landing, he hesitated, peering into the darkness.

It would be impossible to go up the stairs to the roof. The sound of the roof door opening would alert the sniper. At that distance, and as a stationary target for an instant, the shot would be fatal. He needed another way onto the roof.

Moving on tiptoe down the carpeted hallway, he put his ear to the first apartment door. Through it he could hear a television. Someone was listening to a game show, *La Rue de la Fortune*. Wheel of Fortune. He went to the next apartment door and thought he heard someone talking inside. The third apartment was silent. It didn't look like it was wired for an alarm. Just to be sure, he knocked. If someone answered, he'd tell them he was *l'électricien* sent by the concierge to investigate a problem. But there was no answer. Using the Peterson key, he opened the lock and went inside.

The apartment was dark, quiet. He used a pocket LED flashlight to look around, but whoever lived there was out. The window overlooked the Avenue de Wagram. No good, he thought. The sniper was probably right above him, where he could cover the Place des Ternes and the Metro entrance and street. To have any chance, he would need to work his way over toward the other side of the building to try and come up on the sniper from behind.

Provided the sniper was alone and didn't have a spotter. Otherwise all bets were off, he thought, opening the window and climbing out, his toes on the sill so he could reach up to the ledge he had spotted from below.

The night was cool and clear. He slipped his toes into a crevice in the building's facade and pulled himself up by his fingers till his forearms and elbows rested on the ledge. The roof parapet was about a meter above the ledge, so he would have to crouch or crawl, heaving himself up till he could swing a leg over it. For a few seconds he dangled from his arms, gripping the ledge. Don't look down! he told himself.

A moment later he was lying flat on the ledge, staring down at the street four stories below, hoping he hadn't made a sound. He looked up, but saw only the top of the parapet and the sky. He listened intently. There was no way to know where the sniper was; he could be only a meter away.

Slowly, Scorpion moved onto his toes and knees, one foot behind the other, making sure to stay crouched below the top of the parapet. The ledge was barely six inches wide. He felt horribly exposed. Someone honked a horn below. For an instant he looked down, but it was just normal traffic. In the distance, over the tops of the buildings, he could see the upper part of the Eiffel Tower, glittering gold with electric lights. He took a breath. Time to move.

The footing was precarious; he crept slowly, one step at a time. It seemed to take forever to reach the corner of the building. Clinging to the side, he edged around the corner. The parapet on this other side was sloped and he had to hold on as he inched forward, conscious of the sound of traffic on the tree-lined street below. It would be the Boulevard de Courcelles, he thought. About ten meters from the corner he saw a mansard window, though he wasn't sure if it was real or decorative.

Time to decide, he thought. If the sniper was at the Avenue de Wagram parapet, coming over the top he would be to the side and behind him. Then, even if he made a sound, he would have time to aim before the sniper could turn around and shoot. Grabbing the edge of the window molding, Scorpion reached up to the pitched top of the parapet with his left hand. In his right, he held the Glock. It would all depend on which way the sniper was facing, he thought as he put the toe of his shoe into an indented part of the molding. He listened intently. No sound from the roof. Here we go, he thought. Pulling with his left hand, he leaped over the top of the parapet onto the slanted metal roof.

Landing, his feet at an angle, he snapped into a firing position and scanned the length of the parapet just as he heard the snap of a door closing. He whirled, ready to shoot, but the sniper was gone, out the roof door he hadn't wanted to use. He straightened. The rooftop was empty.

He made a tour of the parapet to make sure the sniper hadn't gone over onto the ledge on the Avenue de Wagram side. That was empty too. Then he ran to the roof door, readied himself to fire, and ripped it open. There was no one on the landing, but he could hear the elevator descending. The son of a bitch was getting away!

Scorpion raced to the stairs, took them three or four at a time, leaping down to the landings, then ripped around and down the next flight, racing the elevator. As he reached the second floor, he could hear the elevator door opening, then someone running on the tile floor of the front hallway. Leaping nearly the entire flight of stairs to the landing, he was just in time to see the front door close and an older woman—the concierge—opening her apartment door.

"Retournez à l'intérieur, madame!" Go back inside! he shouted as he raced past her and out the front door. A man with a rifle case was running hard toward the Metro entrance. Scorpion took off after him.

The man leaped down the stairs to the Metro, causing people coming up to stare at him. Scorpion raced across the street, nearly getting sideswiped by a BMW. He ran down the stairs, holding his Glock in his pocket. The man with the rifle case had already gone through the turnstile; he wasn't there.

Scorpion used a one-day ticket to go through the

turnstile, then had to choose which tunnel platform: PORTE DAUPHINE or NATION. No way to know
which platform the sniper had gone to. Trains came
by every couple of minutes. If he chose wrong, he
might give the sniper a shot at him, or the man
would get away and he'd never have a chance to
find out who was after him—whether it was Bern or
something else. Only if it wasn't Bern, how the hell
had they picked up on him in the middle of Paris?

Time to choose. Two passageways: NATION would
be the train heading east into the 11th Arrondissement; PORTE DAUPHINE was the shorter part of the
line, he could see from glancing at the map. The
next stop that way was Charles de Gaulle–Étoile. If
he were the sniper, he would try to lose someone
in all the traffic and people on the Champs-Elysées
and around the Arc de Triomphe, and so he sprinted
down the passage to the Porte Dauphine platform.

He stopped at the opening to the platform and
crouched low. A young woman a few feet away
looked at him, and seeing him take the Glock out of
his pocket, started to run. Scorpion grabbed her by
the arm. She tried to twist away, terrified.

"*J'ai besoin de votre miroir de maquillage,*" he said.
I need your makeup mirror. He took her handbag,
opened it, and poking around, pulled out a small
mirror case. He handed the bag back to her as she
stared at him, wide-eyed. He put his finger to his
lips as she continued to stare as if he was insane,
then bolted and ran toward the exit. He could hear
the sound of her high heels click-clicking behind
him as he bent low and held the mirror out, close to
the floor, angled so he could see the platform.

A train was coming but on the other side, going toward Nation, the noise covering any other sounds. On his side, the platform was long and curved and there were only a dozen or so people waiting. Then he spotted the sniper in the mirror. He was a young man in a black Façonnable jacket, Iranian, by the look of him. Then he turned and Scorpion got a better look.

It was the man with the seaman's cap, the motorcyclist from Hamburg. The one who had killed Harandi.

Scorpion counted eight people on the platform between himself and the sniper, who glanced his way, without being able to see him, in the direction the sniper would have to take were he to come after him. Pulling his hand with the mirror back, Scorpion glanced over his shoulder toward the Metro entrance. There was no way of knowing if there were more of them. The train on the other side pulled away, reminding him that the next train to Porte Dauphine would be coming any second. Once it did, he would have to put himself out in the open on the platform or lose the sniper for good.

He eased the mirror back out again. There were the same eight bystanders and the sniper, for the moment not looking toward him, but down the track. Then Scorpion heard the Porte Dauphine train approaching.

He stepped out onto the platform and sprinted at the sniper, who whirled and frantically began opening the rifle case. He pulled out a large sniper rifle.

It looked like a Russian rifle, Scorpion thought, running; a VKS Vychlop with a silencer. How the hell had the bastard missed?

The bystanders, staring, were about to get killed.

He screamed at the top of his lungs: *"Attention! Fusil! Police!"*

As the sniper swung the rifle into aiming position, some of the bystanders screamed and ran; the others stood there, frozen. Scorpion threw himself onto the platform floor in a prone position, aimed the Glock and fired at the sniper's thigh. He needed him alive.

The sniper staggered but did not go down. He re-aimed as Scorpion fired again, hitting him in the shoulder this time. Scorpion rolled to the side as the sniper fired and barely missed, the bullet tearing a jagged scar in the concrete platform next to his ear, then came up to his feet and ran toward the sniper again.

The man was struggling to raise the Vychlop for another shot. The train was coming fast, not far behind him, the bore of the rifle's silencer opening looking big as a tunnel to Scorpion. But the sniper was too close, and instead swung the rifle at Scorpion's face.

Scorpion blocked it and started the Krav Maga disarm, curling his right arm around the weapon, creating torque on the forearm while smashing his left elbow into the man's face. He twisted the rifle away then smashed the butt of the weapon into the sniper's face, staggering him sideways. As Scorpion reached to pull him close into a choke hold, the Iranian, seeing the train almost there, suddenly lurched sideways and off the platform.

The train came with a roar of air, its brakes squealing above a woman's high-pitched scream as the front car smashed into the Iranian, flinging the body forward onto the track like a rag doll before rolling over it.

He stood in the shadow of a doorway across the street from her building. She had said "third floor," which in France means the fourth floor as Americans count. Her building was brick with wrought-iron window balconies with flower pots, and at the end of the street a stone arch led to the Canal St. Martin. He could smell the water from here.

There was a light in the window of what had to be her apartment. She was waiting for him and he wanted to go up, but he knew this was as close as he was going to get, and that he would remember standing in the street looking up at her window for a long time. He called her on his cell.

"*Allo*," she answered. And in English: "Is it you?"

He didn't answer. Just hearing her voice, knowing he was as close as he would ever get, was like nothing he had ever felt before.

"Where are you?" she asked.

"Across the street."

"Come up, *je t'en prie*," she whispered. Please. "We have to talk."

"I can't. Did you hear?"

"The death in the Metro? It was on the *télé*. Was it you?"

He didn't answer. He could hear her breathing over the phone.

"Witnesses in the Metro said he was going to shoot," she said. "You had no choice. I hate this."

"So do I," he said.

"What are you going to do?"

"You need to leave Paris now. Tonight," he said.

"I could go back to—"

"Don't say it! Don't tell me where. Don't tell anyone. Your phone could be bugged. Just call a taxi and go, now."

"And you?" she said.

"I'm going too. I won't be able to contact you, and don't try to reach me. When it's over, if I'm still alive, I'll find you." With a pang, he remembered those were the same words he had used with the boy, Ghedi. "You'll probably be married with three children."

"I wish," she said. Then softly, "No, I don't."

"If you never want anything to do with me again, I'll understand. It'll probably be the smartest thing you've ever done."

"Who said I was smart?"

"I'm so sorry about this."

"You're sorry. Is that the best you can do?"

"I don't regret a damn thing," he said, and clicked off.

He stood in the shadow of the doorway and waited. He wanted to be sure no one would follow her when she left. A cool breeze came from the canal, and he stepped farther into the doorway, out of the wind. Looking up at the lit window, he saw her shadow moving on the curtains. He hoped to God she was packing. His eyes scanned the street again. There were no watchers at either end or on any of the roofs.

Finally, a taxi pulled up outside her building and its interior light came on. He tensed watching the driver make a call on his cell phone. The light went out in Sandrine's apartment. A minute later she came out of the building, pulling a rolling suitcase behind her. The taxi driver put the suitcase into the trunk and then they were gone.

The street was empty. Checking his iPhone, Scorpion located a youth hostel near the Gare du Nord that catered to backpackers and college students. He walked on the quai next to the canal, where it was virtually impossible for anyone to follow without him spotting them.

Turning up a side street, he walked for blocks past shuttered shops, his footsteps echoing in the deserted street. He had never felt so alone, and all he could think about was Sandrine. How he had upended her life and how quickly she understood what she had to do, even if she didn't understand what was really going on. There's steel in her, he thought. A lot more going on there than just a doctor with a pretty face.

There was traffic on rue du Faubourg St.-Martin. He stepped into the lobby of a cheap hotel and had a sleepy concierge call a taxi that dropped him off at the Gare du Nord train station. Waiting till the taxi left, he walked through the terminal, doubling back to make sure he was completely clean, then walked to the youth hostel.

He spent a restless night in a bunk bed. In the morning, by offering to chip in for gas, he was able to crowd into a beat-up Ford Mondeo, joining up with three young male European backpackers and a college girl from Ohio. They were headed south on the A6 to Grenoble, where all of them except the girl were enrolled at the university.

He went as far as Lyon with them, waving good-bye to the backpackers, and found an Internet café in Old Lyon, a few blocks from the Rhone River. There was only one person he trusted enough to contact, he thought grimly, hoping Shaefer was still in Europe. He sent an e-mail to Shaefer's dummy Gmail account and then used the NSA software on a plug-in drive to delete any trace that he had been on the computer or where the message was coming from, including the deleted items file and the temporary Internet files. It only took four words, but it would reach Bob Harris, whom he and Shaefer had nicknamed among themselves "Turd Face," or "tf."

tell tf im in

CHAPTER SIX

Zug,
Switzerland

It was raining when Scorpion stepped off the double-decker S-Bahn from Zurich. Even before he walked out of the train station in Zug, he spotted the surveillance.

It was a classic six-box shadow detail: two fore, two aft, two bracketing on either side in the center. The center pair—a man with a buzz cut wearing a Burberry trench coat, and a pert blond woman in a sweater and a North Face jacket who looked like a teenager—didn't even bother to pretend they weren't watching him.

Scorpion stood under an umbrella in the Bahnhofplatz in the rain and motioned to the Burberry to come over. At first the man pretended not to see him. When Scorpion persisted, the man threw a glance at the pert blond and came over. He was a big, bulky in his trench coat, a hand in his pocket.

"This is stupid," Scorpion said. "Let's go see Harris."

A minute later he was in the back of a Mercedes

sedan sandwiched between the Burberry and a man in a soccer hoodie. The pert blond climbed into the front passenger seat and turned, flashing perfect teeth and a 9mm Beretta at him. Scorpion handed both his Glocks—the 9mm from the small-of-the-back holster and the small Glock 28 from his ankle holster—to the hoodie. He kept the ceramic scalpel and polymer lock pick—nonmetallic to avoid metal detectors—taped with flesh-colored tape to the sole of his foot.

They drove through quaint alpine streets to the Upper Town and up a winding road toward the green hills. Less than a half hour south of Zurich, Zug looked like what it was: a picturesque backwater. Except for the fact that rented boxes in its local post office served as headquarters for more than thirty thousand international corporations and that most of the world's commodities were traded in offices overlooking picturesque Lake Zug, which made it possibly the richest town in the world.

The Mercedes turned off onto a private road lined with trees and hedges. Scorpion caught a reflection from a scope that someone should have kept covered, spotting a guard in camouflage gear with an M4 rifle hiding in the bushes. There were security cameras and sensors in a 360-pattern around acres of green field and in trees along the road to the safe house, an ultramodern structure of glass and concrete that somebody with money to burn had spent millions on. It stood on its own at the end of a long driveway. A feature he knew he wouldn't find in *Architectural Digest* was the silhouette of a sniper's shoulders and head on the building roof.

Bob Harris was waiting with Shaefer in the living room on the second floor, with its panoramic wall of floor-to-ceiling glass providing a breathtaking view of the town, the blue lake below, and the snow-covered mountains. Shaefer, a lanky African-American, was sitting on a sofa, his long legs stretched out in front of him. Scorpion and Shaefer had been in Delta Force together, the only two survivors of an ambush by the Taliban at Forward Operating Base Echo in the Chaprai Valley in North Waziristan, an area in Pakistan where officially American troops didn't exist, and it defined a bond between them.

"Sorry, I shouldn't have sent Soames to Nairobi," Harris began. For a change, he wore glasses and wasn't in a suit. In his preppy khakis and cashmere sweater, he could have been an aging postgraduate lecturer posing for a Tommy Hilfiger ad.

"Soames is just a prick. It's you I can't stand," Scorpion said.

Shaefer, his old friend, shook his head, grinning. Same old Scorpion.

"Soames is useful," Harris said. "Every executive needs someone everyone can hate, so they don't hate him. Coffee?" he asked, indicating a silver coffee service and several plates of Swiss cookies, a Linzer torte, and what looked like a Black Forest cake on a side table.

"And what's with all the firepower? Who are you expecting? The Chinese army?" Scorpion said, pouring himself a cup of coffee.

"We're talking about people who took out a secure facility manned by specially trained United States

Marines. Some presence is warranted," Harris said, stirring sugar into a cup. "Tell me about Hamburg."

"Harandi went back to his apartment. Warned him not to."

"Did you see who did it? The motorcyclist?" Harris said, sitting in an armchair facing the view.

"Yes."

"Could you spot him again?"

"Not likely. I killed him in Paris."

Shaefer snorted a laugh. Harris looked at Scorpion sharply as the young blond woman with the teeth and the Beretta came in and began working a big-screen laptop computer set up on a dining room table.

"That was you?" Harris said, and when Scorpion didn't answer: "When were you going to tell us?"

"I just did."

"Pity you couldn't have kept him alive for us to question," tapping his finger impatiently on the coffee cup. "That might have been the ball game."

"At the time the only life I was interested in saving was mine."

At that, the young woman glanced back over her shoulder, smiling with her perfect teeth like he was the Black Forest cake, then went back to her work.

"So they spotted you in Paris? How?"

Scorpion shrugged. "You tell me. That's one of the reasons I contacted you. Probably someone with the Kilbane ID photo covering De Gaulle. Or a bent gendarme at Passport Control."

"We'll follow up with the Swimming Pool," Harris said, referring to the DGSE, the French foreign intelligence service, so-called because their headquarters was located in Paris next to the French Swimming Federation.

"Because they've always been so forthcoming in the past," Shaefer growled. He turned to Scorpion. "Did Harandi say anything before he died? Anything on the Iranians?"

"Wait," Harris held up his hand. "Let's get Rabinowich in on this." He looked at the young woman. "Are we ready, Chrissie?" And back to Scorpion: "It's some kind of Skype, only on JWICS," which he pronounced JAYwicks. Scorpion understood. Whereas most U.S. federal agencies, the State Department, and the Department of Defense used both the government's SIPRNET—for classified communications up to the Secret level—or the unclassified NIPRNET network to communicate, the CIA Clandestine Service and NSA used JWICS—Joint Worldwide Intelligence Communications System—the only network designed for highly secure encrypted Top Secret communications on up to the SCI/SAP—Special Compartmented Information or Special Access Program—level, the highest secrecy level in the U.S. government.

They got up and gathered around the big laptop on the dining room table. Dave Rabinowich was already on the screen, picking his nose as the others gathered around.

"Can you see us, Dave?" Harris asked. And to the young woman: "Thanks, Chrissie."

They waited while she left and there were just the three of them in the room.

"Nice girl," Shaefer said.

"She's got a gun," Scorpion said.

"My kind of girl." Shaefer grinned. And to Rabinowich: "You can stop excavating your nose, Dave. It's kind of killing my appetite."

"Actually, the cilia, not the hairs, in your nose help create appetite through the sense of smell. Did you know they continue to beat after death? Their postmortem motility rate actually gives a more accurate reading of time of death than body temperature," Rabinowich said, his face nearly filling the screen. With his close-set eyes behind glasses and bushy eyebrows slanting out at an up angle, he looked like a cartoon of a pudgy Horned Owl.

"Thanks, Dave. I think we've reached our Asperger quota for the day," Harris interrupted. "Scorpion was about to tell us about Harandi in Hamburg." He looked at Scorpion. "What about the Iranians?"

"Nothing. Harandi didn't think it was the MOIS or Hezbollah. Said he would have heard if it was."

"Christ," Harris growled, frustration in his voice. "Was he saying it definitely wasn't the Iranians?"

Scorpion understood his frustration. Things were in motion. While waiting in Zurich's Hauptbahnhof Central Train Station, he had surfed the latest news from cnn.com on his cell phone.

The Americans had tightened security at their embassies around the world. Other Western nations, such as Britain, France, and Germany, were following suit. A news blackout had been imposed in Washington, and the White House, Department of State, and the Pentagon stated there would be no further announcements or press briefings until U.S. and "allied" intelligence sources had identified the Bern attackers, although it was widely speculated that al Qaeda had been behind the attack. The Pentagon did, however, acknowledge that the U.S. military had gone to DEFCON 3 status.

"That's not what I said," Scorpion said. "What about al Qaeda?"

No one said anything, but Rabinowich sat there shaking his head back and forth like a swivel-head doll.

"It's not al Qaeda," Rabinowich said. The fact that neither Harris nor Shaefer disagreed with him meant that as far as the CIA was concerned, they weren't following that thread.

"How can you be so sure?"

"COMINT levels have shown zip. We've been monitoring nonstop. If someone even farts in Rawalpindi we'd have picked up something. It's not them."

"What else did Harandi say?" Harris said to Scorpion. "This thing about a snake?"

"The saw-scaled viper. It's the most poisonous snake in the Middle East."

"Nice," Shaefer said, and to Rabinowich: "Have we heard anything, Dave?"

"Absolutely nothing. Zero. Bit of an outlier," Rabinowich said.

"What about this ayatollah? What's his name?" Harris demanded, turning to Shaefer and Scorpion.

"Ayatollah Ali Nihbakhti. From Qom," Shaefer said, glancing at Scorpion as if to confirm he had it right.

"What do we know about him?" Harris asked.

"It's a cover ID. He doesn't exist," Rabinowich said, wiping his glasses. Without them, his eyes looked softer, more vulnerable.

"Or the Iranians don't want us to know about him," Harris said, pursing his lips. He turned to Shaefer. "What are we getting from the Swiss?"

"You won't like it," Shaefer said, uncrossing his legs.

"They're Swiss. I know I won't like it. What?"

"Nothing."

"That's impossible. There must be something."

"None of the dead attackers had any ID or any papers, anything of any kind," Shaefer said. "There's no record of them ever staying at a hotel or pension or anyplace in Switzerland. Their clothes were cheap, bought locally for cash. No credit cards, debits, anything. According to the Kantonspolizei, it's as if until the day of the attack these guys never existed."

"This is bullshit," Harris said. "There must be something. Dental work, Immigration control photos, a check of Swiss drivers' licenses, Interpol records, something. They didn't just materialize out of thin air."

"They knew we'd be looking," Rabinowich said. "This attack was very carefully planned."

"Impossible. There's always something," Harris said. "Come on, guys. What is it?"

"DNA," Rabinowich said. "On the attackers in Bern. Just preliminary, of course. One of the four bodies from the attack is an Arab. Possibly Iraqi. DNA from the female bomber's foot suggests she may have been Kurdish, possibly a Syrian Kurd;

we need more markers before we can nail it down. The other three bodies are Persian. Give us a couple more days and we can say with 99.999 percent certainty that they're Iranians."

"So that's what we go to war on?" Harris snapped. "Iranians are everywhere. They could've come from England, Turkey, Sweden, even California. We could bomb Beverly Hills. There's not one damn thing to prove they came from Iran."

For a moment no one spoke. Scorpion sipped his coffee and looked out at the view, the trees and fields, the town below, the blue lake and mountains. Thinking the female Kurd was an anomaly, but three Iranians and an Iraqi, ten-to-one a Shiite, wasn't a coincidence. Neither was the Russian VKS rifle of the sniper in Paris, the al Quds Force's sniper rifle of choice. Proving it to the UN and the media on a world stage, though, was something else.

"Red rose," Rabinowich said, pursing his lips and looking more like a horned owl than ever.

"What?"

"*Gol ghermez*," Rabinowich said. "In Farsi it means red rose. According to cell tracking coordinates, someone made a mobile call from Gerten Mountain in Bern to Zurich approximately forty minutes after the attack. All they said was '*Gol ghermez*,' and hung up."

"Could be anything. A guy calling his girlfriend. A florist," Shaefer said facetiously.

"It could be a completion code," Scorpion said. "Maybe signaling success after the attack."

"That's what NSA thinks," Rabinowich said. "They're the ones who picked it up. It just took them a while to sort through all the COMINT traffic in God-knows-how-many-languages in Switzerland.

"And the number in Zurich?"

"Prepaid cell phone purchased with a phony ID."

"Of course. What was the ID?" Shaefer asked.

"According to Swisscom phone records," Rabinowich said, "the purchaser was Ferka Chergari. The name is of Roma origin, obviously. Domiciled in Biasca, southern Switzerland," he added.

"So do we have watchers crawling up this Gypsy's ass even as we speak?" Harris said, his blue eyes glittering.

Rabinowich shrugged. "Difficult, seeing he died in 2007."

"Is that it?" Harris said. "Is that everything we've got? Because I'm beginning to love going back to square one. I may take out a mortgage on it. Come on, guys. Is this the best we've got?" He regarded them defiantly. It made him look older, Scorpion thought, noticing wrinkles at the corners of his eyes in the light from the windows.

"Zurich," Scorpion said.

"What about it?" Harris snapped.

"It was a cutout."

"Of course! Nice one," Rabinowich said, slapping the desk, his head rising up, grinning from ear to ear.

"You two girlfriends want to let the rest of us in on it?" Harris said, suddenly interested.

"Put it together," Scorpion said. "*Gol ghermez*, red rose in Farsi, means the cutout is an Iranian in Zurich. What'll you bet the cutout's a trader doing business for the Revolutionary Guards or one of the factions? Right out in the open, because Switzerland'll do business with Satan himself as long as it ends up in Swiss francs on the Bahnhofstrasse. Can't be that many Iranian trading companies paying the kind of astronomical prices they charge in Zurich's high-rent district."

For the first time, Harris smiled. He rubbed his hands together.

"All right, boys and girls, we are live. You make the approach," he said, pointing at Scorpion. "And let's not alternate this operation with the Ring Cycle. We don't have a lot of time."

"He might have to go to Iran," Shaefer put in. "They're prepping for war over there. The minute somebody climbs over the fence, they'll pop him."

"He's a big boy. He'll just have to watch himself, won't he?" Harris said, looking at Scorpion.

Scorpion got up. He walked over to the plate glass and looked out at the view. Switzerland was like a picture postcard, he thought. So different from Africa, from Sandrine, from everything he cared about. He turned around.

"How much time do we have?"

"None," Harris said. "Things are moving fast. Right now this is our op, but in a little while people with bigger dicks take control."

"For once, he's telling the truth," Shaefer said. "We're talking days, hours."

"I need at least a couple of weeks. Maybe more," Scorpion said. "This isn't some *24* type bullshit where you smack a joe in the mouth and he tells you everything he knows. If it is Iran, penetrating them when they're already paranoid as hell is going to take resources and time."

Harris got up.

"I'll talk to the Director, try to buy you ten days. He'll have to get the President to approve it. After that . . ." He shrugged.

"Three weeks," Scorpion said.

"Ten days. But you better come up with something fast." Harris looked at Shaefer, Scorpion, and Rabinowich on the screen. "As of right now, you three are a special task force. Special Access Program Critical. No one outside us knows anything. Shaefer," he said, nodding at the lanky African-American, "will coordinate. He will speak with not just my authority, but the DCIA's. The Director's already on board, by the way. Use any assets you deem necessary. The entire U.S. military if we have to. Dave," Harris said, turning to the laptop screen. "This is your full-time assignment. And talk to no one inside Langley but me, understood? Anyone gives you shit, send them to me."

Harris looked at all of them.

"We're back in business, guys. Just like old times," he said, winking.

"Better not be," Scorpion said, remembering Rome and St. Petersburg and Kiev.

"You've got the easy job." Harris grinned, the smile that had gotten half the female interns in Washington to drop their pants. "I've got to convince the President to slow-dance with the Washington press corps for ten days in the middle of a crisis."

Harris's L-3 phone chimed. It was a Secure Mobile Environment Portable Electronic Device, a combination cell phone and PDA for Top Secret calls, texts, e-mails and surfing via JWICS. He took the call, holding up his hand to indicate that they should wait.

"Shit!" he said tersely into the phone, then: "Tell 'em do nothing till I get back to Washington tonight," and ended the call. "Shit! Shit! Shit!" he snarled, and looked at them. "Senator Russell got hold of the DNA data indicating it's the Iranians. He's leaked it. It'll be all over tomorrow's *New York Times*."

"That's torn it," Shaefer said disgustedly, getting up. He was supposed to be headed for Bern to dig up what he could from the Swiss federal and cantonal police. "They'll be wanting to declare war before the week is out."

"That's not the only problem," Harris said. "The real problem is not just who wants to pick a fight with the most powerful country in the world. Has it occurred to anyone to ask why? And who in Iran—if it is Iran? And if we don't figure it out, we could be playing right into their hands. There's something going on here that, unless we get it right, is going to come back and bite us in the ass."

"Unbelievable," Rabinowich said.

"What is?" Shaefer asked.

"First time I ever agreed with Bob," Rabinowich said.

Scorpion looked at Harris with his cold, gray eyes.

"Ten days," he said.

"Did you not hear what I said? That asshole Russell just changed the equation. It'll be a miracle if I can get us five," Harris said, heading for the door, then stopping. A nerve in his jaw throbbed. "And Scorpion, they murdered our people in cold blood. No prisoners."

"I wasn't planning on it," Scorpion said.

CHAPTER SEVEN

The two men sat in a corner restaurant near the Schwamendinger-Platz. It was a small place where locals stopped by for a quick lunch or for dinner and a beer after work. Scorpion sat with his back to the wall, facing the street door. Opposite him, Mathias Schwegler, the CIA's man in Zurich, had opened his Armani suit jacket and taken off his Prada tie—as being out of place in the working-class restaurant—and was tearing into an *eintopf*, a veal and vegetable hot pot.

"He's a good guy. You'll like him," Shaefer had said of Schwegler.

"I don't have to like him," Scorpion had replied.

Schwegler was a good-looking man, the kind you'd spot in the first-class lounge of an airline terminal, a sleek blonde beside him. They had chosen this place because it was across the street from the office building on Winterthurerstrasse, where the "Gnomes"—Harris's joke name for the people he had left behind to help out, including Chrissie, she of the perfect teeth and the Beretta, plus two of Schwegler's men—were setting up for the sting. Through the window Scorpion saw that the rain had stopped, the tram wires like black lines drawn on the gray sky.

He leaned forward, holding a green bottle of Feldschlösschen beer close to his mouth, and whispered, "Who put Rabinowich onto Homer? You?" he asked. Named after the Homer Simpson cartoon character, Homer was the code name they'd assigned to Hooshang Norouzi, an Iranian businessman with offices in the Seefeld neighborhood in Zurich's District 8.

"The other way around," Schwegler said, glancing around to make sure they weren't overheard, even though they were speaking English. "About eight months ago, Dave spotted a COMINT from No Such," using the Company slang term for the National Security Agency, known on Capitol Hill as "No Such Agency," because its existence had been denied for years. "A contact code he tied to K.H."

"Good catch," Scorpion murmured. K.H. was Kta'eb Hezbollah, the ultrasecret paramilitary faction within the Iranian Revolutionary Guards he had asked Harandi about that night on the ferry.

"We already had our eyes on this guy because his company, Jamaran Trading International, SA, was negotiating deals for missile components with Rosoboronexport," Schwegler said. "We immediately started full-time COMINT monitoring."

"Surveillance?" Scorpion said, asking if they put a twenty-four-hour watch on Norouzi, his mind going a mile a minute. No wonder Rabinowich had targeted Norouzi as their best bet for the cutout. Rosoboronexport was the big Russian missile company. They made some of the most advanced missiles in the world, including the kind of antiaircraft and antimissile systems Iran was desperate to get its hands on. If Norouzi was negotiating with Rosoboronexport, he had to be tied to the Revolutionary Guards.

"Who has budget for surveillance these days?" Schwegler sighed. "The *dummen* accountants run the world now."

Even more intriguing, Scorpion thought, Jamaran was the neighborhood in northern Tehran where Ayatollah Khomeini, father of the Iranian Revolution, had lived. It could mean that Homer was a true believer or had connections with the Khomeini family.

He leaned in closer.

"Dave's a mathematician," he murmured. "He wouldn't've bet the bank on a pair of deuces. What aren't you telling me?"

Schwegler took a swig of his Eichhof beer and leaned closer as well.

"*Gol ghermez*," he whispered. "The call was received by a cell phone somewhere in or around the Kreuzplatz in District 8."

"So?"

"Homer's office is on Kreuzstrasse," Schwegler said. "You can walk to the square."

Bingo, Scorpion thought. "But it's still thin," he said aloud, nibbling halfheartedly at a salad, then pushing it away.

"I am more worrying about Apple-cake. This is

the most difficult," Schwegler said. "What happens if Homer finds out?"

"You double him," Scorpion said, wiping his mouth with a napkin, getting ready to leave. "We should have had weeks to set this up, not hours." He leaned in. "Are your men tough enough?" asking would they be physical enough and believable enough to fool Norouzi.

"Two of them, Dieter and Marco, are veterans of Einsatzgruppe TIGRIS, Federal," Schwegler whispered. Scorpion took his meaning. Einsatzgruppe TIGRIS was a special tactical unit of the Swiss Federal Police. The Swiss media had dubbed them "supercops." He added, "What about the Gnomes?"

"None of them speaks German," Scorpion said. "They've been told to keep their stupid mouths shut and stay out of sight as much as possible. Where's the extraction?"

"This you will like." Schwegler grinned like he had won the lottery. "Something irresistible. Homer thinks he's hit it big." He whispered the location to Scorpion.

"You're right. I like it." Scorpion smiled as he got up. But all he could think of were the million things that could go wrong.

"And you?" Schwegler asked, meaning what was Scorpion's next move.

"*Apfelkuchen*," Scorpion said, tossing down a twenty CHF note. Apple-cake.

There are private clubs all over the world. Country clubs, golf and tennis clubs, men's clubs, places behind guarded gates or in high rises where celebrities and movie stars go for privacy, knowing the only people they'll run into are other celebrities. And then there's the Club Baur au Lac.

Located in a private mansion across a narrow canal from Zurich's famous Baur au Lac Hotel, the club was a place for business lunches for faceless men in bespoke suits in private yellow salons with yellow awnings on windows overlooking a private garden and the gray waters of Lake Zurich. Members can also repair to the wood-paneled English bar for drinks and Cuban cigars served by silent, efficient Swiss bar men and waiters whose most important skill is their discretion. Membership was by invitation only, and mere millionaires, celebrities, sports stars, and women need not apply.

The men who lunch there are billionaires and the CEOs of major international banks and corporations who value privacy above all else. Most of the world's commodities are represented. Deals worth billions are negotiated over brandy, and a casual nod at the club is considered as binding as the most iron-clad contract.

As he lay flat on the roof of the office building peering through binoculars at the gated driveway to the club across the street, Scorpion mused that when Homer received the luncheon invitation from Herr Matthäus, of the big Swiss arms trading company IWT, SA, he must have thought he had died and gone to Jannah, the Muslim heaven.

The location of the Club Baur au Lac for the grab was to get around the fact that Homer traveled with bodyguards in an armored limousine. An armed confrontation in the middle of Zurich would have made the plan impossible. Scorpion checked his watch. He should have had more time to put this together, he fretted for the twentieth time. It wasn't solid planning, just a last minute, thrown-together improvisation. In a half hour he would have to head to Kloten to pick up Apple-cake at the airport.

Through the binoculars, he spotted Schwegler and three of his men going into the club. They had shown their federal Bundesamt für Polizei badges to the gate guards, parked the BMW SUV, and were now waiting unseen inside the entrance hall. He looked at his watch again. Where the hell was the mark?

His cell phone vibrated. He had a text.

Das Wetter ist heute bewölkt, hoch von 12 Grad

It read: "The weather today is cloudy, high of twelve degrees Celsius." It was from one of Schwegler's watchers on General Guisan-Quai, paralleling the promenade along Lake Zurich. Homer was due any second.

He watched the black armored Mercedes turn in on Claridenstrasse and stop at the gated driveway. The private guards at the club would not allow armed bodyguards on the grounds, and he could see a guard talking to the driver, explaining club rules that they were to stay with the limousine in the parking lot. Only club members and invited male guests would be allowed anywhere inside or near the front entrance. A dark-haired Middle Eastern man in a gray business suit—Scorpion assumed it was Norouzi—got out of the Mercedes, walked by himself to the club entrance and went inside. The limo drove to the lot around the back from the entrance and parked. The bodyguards stayed inside the limo, and Scorpion started breathing again.

If it happened the way it was supposed to, it would happen quickly, he told himself, watching through the binoculars. He was counting on that, and on the fact that the Swiss running the club prized discretion above all else. That, more than anything, was the key to the plan—that they would not call the Kantonspolizei.

Schwegler and his men came out of the club. They were around Norouzi, hustling him into the waiting SUV. A moment later Scorpion watched the SUV come out onto the street, heading toward Dreikönigstrasse. He didn't have to see inside the darkened windows to know they would have handcuffed Norouzi and thrown a black hood over his head. He turned the binoculars to Norouzi's limousine in the parking lot. It didn't move; no one got out. From where they were, they couldn't see the front driveway and what had just happened. Scorpion checked his watch again. Apple-cake time.

CHAPTER EIGHT

Schwamendingen,
Zurich, Switzerland

They were driving into Zurich from the airport. Apple-cake, in the passenger seat, was an Iranian-American in a rumpled gray suit, no tie, and a smile that revealed a gold tooth in place of one of his canines. For this operation, Apple-cake's cover was that he was Hamid Baveghli, a Swiss-Iranian lawyer from Geneva.

"*Shoma Alemani beladid?*" Do you speak German? Scorpion asked in Farsi as he drove the rental car on the autoroute. Traffic was moving normally, the scenery monotonous; trees, power lines, and office parks.

"No, just Farsi and English. Some Swedish," Apple-cake replied in Farsi.

"Swedish." Scorpion frowned. "I need you to speak Schweizerdeutsch." Swiss German. "And French. *Parlez-vous français, Monsieur Baveghli?*" he said, using Apple-cake's cover name.

"No, I don't *parlez-vous.*" Apple-cake grinned, flashing his gold tooth.

What the hell was Shaefer thinking? Scorpion wondered, starting to get a bad feeling. Shaefer must've been scrambling, but still, it was like pitching a Double A ball rookie in a World Series game.

"If you think this is a joke," he growled, "trust me, I'll have you posted to Shit Hole, Alaska, to count rocks for the rest of your career."

"Sorry, I just got pulled into this," Apple-cake mumbled.

"All right. No German," Scorpion said, taking a deep breath. Apple-cake wasn't much, but he was all they had. "We'll have to work something out for French. Ear receiver, maybe," he added, slowing as he turned into the heavier traffic on the A1. "Let's go over the cover. Tell me about yourself, Hamid."

"I'm a lawyer with the firm, Spalding and Cellini, SA. We're in Geneva," Apple-cake said.

"In French, lawyer is *avocat*. Got it? What's the address?"

"Fourteen Rue du Rhône, Geneva."

Bloody hell, Scorpion thought. "For God's sake, say *quatorze* not fourteen. And it's *Genève* in French—not Geneva," he snapped.

"*Genève*," Apple-cake repeated.

"Your client's name is Hooshang Norouzi. Call him Monsieur Norouzi or Hooshang *agha*. You don't know who's holding him, but if he asks you, you can let it drop that you suspect it's the NDB, the Swiss federal intelligence service. You think they've taken him in at the behest of the CIA, though no one's talking. In fact, you don't want to mention CIA involvement specifically, but you can imply CIA all you want. He'll suspect it anyway. Who hired you to represent him?" Scorpion asked, moving into the right lane to exit the autoroute at Wallisellen. He took the exit onto a street of apartment buildings, spindly trees, and strip malls—the part of Zurich where the working people who couldn't afford to shop on Bahnhofstrasse lived.

"I was contacted through an intermediary—can't reveal who—from the Iranian Embassy."

"What's their address?"

"Thunstrasse 68 in Bern."

"Shoma dar Iran al-e koja hastid?" Scorpion asked. Where in Iran are you from?

"I was born in the States—" Apple-cake began.

"Are you out of your mind?!" Scorpion snapped. This guy was pathetic, like a bad *American Idol* audition. He took a breath. "Look, where were your parents—your real parents—from?"

"Northern Tehran."

"Where? What district?"

"Elahieh."

Scorpion studied him out of the corner of his eye. Before the Iranian Revolution, Elahieh had been a Jewish neighborhood.

"You're Jewish, right?" he asked. "Your parents fled when the shah fell?"

Apple-cake looked taken aback. He nodded.

"What street did they live on?"

"I don't know," he said. "It's before I was born."

"All right, listen. Your parents still live in Elahieh, in a fancy high rise on Farzin Street, a block from Fereshteh Street. Everybody in Tehran knows Fereshteh Street. The Jews are long gone. It's all high rises now, very expensive. If he ever asks, it'll impress the shit out of him. And for God's sakes, you're not Jewish, understood?"

"Yes," Apple-cake said, suddenly deadly serious.

Scorpion exhaled. "Look. Here's the key: you're his friend, his best *dust*. You want to help. As an *avocat suisse*, a good Swiss lawyer and fellow Iranian, you are outraged at this violation of Swiss neutrality and at the NDB sucking at the CIA's teat. Be indignant. Cite Articles 173 and 185 of the Swiss Federal Constitution on Switzerland's neutrality to him and anybody who'll listen. Understood?"

Apple-cake nodded.

"And most important—and this is absolutely critical—don't ask him any questions. That's key to this movie," he added, using the intelligence term to describe the creation of a scenario that was presented as real to a mark but in fact wasn't. "Remember, we don't want or need any information from him. We just want him to think we do. You're on his side, his *avocat*. That's it. At most, at the absolute most, you can ask him at the end if there's anything he knows or might have done that you as his lawyer should know about in case it comes up."

"If he says, no . . . ?" Apple-cake asked.

"Good. You're happy," Scorpion said.

"And if he says, yes . . . ?"

"Don't say a word. Just listen. Remember, he's not a joe. He's a client—and a fellow countryman in a place where you're surrounded by infidels and the walls have ears. You're his lawyer. Period. And a loyal supporter of the Iranian government and the Supreme Leader. You're a *baradar* of the Revolutionary Guards and a good Shiite Muslim, and you don't know what this is about. That's who you are," Scorpion concluded, pulling into the parking lot for the office building on Winterthurerstrasse, where, if everything was going according to plan, they were currently putting Norouzi through what was politely called in CIA-speak "enhanced interrogation."

"**H**e doesn't speak French or German?" Schwegler said. They were in the bare office—just two chairs and a table, the windows shuttered and locked—that they would use for Homer to meet with Apple-cake. "*Sheisse*," he muttered. Shit.

"And his suit looks like *sheisse* too," Scorpion grimaced. "I sent Chrissie to get him something decent on Bahnhofstrasse."

"What'll we do about the language?"

"They'll talk Farsi. The Gnomes will set him up with an ear receiver. I'll be on a microphone in case he needs French or I have to tell him what to do."

"We'll use Dieter and Marco as the guards," Schwegler said. "Only German speakers."

"How's Homer doing?"

"Not bad. They beat him up; nothing that shows. Some really good smacks with a rubber baton in the testicles. He'll walk funny for a while. Stress positions. No food, water. Blasting Eurotrash music on earphones so he can't think. Naked. Always in the hood, so he can see nothing; no sense of time. They're waterboarding him now."

"Said anything of interest?"

"Claims to be innocent. Knows nothing. Demands to be able to call his office. He's good," Schwegler said with a touch of admiration.

"Cell phones?"

"He had two: a prepaid and an iPhone. The Gnomes are working on them now."

Scorpion turned the laptop to the hidden camera in the basement room where they were interrogating Norouzi, his head covered by the black hood, hands tied behind his back.

With a flick of his wrist, one of Schwegler's men, Dieter, smacked Norouzi's groin hard with a truncheon.

"*Sprechen Sie, du Stück Scheisse!*" Dieter shouted. Talk, you piece of shit!

"*Ich weiss gar nichts,*" Norouzi gasped, his voice muffled by the hood. I don't know anything.

There was a knock at the door. Scorpion shut the laptop as Chrissie came in. She was holding an expensive men's blue suit and a shirt and tie on hangers, and carrying a shopping bag from Weinberg's on Bahnhofstrasse.

"What do you think?" she said. "The suit's a Zilli. Isn't it gorgeous?" wrinkling her nose. "The tie is Burberry."

"Looks good. Thanks," Scorpion told her, waving her away.

"Don't thank me. I wish I could dress men in expensive clothes all the time. It's the sexiest thing on the planet," she said, flashing her perfect teeth as she left.

They watched her go.

"At least someone's happy," Schwegler said.

"So long as it's not Homer," Scorpion said.

Eleven hours later, at four in the morning, they brought Homer/Norouzi into the room. He was shackled and the hood was still on his head. They had put his shirt and trousers back on but his feet were still bare, and after hours of interrogation they had to support him to keep him upright as they sat him in the chair and ran a chain from his shackles through an eye bolt on the floor. Schwegler's men, Dieter and Marco, checked the room one last time to make sure there was nothing that could be used by Norouzi to orient himself as to who was holding him, what time it was, or where he was. The one window was shuttered and locked; the security cameras were in place.

Watching from an office two offices away on laptops showing multiple security camera views of the room were Scorpion, Schwegler, Apple-cake, and the Gnomes. Scorpion turned to Schwegler.

"How long does he think he's been here?" Scorpion asked. He wore earphones and a microphone set to transmit to an invisible earpiece in Apple-cake's ear. Apple-cake stood next to him, nervously tapping his hand on his thigh.

"Two days. He asked how many days he's been here. Of course, they hit him for asking," Schwegler whispered, even though they had soundproofed the office.

On the screen, they watched Marco leave the room. Dieter was alone with Norouzi. They watched as Dieter removed Norouzi's hood.

"*Ihr Büro muss jemand kontaktiert haben.*" Your office must have contacted someone, Dieter said, going to the door. "Your lawyer is here."

Scorpion tapped Apple-cake's arm.

"You're up," he said. He heard Apple-cake take a deep breath, hesitate for a second, then leave. He watched him walk into the office next door on the monitor, Dieter opening the door for him and then closing it, leaving the two of them, Apple-cake and Norouzi, alone. Apple-cake, looking surprisingly sharp in his new suit, sat across from Norouzi. Around him, Scorpion felt everyone hold their breath.

"Hooshang Norouzi *agha*, *esm-e man* Hamid Baveghli *ast*," Apple-cake said, sitting down at the table, saying in Farsi, Mr. Hooshang Norouzi, my name is Hamid Baveghli. "I'm a lawyer. I was contacted by the Iranian Embassy. They are concerned. Are you all right?"

Norouzi looked at him. Despite being the worse for wear, his hair disheveled and needing a shave, his eyes were clear.

"Where am I?" he asked in Farsi.

"You're in an office in District 12," Apple-cake said. He glanced around and leaned closer. "I'm not sure how much I'm allowed to tell you. My main concern is getting you out," he whispered.

"Who's holding me?" Norouzi asked.

On the laptop screen, Apple-cake looked blank. Christ, Scorpion thought. Apple-cake swallowed; a deer in the headlights.

"You don't know," Scorpion whispered into the microphone in Farsi. "But it's not the *cantonale*. Your office checked."

Apple-cake repeated what Scorpion had said in Farsi, using the French phrase for the canton police. Norouzi stared at him, his face tight.

"Who's holding me?" he repeated.

Apple-cake leaned forward conspiratorially.

"No one's talking. But we suspect the NDB, the Swiss intelligence service. What did they want?"

"What the *goh* is this?" Norouzi growled suspiciously. "Who are you? What company did you say you were from?"

Apple-cake straightened up as if he'd been slapped.

"I told you, Norouzi *agha*. My name is Hamid Baveghli. I'm a lawyer with the law firm Spalding and Cellini, SA of Gen—" Shit, Scorpion thought, thinking he was going to say Geneva. But Apple-cake caught himself: "*–nève.*"

"How'd you find me?"

"It wasn't easy," Apple-cake started, looking around and leaning forward to whisper as Scorpion scrambled to open another window on his laptop and pull up the relevant Swiss legal section. He whispered it into the microphone. "We had to file a writ of habeas corpus under Title 2, Article 31 of the Swiss Federal Constitution. We had to call in favors to find you."

Apple-cake ad-libbed what he'd been told in Farsi, and Scorpion thought, Good. Finally, he's actually thinking.

"Do you have any idea why they brought you in?" Apple-cake asked.

"The attack on the American embassy," Norouzi said. "They think I know something."

Apple-cake nodded. "No wonder all the secrecy. Any idea why they thought you might know something?"

"I know nothing. I had nothing to do with it. I told them," Norouzi said, staring at him without expression.

"Of course. It's because we're Muslims, *jenab* Norouzi *agha*," Apple-cake said sympathetically, using the honorific, *jenab*. "I'll bet it's not just the NDB," he whispered, implying the CIA might be behind it.

Scorpion nudged Schwegler.

"Your cue," he murmured.

Schwegler nodded and took an official-looking writ out of his suit jacket pocket. He went into the next room followed by Dieter and Marco, who carried the rest of Norouzi's clothes.

"Herr Baveghli," he said to Apple-cake, then caught himself and switched from German to French. "Pardon, Monsieur Baveghli. I'm Müller. We have your writ under Title 2."

"Monsieur Müller, *c'est un scandale*." It's an outrage, Scorpion said in French into the microphone, then switched to English. "A violation of Swiss law and neutrality. Monsieur Norouzi must be released at once," watching as Apple-cake repeated it word for word to Schwegler.

"Of course," Schwegler said. And to Norouzi in German: "Herr Norouzi, you're free to go," gesturing to Dieter and Marco to unlock the shackles and give Norouzi the rest of his clothes. "If you wish, Herr Norouzi, my men can take you home or wherever you want."

"No, please," Norouzi replied in German, wincing as he pulled himself up straight. "I've had quite enough of your men."

"I have a car downstairs," Apple-cake said. "I'll take you home, Monsieur Norouzi."

As Norouzi collected his things and dressed,

moving painfully, Schwegler and his men watched, saying nothing.

Norouzi, helped by Apple-cake, limped to the door. As they went out, followed by Schwegler and his men, Schwegler told Norouzi in German, "Don't leave Zurich, Herr Norouzi. Our investigation is not yet concluded."

"Tu goh khordie," Scorpion heard Norouzi mutter in Farsi as he left. *Go eat shit.*

Putting his finger to his lips to alert the others, Scorpion put his ear to the office front door. He heard the elevator go down and went to the window, peering out from behind the curtain.

He watched as they came out of the building. Norouzi waited on the sidewalk below with Schwegler, Dieter, and Marco, while Apple-cake brought the car around. Norouzi got in, throwing off Dieter's helping hand, and a moment later the car disappeared down Winterthurerstrasse, the overhead tram lines swaying slightly in the wind. The sky was beginning to turn the faint purple-gray of predawn, still too dark to see the distant Alps.

The others had gone back to work or had left. Only Chrissie stood next to him.

"Now what?" she asked.

"We wait," Scorpion said. "You go join the surveillance team."

Forty minutes later Scorpion got the call. It was Glenn, the buzz cut in the Burberry, whom he had assigned as the lead bird dog.

"We lost Homer," Glenn said, panic in his voice evident even with a bad cell connection and the sound of a tram in the background.

"Impossible," Scorpion said, a sick feeling growing in the pit of his stomach. It couldn't be. They were using GPS and COMINT tracking three different ways, plus 360 surveillance on Norouzi's apartment house. "What the hell are you talking about?"

"He's gone. Disappeared," Glenn said.

CHAPTER NINE

Barcelona,
Spain

"Sagen Sie dem Gärtner, muss das Gras zu schneiden."
Tell the Gardener, the grass needs to be cut.

Scorpion kept going over that single sentence again and again in his mind on the flight from Zurich to Barcelona. "Tell the Gardener." The Gardener. And the sound of it. A woman's voice on a cell phone call speaking German, but with a hint of Slavic in her accent; not a native German or Swiss-German speaker.

Because they were still working out JWICS logistics, Shaefer had forwarded the MP3 of the woman's voice to Scorpion during their chat in a European singles Internet chat room so highly trafficked that chances of interception were remote. In the chat room, Shaefer was a forty-something Italian woman named Liliana from Bari in Apulia, the heel of the Italian boot, and Scorpion was Claude, a high school teacher in St.-Étienne in France with a thing for women's high heeled shoes, *avec des sangles.* The strappy kind.

Glenn's call had sent them scrambling. From the moment Apple-cake dropped Norouzi off at his apartment building in Leimbach until they had eyes on the building, barely one minute forty seconds had elapsed. The video camera planted in a tree across the street showed no one had exited the building during those critical seconds. Plus there was electronic surveillance. While they had been interrogating Norouzi, two of the Gnomes set up bugs and hidden cameras for 24/7 monitoring of Norouzi's apartment; in CIA-speak, a 360 black-bag job.

Except the monitors showed there was no one in Norouzi's apartment. The bugs they had planted on Norouzi's cell phones, plus an additional bug sewed into the seam of his pants, indicated no movement. So Norouzi was stationary and in the building.

Except he wasn't.

To confirm, Dieter had knocked on the apartment door and, when no one answered, picked the lock and went inside. It was empty. There was no sign that after Apple-cake dropped him off, Norouzi had ever returned to his apartment.

They would have to search the entire building. While Schwegler set up a power outage as an excuse so Dieter and Marco could go in as electricians to "check" every apartment, Scorpion pulled up on his laptop the file Rabinowich had put together on Norouzi. The bottom line, was, as Schwegler put it: *"Unmöglich."* Impossible. "People don't just disappear."

Scorpion scoured the files on his laptop from both Rabinowich and Schwegler, focusing on Norouzi's company, Jamaran Trading International.

But he didn't see anything that would provide a lead on Norouzi's disappearance. It didn't compute anyway, he told himself. They had taken him home. Whatever disappearing act Norouzi pulled off had happened inside the apartment building.

One thing: the fact that Norouzi had bolted suggested they were on the right track. He wasn't some innocent foreign businessman in Zurich.

Scorpion went back over what they had on Norouzi's personal life. He lived with his wife and son, a ten-year-old. At the moment, according to Schwegler, the wife and son were visiting relatives in Iran. There was also a teenage daughter in boarding school in Lausanne. He called Schwegler and told him to check with the school and make sure the girl was at the school where she was supposed to be.

And a mistress—a twenty-year-old girl from Kharkov in eastern Ukraine named Oksana—Scorpion feeling a twinge, the reference to Ukraine reminding him of Iryna and Kiev. A Facebook photo of Oksana showed a pouty blonde in a short skirt and white boots barely older than Norouzi's daughter. He looked for the girlfriend's address in the file. It wasn't there.

How the hell had they missed that? he wondered, texting Shaefer on JWICS. As he did so, Glenn called to tell him a young woman in a red VW CC was driving out of the apartment building's underground garage.

Scorpion texted furiously to Shaefer: *homeys girlfriend. whats her address?*

At the same time, on his cell to Glenn, he said: "Describe her."

Why? Is she hot? Shaefer typed back.

"Blond. Long straight hair. Not bad looking," Glenn said. "Do we tail?"

Need address now! Scorpion typed.

Seconds ticked. Then Shaefer responded, and there it was.

Oksana's address was the same as Norouzi's, only his apartment was on the second floor, hers on the fourth. Norouzi had had the balls to install his girl-friend in an apartment in the same building as his wife and family.

"Front and back tail," Scorpion told Glenn. "Don't lose her. Take Chrissie." Norouzi must have gone straight to his girlfriend's apartment in the same building instead of going back to his place. If she was leaving now, it was on an errand from him and he was at her apartment, or he was hidden, pos-sibly in the trunk or backseat of the VW.

Scorpion got the text from Glenn half an hour later.

Stopped. Rudenplatz. Hair salon. The girlfriend, Oksana, had parked in or near the Rudenplatz in Zurich's Old Town and gone into a hair salon.

Send Chrissie in after her, he texted back.

She's already on it, Glenn responded. Good girl, Scorpion thought.

It didn't take long. Oksana made a call from the ladies' room in the hair salon. She spoke the single sentence in German that had whole departments at both the CIA and NSA working overtime, then hung up. Fortunately, Chrissie had been at the sink outside the stall and done a swipe, technology that enabled you to hack someone's cell phone with an appropriately configured cell phone just by coming within a few meters of them. Once she had the message, Chrissie linked it with NSA-based SIGINT; it was "slaved," to be able to eavesdrop on everything said or done with that person's cell phone.

Within minutes the MP3 file of Oksana's call in German had been forwarded via satellite to the Black House, the NSA headquarters in Fort Meade, Maryland. Ten minutes later both Scorpion and Shaefer had the original message in German and the translation. Shaefer texted Scorpion that she had made the call to a cell phone in Barcelona, Spain.

The business heard on the cell phone about cutting the grass was probably their equivalent of a Flagstaff-type message, indicating to whomever was running Norouzi that he'd been taken in for questioning on the Bern attack. Or maybe Norouzi was pulling the pilot eject handle, telling them to pull him out. He'd leave that to the cryptologists, Scorpion thought. Bottom line, it was a distress call. The key was the Gardener, whoever or whatever that was. Shaefer had indicated that according to Rabinowich, Langley had never heard of the Gardener.

Shaefer had texted that *pikl @ ful boyle*, the Pickle Factory, insider slang for the CIA, was at full boil, running around like crazy trying to come up with something.

Rabinowich indicated that Harris suspected the Gardener—presumed to be a previously unknown spymaster—was the person behind the Bern attack. Scorpion could already see where Harris was going with that. If he could pin the blame for Bern on the Gardener—and if he, Scorpion, could identify who this Gardener was, preferably someone in the Iranian government—the generals and the hawks would be able to bomb Iran, and no one at the UN or anywhere else would raise a finger against it.

"Find the Gardener," was the Company's new imperative. Their top priority, Shaefer had told him.

"Maybe he didn't do it. Maybe it's a cover and there is no Gardener," Scorpion said. That wasn't the least of what was troubling him.

"Find him anyway," Shaefer replied.

At Zurich Airport, waiting for his flight to Barcelona, Scorpion watched a TV monitor showing a U.S. aircraft carrier moving into the Persian Gulf. The announcer looked meaningfully into the camera and pronounced: *"Iranische DNA. Heist das, Krieg?"*

He had just enough German to know he was saying: Iranian DNA. Does this mean war?

War, he thought. The Iranians had to be feeling it too. He had to talk to Shaefer. As the gate loudspeaker announced his flight, he held back, taking out his L-3 SME PED device and dialing. Shaefer picked up at the first ring.

"Mendelssohn," Shaefer, a music lover, answered, using the agreed-upon code name. His voice was faintly slurred by the encryption on the line.

"Flagstaff," Scorpion said. "Listen. We need to pull the Gnomes. Just use COMINT."

"Negative," Shaefer said in such a way that Scorpion sensed he had already been arguing with Langley about it. "Soames says no."

"Soames? How the hell did he get into this?"

"Harris had to deal with— Never mind. There's a pissing contest going on with the alphabet soups."

Scorpion could only imagine the turf wars as the different agencies, the CIA, the DIA, SOCOM, the State Department's INR, and for all he knew, the Girl Scouts, fought over the operation.

"I don't give a damn," he said through clenched teeth, glancing around to make sure he wasn't overheard. "Pull 'em. It isn't going to take whoever's behind this two minutes to figure out that the Iranian Embassy never sent a lawyer to free Homer." As it was, they were damn lucky Apple-cake was safely on a flight back to Stockholm.

"That point's been raised," Shaefer said evenly, and Scorpion sensed the battle behind the scenes. He imagined Shaefer sitting in front of his computer in his office in Bucharest, or maybe he was still at the safe house in Zug, staring out at the view of the hills and the town and the lake. "Soames says what if Barcelona's a feint?"

"Is he completely insane?" Scorpion growled. "Homey's so scared shitless he has to send his girlfriend to broadcast an SOS from a hair salon in the Rudenplatz, and this idiot thinks it's a feint?"

"Politics. He's covering his ass. He wants the Gnomes here so whatever happens, it won't come back to bite the great you-know-who," and Scorpion knew he was talking about Harris. In the background, he heard the gate loudspeaker announce the final boarding call for his flight.

"Jesus," Scorpion breathed. "Didn't that jerk go to high school? Every action has an equal and opposite reaction. Listen, there's some protocol here. I'm the field op, the one who requested them in the first place. This is an order. Pull them out now!"

"They don't want to be pulled. What if someone contacts Homey?" Shaefer said. It sounded like Shaefer wasn't sure. He was being pulled in two directions.

"Do it," Scorpion said, ending the call, and immediately calling Mathias Schwegler.

There were street sounds in the background when Schwegler answered. He must be walking, Scorpion thought.

"Flagstaff," he said. "There's a storm coming. I told Shaefer to pull the Gnomes."

"It appears there is confusion on this," Schwegler said carefully, clearly aware of the disagreement going on back at Langley.

"I'm the field op. You don't want your people walking in a mine field." In the background, he could hear the final boarding call for his flight.

"My feelings also. *Ein genuss*, my friend," Schwegler said. It's been a pleasure.

"See you around," Scorpion said, ending the call and slipping onto the boarding bridge as they were about to close the gate.

Flying into Barcelona at dusk, he could see the strings of lights on the boulevards and along the line of the shore, the spires of the Sagrada Familia church and the phallic shape of the Agbar Tower lit up like gold against a pink and purple sky.

He had a bad feeling about leaving the Gnomes behind in Zurich. Soames didn't get it. They were doing 24/7 surveillance on Norouzi, which made them easy to spot. And they were so obviously Americans, they stuck out like African-Americans at a Mormon convention. They couldn't even speak German. It made the hairs on the back of his neck stand on end. All he could do was hope to God he was wrong and that Shaefer was able to change Soames's mind, or even better, get to Harris and pull them out.

The mission was getting to him. He thought about pulling out himself. It was all too improvised, too catch as can. Too much could go bad very fast— and no time to fix it. Think of something else, he told himself. Think of something good.

He leaned back in his seat and thought about Sandrine. He pictured her back in Africa outside the hospital tent at dusk, the refugee families around cooking fires, an acacia tree in the distance. A fantasy, he thought. She could be anywhere. For all he knew, she had gone back to her millionaire fiancé. Be a damned sight more sensible than waiting around for him. Except he didn't think she had. That wasn't her.

The flight attendant announced on the intercom in Spanish, German, and English to prepare for landing. The plane made a wide turn as it descended to approach the airport. Through the window, he could see lights of the islands of Menorca and Mallorca against the darkening sky. Out of habit, he glanced at his watch: 6:14 P.M. local time.

He had at most eight or nine days, probably less.

CHAPTER TEN

Zurich-Höngg,
Switzerland

For Scale, the problem was the twenty-four-hour surveillance. They—he assumed it was the Swiss NDB, although for all he knew it was the CIA—were watching Norouzi so closely that, as the Persian saying went, they had eyes in their asses.

During a drive-by earlier that day, Scale had spotted not only the parked VW with watchers, but security cameras set up for complete coverage of the apartment house in the Leimbach quarter where Norouzi was holed up with his Ukrainian whore. They also likely had surveillance equipment and maybe even a watcher hiding on the hill behind the apartment house.

Problem one: Norouzi had sent them a message. So how were they to get a message back to him? They were not only watching him round-the-clock, he had to assume they had an invisible net over him to bug all electronic communications. The Swiss and the Americans were good at that sort of thing, he acknowledged. Any kind of call, e-mail, text, anything electronic was impossible.

Problem two: even if they did get a message through, would Norouzi show up? And if he did, what to do about the watchers?

Problem three: what to do about the Ukrainian whore?

He thought about the apartment house. They were holed up in there. Did either of them go out at all? Of course. The whore went to the Migros supermarket every day to shop.

Scale smiled to himself as he looked up the hill through binoculars toward Norouzi's apartment house on Maneggpromenade and took out his cell phone. He had the solution. All he needed was a junkie, preferably female; less threatening.

He picked the girl up on Langstrasse, the main street of Zurich's red light district. At night it was filled with the lights of bars, clubs, passing trams, and men of all nationalities crowding the sidewalks, but the morning belonged to the junkies and prostitutes too desperate for a fix to wait for nighttime. She was thin, a Brazilian with long dark hair and coffee-colored skin, arms scarred by needle marks, and if she hadn't been desperate, she wouldn't have been working the street at eleven in the morning for a quick forty Swiss francs.

Scale offered her a hundred.

"For a hundred I do anything you want, *schatz*," she said, inclining her head toward a nearby hotel with a neon sign, pale in the morning light, that read THE VEGAS. "Whatever you want. Mouth, anal, I'll let you hit me," she whispered, pressing her thin body against him.

"I need you to come with me," he said in English. "Only for a few hours."

"What is this?" she said, drawing back. "Are you a *bulle*?" German slang for cop.

"Look at me," Scale said, standing there. Small, wiry, Middle Eastern. "I'm not even Swiss."

"What do you want?" she said, her eyes narrow with suspicion.

"I need you just to give something to someone. A woman."

"Give what?"

He showed her. A chocolate candy bar called "Tourist" he had spent a quarter hour rewrapping carefully so it looked like it had never been opened. He put it back in his pocket.

"Just that? A hundred?" she said.

He nodded.

"I can't wait, *schatz*. Give me the money now," she said, her pink tongue darting between her lips. Scale knew if he gave her any money, he'd never see her again.

"Get your—" He hesitated. "You get whatever you need, but I come with you. Then you come with me and I'll give you the rest of the money."

"You don't know these *jungs*," she said, holding out her hand, implying the guys she was talking about were dangerous. "Give me the money. I'll be right back. I'll give you a *blasen*," meaning a blowjob. "No charge, *schatz*," her hand caressing and squeezing his crotch. He grabbed her wrist and started to twist and apply pressure. She cried out and tried to pull away, but he held her hand imprisoned in his powerful oversized hand like a vise.

"A hundred and fifty," he said. "Fifty now—we go wherever you need to, but together—and a hundred after you give her the candy."

An hour later, after she'd had her shot of heroin in the unisex bathroom of a Langstrasse bar lit by blue light so it would be easy for junkies to find their vein, they were in a Migros supermarket in the Leimbach district pretending to shop. Maziar had called him to let him know the Ukrainian woman, Norouzi's mistress, was on the way.

He watched in the overhead aisle mirrors as the Brazilian girl—Yara, she said her name was—walked by the canned vegetables section for the third time, her hand in her handbag holding the candy bar. He had told her to pretend she didn't know him.

Norouzi's blond whore, Oksana, entered the supermarket, and he had to force himself to ignore her. His nerves felt tight as violin strings. He watched her go to the produce section. Yara paid no attention to the blond woman. Stupid junkie whore, he thought. Get her before she leaves.

He just started toward Yara when she turned and walked over to the mistress, Oksana. He watched them out of the corner of his eye in the aisle mirror. Two whores, he thought, watching Yara take the candy bar out of her handbag and hold it out to give to the Ukrainian.

Make it fast, you stupid whore, he thought, as a big man wearing a Burberry came into the supermarket and picked up a shopping basket. An American, by his shoes and crew cut, Scale thought. CIA *madar sag* son of a bitch. So they were the ones who had arrested Norouzi. It wasn't the NDB; it was the CIA after them because of Bern. He would have to alert the Gardener.

He watched Yara in the mirror say in German what he had told her to say:

"A friend says Hooshang likes chocolate."

The woman, Oksana, looked around nervously then took the candy bar and slipped it into her pocket. The two women walked away from each other. Scale didn't think the American, still on the canned goods aisle, had spotted the exchange. They were all over Norouzi, he thought. It was going to be difficult, watching as Yara, throwing him a sideways glance, walked out of the store. For a second he thought the American might go after her. Scale moved over and bumped into him as if by accident.

"*Entschuldigen Sie, mein Herr*," Scale muttered, and paying for a pack of cigarettes, headed out the door. He waited a minute in case the American followed, but the idiot stayed as he had been taught with his primary target—the Ukrainian woman—inside the supermarket. When Scale was sure the American wasn't coming out yet, he went around the corner where Yara was waiting, hugging herself although it wasn't cold. He wondered if she needed another fix so soon. She held out her hand for the money and he handed it to her, then watched her count it.

"Do you want *blasen* now? A quick one. No extra charge," she said, pocketing the money and eyeing

a doorway near the parking area behind the supermarket.

"I need you to forget you ever saw me," Scale said.

"This is easy, *schatz*," she said, already walking
toward the tram stop. "I never look at your faces
anyway."

From his position behind a fallen log at the edge
of a clearing, Scale scanned the approaches through
his night vision goggles. There had been a brief
drizzle earlier that afternoon and the log was still
wet. He could smell the damp leaves and earth. He
studied the small reflector he had set on a stake in
the ground in the center of the clearing for distance
sighting for their weapons. Then he verified the cell
phone numbers for each of the three IEDs he had
set, planted in brush beside the hiking trails. Done.
He pulled his sleeve back to check his watch. Twelve
minutes to go.

The meet was for ten that night. Scale had
written a message to Norouzi in Farsi on a slip of
tissue-thin, water-soluble paper, so it could easily
be disposed of or swallowed in seconds. He'd put it
inside the Tourist candy bar wrapper:

Park-e Bergholz. 300m shomal Kappenbühlstr;
Sa'at 22-e. B.

Bergholz Park. 300 meters north of Kappenbühlstrasse; 2200 hours—10:00 P.M.—and the Farsi letter
be, B, for Baghban, suggesting it was coming from
the Gardener himself. If that didn't make Norouzi
want to shit himself and ensure that he would show,

nothing would. The park was a large wooded area of bike and hiking trails in Höngg, a western suburb in Zurich's District 10, south of the A1 motorway.

Scale knew he would have to deal with the CIA watchers. Norouzi would probably try to lose them in a shopping mall or movie theater, but he didn't know how good Norouzi was and had to assume they would still be on Norouzi when he tried to make the meet. The question was, how many? Best guess was a front and back box, four watchers, but he would plan for more. There was also the matter of Norouzi's whore, Oksana. She would have to be dealt with at the same time, though there was virtually no chance she would be at the meet.

Scale took off his goggles and checked the sensors he had placed on the approach trails. He guessed that Norouzi would be taking the tram, not his car, which meant his most likely approach would be to get off at the tram stop on Michelstrasse and walk to Kappenbühlstrasse, where the entrance to the hiking trail was located.

Scale knew that if he—or the CIA *seyyedan* bastard agents—took another route, his plan wouldn't work and within the hour he would most likely be dead. Nothing he could do about that, he thought. He had four men in place—plus himself, the IEDs, and the element of surprise. And he had sent Danush to take care of the whore. It should be sufficient, he decided. It would have to be.

His cell phone vibrated. One-word text messages from Maziar, then Armin, then Ebrahim, saying yes, meaning they were in position. Nothing from Mohammad. He texted a question mark to Mohammad. No answer. He was about to text Ebrahim to check on him when Mohammad texted back that he was in position on the opposite side of the clearing. Scale scanned the trees on that side through his night goggles. At first he saw nothing. Then he spotted the sound suppressor mounted on the HK G36K assault rifle muzzle peering out of the foliage. *Inshallah*, God willing, he said to himself.

He opened the laptop and saw them. The sensors were working. There were indications of someone, a dot on the screen, coming up the trail from Kappenbühlstrasse, followed a hundred meters behind on the trail by two more moving dots. If there were more, there was no sign of them. He closed the laptop and adjusted the night goggles, his HK rifle, and Beretta with the sound suppressor ready. Idiot, he thought, wondering if Norouzi could really be so stupid as to not know he had CIA agents trailing him.

He searched the far side of the clearing by the gap in the trees where Norouzi would emerge any minute. His cell phone vibrated with another text message. It was from Mohammad and read: *2 in Audi*. So the two American agents tailing Norouzi were backed up by another pair in an Audi, probably parked on Kappenbühlstrasse. The cell vibrated again, but there was no time to look because he saw Norouzi emerge, a lighter green moving figure in the night vision goggles silhouetted against the darker green of the trees. He watched Norouzi walk to the middle of the clearing, stop by the marker and turn, looking around, uncertain what to do next.

Scale waited. He watched the trees at the other end of the clearing. And then he saw two green figures. They stopped by the edge of the clearing and dropped to the ground, making a single green form that didn't move. They wanted to see who would show up. At the same moment, Scale's cell phone vibrated. He didn't have to look at it to know it was coming from either Maziar or Ebrahim, both already concealed on that side of the clearing, letting him know about the two CIA *seyyedan*. He scanned the tree line one last time to see if he could spot his four men, but they were too well hidden. He took a deep breath, and unfastening his Beretta in his shoulder holster under his jacket, stood up.

He walked toward Norouzi, who turned to face him.

"What time does the plane leave?" Norouzi asked in Farsi. The standard contact sign.

"The plane to Isfahan left yesterday," Scale said. "You know you were followed?"

Norouzi nodded. "Are you him?" he whispered, wide-eyed. "Baghban?" The Gardener?

"*Saket, baradar.*" Shut up, brother. "You think they're not listening now?" Scale hissed, his eyes on the tree line.

"They arrested me. They tortured me. My family is in danger. I've got to get out," Norouzi said.

"Who arrested you?" Scale said, watching the trees.

"I'm not sure. They didn't say. The NDB, I think."

"What makes you think NDB?"

"My lawyer thought so. There were a number of

them, but the two who spoke to me spoke Schweizerdeutsch. The lawyer, *inshallah*, spoke Farsi."

"What lawyer?" Scale demanded.

"The one from Geneva. The one the embassy
sent."

You donkey, Scale thought. There was no lawyer
from the Iranian Embassy. It was a "movie." The
CIA had set Norouzi up to see who he would contact, and the idiot had fallen right into their trap.
Keep it calm. Just question him, Scale told himself,
and then he saw them.

Two CIA *seyyedan*, except now he saw that one
was a woman. They had gotten up from where
they had been hiding in the trees and were walking
toward them.

"Listen to me, *baradar*," Scale said. "Your life depends on it. When I say *'pay'in'*"—Farsi for down—
"drop instantly to the ground." It was all happening
very fast. The Americans were getting closer. A big
man with short hair in a Burberry—the one from
the Migros market—and a pretty blond woman.
Both holding pistols aimed right at him and Norouzi.

"Put your hands up!" the American shouted.

"I don't—" Norouzi began.

"Pay'in!" Scale hissed and dived to the ground,
pulling Norouzi down with him with one hand as
he took the Beretta out with the other. He aimed at
the woman and fired, hitting her in the shoulder as
the woods erupted with automatic gunfire from his
four men in concealment, cutting the big American
and the woman down.

Scale got up and, tugging at Norouzi to follow,

ran back to the log where he had left his laptop and opened it. The sensors showed two moving dots approaching the location of the IED at the beginning of the trail.

"You killed them," Norouzi said, his eyes stunned.

Scale didn't answer. He watched the dots approach the IEDs. As they came up to it, he pressed the Send on his cell phone. Instantly, they heard the loud bang of an explosion. It echoed across the clearing. He selected a second contact number, called, and there was a second explosion.

"*Vay Khoda!*" Norouzi said. My God! "What's happening?"

"They were CIA, not NDB, *baradar*," Scale snapped. "What did you tell them?"

"Nothing. I told them I had nothing to do with the attack on the embassy."

Scale smacked him hard, backhanded, across the face.

"The truth! Don't lie!" he shouted.

"I knew nothing!" Norouzi cried. "I told them nothing! *Inshallah*, not a word."

Scale nodded. He grabbed the laptop and his HK assault rifle and walked back to the center of the clearing, where one of his men, Maziar, was standing over the bodies. Norouzi followed.

"This one," Maziar said, touching the blond woman with his foot, "is still alive."

Scale looked down at the woman. She was breathing heavily, looking straight up into his eyes, something no decent Persian woman would do. These Western whores, he thought. He took his HK, aimed, and squeezed two shots into her head.

He handed his HK to Maziar, bent down and retrieved the woman's pistol from the ground, a Beretta, then turned and shot Norouzi once in the chest, and as he collapsed to the ground, again in the head. He put the Beretta in the dead woman's hand and his HK next to Norouzi. With any luck, the *polis* would first assume they shot each other, until they did a full crime scene and forensics analysis, and that would take time.

"Collect everything. Call Danush and make sure the Ukrainian *jendeh* whore is dead," he told Maziar. "We have to go. The *polis* will be here any minute."

They were back in the Mercedes driving on Emil-Klöti-Strasse toward the A1 motorway when Scale got the text from Danush on his cell phone.

"Ghat' shod." Closed. The mistress, Oksana, was dead.

They drove into the center of Zurich, parked and gathered their things. Scale reminded them to meet him as planned at the Hauptbahnhof, Zurich's central train station. He went back to his room—rented with a false ID—packed and used a sterile wipe to wipe down everything he had touched before he left. Then he took the tram to the Hauptbahnhof. As he walked into the station's main concourse, near the big board listing departures and arrivals, a man in a windbreaker—he looked Iranian—asked him in Farsi for a cigarette.

"I only smoke 57," Scale said, naming the popular Iranian cigarette brand named after 1979, the year of the Revolution; the year 1357 in the Iranian calendar.

"Take one of mine," the man said, handing him one and walking away.

Scale went to the public men's room, found an empty stall and closed the door behind him. He carefully opened the cigarette and shredded the tobacco into the toilet. Written on the inside of the cigarette paper were just two words in Farsi, but for Scale as he rolled the cigarette paper into a tiny ball and flushed it down the toilet with the tobacco it was as if a window had opened. He finally began to understand what the operation was really about.

It read: *Barcelona. Scorpion.*

"Where are we going, *baradar*?" Maziar asked when he came out of the men's room.

"Barcelona," Scale said.

CHAPTER ELEVEN

Ciutat Vella,
Barcelona, Spain

Scorpion sat over coffee and an omelet *bocadillo* sandwich at an outdoor café, tables lit by candles under the arches of a quiet square with trees, the Plaça Vicenç Martorell. The night was clear, and with the arches and the candles, it seemed medieval, for all that it was only a few blocks from the noisy, crowded Las Ramblas. From somewhere, someone's radio or iPod, came music, an enticing mix of flamenco, dub, and hip-hop that was uniquely Catalan. He was there to meet with Juan Marchena, an agent from the CNI, the Spanish intelligence service.

Shaefer had set up the RDV and it looked like the Spanish would cooperate. Going through Passport Control at Barcelona's El Prat airport, the female Immigration agent checked his Richard Cahill Canadian passport, checked again, and asked him to wait. Two armed Spanish CNP uniformed officers appeared and asked him to follow. They led him to an office, handed his passport back to him and told him he could go, pointing to a side door. There would be no record of his ever having been in Spain.

Except Marchena hadn't showed. The waiting was getting to him. In his hotel room, getting ready to come to the RDV, he had caught the latest news on television. Iranian foreign minister Gayeghrani was shown at a news conference, stating that not only was Iran innocent of any complicity in the attack on the American embassy in Switzerland, but if Iran detected any coercive or military action against it, they would not hesitate to act.

"We will not wait for the American Satan and their yapping dogs, the imperialist British and the Zionists, to attack the innocent Iranian people. If America dares consider action, Iran will strike first," he declared.

They were running out of time, and for all he knew, he was chasing a ghost called the "Gardener." The whole thing didn't add up. If this Gardener was a major spymaster, how was it that no one had ever heard of him? Even more puzzling was the question Harris had hinted at: Why would the Gardener—if he even existed and was behind the Bern attack— want to provoke the world's military superpower into attacking his own country? To use Harris's catch phrase: "Where's the profit?"

He sat an extra twenty minutes, growing more frustrated by the second, and was about to leave when a young woman who looked like a college student in shorts, carrying a backpack, brushed by his table and, as she passed, murmured in English, "Go left on Carrer de les Ramelleres to Elisabets."

Scorpion watched her walk to a line of parked motor scooters, hop on one and take off on the narrow street bordering the plaza. He left money on the table and walked according to her instructions in the opposite direction toward the corner, where he stood and waited. A blue Seat Ibiza, a compact crossover SUV, stopped next to him and the rear door opened.

"Get in," a stocky man in his sixties in the back-seat said in English, beckoning him. Scorpion checked the street, then got into the SUV, which immediately took off down the narrow street. They went around the block several times, making turns to make sure no one was following, before heading toward Las Ramblas.

"*Buenas tardes*, Scorpion—" the man began.

"Where's Marchena?" he interrupted, crossing his leg so his hand rested on his lower calf, near the hidden ankle holster with the Glock 28 pistol. They drove past lit shop windows and cafés, and the closer they got to Las Ramblas, the more it seemed like everyone in Barcelona was out in the streets. The driver, a fit-looking young man, had to honk a number of times to squeeze the SUV past people walking on the narrow cobblestoned street.

"How do you know I'm not Marchena? You never met him," the man said.

"Your accent is Israeli, not to mention your lack of a Castilian lisp or any hint of Catalan when you said—or should have said—'*Bona tarda*,' not '*Buenas tardes*.' So you're not CNI. But you are in intelligence, and judging by your age, fairly senior. So what the hell is the Mossad doing in the middle of this?" Scorpion said, hand resting casually on top of his ankle gun.

"You see?" the man said to the driver, as if he had just proved a point he'd been trying to make. "I understand now your reputation," he added, his eyes on Scorpion's hand resting near his ankle. The driver's eyes watched them in the rearview mirror. "Call me Avram," the man said to Scorpion. "It's not my real name, but then neither is yours. Is it, Mr. Cahill?" he said, using the cover name on Scorpion's Canadian passport.

"Why don't I call you, Yuval? Yuval Ofer, head of the Mossad," Scorpion said. Who else, he guessed, would have knowledge of a Special Access operation or know his CIA 201 code name, Scorpion?

"Better still," the man smiled, "Yuval."

"Now that we're all buddies, what do you want?" Scorpion said.

"To help," Yuval said as they turned right onto the wide Las Ramblas, in the direction of the port. The kiosks on the promenade that ran down the center of the boulevard were brightly lit. The pedestrian area was crowded with people, street musicians and performers, tourists, Gypsies, pickpockets and thieves, stalls selling flowers and souvenirs, music blasting from loudspeakers; the human parade under strands of lights strung between the trees.

"Why?"

Yuval shrugged. "We're allies, after all. Mind?" he said, pulling a crumpled cigarette from a pack in his shirt pocket.

"Go wave the flag at somebody else. What do you want?" Scorpion said.

"I understand," Youval said after lighting the cigarette. "Top Secret Special Access op, and all of a sudden another player steps on the field. Except when it comes to the attack on the embassy, we're all thinking the same thing, aren't we? Iran. And that, you must admit, concerns my little part of the world," he added, picking a tobacco shred from the tip of his tongue.

"Not my problem," Scorpion said, looking ahead. As they approached the port, the buildings were grander, more baroque, and on the promenade there were outdoor cafés under awnings strung with lights.

"No. Mohammad Karif is your problem," Yuval said.

"Who's he?"

"Someone we've had our eye on. An engineer, graduated with honors from the Universitat de Barcelona—and don't tell me. I'm sure I didn't pronounce it right," he said, exhaling a stream of smoke.

"And I should care because . . . ?"

"He's Kta'eb Hezbollah. At least we believe so."

Scorpion was instantly alert. It had been a contact code from Kta'eb Hezbollah that first alerted Rabinowich to Norouzi in Zurich in the first place. It meant either the Iranian Revolutionary Guards were indeed behind the embassy attack or—and this was the dangerous part—that their focus on Kta'eb Hezbollah was leading them from a single assumption further down the wrong path, And no way to know which was right. He wouldn't put it past the Israelis to do that for their own purposes.

"Where's this coming from? Who got Shaefer to set this little drive up?" Scorpion said. "Tell me now or I'm getting out. Was it Soames? You!" Calling out to the driver. "Stop the car."

Ahead, a wide area fronting the marina and the sea was brightly lit, with massive columned government buildings and traffic circling the base of a column at least fifty meters high, topped by a large statue with an outstretched arm pointing out to sea. The driver slowed to pull over. Someone behind them honked his horn.

"That's Columbus," Yuval said, indicating the statue as the SUV turned right, heading, according to the sign, toward the Plaça Drassanes and the port. "They say that's the spot he landed when he came back from discovering America."

"Just pull over anywhere," Scorpion said, and put his hand on the door handle to get out.

"No, it was Dave. David Rabinowich," Yuval said.

Scorpion settled back in his seat. It meant Rabinowich had been liaising with the Israelis, which neither Harris or Shaefer had told him. Need to know and all that Company baloney, he thought. Except he was the one on the line—and not knowing there was another player in the game could get him killed.

"Why?" he said.

Yuval said something in Hebrew to the driver and they started moving with the traffic again, down a wide palm-lined street parallel to the port.

"For years we've been warning Washington that the Iranians were creating resources in Europe and the U.S. to use against America and her allies,"

Yuval said. "Dave's one of the few who paid attention. Now it's come." He lit a new cigarette from the first and crushed the burning end of the first out on his thumbnail with fingers stained yellow by nicotine. He caught Scorpion looking at his hands. "I know," he said. "These things will kill me. But given the fact I live in the Middle East, the odds are something else will kill me first."

"Who's this Karif?" Scorpion said.

"Smart, serious. A Bahraini, from Manama."

"Shiite? Opposes the Al-Khalifas?" Scorpion asked. If Karif was a Shiite opposing the Bahraini ruling Al-Khalifa family, Sunnis allied with Sunni Saudi Arabia, it would make him an obvious recruiting target for either the Iranian MOIS or the Kta'eb Hezbollah; particularly since Bahrain served as the key base in the Persian Gulf for the U.S. Navy.

Yuval nodded. "He lives in Les Corts. Doing his MBA at ESADE."

"And that matters because why?" Scorpion asked as they drove around a roundabout. On the left a big cruise ship docked at the port was lit up like a Christmas tree.

"Listen," Yuval said. He held up a cell phone. Then Scorpion heard it again. The same German sentence in the same woman's voice he had been going over and over in his head since Zurich. Norouzi's mistress saying, *"Sagen Sie dem Gärtner, muss das Gras zu schneiden."* Tell the Gardener, the grass needs to be cut. "We recorded this earlier today on Karif's phone."

Scorpion looked at the Israeli. If they recorded it, it meant they had Karif bugged.

"Who's the Gardener?" he asked.

"We were hoping you could tell us," Yuval said.

Scorpion shook his head. "What indicator do you have that Karif's working for Kta'eb Hezbollah?"

"This man," Yuval said, pulling an iPad out of his briefcase and turning it on. He scrolled till he found the photo of a smallish man in a rumpled suit, unshaven, with what looked like outsize hands. He was talking to someone on what appeared to be a European street, but because a fraction of a billboard at the edge of the photograph advertised Bonjus, a popular Lebanese juice drink, Scorpion assumed it was taken in Beirut. "Our agent—"

"Where? Beirut?"

Yuval smiled. "Good," he said appreciatively. "Yes, Beirut. Our man heard him called 'Said Dekhil Flauban.' We suspect he was involved in the Ghanem assassination a few years back. Inside Hezbollah, mention of the Flauben is associated with Kta'eb Hezbollah."

Scorpion's mind was going a mile a minute. Said Dekhil Flauban was Arabic for the saw-scaled snake, the deadliest snake in the Middle East. Ghanem had been the Lebanese prime minister assassinated by a terrorist bomb that everyone assumed had been planted by Hezbollah. What Yuval was also telling him was that the Israelis had a mole inside Hezbollah in Lebanon. It was the only way they could have known about the Snake.

"What connects this 'Snake' to this guy Karif?"

"Karif was in Beirut at the same time. Apparently meeting with Salim Kassem. I believe you may have encountered him," Yuval said carefully. "That's how we got onto Karif in the first place."

Scorpion understood. His encounter with Salim had been during the Palestinian operation. Salim was Nazrullah's deputy secretary and a member of Al-Majlis Al-Markazis, the Hezbollah Central Council. Ghanem could not have been assassinated without Salim's involvement. Yuval was saying his Lebanese mole tied Salim and Hezbollah to both the Snake and Karif.

"Why come to me?" he asked. "Why am I so deserving?"

Yuval nodded as if he understood Scorpion's cynicism. Intelligence services only liaised because they had to, and they never gave anything away for free.

"Two things," he said, staring ahead at the traffic. They had turned from the port and were heading up Avinguda del Parallel, a broad avenue bordered by apartment buildings and stores. "First, we're limited here. The Spanish don't like us."

"Not since Cast Lead," Scorpion said, referring to the 2009 Israeli military incursion into Gaza, when there had been massive demonstrations in Madrid against Israel.

"Not since the Spanish Inquisition." Yuval grimaced, a sour expression on his face as he gestured for the driver to pull over. They stopped at a spot not far from a Metro station. "This is your operation. Also, Ahmad Harandi. It wasn't his real name, of course. It was Avi. Avi Benayoun. He had a wife and daughter in Netanya. We appreciate what you tried to do."

The Israeli mole in Hamburg, Scorpion thought, feeling a stab of regret, recalling their last meeting on the ferry. He had liked Harandi and failed to save him. It wasn't a victory.

"I didn't do it for you," he said.

"No," Yuval agreed. "Here," handing him a flash drive. "Everything we have on Karif. Photos, address, even a video. Everything."

"Including spy software. A Trojan horse perhaps?"

Yuval smiled. "You have a suspicious mind."

"Can't imagine why," Scorpion said, pocketing the flash drive and putting his hand on the door handle. "You're out of it," he told Yuval, getting out of the SUV. "Keep your people away. If I see an unknown on the field, as far as I'm concerned it's the opposition. I'll kill him, understood?"

Yuval raised his hands, a sign of surrender.

"It's out of our hands. *Kol tov*," he said as Scorpion got out and closed the car door.

Scorpion waited for a moment, watching the SUV pull into traffic and drive away, then turned and headed to the Metro station.

Going down the stairs into the Metro, he kept glancing over his shoulder, though he hadn't spotted anyone tailing him. He had a prickly feeling at the back of his neck as if something terrible were about to happen. Already on this operation Harandi had been killed and they'd nearly gotten him and Sandrine in Paris. And you couldn't turn on a TV without hearing war talk. It felt like he was blindfolded on a battlefield, something bad coming at him and he didn't know what or from which direction, as he stood on the platform and watched the train with a sign that said L3 coming into the station. He had a lead. Karif. But was it a real lead, or were the Israelis pointing him at someone for their own reasons?

It was all coming down to one thing: Who was the Gardener?

CHAPTER TWELVE

Les Corts,
Barcelona, Spain

Karif's apartment was on the sixth floor of an apartment building in the Les Corts district, a few blocks from the tram stop. Normal protocol would have been to watch Karif and pick him up when he was isolated or go into his apartment when he wasn't at home and wait for him to show up. But they were up against the clock. Scorpion checked the street one last time. From the get-go they'd been on the defensive, rushed and desperate to pull a rabbit out of the hat so the administration in Washington would be able to prove to the world and, most of all, to the American public, that if they were going to bomb someone, it was justified, and that they had the right bad guys in their gun sights.

He decided to simply knock on the door. If Karif was home, he would try to persuade him that the Gardener had sent him from Tehran. If not, he would pick the lock, black-bag the apartment and wait for him. While on the tram, he had plugged Yuval's data into his iPad, and after studying half a dozen photos and a blurry eight-second time-stop video, was sure that if he saw Karif—a clean-shaven young man with dark hair and a gap-toothed smile—he would recognize him.

Looking up at the apartment from the street, he couldn't tell if anyone was home. The curtains were drawn and no light escaped. The street wasn't busy, only a few people out though it was not yet ten o'clock, early for Barcelona. It was just a normal weeknight in a residential neighborhood, light from a small *pasteleria* bakery-restaurant spilling into the street.

He used a credit card slipped between the door and the jamb to open the front door of the apartment building. There was a small lobby and an elevator, which he ignored, instead taking the stairs to the sixth floor. He walked down the hallway, stopping at every apartment door to listen. Inside each one he could hear a television, but when he got to Karif's apartment—listening intently, his ear on the door—there was nothing. No TV, no one talking, no sound of any kind. He reached into his pocket for his Peterson universal key.

Just then the door of the apartment next door opened and two teenagers, a boy and a girl, came out, the sound of a sitcom with a loud laugh track blaring as they closed the door behind them. They looked at Scorpion curiously. Quickly improvising, he nodded at them and knocked on the door, unable even to put a hand behind him on the Glock pistol in the holster at the small of his back. He didn't expect a response but the door suddenly opened.

It wasn't Karif. A burly Iranian-looking man with

a thick mustache, wearing a windbreaker, stared back at him. His shoulders were huge. Scorpion would have bet he'd done some wrestling, a national sport in Iran.

"Qué quieres?" the burly man said in non-Catalan, heavily accented Spanish. What do you want?

"Where's Mohammad?" Scorpion said in English, sensing the teenagers walking away down the hallway.

"Here. You coming in," the man said, his English as bad as his Spanish, opening the door for Scorpion to enter.

He stepped into the apartment and started to turn to confront the man, his hand going back to the gun at the small of his back, when he felt a tremendous blow to the side of his head. For an instant the room tipped sideways, and then he saw nothing.

The first thing he saw was his hand, covered in blood. And then the knife in his hand, dripping blood. He was lying on the carpeted floor. How long had he been out? he wondered. Then the panic hit. The man who hit him might still be there. He jumped to his feet and whirled around, the bloody knife in his hand. He didn't see him as he ran to the kitchen, holding the knife as far away from him as he could so the blood wouldn't drip on his clothes. The apartment felt like the man with the mustache had gone.

He dropped the Spanish Navaja-style folding knife into the sink and ran the water, washing the blood off his hand and watching it stain the basin pink. He looked to see where he had been cut but couldn't find anything. Using dishwashing liquid, he washed his hands, went to the bathroom and dried them off with toilet paper, then flushed the pink-stained paper down the toilet.

He felt for his guns, the one at the small of his back and the one in his ankle holster, which were still there. Odd, he thought. Then it hit him. He wasn't thinking straight; the blow might have caused a concussion. If he wasn't cut, where did the blood come from? And how long had he been out?

Checking his watch, he saw that he couldn't have been out more than a minute or two. Maybe less. His head throbbed and there was a painful lump on the right side at the back. It felt like someone had been using it for a golf ball. Then he pulled the Glock from his back holster and started to go through the apartment.

There was just the living room, the kitchenette, a single bedroom, and a bathroom. A student's apartment. Cheap furniture, a pile of books, college texts, a laptop on the coffee table in the living room. He inserted a flash drive into the laptop. Its NSA software would suck all the document files, e-mails and contacts, and Internet temporary files and history from the laptop in seconds. Then he saw the bottom of a shoe beside the bed. He crept into the bedroom, ready to fire.

There was no need. Karif was lying on the carpet next to the bed. He recognized the young man immediately from his photos and video. His throat had been slashed from ear to ear, and the carpet where he lay was soaked with blood. Scorpion backed away, trying to keep the blood off his shoes.

What the hell was going on? Did the Israelis set him up? He didn't think so, but he couldn't exclude the possibility. Or was Kta'eb Hezbollah, the saw-scaled snake maybe, shutting down the network? The call Norouzi's girlfriend had made about the Gardener was proving fatal for everyone involved, so it was more urgent than ever that Shaefer pull the Gnomes off Norouzi. He would demand it or call Harris at Langley direct himself, he thought. So if it wasn't the Israelis, then it was unbelievable timing that he had knocked on Karif's door just after he was killed, before the murderer could get away. If so, why had the murderer left him alive?

From outside he heard the wail of a police siren. More than one. He ran to the living room window and pulled back the edge of the curtain. Two white bullet-shaped police cars had just pulled up in front of the building and police were getting out of the cars. Scorpion stepped back. Either he had been set up or the murderer himself had called it in to cover his tracks. Realizing he only had seconds to get away, he started toward the door, then stopped.

The knife! His fingerprints were on it. He ran to the sink, grabbed the knife and dropped it into his pocket. What else had he touched? The dishwashing liquid. He rubbed it down with the liquid soap and toilet paper and flushed it down the toilet. Had he touched the door handle? No, the killer had opened the door, he thought, as he opened the apartment door with toilet paper.

Scorpion started for the stairs and heard men's voices and panting as they came up. In a few seconds he'd either be arrested or dead. He ran up the stairs on the tips of his toes. The roof door was locked, but he frantically managed to open it with the Peterson universal key. He stepped out onto the roof, closed the door as quietly as he could behind him, and ran to the edge. The roof of the building next to this one was just a few feet lower. He jumped down and raced across it to the next building. There was a narrow alleyway, perhaps two meters, between the buildings. If he missed, it was a seven-story drop. No other way, he thought, backing up five or six meters.

From behind, he heard sounds and glanced over his shoulder. Two policemen had run out on the roof of Karif's building, guns drawn. They spotted him.

"*Policia! Détente!*" one of them shouted in Spanish, telling him to stop, then going into shooting position.

Don't think about it, he told himself. If he thought about it, he wouldn't do it. Just as he neared the edge he leaped off his right foot as hard and high as he could, and as he did so, heard a shot and sensed something whiz by his flailing arm.

He sailed over the alleyway, having only the briefest glimpse of the concrete and trash cans far below, and then he landed on the other roof, stumbling and waving his arms for balance. Even before he could right himself he scrambled to the roof door.

It was locked. He felt in his pocket for the Peterson key, glancing back at the other roof, where the two policemen were running across toward the gap between that building and his. He darted a glance over the parapet at the street below. There were at least a half-dozen policemen, hands on guns, watching the front door of Karif's apartment building, one of them saying something to bystanders, who were starting to gather across the street.

The burly man with the mustache, the one who had clobbered him and had no doubt murdered Karif, was standing with the people on the sidewalk, watching the police. There was still had a chance to get him, he thought, pulling the Peterson key out of his pocket and going to the roof door. He tried the key, giving it a tap to jump the lock. He felt it click but the door still didn't open. It was jammed. He turned the key and handle and slammed against it with his shoulder. It made a cracking sound but was still jammed. He looked back over at the other roof. There was no more time. Both policemen were lining up to shoot him.

He tried the lock again, slamming against the door with all his might, heard something crack, and then the door banged open with a loud snap. Anyone on the floor below would have heard it. Bullets cracked into the doorpost behind him as he dove through and raced down the staircase, no longer bothering about making noise.

An apartment door near one of the landings popped open and a woman in a robe, her hair up in curlers, popped out. One look at his face and she dived back into her apartment, shutting the door and shouting for her husband. Scorpion jumped down the last few stairs to the ground floor, where the hallway was dark. He left it that way and peered out the glass in the front door, the Glock in his hand inside his jacket pocket.

The crowd of spectators across the street from Karif's building had grown larger, but he couldn't spot the mustache guy. Someone upstairs in his building was shouting something. He couldn't stay there any longer, he realized, and still had the murder weapon in his pocket. For the moment, no one among the spectators and police outside seemed to be looking at this building. They were all looking up at the other roof, where the shots had been fired. Heart pounding, he opened the door and walked slowly, carefully, across the street to the edge of the crowd.

Mustache guy was no longer standing among the spectators. Peering over the heads of other spectators, Scorpion saw the back of a burly man in a tan-colored windbreaker walking toward the corner. One of the police *mossos* glanced at the burly man but otherwise didn't react. The *mosso* looked back toward the crowd and then up at the roof of the building, like the other spectators.

He only had a few seconds to decide. If he tried to push through the crowd to follow, he'd be sure to attract attention. That *mosso* might be too dumb to do anything now, but if he was to chase Mustache, even the *mosso* would be able to figure it out. He watched out of the corner of his eye as Mustache turned the corner. Probably headed toward Avinguda Diagonal, he thought, one of the main streets.

Edging away from the crowd, Scorpion walked in the opposite direction, toward the next corner. Checking the reflection in a store window, he saw no one following him and began to believe he might get away when he heard shouts. The police *mossos* on the roof were pointing at him, and several *mossos* and spectators on the street were now chasing him. He turned the corner to a street parallel to the one Mustache had gone and ran toward Avinguda Diagonal.

People in the street stared curiously at him as he ran by. He looked around, feeling conspicuous. It was a one-way street of brick apartment houses with shops on the ground floor. There were lights on some of the balconies, where people were eating or drinking despite the cool evening. There was nowhere to get rid of the bloody, incriminating knife. Glancing over his shoulder, he saw that no one chasing him had turned the corner yet, but that would change any second and then people on this street would start chasing him as well. He had to change the equation—and fast.

A yellow Seat Mii, a tiny three-door subcompact car, emerged from an apartment building underground parking garage, a young woman at the wheel. As she stopped to check the street traffic, Scorpion ran over and rapped on the driver's window with the Glock. For an instant, the woman froze. He pointed the gun at her, motioning for her to roll down the window. She hesitated, then complied. Out of the corner of his eye he could see a *mosso* round the corner and shout, followed by a dozen or more men and *mossos*.

"Get out!" Scorpion told her in English, and when she didn't move, shouted *"Fuera!"* and pressed the Glock's muzzle to her head.

Eyes wide, she unfastened her seat belt with trembling fingers and opened the car door. Before she could get out, he yanked her from the seat and got in. Scorpion jammed the gear stick into first and took off, turning into the street. He hit the accelerator and upshifted, the little car's engine revving into the red-line RPMs. In the rearview mirror the running *mossos* were falling behind, everyone in the street staring at him, but in the distance he could hear the *wee-you wee-you* of a police car siren in pursuit.

A man on a motorcycle was pulling out between parked cars, and Scorpion hit the horn and the accelerator simultaneously, swerving to squeak by him. With parked cars on both sides of the narrow street, there was only a single lane. Ahead, a Renault sedan was stopped at a traffic light. Scorpion upshifted to the top gear and, horn blaring, turned and bounced up onto the sidewalk, around the Renault, and into the intersection, just missing an oncoming sedan, the driver's eyes wide with terror. Cross traffic all around him was screeching to a halt, cars crashing into each other and horns blaring as he tore across one street and on down another, which was one-way. Ahead he could see a commercial van stopped, blocking his way.

He swerved diagonally into a no-parking zone and again up onto the sidewalk. Blasting on the horn, he downshifted and dodged to get around pedestrians who froze in place, staring. A man and a woman walking just ahead stopped when they heard the horn as he came right at them. Yanking hard on the wheel, he swerved back into the street, the little car coming up on two wheels, teetering precariously before slamming down onto the pavement. Ahead he could see trees and traffic at the Avinguda Diagonal intersection.

Making the turn into traffic on the wide avenue with its grassy divider and car and tram lanes in the center, Scorpion glimpsed Mustache boarding a red and green tram at a stop barely a hundred meters ahead. He gunned the little engine and upshifted, shooting the car diagonally across traffic. He felt a nudge as someone hit his rear fender, threatening to spin the little car completely out of control. Fighting the wheel, he compensated for the hit, fishtailing onto the grassy center divider, slaloming between trees and onto the tram tracks in the center of the avenue. Wheels skidding on the metal tracks, he followed the tram as it picked up speed. Although the little Seat's engine was desperately underpowered, he dodged left and right between cars, trying to weave between lanes and catch up.

After whipping around two cars, he saw another tram coming straight at him. He could see the driver's wide-eyed horror as, at the last second, he slotted in behind the red and green tram, slipstreaming behind it. The sound of sirens came blasting from behind. He spotted a police car in the rearview mirror shooting out from the street he had come from. Siren wailing, it swerved onto the outer traffic lanes of Avinguda Diagonal.

As the tram ahead began to slow for the next stop, Scorpion scanned the street. It wouldn't take long for the police to catch his little yellow subcompact.

Inside the brightly lit tram, he could see Mustache looking around before taking his seat.

Scorpion pulled around the tram, skidding on the tracks before sliding ahead of the tram car, which for an instant blocked the police car from spotting the little yellow Seat. He pulled ahead then, moving with the flow of traffic, watching the tram recede behind him as the wailing of the police siren grew closer.

The tram behind him was moving again. As he watched it grow in his rearview mirror, he heard the deafeningly loud police siren right behind him. It swerved right next to him. A helmeted *mosso* looking out the passenger window motioned furiously for him to pull over. Scorpion looked around.

Ahead there was a roundabout bordered by office buildings, traffic feeding from multiple side streets joining the flow, curving around trees and grass in the center of the roundabout. He hit the accelerator, shifting to the top gear and feeling it catch as the little car hurtled forward into a gap between two lanes of traffic. Cutting across the center circle, he bounced up onto the grass, barely scraping between two trees. The police car tried to follow but was too big to get between the trees. The driver, jamming his brakes on the grass, hit one of the trees, then had to back up and swerve back onto the roundabout to follow him.

The next tram stop was a block ahead. Behind Scorpion, despite the police chase, the tram was coming steadily on, as was the police car. He slammed on the brakes and braced for the impact as the car behind him plowed into the back of the little Seat, smashing it forward into another car. People were honking their horns and shouting as he unbuckled and leaped out of the car, pulling out his Glock. He ran to the tram, which had stopped, banged on the door, and showing the driver his gun, shouted, *"Policia! Policia!"*

The driver opened the doors and Scorpion climbed in. He shouted *"Policia!"* again and showed the Glock to the passengers while searching for Mustache. He was in the middle of the car, already getting up. Scorpion moved toward him, pointing the Glock. Mustache grabbed a middle-aged woman and hurled her at him as easily as tossing a Frisbee, then leaped from the train and ran toward the street corner. It took a second for Scorpion to disentangle himself from the woman, and when he got out of the tram, Mustache was already a good thirty meters ahead. He was running hard toward a lit-up Metro sign, glowing red, like a traffic light in the night.

Scorpion took off after him. Behind him, he heard shouts and a *mosso* screaming, *"Détente! Stop! Policia!"*

Over his shoulder he saw the *mosso* in a shooting position, a pistol aimed at him. Scorpion dodged left, then around a man with a boy so that they were between him and the *mosso*, who resumed chasing him. When he looked ahead, Mustache had already gone into the Metro station.

Scorpion ran to the entrance and using his free hand for leverage leaped over the turnstile. Mustache was shoving people aside on the escalator, pushing his way down to the platform. Scorpion could hear the sound of a train coming into the station. He leaped onto the incline by the escalator handrail, jumping and sliding down beside the escalator to the platform, people shouting at both Mustache and him and shaking their fists.

By then a train was waiting at the station, its doors about to close. Mustache ran to it, shoving at a door with his meaty hand so he could get through. The closing doors stopped and opened for a second, then started to close again. Scorpion leaped, just getting his hand between the two doors. It felt like the train was going to start with just his forearm inside as he strained to spread the doors open. They did open then, a few more inches, and he managed to slip in before they slammed closed and the train began to move. Behind him, he saw the *mosso* bursting onto the platform, and seeing the train pull out of the station, call on his cell phone.

Then Scorpion turned and scanned the car for Mustache. The car was full, about twenty or so passengers standing and swaying as the train picked up speed. There was no sign of Mustache, but at the far end of the car he saw the door to the next car open. He couldn't see who it was, his view blocked by a group of high school or college students standing near the door, but thinking it might be Mustache, heading toward the front of the train, he followed.

Hand on the Glock in his jacket pocket, he made his way through the car as it sped through the tunnel. He knew he might come upon Mustache at any time, and the bulky Iranian had already shown how fast he could move. The floor space between cars was covered with an accordionlike material, binding the cars together. After opening the door, but before stepping into the next car, he scanned ahead, spotting Mustache standing at the far end of the car, holding onto a steel pole and staring right at him, his hand in his pocket.

As Scorpion stepped into the car, the train slowed as it pulled into a station and he felt the momentum pulling him forward. Mustache's gaze flickered for a moment at the station platform moving by, then back to him. If there was shooting, Scorpion thought, people were going to be killed, his eyes darting at the platform, knowing there would be a bunch of *mossos* waiting for him. If shooting started, both he and Mustache, plus a bunch of bystanders, would be dead. In any case, he was trapped. The only question was what to do about Mustache.

He struggled to push toward the burly man through the crowd of people getting up to leave the train, the momentum as it stopped lurching him forward. Pushing through, he saw Mustache join those people getting off through the far door. He started to push out through the nearest door but was met with a scrum of passengers coming onto the train. There was no way through, and he watched desperately as Mustache walked past a large squad of *mossos*, who ignored him as they scanned the train.

He had to wait for the crowd boarding the train to ease, and then, as he started to get out, one of the *mossos* pointed at him, shouting, *"Ahi está! Es él!"* It's him!

Seven or eight *mossos* rushed the train, shoving their way into the car, their guns drawn. People shrank away from them as two of them ran up to Scorpion, who took his hand out of his pocket and just stood there, while the train loudspeaker announced in Catalan and Spanish that the train would not be moving because of police activity.

Two of the *mossos* roughly grabbed his arms, and a third put handcuffs on him.

"*Vostè està sota detenció,*" one of them said. You're under arrest.

CHAPTER THIRTEEN

Eixample,
Barcelona, Spain

The handcuffs were made of nickel-coated steel and not connected by links but a hinge that allowed less movement. The keyholes for each cuff were in the extensions that formed the hinge. He thought about escaping, but there was no chance after they brought him out of the Metro and put him, along with a *mosso* to watch him, in the back of a *mossos d'esquadra* van to the police *comisaria* in the Eixample business district. It was a gray concrete fortress of a building off a smart, tree-lined street, Via Augusta, that he only caught a glimpse of before they hustled him inside.

They brought him to a room with no windows, empty except for a table and chairs, and frisked him. A *mosso* went through his pockets, dumping everything onto the table. When they found the knife and the bloodstained pieces of toilet paper, they looked significantly at each other. One of the *mossos* pulled on latex gloves and placed the knife and the toilet paper in separate see-through plastic bags. Throughout it all Scorpion said nothing. He barely glanced at the one-way glass on the wall or the video camera near the ceiling, but registered their locations.

They sat him in one of the chairs facing the one-way glass. One of them, an older, tanned police sergeant with long iron-gray hair, sat opposite him.

"Quin és el teu nom?" the sergeant asked him first in Catalan, then in Spanish, then English. What is your name? Scorpion didn't answer.

The sergeant stood up, leaned across the table and smacked him hard across the face. The tiniest flicker of a smile ghosted Scorpion's lips. "If you do that," he remembered Sergeant Falco saying about smiling at his first interrogation during his Level C SERE training at Fort Bragg, North Carolina, when he was in JSOC's First Special Forces Operational Detachment Delta Force, "you're letting the interrogator know he's in for a fight." At Level C SERE, interrogators were allowed to break no more than one major and two minor bones. In comparison, most other interrogations, even brutal ones, were walks in the park.

"Who are you?" the sergeant asked. Scorpion had left his Richard Cahill Canadian passport in the hotel safe and was carrying no ID. "Why did you kill Mohammad Karif? What was he to you? Did you know him? Where are you from? Are you Catalan? Spanish? I think you are a foreigner, yes?"

Scorpion just looked at him.

"We have you," the sergeant said. "We have witnesses. We have the knife, the bloodstains. We will do scientific analysis and have a lot more. If you talk now, it will go more better for you."

Scorpion didn't respond.

"Say something!" the sergeant shouted, smacking the table with his hand. *"Fill de puta!"*

Scorpion stared at the one-way glass, where he knew others were watching. Think nothing, he told himself. Show nothing. Be nothing. Sooner or later they'd leave him alone for a minute and he could escape.

The sergeant went out, leaving him alone. There was no point doing anything; he knew they were watching. Probably trying to decide whether to send in someone else to question him. Good cop, bad cop. Meanwhile, his mind was racing ahead.

When he had knocked on Karif's door, both he and Mustache had been surprised. Mustache had improvised, and it was likely he'd called the police to pin the blame on him for the murder. Assumption: Mustache worked for the Gardener, who was shutting his network down.

Why?

Because he didn't want the attack on the embassy to be traced back to Kta'eb Hezbollah, thereby allowing the Americans to justify an attack on Iran, he decided. No witnesses, no proof. Total deniability. If the U.S. attacked, Iran could turn to Russia, China, and the rest of the Muslim world and talk about U.S. aggression.

He was getting a sense of the Gardener. He was careful, smart, devious, and ruthless as hell. The Gardener was as dangerous an adversary as he had ever faced, he decided as the sergeant came back into the room with four more policemen.

"We have two eyewitnesses who say they saw

you go into Mohammad Karif's apartment," the sergeant said in Catalan, then in Spanish and English. "Unless you talk to me now, you will not leave prison for many years."

Scorpion just looked at him.

The sergeant gestured to the policemen, who took him out of the room and down a long hallway to another room, where they prepared to photograph and fingerprint him. A television on top of a file cabinet was on. It showed a newscaster from Antena 3 Noticias in front of a screen showing a floodlit police nighttime scene. It was a European country, but not Spain, Scorpion thought. A subtitle on the screen read: ZURICH, SUIZA. Switzerland. One of the Swiss policemen on TV pointed at a body in what looked like a wooded or park setting. Then the camera showed more bodies. They started to turn Scorpion toward a table to be fingerprinted.

"*Espera*," Scorpion said, the first word he had spoken. Wait.

Surprised, they stopped, and like him, they turned to watch the TV.

Although he couldn't follow the rapid Spanish, he could catch some of it from the news ticker crawl at the bottom of the screen. It was Bergholz Park in Zurich. Five men and one woman found dead. Murdered. Some of the dead may have been Americans. They showed the face of the dead woman taken from a passport photo, a pretty blonde, and even before they showed it, Scorpion knew it was Chrissie.

It hit him like a pile driver. The Gnomes. Chrissie. Glenn. All four of them dead. He felt like throwing up. He'd warned Shaefer! Told him to pull them off. It was his fault. He'd asked Harris to leave the Gnomes in Zurich to help him pull off the movie for Norouzi. Soames, he thought. If he got the chance, he'd rip his guts out.

Five men dead, the announcer said. Who was the fifth?

Norouzi, he thought. It had to be.

The announcer's next words, which he read in the crawl at the bottom of the screen, confirmed it.

"According to Swiss authorities, one of the dead has been tentatively identified as an Iranian businessman, Hooshang Norouzi, whose company had an office in Zurich."

First Norouzi, then Karif, he thought. The Gardener was covering his tracks. He felt an anger grow inside him, a sick rage that almost made it impossible to think. He was as angry as he had ever been in his life. Breathe, he told himself. Control it. Use it.

"*Bueno*, let's take his photo," the photographer said in Spanish, assuming the prisoner would understand Spanish if he didn't speak Catalan.

Two of the policemen faced Scorpion away from the TV. One of the them stood him against a wall in front of the camera. He tried to control his breath as he took in what had happened in Zurich. He had to get out of here now, he thought. As the guard positioned him for the photograph, the man grabbed between his legs as if to frisk him again but whispered in Scorpion's ear in Spanish, "*Estaré esperando por ti, puta.*" I'll be waiting for you, bitch.

Thinking, Boy, did you pick the wrong time, asshole, he slipped his leg behind the guard's leg and swung his handcuffed hands with all his might at the side of the man's head, smashing him so hard into the wall with the cuffs that he could hear the skull crack. He didn't wait for the guard to fall, the legs already buckling, but turned toward the other three policemen. Two of them had started toward him, while the third fumbled for his police whistle. The police photographer, who had been about to take his mug shot, reached for a telephone.

As the biggest guard reached out to grab him, Scorpion executed a Brazilian high kick to the head while using an aikido grab and throw to take down the other charging guard. With the two of them on the ground, he jumped with both knees on the first guard, knocking the wind out of him, and smashed his cuffs across the bridge of his nose, effectively blinding him. Jumping to his feet, he kicked the man in the head to finish him, whirling to face the second guard, who was getting up from the floor.

A straight-fingered thrust to the windpipe with both handcuffed hands had the second guard gasping and choking. Then he grabbed the man by his hair and smashed his head against the corner of a desk. The guard crumpled, the side of his head pouring blood.

The fourth guard had managed a small bleat with his whistle and was starting to blow again, his cheeks bulging, when Scorpion caught him with a knee to the groin. As the doubled over, expelling air with a whoosh, Scorpion smashed him into the photographer, taking both men and the camera down. He jumped on top of the photographer, landing on his face with his knees, ramming the man's head against the floor. The fourth guard, getting up, swung at him. Scorpion sidestepped the punch and caught him in a guillotine choke hold in the crook of his elbow, cutting off his air and, more critically, the flow of blood in his carotid artery. The guard went unconscious within a long fifteen seconds. Then Scorpion got up, saw the photographer stir, and kicked him in the side of the head, finishing him off.

He looked around. The entire fight had taken less than forty-five seconds. Catching his breath, he searched the first guard's pockets and found the handcuff keys. The fact that the cuffs were hinged made the positioning of his hand and wrist awkward, but not impossible. The lock clicked and the first cuff opened. With his left hand free, it was even faster opening the second cuff.

He took off his clothes down to his underwear. The fourth guard, the one with the whistle, was closest to his size. He stripped the police uniform, ID, and the PK380 pistol and holster off the man, checking the magazine before putting on the uniform, then walked out of the room and down the hall to the stairs. By the time he reached the ground floor he could hear shouts from above. At the main entrance he nodded to the desk sergeant, who looked at him oddly, as if trying to remember who he was, but didn't say anything. As he walked out the front door he felt a tingling in his back, as if any second the desk sergeant would call him back.

He passed a pair of *mossos* dragging in a Gypsy, who was shouting in Catalan, *"Creus que tots els gitanos és un lladre!"* Something about the cops thinking every Gypsy was a thief.

"Only because it's true," the *mosso* said as Scorpion passed them. Walk, don't run, he told himself, coming around the corner to Via Augusta. He knew there wasn't much time. The police would be after him any second.

There were dozens of motor scooters parked in a line in the tree-lined passageway bisecting the street. He was about to steal one when he spotted a taxi and waved him down. The driver hesitated, perhaps wondering why a *mosso* needed a taxi, but picked him up. As they drove down the avenue, the driver kept eyeing his uniform. When they were a good kilometer from the *comisaria*, he told the driver to pull over.

"Take off your clothes," Scorpion told him in his bad Spanish.

"*Que?*" the driver asked.

"Your clothes. I want them," he said.

The driver shook his head. "No, *senor.*"

Scorpion fished in the pockets of the uniform, found forty-five euros in the wallet and pointed the Walther at the driver.

"I'll give you forty-five euros," he said, "*o te mato.*" Or I kill you.

The driver hesitated. He looked at the Walther, then at Scorpion's eyes, and nodded slowly. They sat in the taxi and took off their shirts and pants. In a few minutes the driver wore the police uniform and Scorpion was in the driver's clothes. He handed the man the money, got out of the taxi and motioned him to drive away.

When the taxi was gone, Scorpion walked for several blocks. He was on a quiet street of older apartment buildings with balconies and wrought-iron railings. Here, as in many places in the city, scores of motor scooters were parked in rows on the street. Looking around to make sure no one was watching, he used the lock pick taped to the bottom of his foot to unlock one and start it. He drove down the street, crossing Avinguda Diagonal, not far from where he had run from the tram, and drove on for several kilometers. In a narrow street, almost an alley, he left the scooter and walked back to his hotel.

The minute he got back to his room—before he even washed his hands, which still had traces of Karif's blood—he grabbed one of his prepaid cell phones and called Shaefer's number. Although it was after midnight, he wasn't surprised when Shaefer picked up on the first ring.

Before Shaefer could speak, Scorpion said between clenched teeth into the phone: "Flagstaff. I told you to pull them, you son of a bitch."

"You realize this is an open line?" Shaefer said.

"Go to hell," he said.

"I'm already there," Shaefer said, and Scorpion knew the deaths of the Gnomes had hit him hard too. "The Pickle Factory's going nuts," suggesting the CIA, not to mention everybody in Washington, was scrambling trying to find someone to blame for the deaths of four agents.

"They deserve it," Scorpion said.

"You're on hold, pending further notice," Shaefer told him. What Shaefer didn't say was that he was in the crosshairs of someone higher up looking to hang him out to dry for the four deaths.

"No, I'm not," Scorpion replied.

For a long moment Shaefer didn't say anything. He was Scorpion's closest friend in the CIA and knew him well enough to know that regardless of what the DCIA ordered, Scorpion was going forward. Scorpion could feel Shaefer trying to decide. Because of orders from higher-ups, Shaefer had betrayed their friendship in the Ukraine operation and regretted it. Now he had to make the same decision again. Scorpion waited for him to figure it out.

"What do you want?" Shaefer said finally.

"Get rid of Soames."

"Not happening."

"Do it—or I will."

"I'll see what I can do," Shaefer muttered. "Anything else?"

"I need an SOG," Scorpion said.

CHAPTER FOURTEEN

El Born,
Barcelona, Spain

"You were there?" Scorpion asked.

"You kidding, hombre? I helped with the cooking," Shehi said. The Albanian was a short man with a close-shaved head and a three-day beard that didn't disguise the knife scar that ran down the side of his face from the hairline to the jaw.

They were in the back room of a small bar on the cobblestoned Carrer de l'Argenteria in the gothic El Born district. Starting with a Romanian whore on Calle Ramon in El Raval, it had taken Scorpion just four hours to work his way up the criminal food chain to the Albanian. It seemed odd for him to be there in the tiny room, dark and smelling of beer and mold, when the day had turned sunny, the trees green, and in an early sign of spring, girls were on the Ramblas in tank tops and brighter colors.

"How'd they kill him?" Scorpion asked. They were talking about a notorious incident that had echoed around the police and intelligence world in which the members of an Albanian Spanish mafia gang had killed, cooked, and eaten one of their own they considered a traitor.

"With a hammer," Shehi said. "Why do you think they call Hayir 'El Martillo'? Here." He poured brandy from a bottle of Fundador and pushed the glass at Scorpion. "Stop with that *cava* piss and drink like a man." Scorpion traded the sparkling wine for the brandy.

"*Salud,*" he toasted, and they drank. "So how'd you cook him?"

"We ground him up in a meat grinder. Then we made *pimientos rellenos de carne*. Stuffed red peppers. Everyone at a big table. Must have been at least twenty of us."

"How was it?"

"You know . . ." The Albanian paused to reflect. "We fried the peppers, and let me tell you, with a nice onion sauce and *vino tinto*, he was pretty good. Better than he ever was alive, that *culero*." He laughed, then looked at Scorpion speculatively. "So what kind of *joda hijo de puta*"—cop son of a bitch— "you looking for?"

"A *joda* who likes to *chupame la polla*." A cop who'll do oral sex; in slang, someone willing to do anything for money. "Even Muslims."

Shehi looked at him sharply. "What kind of Muslims?" For Albanians, religion was dangerous territory.

"Shia," Scorpion said.

"Hezbollah? You talking Hezbollah? That's serious *mierda* you talking, hombre."

Scorpion put a hundred euro bill on the table. Shehi didn't respond. He put another hundred down, then a two hundred. Shehi put his hand over the money, and Scorpion stopped him from taking the money by touching his index finger to the back of Shehi's hand. Neither of them moved.

"The *joda* you want is Pintero. Victor Pintero. A *sotsinspector* in the *mossos d'esquadra* in El Raval," Shehi said, taking the money.

"He'd sell information to Hezbollah?"

Shehi shrugged. "For the price of a stink-faced whore, he'd sell his mother."

"What makes you so sure he's Hezbollah's *puta*?" Scorpion asked, letting his right hand drop below the table to the pocket where he carried the Walther PK380 he had taken from the police station. Shehi was holding something back; he wasn't sure what. He put his hand on the gun. "You don't want me to come back," he added quietly.

"I shit on you too," Shehi said. Then looking into Scorpion's cold gray eyes, he reconsidered. "He's on our payroll. I know definitely one hundred percent he deals with Hezbollah. So do we."

"Like what?"

"Guns, drugs, money washing, *putas*. Romanian women, Moldovan, Russian. Good business," rubbing his thumb on his fingers in the universal sign for money.

"And I should believe you because . . . ?" Scorpion said.

"Like you say, hombre," Shehi said, taking a swig of the brandy and wiping his mouth with his hand. "I don't want to see you again. You too hot. Too many people looking for you," looking directly at Scorpion. "No good for business."

So Shehi had recognized him from the police sketch shown on TV and in the newspapers, Scorpion thought. He would have to change his appearance beyond just growing a Van Dyke type beard. It also meant Shehi knew about the four policemen he had taken out at the *comisaria* who were all in serious condition at Clínic de Barcelona hospital. That's why the Albanian didn't want to mess with him.

"Except maybe you'll think to call the *mossos* the minute I leave."

Shehi grinned. "The thought occurred."

"Sure. Kill two birds with one stone. Make a little extra." Scorpion winked, easing the Walther out and pointing it, under the table, at Shehi's belly. Another word and he would have to kill him.

Again Shehi shrugged. "Not a bad idea."

"It's a very bad idea," Scorpion said, finger tightening on the trigger.

"You think I don't know, hombre? I shit in the milk of any *joda's* mother," Shehi said, giving no sign he knew how close to death he was. "I never tell *mossos* nothing. *Nada.* And if I did, what would I tell them? We talk. 'And where did he go?' they will ask. What can I say? I don't know nothing. I don't want to know nothing." He looked shrewdly at Scorpion. "We finish, hombre?"

Scorpion slid the Walther back into his pocket as he got up.

"Cell phone," he said, holding out his hand. Shehi handed his over.

Scorpion stood over him. "So long as you forget you ever saw me, that we ever had this conversation, we finish," he said.

When he got outside, the sun was so bright he had to shade his eyes. As he walked the narrow street toward the Santa Maria del Mar church, he used Shehi's phone to make a call. When he was done, he took out the SIM and battery, tossed the cell phone into a trash bin, then dropped the SIM and battery into a storm drain a block away before heading to the Metro.

The clock was ticking. And all he could think about was not the mission, but Sandrine. He wondered where she was now and if she was safe.

CHAPTER FIFTEEN

Dharkenleey,
Mogadishu, Somalia

She was being watched. It was the South African, Van Zyl, a lanky bearded man with blue eyes. He was from UNHCR, the United Nations refugee agency, at the improvised horror show called Badbaada Camp on the western outskirts of Mogadishu. The Badbaada refugee camp made the one at Dadaab in Kenya seem like the Ritz Carlton. Plastic sheeting was the only shelter, no food or toilet facilities, nothing; just dirt on the wrong side of Dharkenleey Road and a single water faucet for sixty thousand people and hundreds more arriving every day to escape the fighting and starvation in Afgooye and Lower Shabelle. Van Zyl had shown up just three days after she arrived.

She had flown in from Nairobi. Coming in from the airport, Mogadishu was a city of blazing sun and battered white Toyota vans so packed with people that men and boys rode clinging to the outside, standing on rear bumpers as they bounced along the rutted streets; a city of open-air markets selling vegetables, guns, and ammunition; concrete cinderblock buildings, some blasted to ruins by the recent fighting, women in multicolored *direhs* with children moving among the armed green-bereted African Union troops and Somali government soldiers that were everywhere.

Whenever Van Zyl was around, she sensed his eyes on her. Not the normal way men looked at a woman, particularly if she was reaching or bending over to get something. She was a grown woman and understood that kind of a look. This was different. As if he was watching to see what she would do.

The boy, Ghedi, the one saved by the American she called David Cheyne, even though she knew it wasn't his real name, noticed it too. When she had come back to Dadaab from Paris, the boy was gone. He disappeared after learning his little sister might still be alive in Mogadishu. God only knew how he'd made it through the war zone, but somehow he was here now, still looking for his sister.

"That *mzungu*," Ghedi said, using the Swahili slang word for a white man that he had picked up in Dadaab, "he watch you."

"Yes," she nodded, wiping her forehead with her forearm. Under the stretch of plastic tarps that served for a hospital tent, it was unbelievably hot, at least forty-five degrees Celsius. If her patients weren't already dying, the heat and the flies only compounded the misery. But they never complained. Even though she could do so little for them, they were grateful. They were wonderful, and it was hopeless, and what was she doing here and where was the American and why couldn't she get him out of her mind?

The Hawiye women in their beautiful *direhs* and graceful gestures would say she was bewitched. Maybe it was true, she thought. Why else was she here?

"Should I kill him, *isuroon*?" the boy asked, using the Somali word for a woman deserving of respect, holding up the *belawa* knife he wore on a leather thong around his neck. He had seen her with the American and had appointed himself her protector till the American returned.

"*La*," no, she said, touching his hand with the knife. "Not yet."

"If you say, I will kill him," he said, looking at her.

"I know," she said. "But now you must go. This is for women. A *ragol*," a man, "may not be here."

She felt him leave as she turned back to the patient, a little girl on a shred of blanket on the ground. Small, shriveled with a swollen belly, she looked barely four years old, though her mother said she was seven. The child was severely malnourished and dehydrated. Too malnourished to use an IV, which could overhydrate and kill her. And she was dangerously lethargic. It could be shock or sepsis, she thought, looking at the mother, whose face had so little flesh it was like looking at a skull.

"*Voici*." She gestured to the mother, handing her one of the few Baggies of liquid ReSoMal she still had left and showing her how to give it to the girl orally, even as she debated with herself whether to use it or save it for another because this child was so far gone. Except she couldn't do that, could she?

she told herself. She raised the tiny torn *direh* and then saw it. The gaping bloody wound at the child's genitals.

"*Mada? Mana?*" What? Who? she asked the mother, pointing at the wound and using two of the few words of Arabic she knew.

"*Digil, Al-Shabaab,*" the woman said. Al-Shabaab soldiers from the Digil clan.

It was rape, Sandrine thought, feeling nauseous. The thought of grown men with this tiny child made her try to swallow to keep from throwing up. I can't do this anymore, she thought, looking at the girl's wasted body. She took a breath. This *petite* didn't do anything to have this happen to her, she thought, pulling out a thermometer strip to take the girl's temperature: 40.2 degrees Celsius. High fever. Sepsis from the wound. She looked around despairingly. By rights she should order a CBC, start skin tear repair, but the only thing she had—and damn little of it—was penicillin. This wasn't medicine, it was witch-doctoring!

She took out the ampule, gave her the injection, and bandaged the wound as best she could. The child barely reacted to the needle. She had to get out of here, Sandrine thought. She patted the mother on the arm and ran out into the blazing sun.

Van Zyl, in his ratty Kaizer Chiefs football T-shirt and shorts, was standing there. Not doing anything, just standing there.

"Stop watching me, you bloody son of a bitch!" she screamed at him. "So help me, I'll have someone shoot you! And do something useful for once! Get the medicines I ordered!"

"Take it easy, *bokkie*. I'll catch you later," he said, holding up his hands in mock surrender and walking away.

She put her hands to her face. She wasn't helping these people or herself. Why was she here? And an inner voice whispered: *Because you know he'll find you here.*

She shook her head. *Ce n'est pas moi*, she told herself. It's not me. She went back into the hospital tent. The heat and stench were overpowering.

"*Merde*," she said aloud, and went back to work.

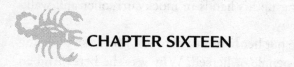

CHAPTER SIXTEEN

Gràcia,
Barcelona, Spain

Marchena, the CNI agent who hadn't showed at the RDV set up by Shaefer at the Plaça Vicenç Martorell, was a tall balding man in a gray suit and dark shirt. He had the look of casual authority, like a professional soccer coach, Scorpion thought as he watched him get into his car, a bright red BMW Series 6 coupe in the office building's underground garage. The Barcelona branch of the Spanish intelligence service, the Centro Nacional de Inteligencia, was headquartered in the building, using the cover of a construction machinery company, Grupo Puentas y Gracia. He treats himself well, this Marchena, Scorpion mused as he walked over and rapped on the driver's window with the Walther pistol.

"Qué diables!" Marchena exclaimed in Catalan. What the hell!

Scorpion motioned with the Walther for Marchena to unlock the passenger door. It took Marchena a second to figure it out that there wasn't enough time to start the car and drive before the stranger with the gun and wearing a blond surfer boy wig could shoot. Marchena pressed the unlock button and Scorpion got in.

"Drive. I'll tell you where," Scorpion said in English.

"The hell I will. Who are you?" Marchena replied in good English, not moving.

"I'll shoot you," Scorpion said, pointing the Walther at Marchena's head.

"No, you won't," Marchena said confidently, looking around. There were a few other people going to their cars in the garage.

Scorpion fired a shot, the bullet shattering a hole in the driver's side window, just past the tip of Marchena's nose. The sound of the shot echoed loudly in the garage, and two people who had been going to their cars froze and looked around.

"Last chance," Scorpion said, shoving the muzzle against Marchena's ribs. "Drive."

Darting him a quick sideways glance, Marchena started the BMW and drove out of the garage into the bright sunlight. Both men put on their sunglasses as they drove on the broad Passeig de Gràcia, past fashionable stores and office buildings.

"Where are we going?" Marchena asked.

"Just drive. Go someplace where I can shoot you if I don't like what you say," Scorpion said as they slid into the traffic circling the stone obelisk in the center of Plaça de Juan Carlos I where the two broad boulevards, the Passeig and the Avinguda Diagonal, intersected.

"Why? Who are you? What do you want?"

"We had a date, remember?"

"Date? What the hell are you talking—" Marchena went suddenly pale. *"Déu,"* he breathed, glancing at the man beside him. "You're Scorpion."

"Why didn't you show?" Scorpion asked.

Marchena took a deep breath. "How am I still alive?" he muttered, his eyes flicking sideways at Scorpion. "Was it you?" he asked. "It was, wasn't it? You put five *mossos d'esquadra* into the hospital while handcuffed. Unbelievable," shaking his head while watching traffic. "Did you kill Mohammad Karif?"

"Don't be stupid. Karif was the only link to what happened in Bern. I'm the last person on the planet to want him dead."

"So who killed him?" Marchena asked, forced to make a left turn as the wide boulevard dead-ended and then a right turn into a narrow residential street.

"A man with a mustache. Looked Middle Eastern. I got there maybe a minute after he killed Karif. He caught me unawares."

"I wouldn't have thought that was possible," Marchena said cattily.

"I try not to make a habit of it," Scorpion said. "If I did, I'd be as dead as Karif."

Marchena glanced over at him.

"This mythical man with a mustache—" he began.

"He's not mythical. Somebody killed Karif," Scorpion said.

"All right, I'll bite. Why didn't he kill you?"

"To frame me for Karif's murder. He's the one

who called the *mossos d'esquadra*. He must've figured if they were chasing me, they wouldn't be chasing him. They got there as I was leaving."

"Why'd he kill him?"

"Don't you watch TV? The Americans want to bomb the hell out of somebody for what happened in Bern. Someone's trying to avoid it being them."

"What did Karif have to do with it?"

"Karif was a contact. An Iranian named Norouzi called Karif from Zurich. That's what brought me to Barcelona. Last night Norouzi was also found dead."

"They're shutting down the network. Is that it?" Marchena said, making his way around construction and then turning onto Travessera de Dalt, a long straight street lined with apartment houses.

"Where are we going?" Scorpion asked.

"You wanted to talk. I thought maybe Park Güell. We could walk."

He wants people around, Scorpion thought. Someplace where he feels safe.

"If I decide to terminate you, having people around won't make any difference," Scorpion said. "And you didn't answer my question. Why didn't you make the RDV?"

"Spain is a leading supporter of Palestinian rights. We have more than a million Muslims. If America—or Israel—want to make war with Iran, NATO or no NATO, it's not good for us. We don't want any Berns—or Zurichs—in Barcelona," he said, glancing pointedly at Scorpion. "My bosses ordered me not to meet you, and they were right. You've been in Spain less than twenty-four hours,

Scorpion, and already we've got a dead Muslim and five policemen in the hospital. Whatever you're here for, Senor Cahill," making sure Scorpion knew he knew his cover ID, "we want no part."

For several minutes they didn't talk. There was a tunnel up ahead. Marchena glanced at Scorpion, who nodded. They drove through the dark tunnel and out into the bright sunshine.

"It's not that simple," Scorpion said. "You can't ignore us," implying he was speaking not just for the CIA, but for the entire U.S. government. Total bullshit, he thought. The reality was, except for Shaefer and maybe Rabinowich, he was on his own.

"Meaning?" Marchena said, turning left into a narrow street going up a hill. He's heading for the park, Scorpion thought. Human instinct. In danger, people always head up, and if possible, toward other people.

"It's not that simple," Scorpion repeated, letting the implied weight of Washington sink in.

"What do you want?" Marchena said finally, pulling the car into a parking space on the street. Ahead, they could see the entrance to Park Güell, the gate flanked by two gingerbread gatehouses designed by the famed architect, Gaudi, after whom the word "gaudy" was coined.

"I want you to get a message to a certain *mosso d'esquadra*, but it has to be done the right way."

Marchena shut the ignition and turned to face Scorpion.

"Who is this *mosso*? A mole—or is he simply a corrupt *policia*?"

He's good, Scorpion thought. The Spaniard had figured it out in a second. He would have to keep that in mind when dealing with him.

"Haven't a clue. He's probably just a bad cop, but honestly, it doesn't matter." Scorpion shrugged.

"What does matter?"

"That he passes information to certain Muslim interests."

Marchena looked at him sharply.

"Hezbollah? Mind?" he asked, taking out a pack of Fortuna cigarettes. Scorpion nodded, and Marchena pulled one out and lit it. "Or maybe Kta'eb Hezbollah?" exhaling a stream of smoke.

"You're good. We should have met when we were supposed to. Would have saved us all a lot of trouble—and those cops wouldn't be in the hospital. What else do you know?" Scorpion said quietly, keeping the Walther still pointed at Marchena.

"Shall we walk?" Marchena asked, indicating the park.

"Give me the car key—and don't be stupid," Scorpion said. They were talking. If Marchena felt more comfortable in the park, he thought, all the better. In the sun visor mirror, Scorpion checked the blond wig he had picked up in a theatrical supply shop in the Raval. Now that he was clean-shaven, the change in his appearance was astonishing, he thought, putting the gun in his pocket.

Marchena handed him the key. They got out of the BMW, walked into the park and up broad stone stairs curving past a fountain with a sculpture shaped like a dragon covered with bits of colored tiles like a mosaic. A crowd of tourists posed for photos on the steps and around the fountain. They went up to an undulating stone pavilion lined with columns and past a long serpentine stone bench covered in colored tiles, all designed by Gaudi. At the top was a terrace with a snack stand. People crowded at tables, eating and enjoying the view.

If Marchena was going to make a move, he would do it here, Scorpion thought, but by now it seemed the Spaniard was as interested in what he had to say as he was in getting the man to help him.

They kept walking, following curving paths through stands of trees. The day was sunny and clear, and for a time they said nothing. They climbed to a stone cross at the top of a hill. From there, they could see over the city to the Mediterranean, the sun sparkling on the sea.

"So what is this information you want this *poli malo*"—bad cop—"to pass to these Islamic *capullos*?" Marchena asked.

"Careful. You're letting your prejudice show," Scorpion said.

Marchena shook his head.

"You Americans. We've been fighting Muslims for a thousand years. You're Johnny-come-slowlies, believe me." He stopped walking and looked directly at Scorpion. "I don't want my city turned into a war zone," he added before starting to walk again. "What do you want him to know?"

"Just tell him where I am. I've been spotted. Very hush-hush. Use my code name, 'Scorpion.'"

"You're painting a target on your back . . . Of course," the Spaniard smiled, taking a deep drag of the cigarette and exhaling, "you're setting a trap."

"The key to all of this is that this *policia*—his name is Victor Pintero; he's a *sotsinspector* in the El Raval district—has to believe he got this information on his own. That it's top secret. Shouldn't be hard. Everyone's hunting me. I'm Karif's killer. Make it part of the *policia* manhunt. Except you let him know the CNI knows something the ordinary *policia* don't."

Marchena's eyes narrowed. He flicked the ash from his cigarette.

"What's that?" he asked.

"Karif was a Kta'eb Hezbollah agent. He was killed by the American agent, Scorpion," Scorpion said.

"And where will whomever they send find you?" he asked.

Scorpion told him.

"Why there?" Marchena muttered, half to himself.

"To minimize civilian casualties."

"*Jesús Cristo*," Marchena swore, shaking his head. "And I should do this because . . . ?"

"Right now the trail ends in Barcelona," Scorpion said. "One way or another, America will have its justice for Bern. Trust me, this city isn't where you want the war to happen."

Marchena dropped the cigarette and stepped on it.

"I was ordered to stay out of this, so no Spanish will be involved. But I have to tell you, two of the *mossos* you injured at the *comisaria* are in critical condition. They may not survive. They had families."

"I know. I'm sorry," Scorpion said. "For what it's worth, if I wanted to kill them, they wouldn't be alive."

"It would be best if you were to leave Spain soon, Scorpion," Marchena said. "I'd say the quicker you are out of my country, the better, but the truth is, if these are the same hombres who did Bern and Zurich, I suspect you will not be alive much longer."

 **CHAPTER SEVENTEEN**

Girona,
Costa Brava, Spain

Driving on the E-15 toll road in a rented Citroen on a sunny morning, wearing a white polo shirt, sunglasses, and the blond surfer boy wig, the radio tuned to the BBC World Service, Scorpion could have been any vacationer on the Costa Brava. When the announcer commented on the Bern attack crisis, he turned the volume up. The news was grim.

There were reports from Washington that the President's National Security Council was meeting in emergency session. Lights were seen in offices in the West Wing of the White House far into the night. In Brussels, NATO ministers were affirming their support for the United States, although the French representative warned that no military action should be taken until it was definitively established who the perpetrators of the Bern attack were.

"Without sufficient proof, it will be impossible to justify any diplomatic or military action," he declared, reading from a prepared text. Meanwhile, the

AP reported that satellite cameras had spotted an additional U.S. aircraft carrier group in the Indian Ocean, apparently heading to the Persian Gulf. In Tehran, in a speech to the Iranian parliament, the *majles*, Foreign Minister Gayeghrani, stated that if it appeared an attack was imminent, Iran would not hesitate to act first and mine the Straits of Hormuz, cutting off the flow of oil from the Middle East for the entire world. The actions in the Gulf were having an impact on global oil prices.

The BBC announcer stated: "As a result of the escalating crisis, the benchmark price of Brent crude oil has risen to $165.33 a barrel at today's closing. Economists at the World Bank have forecast a severe impact on the global economy if the crisis cannot be resolved quickly. The Dow Jones Industrials dropped 342.67 points in the final hours of trading on the news. In London, the FTSE was off 101.67, and analysts are warning further possible declines as the crisis continues."

Scorpion's latest prepaid cell phone, bought under the name of a Spaniard who had died twenty-one years ago, vibrated three times and stopped. He turned off the radio. It meant the six-man SAD/SOG, Special Activities Division/Special Operations Group squad arranged by Shaefer was in position at the villa. He would RDV with the team's leader, Webb, in Girona.

Within the CIA it was widely understood that SAD was the most dangerous assignment in the Agency. Such were the nature of the Top Secret missions they were sent out on that their casualty rate was higher than for any other group of its kind in the world, even though every member of SAD was an experienced, tough-as-nails U.S. Army Delta or Navy SEAL veteran, who underwent further extensive training than even those formidable groups. Once an SAD Special Operations Group team, or SOG, was activated, they were dedicated to complete their mission or die—and more of them had than all the rest of the CIA's other operatives combined. Scorpion's initial assignment when he first joined the CIA had been in SAD.

He had personally gone over the 201 files of every member of the team, code-named "Sangria," before accepting them for the mission, and he had little doubt that before it was over, he might well lose some of them. Driving on the E-15, traffic easy during the Costa Brava's off-season, well-tended houses and villages on the hillsides hidden by dense thickets of trees along the highway, it seemed insane that he was heading into a battle, but there it was.

This time, if it went off the rails, he couldn't avoid knowing it was his fault. The whole thing was his plan—and it all hung on the word of an Albanian gangster and the avarice of a bent policeman.

They met in the tiny hotel room that Webb, leader of the Sangria team, had booked in the Hotel Europa. The small hotel was near the train station in Girona, a town on the way to Begur, a coastal village where the villa Shaefer had rented was located. Webb was a big man with buzz-cut hair who looked like he spent plenty of time at the gym and a blade of a nose that he thrust at you like the bow of a ship. He had no-nonsense Delta Force written all over him.

Scorpion started to scan the room with an electronic surveillance detector and Webb waved it away.

"It's clean. I fine-tooth-combed it," Webb growled. He jerked his head at the door to indicate the hotel's owners. "They probably think we're pansies."

"Costa Brava," Scorpion said. "This is the place for it." The two men sat on the twin beds, facing each other. "You came in through Morón?" the U.S. Air Force base near Seville in southern Spain.

"Yeah. Drove all night to get here. Shaefer said you like Glocks," he said, tossing two Glock pistols and an H&K MP7A1 compact submachine gun on the bed.

Scorpion picked up the weapons and checked them.

"What did Shaefer tell you?" he asked, putting one Glock in the holster at the small of the back and the other in an ankle holster, pulling his shirt down over the back holster. The MP7A1 he put back in its carrying case.

Webb watched him, his arms folded across his chest. Defensive posture.

"He said this was your show. You'd be running it. We're here for if and when the nasty brown stuff hits the fan."

Scorpion nodded. "You don't like it?" he said.

"I'm military. This is my team. We've trained together, been together," Webb said. He didn't say "turf issue." He didn't have to.

"So was I," Scorpion said, meaning military. "We'll go over the disposition together. When the shooting starts, you run your team however you see fit."

Webb took a breath and put his meaty hands on his thighs, clearly relieved.

"Better," he said. "Shaefer said these guys might be the ones who hit Bern."

"There's a good probability," Scorpion said. "So yeah, there's payback. But don't underestimate them—or me," his eyes narrowing. "These guys took out a highly trained U.S. Marine detachment in Bern and four good CIA agents in Zurich. They don't come in shooting and hoping for the best. They think."

"Meaning?"

"I don't care what kind of superstars you guys think you are. This is no slam dunk. Got it?"

Webb nodded. He took out an iPad and displayed a satellite aerial video of the villa and grounds, showing Scorpion where he planned to place men and devices. From the image, Scorpion could see the grounds were encircled by a stone wall and ended on a cliff overlooking a rocky cove opening to the sea.

"What are your people packing?"

"MP7A1s with sound suppressors, chambered for DM11 4.6-x-30mm cartridges in thirty-round and forty-round box magazines. Penetrate any CRISAT," Webb said, meaning the bullets would drill through a target made up of twenty layers of Kevlar with 1.6mm titanium backing at two hundred meters; they were the ultimate small arms body-armor-piercing rounds. "Glocks, M67 grenades; C-4 with remote-controlled detonators for IEDs, one M25 sniper rifle, and two XM25 grenade launchers. Those two are the real game-changers. Should be plenty."

"I'm not so sure," Scorpion said, studying the iPad image. "I need eyes. We could use a drone."

"What the hell are you expecting? World War Three?" Webb said.

Scorpion sat up straight. "I need you to be more worried than you are," he said. "How much C-4 have you got?"

"Plenty. Why?"

"I'll need about five kilos and two detonators."

"Jesus! What the hell are you planning to blow up?" Webb exclaimed. In a way, Scorpion understood. A half kilo of C-4 would completely demolish a large military truck. Five kilos would vaporize it and a whole lot more.

"My car," Scorpion said. "Put a cork in the bottle. Block the road. Once they're in the villa grounds, they stay in."

Webb nodded grimly.

"You are taking them seriously," he said. "How are you going to get them to the villa?"

"No problem. They'll just be following the moving dot."

"What's the moving dot?" Webb asked.

"Me," Scorpion said.

CHAPTER EIGHTEEN

El Raval,
Barcelona, Spain

Scale was at an Internet café on the Calle Barra de Ferro near the Picasso museum. There was no help for it, he thought. The information was too critical. He would have to contact the Gardener himself. A website for the Iranian Dried Fruit Exporters Association was the gateway. He could sign in with a password and an RSA token that provided a two-way authentication and send a text to the Gardener's contact alias.

For five euros he bought a mug of tea and an hour on an older PC in the corner. The café was about half full, mostly young people, travelers, and students. At the PC next to his, a male student was playing a video game. Secure enough, he decided. Before he logged in, he went over the information in his mind. The Gardener did not tolerate long texts. It would have to be direct and just circumspect enough to resist easy interpretation in case of electronic eavesdropping, beginning with the code word that would let the Gardener know it was him and that it was urgent: *kerm-e shab tab.* Firefly.

Scale had met the *policia* in a brothel on a narrow trash-strewn street in the El Raval slum. When he knocked on the door to the room and went in, the *policia* was seated on the edge of a disheveled bed. There were two half-naked women in the room: a dark-haired woman whose head bobbed up and down as she gave the *policia* oral sex, and a bored-looking young African woman sitting in the corner, smoking a cigarette.

The *policia* was a stumpy middle-aged man in uniform with a pencil-thin mustache under a pointed nose that gave him a ratlike look and a belly that sagged over his belt. He made Scale wait while the woman finished him, biting his lip and wheezing *"Basta ya!"* then pushing her aside as he rearranged and zipped up his fly and adjusted his pistol belt.

"From these two, I take my *tarifa* in exchange," the policeman, Pintero, said. "They like it, don't they?" he growled, grabbing the white woman's face with his hand. He twisted her face to Scale. "You want either of them? Be my guest." He grinned. "They like doing favors for me. That one," pointing at the African, "she's got the best *culo*," kissing his thumb "in Barcelona."

"We have business," Scale said.

"Por supuesto." Sure. *"Fuera!"* Beat it, Pintero told the women, who gathered their clothes and left. There was a bottle of Fundador on the nightstand. Pintero poured himself a glass. He waved the bottle at Scale, eyeing the bulge under Scale's jacket that could only come from a gun. "You want? Or are you one of these Islamistas who only drinks piss?"

There were no chairs in the room. Scale leaned

against a wall, his outsize hands clasped in front of him, seemingly relaxed but keeping his hands close enough to be able to grab his gun from his shoulder holster.

"I'm told you have information," he said.

"I piss in your mother's milk," Pintero said. "You think I just give it to you?"

Scale crossed the space between them with a speed Pintero could not have believed possible and jammed his thumbs into the corners of Pintero's eyes. Pintero screamed.

"You want me to pop them out?" Scale hissed. "I can do it—easy."

Pintero struggled, but Scale's massive hands were immensely strong. Pintero reached down for his gun. Scale twisted it out of his hand and threw it on the bed. He smacked Pintero hard across the face and began applying pressure again to his eyes.

Twenty minutes and two thousand euros to Pintero later, he had what he wanted. If the slimy Spaniard could be believed, the American, Scorpion, was wanted by the police for the murder of Mohammad Karif. Of course, Scale knew better. It was his man, Danush, who had killed Karif, and then when the American had shown up unexpectedly, managed to get away and mislead the police into believing the American had done it.

Pity, Danush didn't know it was Scorpion at the time, or he could have terminated him then and there, Scale mused. But the fact that the American had gotten so close to Karif, almost at the same time as Danush, only proved how right the Gardener had been to shut the network down.

Even more to the point, Pintero told him the Spanish CNI were GPS-tracking a cell phone this Scorpion was using. Pintero said that according to the CNI, the American was heading toward the Costa Brava, possibly running for the French border. Scale gave him the two thousand for the cell phone number.

The question was—the reason why he had to contact the Gardener—was it a movie? The CIA and the CNI sometimes worked together and they both hated Iran. It could be a trap, he thought as he logged into the Iranian website.

Kerm-e shab tab. The one we seek ran away. I've discovered where, but I have concerns, he typed and waited. A minute later came the response.

You think it is ab nabat? Candy—the code word for a trap. The Gardener was brilliant, Scale thought. He had grasped the situation and all its implications immediately. Scorpion's escape could be a movie created by the CNI working with the CIA. They might be walking into a trap.

I don't like candy, Scale texted back. *Maybe I shouldn't have any. Of course, it may not be,* he felt compelled to add. There was no certainty here, only guesses. The Gardener would know what to do.

It is ab nabat, the Gardener replied. In other words, it was a trap. No question.

Should I abstain?

Candy is bad for children. You should eliminate it, the Gardener replied, ending the session.

CHAPTER NINETEEN

Begur,
Costa Brava, Spain

The villa was on a cliff overlooking a spectacular view of the lower town and a rocky cove opening to the sea. It was made of stone and glass, large, modern, and expensive, with at least a half acre of landscaped grounds and a stone pool terrace with a rectangular swimming pool. The terrace was on a level with the colonnaded back of the villa and stood a half meter above a garden of rosebushes and trees that led down to a wrought-iron railing at the edge of a thousand-foot cliff, overgrown with wildflowers. The villa was surrounded by a high ivy-covered stone wall with a drive-in wrought-iron front gate. On the land side it was backed by a pine forest that isolated it from the other holiday villas, and could only be approached by a winding single-lane road that made it ideal for defense and would hopefully limit any civilian casualties, Scorpion thought as he stood on the pool terrace and used Webb's binoculars to survey the terrain.

Below was a part of the town of Begur with its

medieval stone buildings and palm trees, and below that the cove, with stone steps carved into the side of the cliff leading down to a small sandy beach. The water was so clear that when the wind died, you could see rocks on the bottom a hundred feet deep. The beach was deserted, umbrellas stacked and furled this early in the season, especially with a Tramuntana, the wind that in the early spring blows from the Pyrenees. The wind whipped the sea to whitecaps, rocking a lone sailboat at anchor in the cove like a metronome.

From the terrace, Scorpion could see a good stretch of the Costa Brava, trees bending in the wind and beyond, the wild jagged coast and the sun shining on the choppy blue of the Mediterranean. It was the most beautiful place he had ever seen.

In a way, his part was done, he thought. Webb had hinted as much. He was the bait. He'd driven into Begur, with its narrow cobbled streets and ivy-covered stone walls, dominated by the ruins of twelfth century castle perched atop a hill like the Acropolis in Athens. He stopped in at cafés and little *tiendas* in town, talking loudly and generally doing his best to draw attention to himself so people would remember him, though in his blond surfer boy wig, he thought it would be hard if they didn't, making sure everyone knew which villa he was renting and that he would be there for a week. Several of the townspeople had thrown him looks that let him know they thought he was full of himself. Good. They would remember him.

Now all he had to do was leave the cell phone turned on at the villa, whose number he hoped

Kta'eb Hezbollah was GPS-tracking, and let the SOG team do the rest. All they could do was wait for Kta'eb Hezbollah to commit. Because otherwise the trail ended with the dead Karif and the mission was over.

He met the SOG team in the villa's upper master bedroom, whose windows had the widest views. All of them were like Webb: lean, muscled, intense. They were a team; he was the outsider. He tried to break the ice with stories about SAD training at the CIA Harvey Point facility, aka "the Point" in North Carolina; in particular, about a certain well-endowed female bartender named Melissa in Elizabeth City, about whom everyone had a tale to tell. On the surface they accepted he was a warrior, but their looks let him know they didn't think they needed him.

Scorpion knew otherwise. If their ruse worked, the Saw-scaled Viper and his team would be coming. They had been ahead of him every step of the way. They had killed Harandi and the Gnomes, and whatever happened, Scorpion knew he had to be here.

"When do you think they'll hit?" Webb said.

"Tonight, probably 0200, 0300 hours," Scorpion said. "It's when either of us would."

Webb nodded. They went over the layout and deployment of men—who would be where, weapons and sensors—on the iPad with the team. The comm, a mid-sized welterweight with a crooked nose called J.G., passed around the satellite-based TactiCell EV-DO phones they would use to communicate. In honor of the Point, the password would be "Me-

lissa" and the countersign "Elizabeth" for Elizabeth
City. A lanky Kentuckian, Rutledge, passed around
the night vision goggles. Rodriguez, a Latino from
East L.A., was on the M25 sniper rifle. A six-foot-
six African-American linebacker type with a shaved
head that everyone facetiously called "Mini Me" set
up the C-4 IEDs. Webb and a tough New Jersey-
ite, Delucca aka "Spartacus Balls," would have the
XM25s, plus they would all have H&K MP7A1
compact submachine guns, plus grenades and pistols, including Scorpion.

"Where will you be?" Webb asked him.

"In the house, nice and lit up where they can see
me till it gets late and they'll figure I'm asleep. Then
I'll make my way down to the car in the woods off
the road. Once they attack, I'll move it to block the
road set with C-4 so they can't get out."

Webb looked around.

"Anything else?" he asked.

"Yeah," Scorpion said to all of them. "These are
probably the guys who lit up Bern. I know we all
want to kill these Mike Foxtrots," Army slang for
motherfuckers, "but if we can keep one of them
alive, we can get intel the White House would kill
to have right now."

"We're not going to give these dicks the chance
to shoot back," Spartacus Balls growled in his Jersey
accent. They all looked at Scorpion, and he looked
at each of them in turn.

"No, we're not going to do that," he agreed.

They nodded. Professionals. Everyone began
to move to their assigned locations. Webb walked
Scorpion down the stairs and out to the pool ter-

race, the water in the pool spilling over the edge because of the wind.

"How do you figure they'll come?" Scorpion asked.

Webb inclined his head toward the pine forest on the hill behind the villa.

"That's how I would."

"What about the cliff?" Scorpion asked.

"Too steep. Especially with equipment." Webb shrugged. "But just in case, I've got Mini Me there. He's big enough to take them all by himself. So," he hesitated, "what do you think?"

"It's going to be a long night," Scorpion said.

He watched the three-quarter moon rise over the sea from the dining room of the villa, painting a rippling silver path on the surface of the water. The night was clear, cool, the Tramuntana blowing about twenty miles per hour, stirring the trees. Although he seemed alone, he was conscious of Rutledge in the hall closet, the door cracked just a little to let the sound suppressor on the MP7A1's muzzle peek out. The living room was well lit. From the outside anyone could easily spot him as a target. That was the idea.

He checked his watch one last time. A little past 2330 hours. Time to go. He hit his EV-DO phone.

"Melissa. This is Scorpion. I'm heading out to the road," he said, and clicked off. The others would be tracking him with their night vision till where the road curved and they lost sight of him. Not for the last time, he wished he had a drone for eyes above. His mission sense told him they would absolutely hit the villa tonight; he could feel it.

He grabbed his gear, went out by the pool terrace and around to the front of the villa. The back of his neck prickled. He could feel them watching him as he got into the Citroen and drove down the road, shrouded by overhanging trees. The headlights carved a tunnel of light in the darkness bordered by shadows that seemed to move as the trees rustled in the wind. As he came around the curve and saw the road empty ahead, he switched off his headlights and put on the night vision goggles, turning the road into an eerie green lane between the trees.

The gap in the stand of pines he had spotted earlier that day was on his left. He stopped, turned the car around, and backed in far enough so it was well hidden from the road but facing it so he could drive it out in seconds. It took a few more minutes to set the detonators for the C-4 rigged to a cell phone set to Vibrate. If he called it, the vibration would create sufficient amperage to set off the detonators. He gave his weapons a final check, then got out of the Citroen and hid on the ground at the edge of the trees beside the road, lining up so he could watch the road through tree branches he pulled into place to camouflage his position.

He settled in, the MP7A1 with its sound suppressor steadied on a downed tree limb. From where he lay he could not see the moon, only its light on the road, a slash of pale green in the goggles, and the moving shadows of the trees stirring with the wind. They wouldn't hit from this side, he thought. Of all of them, he would probably have the least part in this fight.

As the minutes stretched he thought about Sandrine and whether he'd ever see her again. Probably not. If they were successful tonight, the mission would get much more dangerous and he would be going it alone. And if they were unsuccessful, he'd be dead. Don't think about that, he told himself, thinking like that never brings luck. He shivered inside his jacket. It was getting cold. It was going to be a long night.

Come on, he thought, calling to Kta'eb Hezbollah in his mind. He'd planted the cheese in the trap. He'd set the table for them. All they had to do was take it, not wanting to think about how much could go wrong. Everything depended on a dubious CNI agent and a dirty Spanish cop.

It was just after three in the morning when he was alerted by his EV-DO phone vibrating. By the voice, it sounded like the sniper, Rodriguez. He and Webb were stationed in prone positions on different sides of the villa's roof.

"Melissa. Movement in the trees," Rodriguez said, and clicked off. Almost at the same moment, Scorpion heard the sound of an engine coming up the road. A white van loomed in the night vision goggles; IBERDROLA, the electric company, was painted on its side as it raced past. He called on his EV-DO.

"Melissa. Van approaching fast. Could be explosives. Don't let it get close."

"Elizabeth," Webb started to say. "Romeo tha—" He was cut off.

There were two or three shots, then a fusillade of gunfire—the rattle of sound-suppressed MP7A1s and the unmistakable staccato of AK-47s—from somewhere close to the villa. The shooting sounded like it came from the woods behind it. Then a loud explosion echoed through the trees and a bright white flare of light filled the night goggles.

Scorpion ran to the Citroen. The gunfire didn't sound like it was coming from the front of the villa where the van would pull in, but from the pool terrace.

Mini Me! The sons of bitches came up the cliff! Scorpion thought as he jumped into the Citroen and started it. He moved the car so it was parked horizontally across the road, preventing anyone from getting past. Locking the Citroen, he ran back to the woods, moving on all fours, Delta style, through the trees and toward the villa.

The Saw-scaled Viper—it had to be him—must've launched a three-pronged attack: from the pine woods behind the villa, up the face of the cliff, and with the electric company van. There was a sound of metal crashing—maybe the van smashing through the villa's wrought-iron gate and then the bang of a single shot that could only have come from Rodriguez with the M25 sniper rifle. Taking out the driver of the van, Scorpion hoped.

Ahead, through the foliage in his night vision goggles, he could see the high stone wall that went around the grounds of the villa. On the other side came the sound of intense gunfire. It was coming from all over. No way to tell who was shooting at whom or from where, but he could hear the sound of bullets hitting the stone wall, some ricocheting, some of them—probably the MP7A1's DM11 4.6x30mm bullets that could go through damn near anything—ripping holes in the wall, he thought, hitting the ground to try to avoid being tagged by one of them.

As he wriggled on the ground along the wall, he heard the crump of two grenades going off, one right after the other, then the crash of the M25 and more automatic fire. It was like a war on the other side, he thought, angling through the leaves on the ground toward where the wall ended at the edge of the cliff. Just as he reached the cliff edge, the sight of the cove and the sea and the moon eerily bright through the night vision goggles, a giant explosion hurled shards of metal, glass, and bodies like shrapnel against the other side of the wall, ripping trees, tearing down limbs and leaves, even taking down a part of the stone wall about twenty meters behind him.

He took out the EV-DO.

"Melissa. Scorpion. Do you copy?" he whispered into the device.

No one answered. He tried again. Nothing. My God, he thought. Have I lost all six of them? He had to find out!

Ears ringing from the explosion, he slid feet first over the edge of the cliff, feeling with his toes for a foothold. Nothing. He stretched his toes out as far as he could while keeping the weight of his upper body on level ground so he wouldn't go over the rocky edge of the cliff, especially with all his gear. He had to get around to the other side of the wall and see what was happening.

He felt something. A crevice in the rock face for his toe. It would have to do, he thought, putting his weight on the toes of his left foot pressed into the crevice and swinging his body over and around the edge of the wall. With his right foot, he desperately felt on the rock face for something he could gain a purchase on. He clung to the wall with both hands, feeling blindly with his right toe. Then he felt something, a root or something else sticking out perhaps half an inch from the surface. Here we go, he thought, rested his weight on it and swung over with his upper body while clawing at the iron terrace railing. Pulling himself up, he rolled over the railing into the bloody mess that was all that was left of Mini Me and whoever had been wearing the suicide vest that killed them both.

That had been the first explosion he heard, he thought, scanning for movement and cover. All around there were flashes of light from gunfire. A bullet zinged off the iron railing. He dived into a rosebush and crawled on the ground below the side of the stone pool terrace. Cautiously raising his head, he peered over the terrace edge.

The electric company van was obliterated down to the chassis. That had been the big explosion. The back of the villa was completely demolished, upper floors buckled and exposed as if someone had cut away the entire wall. There were flashes of gunfire between someone next to the side of the villa and at least two persons, maybe more, firing from behind a stone flower urn on the terrace. Suddenly, from the battered roof of the villa, came a laser aimed above the urn. In the night goggles, Scorpion saw as a straight line of white light. It was followed by the crump of a weapon and an explosion as a grenade exploded above and behind the urn. Webb with the XM25 grenade launcher, he thought. The game changer. It calculated the distance and trajectory to the target from the laser and exploded the grenade so it took out those hiding behind an obstacle. The guns firing from behind the urn fell silent.

"Melissa. More from the woods," someone said in the EV-DO.

A second crump came from someone hiding up in a tree next to the villa, followed by an explosion and screams from the woods. Delucca and the second XM25, he thought. There were moving shadows and flashes of rapid fire, the shattering staccato of AK-47s and the crackling of an MP7A1, followed by another grenade explosion inside the house that for an instant lit the entire scene in harsh light. Two more dead attackers and one of the SOGs—no doubt Rutledge, who'd been hiding in the closet— whirling in a kneeling firing position as two figures streaked toward the villa wall. Rutledge cut them down with a long burst from his MP7A1. But an RPG fired from the vicinity of a tree in the front courtyard came streaking into the shattered villa and exploded in a blaze of light, and when Scorpion, blinking, could see again, Rutledge was gone.

Scorpion looked back toward the tree and thought he saw one of the attackers moving. He took a breath and started to aim. Before he could fire, there was another explosion by the shattered front gate to the villa property. An IED, one of those laid by Mini Me, he thought, and saw four shadows running toward him. They leaped from the pool terrace down to the garden and ran toward the cliff. He pressed against the stone side of the terrace and after they passed him sat up and fired his MP7A1, cutting down two of them. As the other two leaped over the iron railing, something came flying through the air back at him. A grenade. He barely had an instant, hearing it bounce on the stone surface of the pool terrace as he pressed himself against its side.

The hard shove of the blast ripped the air above him, shrapnel shredding a nearby hedge. Incredibly, he was okay. It had come within a hair of taking him out. Being below the blast and against the side of the terrace had saved him. He grabbed the EV-DO phone and clicked on.

"Melissa. Scorpion. Two of them went over the cliff edge," he said.

Not waiting for a response, he ran to the iron railing and peered over. Already a few hundred feet below, two men were rappelling down the face of the cliff. He looked around, spotted the climbing ropes and carabiners tied to the rail, and ran over. It took him longer than he wanted to find his Leatherman pocket tool, and by the time he used its knife to cut the ropes, he could no longer see them or tell if he had done any damage. From far away he heard the distant wail of police sirens. The Costa Brava was remote enough that although the gunfire and explosions had to have aroused dozens of emergency calls, it would take the *policia* time to reach the villa.

And speaking of reaching, how were any of the surviving attackers going to get away?

"Melissa. Scorpion. I'm heading for the road," he said into the EV-DO phone, then ran toward the front gate, the gateposts blasted and what was left of the wrought-iron twisted and mangled on the ground. He ran out into the road and down the hill toward the curve where he'd left the Citroen. Without the goggles in the pitch-darkness, he would have seen nothing, but far ahead he saw two figures running on the road.

One of the figures turned and fired a burst from an AK-47 at him, but it was wild and went wide. Scorpion zigged and zagged a little and ran faster. Rounding the curve, he could see them approaching the Citroen some two hundred meters ahead. Scorpion hit the asphalt, pulled out his cell phone, found the contact number for the IED and pressed Send.

The explosion lit the night with a giant fireball that shattered everything around it for a hundred meters and set nearby trees ablaze, bits of metal and glass stripping leaves from the trees. The force and a wave of heat rolled over him. He stood up and took off his goggles. The shooting had stopped. Whoever had been near the Citroen no longer existed. He walked slowly back up the hill to where Webb and the other remaining men of the SOG team were standing on the grounds in the front of the villa.

They had lost two men, Rutledge and Mini Me. Rodriguez was wounded and limping from the blast from the electric company van. J.G. and Spartacus Balls Delucca were stripping and packing their weapons.

"How soon before the *policia* arrive?" Webb asked.

"Ten minutes. Not more," Scorpion said.

"We'll be gone," Webb said, motioning to his men.

"We need to sweep the bodies for intel," Scorpion said, heading toward the pool terrace. The two bodies of the attackers he'd shot were both lying facedown near the railing. He pulled an iPad out of his backpack and began checking their pockets, using the iPad to photograph and fingerprint the dead attackers, what was left of them. The first body was of a small man, obviously of Middle Eastern origin. Nothing in the pockets. When he rolled the second over, he had a brief moment of satisfaction when he saw it was Mustache, the man who had killed Karif. He took his photo and fingerprints, and in one of the pockets found a small plug-in drive. Perhaps Mustache had intended to use it on intel he found inside the villa. Langley could handle it, he thought, heading to what was left, a foot and part of an arm and skull of the attacker with the suicide vest who had taken out Mini Me. As Scorpion took the fingerprints of the surviving hand, his EV-DO sounded.

"Melissa. Time to go, ladies," Webb said.

"Elizabeth. Romeo that," Scorpion said, gathered his things and went back to the front of what was left of the villa, where the others were already carrying their gear. J.G. and Rodriguez carried Rutledge's body on a stretcher. They could hear the sirens of *policia* cars coming closer up the hill. They headed into the pine woods where they had hidden their getaway ride, a square-angled Mercedes G SUV. Before they got in, J.G. checked the traps—thin black threads tied between the doors—and under the chassis—branches in specific positions and angles to camouflage the vehicle—to make sure they hadn't been tampered with and that no one had booby-trapped the SUV.

Twenty minutes later they were riding on a side road they had reconnoitered the previous day toward the *autopista*, AP-7, to Figueres and the French border. They sat cramped next to each other, legs on their gear and weapons. They had laid Rutledge's crumpled body in the back. For a time none of them spoke.

"How long till they shut the border?" Rodriguez asked.

"Our contact from CNI," Scorpion said, not using Marchena's name, "said the *policia* request would have to be routed through CNI. He said he would be watching for it and hold off closing the border till 0430 hours." He checked his watch. "We've got fifty minutes."

"Step on it, J.G.," Webb told J.G., who was driving. "How many *hajjis* did we get?"

"One in the van," J.G. said.

"One plus three in the woods," Spartacus Balls growled.

"One with the suicide vest," Scorpion said, not wanting to mention Mini Me. "Plus two in the garden and two with the IED in the Citroen."

"Confirm two more in the garden with the XM25," Webb said.

"Four for Rutledge: two inside, two outside," Scorpion added. "Two got away."

"Seventeen dead Mike Foxtrots," Webb said.

"Fucking van," Spartacus Balls snarled, hitting the back of the seat in front of him, and for a time there was only the sound of the engine and the tires on the road, headlights carving the way in the darkness.

"Well, you said not to underestimate them," Webb muttered finally, not looking at Scorpion. "I'll give you that."

"Rutledge and Mini Me didn't underestimate them," J.G. said, and no one said anything after that. In a way, Scorpion couldn't blame them. He was the outsider, and so far on this mission, he had brought everyone associated with it grief. God, he was glad Sandrine was out of it.

As they approached the border at Le Perthus Scorpion got the call on his SME PED phone from Shaefer.

"Mendelssohn," Shaefer said.

"Flagstaff," Scorpion answered, his hand covering his mouth to minimize being overheard by the others in the SUV, though from their thousand-meter stares, he didn't think they gave a damn.

"We got a hit. A cell phone call from one of the coves in Begur. Aiguafreda," Shaefer said.

"What have you got?" Scorpion asked.

"A phone number in Tehran."

"Do we know who it belongs to?"

"Romeo that," Shaefer said. "But we need confirmation. The good news is you're legit again." The mission was back to being authorized by the DCIA.

"We left a mess here. Killed some Bravo Golfs." Bad guys.

"We'll handle it. Casualties?" Shaefer asked.

"Two," Scorpion said, looking at the dark silhouettes of Webb and the others.

"I'll pass it on," Shaefer said, meaning Harris and the upper echelons. "What about collateral damage?"

"Negative, but there's some property and a road pooched."

"Christ," Shaefer muttered. "Everywhere you go, do you have to blow every goddamn thing up?"

"What'd you want a SOG to do, kiss 'em? How're we doing?" Asking what was happening behind the scenes in Langley and Washington.

He could hear the tension in Shaefer's voice. "We got their attention. The whole damn NSC, the Pentagon, everybody's on stand-by."

"I'll tell them," Scorpion said. Webb and the SOG team. They'd earned it, he thought. Shaefer's message meant that the U.S. was ready to attack Iran and if necessary go to war as soon as he provided proof as to who in Iran had ordered the Bern attack. "I'm not sure they'll give a shit, but I'll tell them. How soon do I have to be there?" Thinking Tehran. The belly of the beast. The odds of ever seeing Sandrine again were getting longer by the second.

"Yesterday," Shaefer said.

CHAPTER TWENTY

Imam Khomeini Airport,
Tehran, Iran

She was attractive, with a knockout figure not hidden by a paisley manteau, a wide mouth that spelled trouble, and obsidian-black hair peeking out from under a bright fuchsia-colored *rusari*, as *hijab* head scarves were called in Iran. A girl who likes to be noticed, Scorpion thought as he exited the customs control line. Her clothes were designer-made or good copies and she carried a hand-lettered sign with the cover name he was using: Laurent Westermann. A hundred-to-one, he thought as he walked over to her, she was VEVAK, Iranian internal security.

"*Salam*, Mr. Westermann. Welcome to the Islamic Republic of Iran," she said in good English. "We have you booked at the Espinas. There's a party tonight. Just a few people from the ministry. General Vahidi would be honored beyond words for you to come, and expresses his regret on his eyes he couldn't greet you in person." She gestured to a tough-looking man in a windbreaker and khakis to take Scorpion's rolling suitcase while leading him toward the airport terminal exit. "I'm Zahra," she added, a sideways glance taking in his Burberry raincoat, Armani suit, Hermès tie, and Ferragamo shoes like he was a baklava she couldn't wait to bite into.

I'll bet you are, he thought, glad they had paid attention to detail.

"**G**hanbari. Muhammad Ghanbari," Shaefer had told him during his stopover in Dubai. They met in a safe house apartment in an ultramodern building near the Deira City mall, shades drawn against the afternoon sun and anyone who might be peering in with a telescope from another building.

"He's the target?" Scorpion had asked.

"We don't know. But that's who the cell call from Begur was made to," Shaefer said, rubbing his hands together as if he was cold. He's fidgety, Scorpion thought. Something was up. Pressure from higher up maybe.

They had already gone over the cover and communications. It was going to be tricky as hell. The crisis had only made things worse. Any kind of SME PED or other device or even a gun would be a dead giveaway, and normal Internet or other COMINT was out. Both VEVAK and the Revolutionary Guards had the city of Tehran blanketed for coverage and they'd pick him up in a heartbeat. The only thing he brought in was a plug-in flash drive and electronic bugs, all disguised as components of a spare cell phone and his laptop computer.

"You think he's the Gardener?" Scorpion asked.

"You tell us."

"What do we know about him?"

"I told you. Nothing. Zilch. *Nada*."

"Are you kidding me? You're telling me Dave Rabinowich doesn't have a clue who this guy is?"

Shaefer shook his head. "In theory, except for a cell phone in his name, he doesn't exist. Except," holding up a cautionary finger, "there was a student by that name who graduated from Tehran University eighteen years ago. Then, nothing."

"Revolutionary Guards?" It was a pattern with the Iranian elite. Recruit top candidates or those who were well-connected from the university, and nearly all records or mention of the person suddenly and forever disappear.

"Bingo," Shaefer nodded.

"So that's the mission?" Scorpion asked. "I find out if this Ghanbari's the Gardener and who he's connected to so the U.S. can justify the hell out of it worldwide when they drop bombs on them?"

Shaefer leaned closer. "Who ordered the attack? That's what the DCI and the White House want. Give them the tiniest shred of evidence and they're good to go. Harris wants to know about the Gardener. Rabinowich wants more. He says it doesn't compute."

"It doesn't," Scorpion agreed.

"I know. The Iranians and their surrogates don't mind killing Israelis or anyone else who gets in their way, but this was an attack on an American embassy. Someone deliberately wanted to pick a fight with the biggest, baddest dude on the block."

"He wants to know why?"

"Don't we all," Shaefer said. "What do you think we've been working on while you've been off having fun in Spain?"

Fair enough, Scorpion thought. From the moment he had met with Harris and his team in Zug, Shaefer and Rabinowich had been working on his cover, going deep enough to set up a special office in Geneva, staffed by French and German-speaking agents supplied by Schwegler, just to deal with the inevitable Iranian vetting. That office had arranged for his visa for Iran, while Rabinowich dealt with how he would enter the country without getting nailed by VEVAK or the MOIS or any of the various factions of the Revolutionary Guards or God knew who else because of the Kilbane photograph from the Bern computer.

His cover name was Laurent Westermann, a Swiss businessman employed by Glenco-Deladier, SA, a secretive Swiss arms trading company, headquartered in Geneva. The company was privately held, powerful and extremely discreet. It was known to act as a middleman for the biggest, most sophisticated military deals for major players, including Pakistan, North Korea, and China. In particular, they were the exclusive non-Russian agent for Rosoboronexport, the giant Russian arms company.

The agreement he was supposedly brokering involved Russia's most advanced ballistic missile, the SS-27 Topol-M3. The SS-27 was nuclear-capable to 550 kilotons with up to six MIRV warheads, had a 10,500 kilometer range, and could be launched from TELs; mobile Transporter Erector Launchers. It was invulnerable to any modern antiballistic missile defense including lasers, which only existed as prototypes. The deal would cost the Iranians tens of billions of dollars, and if completed would change the balance of power in the world. So it wasn't surprising the Iranians were giving him the five-star treatment, Scorpion mused as they got into a black Mercedes sedan for the drive into Tehran.

The key was his face. Because of Bern, someone in Iran, presumably the Gardener, knew what he looked like. Depending on how widely his photo had been dispersed, they could stop him at passport control or pick him up whenever they liked. The alternatives were hair coloring, plastic surgery, colored contact lenses, major self-alteration—such as gaining or losing a lot of weight—but there was too little time, and with more advanced facial recognition software it might not work. Rabinowich's solution cut through all that; it was both brilliant and simple.

Olympic Torch. A genius-level, virtually undetectable piece of viral software jointly developed by the National Security Agency, Central Security Service, and the Israeli Defense Force C41 and Sayeret 8200 cyberwarfare units. The computer virus had been infiltrated into Iranian government and research computers. With it, they had supposedly located the Kilbane image taken from Bern that had been distributed to MOIS, VEVAK, and the Iranian border control and had modified the features, hair color, eye color, and facial structure of the computer image just enough so he was no longer recognizable. As Rabinowich put it: Scorpion's face hadn't changed; who they were looking for had. At least, that was the theory.

"This better work," he had told Shaefer in Dubai.

"It will. The cover's solid," Shaefer assured him.

"Better be. Iranians notice everything," he had replied. "The tiniest detail and they'll be frog-marching me to Evin Prison."

"**H**ave you been to Tehran before, Mr. Wester-mann *agha*?" Zahra asked in the Mercedes as they drove past desert on the modern Tehran-Qom Freeway.

It was a test, Scorpion thought. His Swiss passport showed he'd been to Tehran once before three years ago. The Olympic Torch software supposedly had made sure that the visa, passport, and hotel information in the Iranian Ministry of Interior and VEVAK databases matched the information in his passport. He was in the backseat, sandwiched between her and the man in the polo shirt, while another man drove. It felt somewhere between being an important guest and being arrested.

"Just once. Three years ago," he answered in English with just the barest hint of a French accent to help support his cover that he was from Geneva.

"*Aya shoma Farsi baladid?*" she asked. Do you speak Farsi?

"Sorry?" he asked, making his face go blank as if he didn't understand. A lie, of course. He had been in Iran on a number of ops and also spent a year as a student at Tehran University because his foster father and mentor in Arabia, Sheikh Zaid, had foreseen the coming crisis between Shiites and Sunnis, and in particular, between the Arabs and the Iranians. *Learn everything*, Sheikh Zaid had said. *To un-*

derstand your enemy's thoughts and language is worth ten thousand men with rifles.

She frowned. "You come at a difficult time." Talking about the crisis. "I hope it won't interfere with your enjoyment of our city," she added so flirtatiously, he wondered if she was going to take off her clothes right then and there.

"We Swiss are neutrals," he said. "It's written into our Constitution. Conflicts of others are not our concern."

"You like money, though?" she said.

"Doesn't everyone?" he said, peering through the tinted windows at the desert giving way to farmland. A lot of this had been built up in the years he was away. Ahead, in the distance, he could see the dark smudge on the horizon from the dense layer of smog that hung like a permanent brown tent over Tehran.

"If you really wanted to make money in Iran," she laughed, "you wouldn't deal in technical things. You'd set up a plastic surgery concession. Every woman in Tehran gets at least one nose job." She tilted her head as if to show off her nose and grinned, showing perfect white teeth. "You're surprised my talking about it? Not strictly *ta'arof*," describing the elaborate code of courtesy that governed all social interactions in Iran.

"Curious," he said. "In my very limited experience, Iranian women don't talk that way."

"No . . ." She paused, thoughtful for a moment as they passed the cloverleaf interchange where the freeway intersected with the Azadegan Expressway and entered the city proper; the freeway bordered by clusters of apartment buildings, factories, and a billboard showing a pretty girl in a *rusari* advertising Zam Zam Cola. "I'm different."

Another twenty minutes and the freeway gave way to the Ayatollah Saeedi Highway and the dense, smoggy city of high-rise apartments and streets thick with traffic. On their left was the city's other airport, Mehrabad, slowing traffic as they headed into the roundabout around the Azadi Tower, the massive splayed-leg, flat-topped monument that was the symbol of Iran.

"Welcome to Tehran," she said, pointing a small Beretta pistol at him. "I'm afraid Rostam here," gesturing at the muscular man sitting next to him, "is going to have to search you rather thoroughly."

Scorpion smiled. "I'd rather have you do it."

"You're a naughty man, Mr. Westermann *agha*," she said, her dark eyes unreadable.

"You have no idea," he said.

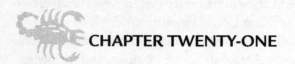

CHAPTER TWENTY-ONE

Elahieh,
Tehran, Iran

"She pulled a gun on you?" General Vahidi said, handing him a glass of Johnnie Walker Blue on the rocks and pouring one for himself. A big man, clean-shaven, fighting a belly in a white silk shirt and plaid sport jacket. He could've been a sports announcer. "Fascinating woman. She has her own ideas of doing things. Cheers." They touched glasses.

"Not very *ta'arof*," Scorpion said, sipping the whiskey, taking in the spectacular view of the city at night. They were in Vahidi's study on the second floor of a two-story penthouse apartment in a white high-rise building in the fashionable Elahieh district. Through a wide window behind a mahogany desk there was a view of the Milad Tower dominating the skyline, rays of blue light pointing skyward from the knob near the pinnacle of the slender tower. Through a matching window forming a corner with the first, the lights of the city stretched north to the snow-covered peaks of the Alborz Mountains towering over the city.

"She acts purely on instinct. It would be interesting exploring those . . . instincts." Vahidi hesitated, index finger stroking his glass, and Scorpion got the sense the general was offering her to him, if only in an exploratory way. The Iranian was feeling him out on his sexual preferences—and if it meant giving him the woman, clearly that, and probably a lot more, was on the table. This contract was critical to the Iranians, he thought. And they were world masters at negotiation.

"My wife might feel differently," Scorpion said. Shaefer had supplied him with a wife and two children, a girl and a boy, nice photo in his wallet as part of his cover backstory.

"We were speaking hypothetically, of course," Vahidi said in a way that let him know the conversation was anything but hypothetical.

"She asked me who we were interfacing with at Rosoboronexport."

"What did you say?"

"Told her it was none of her *putain* business," slipping in the French swear word to reinforce his cover.

"Such language? With an Iranian woman? Most definitely not *ta'arof.*" Vahidi smiled.

"Well," Scorpion said, "I did it with a certain Swiss charm. Not that it matters which *fils de pute* we deal with at Rosoboronexport."

"Because the only way Iran will get the missiles will be decided in the Kremlin," Vahidi said.

"It's a privilege doing business with a man who understands these matters," Scorpion said, raising his glass.

"*Bashe*, now the flattery. You see, you do understand *ta'arof*. And much more, I suspect," raising an eyebrow.

"Such as?"

"Such as what you already know. That there are two Irans. On the outside, the one the world sees. The Iran of mullahs and women in chadors and men shaking fists against America at the Friday *dhuhr* prayer. And then there's the Iran *posht-e pardeh*. The behind-the-curtain Iran, where everyone drinks Johnnie Walker and women take off their *rusaris* and let us see how beautiful they are and everyone watches American television broadcast from Dubai."

"Despite which, everyone is a good Shiite Muslim," Scorpion murmured.

"Indeed. Allah . . . " Vahidi smiled, " . . . is very understanding."

True enough, Scorpion thought. When he had come into the apartment with Zahra, she had stripped off her *rusari* and manteau to reveal a form-fitting strapless red dress matched by her blood-red lipstick and nail polish. The ultramodern apartment was filled with a Who's Who of North Tehran, including Mahnaz Banoori, a well-known Iranian TV actress; Gholem Bahmani, a billionaire member of the Expediency Council; Nazrin Rahbari, a spokesman for the Foreign Ministry often seen on al Jazeera; as well as a number of men in suits with bulges in their jackets who were clearly from VEVAK, MOIS, or other agencies.

Around the luxurious main salon downstairs there were bowls of pomegranates, fresh-cut flowers in Waterford vases, and a giant flat-screen television showing a rerun of *Everybody Loves Raymond* with Farsi subtitles. Interspersed among the movers and shakers at the party, there were enough pretty female twenty-somethings in stylish outfits sipping cosmos for a Middle Eastern remake of *Sex and the City*.

"So what is it Moscow wants? Really wants, Monsieur Westermann?" Vahidi said, putting down his glass.

"You mean between you, me, and whoever else is listening in to our conversation," Scorpion said. Although he hadn't been able to check the room, he didn't doubt for a second he was being recorded.

"You lay your finger on the problem. Let's just say trust is difficult to come by these days. Even among friends." Vahidi grimaced. "The Russians. What do they want?"

"You mean besides money?"

"Of course." Vahidi shrugged.

"A lot of money," Scorpion said.

"Is that all? Surely not," Vahidi said, eyeing Scorpion carefully.

"They don't want a war."

Vahidi's face grew hard. Suddenly, Scorpion was seeing the real man.

"Tell that to the Americans. We're not the ones threatening them. Moving aircraft carriers into the Persian Gulf just off our shores," he growled. "Besides," he added, "why should you care? Isn't war good for your business?"

"Not really," Scorpion said. "War disrupts business. It's the threat of war that's good for my business."

"*Barikallah!*" Vahidi raised his glass. Bravo!

"We begin to understand each other. So who are you really, Mr. Laurent Westermann? NDB? Russian SVR? For all I know you could be CIA. Israeli even," he said, his eyes narrowing.

"You give me too much credit, General. I'm just a simple Swiss merchant in the bazaar, trying to earn a dishonest dollar," Scorpion said, and Vahidi laughed.

"Good. A simple merchant. I'll have to remember that." Vahidi nodded. "So Moscow wants nothing? Just money?"

"There is a concern," Scorpion said, sipping his whiskey. "A name came up. If it could be definitively tied to the attack on the American embassy in Bern, that would be a problem for Moscow."

"Why should Moscow care *goh* about the Americans?" Using the Farsi slang word for shit.

Scorpion got up and gazed at the view of the Milad Tower, then turned to Vahidi.

"Let's not play games with each other, General. Do you really imagine that Moscow would be indifferent if all of a sudden the United States discovered that the Russians were supplying the most advanced ballistic missile in the world to a country they were about to go to war with? A missile capable of reaching not just Tel Aviv or London, but New York. If you do, you've got more up your ass than *goh*."

"I won't pretend we aren't interested. But if necessary, we have our own missiles. More than any other country in the Middle East," Vahidi said, his face set. They faced each other like gunfighters.

"Except it's about a lot more than nuclear enrichment, isn't it?" Scorpion said, going over and leaning back on the desk, one of his fingers casually attaching an electronic listening bug to the underside of the desktop with a smidge of glue stick paste. "Let's be honest," thanking his stars Rabinowich had prepped him via JWICS in Dubai. "You could have all the uranium in the world enriched to ninety-plus percent and it wouldn't mean *goh*, since neither the Shahab 3—or the Sajjil 3 that you're secretly building that nobody's supposed to know about—have the capability of carrying a nuclear warhead because you Persians don't know how to build it small enough and smart enough to fit on the top of your rocket."

"You know about the Sajjil 3?"

"It's my business to know. It won't solve your problem with warheads."

"We can put a metric ton of explosive up there," Vahidi said.

"Not enough. And you don't have the two to three years you need to figure it out. So for both of us it's this deal or nothing. If the Americans pin the attack in Bern on you, they can spike the whole thing. Cheers," he said, then sat down again and downed the whiskey in his glass. Vahidi stared coldly at him, as if over a gun sight.

"Who are you? NDB? SVR?"

"Please," Scorpion said. "You know exactly who I am and who I represent or I wouldn't be sitting here. But I'm also a Swiss citizen acting as a middleman for the Russians. There's no way I could be having this conversation with you without both the organizations you mentioned, the Swiss, and the Russians knowing about it."

"This is dangerous talk," Vahidi said.

"We're in a dangerous business."

"You realize I could have you arrested and shot in a second? You would be in Evin Prison with a single word. Like this!" he said, clapping his hands once sharply, like a pistol shot.

"I know."

For a long moment neither of them spoke. Finally, Vahidi brought the Johnnie Walker bottle over to Scorpion and refilled both their glasses.

"A thousand thousand apologies, *ghorban*. I'm being a poor host to an honored guest," Vahidi said.

"We're back to *ta'arof*, are we? So much nicer," Scorpion said. He exhaled. "We're on the same side, you know. My company, our Russian friends, none of us can afford the blowback, especially if things were to escalate out of control."

They sipped their drinks in silence. Scorpion looked out at the city lights. A few drops of what might be rain dotted the window. He'd made his play, he thought. Either Vahidi answered or he was on the next plane out of Iran.

"What's the name?" Vahidi asked.

Scorpion took a breath. Here it was. Moment of truth. If he were in Las Vegas, he'd be pushing in his chips and saying, "All in."

All at once there was a sound of people shouting from the main salon downstairs. Something was wrong. They could hear someone pleading loudly, *"Sokut! Khahesh mikonam!"* Silence! Please!

"We better go see," Vahidi said. They went out of the office, down the stairs to the foyer and into the main salon. People were trying to quiet each other as everyone gathered closer to the TV screen, where an Iranian announcer was talking, while on a split-screen there was a video of Iranian boats and an American warship. As they stood there, Zahra came up.

"What's he saying?" Scorpion said to her, still pretending he didn't understand that an American warship had presumably sunk an Iranian boat.

"An American destroyer, the USS *McMannis*, has sunk an Iranian Revolutionary Guards Peykaap Class Missile/Torpedo Boat, the *Sanjaghok*. It happened in the Straits of Hormuz. Twenty-two Iranian sailors are feared dead," she said, looking at him. "Is it war?" she whispered.

"Quiet," Vahidi hissed, his eyes riveted on the screen. It showed a small sleek ship slicing through the waters of the Gulf, but nothing of the Americans. Stock footage, Scorpion thought mechanically, as the announcer said something. A bearded man in a black turban came on the screen. He read a statement, not looking at the camera until he finished. When he glanced up, his eyes looked stupid and fierce, like a hawk's.

"Who's that?" Scorpion asked.

"Hamid Gayeghrani. The foreign minister," she whispered, listening intently. "He says the Americans sank our ship without provocation in Iranian waters. He says it's an act of war. He says Satan America will have our response in blood."

Suddenly the TV screen went blank except for an Iranian flag and military music. A young man came over to General Vahidi and said something to him. He looked at Scorpion.

"I have to leave," Vahidi told him.

"We need to finish our conversation. Now, more than ever," Scorpion said.

Vahidi's eyes blinked rapidly.

"Yes, but just for a minute," he said as conversation began to buzz around them. Vahidi told the young man to wait, pushed his way back to the stairs and went up. Scorpion followed him back to the study.

"If we were to agree—a big *if*, my friend," Vahidi began, "how quickly could we get even five SS-27s?"

"Five SS-27s would change the equation," Scorpion said.

"How long?"

"How long can Iran hold out? If you think life is *goh* with economic sanctions, wait till you see what an American naval and land blockade will do. Not to mention if the Americans start bombing."

Vahidi looked at him hard, obviously calculating.

"What's the name of the man you want to know about?" he said finally.

"Muhammad Ghanbari. Do you know him?" Scorpion asked, although he could see by Vahidi's eyes that the instant the words came out, Vahidi knew who it was.

Vahidi sat on the edge of a mahogany desk and rubbed his face with his hand. "And this name came from the SVR? Or perhaps the CIA?"

"What difference does it make? Moscow needs to know their exposure. Frankly, so does my company. Neutrality only goes so far. We do business with the Americans too. Who is he?"

"What I'm about to tell you—" Vahidi began, and stopped. He took a deep breath. "In this country we have two different factions competing for power. In an odd way, we're like the Americans with their Republicans and Democrats. These days the battle is between those like the head of the Expediency Council, Abouzar Beikzadeh, who want Iran and Muslims worldwide to move aggressively against the Americans and their Zionist lackeys in Israel, even if it means all-out war, and those in the Guardian Council who urge restraint, particularly in light of the Bern embassy attack and the American and European sanctions and now this latest incident. This everyone knows." He waved his hand dismissively.

"Can I ask which faction you support?" Scorpion asked carefully.

"No, you may not," Vahidi said, getting up and motioning Scorpion to follow him. They went into a large gleaming white marble bathroom. Vahidi put his finger to his lips and closed the door. "It's important we understand each other or there will be no missiles."

"Yes," Scorpion murmured.

"This rivalry seeps down to all levels, particularly in the Revolutionary Guards. Do you understand?" he asked.

Scorpion's mind was racing. Vahidi was suggesting the attack on Bern was part of the rivalry between factions in the Revolutionary Guard vying for power.

"Who is Ghanbari?" he asked.

"Have you heard of Asaib al-Haq?" Vahidi asked.

"No. Who *le diable* are they?" he lied. He knew exactly who they were. Asaib al-Haq. The League of the Righteous aka the Khazali Network. A Shia

Iraqi guerrilla force responsible for hundreds of terrorist attacks in Iraq and elsewhere. In Dubai, Rabinowich had told him he had indicators but no proof that Asaib al-Haq was being run and financed from Iran by the al Quds Force of the Iranian Revolutionary Guards.

"An Iraqi arm of the al Quds Force, which is as you know a special paramilitary unit within the Revolutionary Guards designed for secret operations anywhere in the world. But they are expanding what they do. There is a rift within the Revolutionary Guards between the al Quds Force and Kta'eb Hezbollah."

"And this man, Ghanbari, is a leader in al Quds and Asaib al-Haq?" Scorpion asked, his voice echoing slightly off the marble walls. If there was a battle for control of the Revolutionary Guards, he thought, Ghanbari might have attacked Bern as part of it.

Vahidi didn't answer.

"I have to give my partners something," Scorpion said.

"You mean Moscow?"

Scorpion nodded. "Did Ghanbari attack Bern?"

"Impossible! This could not have happened without approval of the Expediency Council. I would know about it," Vahidi snapped.

"Where can I find him?"

"I have no idea. I deal with missiles and the defense of my country," Vahidi said stiffly. "This is Revolutionary Guards business. You should ask —" he started to say, then stopped. "I've said all I have to say. Iran did not attack in Bern. If Asaib al-Haq did something, blame the Iraqis."

"What about the Gardener?" Scorpion asked.

"What?" Vahidi snapped.

"The Gardener? Is Ghanbari the Gardener?"

Vahidi shoved past him, opened the door and walked out to the office. He turned and glared at Scorpion coming out. If Scorpion didn't know better, he could have sworn he saw fear in Vahidi's eyes the minute he mentioned the Gardener.

"Look, General—" he began.

"I think you should leave, Monsieur Westermann," Vahidi said. "Our conversation is over."

CHAPTER TWENTY-TWO

Farmanieh,
Tehran, Iran

Zahra was driving, bumping the Mercedes along in stop-and-go traffic, heading for Sadr Highway; the only way to get across North Tehran this time of evening, she said. Just the two of them in the car taking him back to his hotel, the street lined with plane trees and a few people still out walking despite the rain.

"What happened with General Vahidi?" she asked. "He seemed upset."

"We talked. Obviously, the sinking of the missile boat is not good," Scorpion said. He kept going back in his mind to what Vahidi started to tell him about Ghanbari before he stopped himself. He had said, "You should ask . . ." then stopped. For Scorpion, it had to be Zahra. She and Vahidi were the only people he knew in Tehran.

"*Beshoor*," idiot, she muttered, swerving to avoid a Samand compact car weaving between lanes, which in Tehran were theoretical at best. She darted a glance at him. "What do they want from us, the Americans?

Sanctions. UN resolutions. Threats. Whatever happened between us was a long time ago."

"Maybe they don't like people getting killed in their embassies. We Swiss don't like it either."

Headlights from a passing car briefly swept across his face. The rain got heavier. She turned her wipers on faster.

"What has that to do with us?"

"Don't be naïve," he said, glancing casually back over his shoulder at the rear window, stippled with rain. The dark Peugeot that had been following them since they left the party was still on their tail. "Moscow takes what happened in Bern very seriously. If the Americans can prove an Iranian link to Bern, any possibility of missiles for Iran may be off the table."

"Meaning what?" she asked, the sound of the windshield wipers punctuating their conversation.

"We're being followed," he said.

"Are you sure?"

"A Peugeot sedan. It's been with us since we left the party."

She bit her lip. "Maybe it's from the general. To protect you."

"From what? Tehran traffic? It's no good, Zahra. I can't do business this way," he said.

"What do you want to do?" she asked softly.

"Better not go back to my hotel. Where else can we go?"

She thought for a moment; a touch too casual about them being followed. They're hers, he thought. Everyone in Iran is a little paranoid. Why wasn't she, unless they were hers?

"There's Chai Bar Coffeehouse," she said. "It's on Salimi Street in Farmanieh, not far from my flat. It has a nice garden under umbrellas for the rain, good food."

"Too public. Someplace private," he said, looking at her with what he hoped was a seductive gaze. Glancing over, she caught his drift immediately.

"I was right. You are a naughty man," she said.

"We need to talk. It's important." When she gave him a *This is just a line to get me into bed* look, he added, "I'm a married man."

"Aren't they all?" she said. "How do I know I can trust you? Don't be fooled by what goes on 'behind the curtain' in North Tehran, Mr. Westermann. This is a very conservative country. I'm an unmarried woman."

"Are the men in Iran blind? You're a beautiful woman," he said, checking the side mirror as they turned onto Sadr Highway. It was a wide road, four lanes in each direction. They drove past a parade of high-rise apartment buildings, the Peugeot still behind them.

"I'm divorced," she said. "Damaged goods. Who do you think they are?" Meaning the Peugeot.

"I know who they are. So do you," he said. Oncoming headlights from cars on the other side of the highway sprayed the rain-spattered windshield with light like broken glass.

"VEVAK," she said. "You're an important man, Mr. Westermann."

"Call me Laurent," he said, touching her bare arm with his fingertips.

"*Vay,*" she breathed. Oh my.

Her apartment overlooked a quiet tree-lined street. From behind the window curtain he could see the Peugeot parked in a No Parking zone. No one had gotten out of the car.

"Still there?" she asked about the Peugeot, opening a bottle of pinot grigio in the kitchen. He looked around the living room. It was nicely furnished, with a good Kashmar rug on the floor. Whatever she did at the ministry, the money came from somewhere else, he thought.

"Afraid so," he said. "I'm ruining your reputation."

"For my parents, I'm a lost cause," she said, coming over and handing him a glass. "Cheerio."

"*Santé*," he said, keeping the French cover going. His hand in his trouser pocket was fingering the Tylenol gelcap containing Ketamine, a powerful knockout drug. He'd brought it along just in case and had been hoping to use it since General Vahidi implied that she knew something about Ghanbari.

"Now what was so important you had to get me alone?" Zahra said, coming seductively close to him. He could smell her perfume. Joy, by Jean Patou. He put his hand to her cheek.

"Are we going to do this?" he asked.

"I don't know," she said. "Are we? You. The Russians. The Americans. It's crazy. When comes the part when you tell me it's been nice and how you love your kids?"

"Vahidi said you know a man named Muhammad Ghanbari. Who is he?"

"You bastard!" she snapped, and threw her wine in his face. "I thought you were interested in me. I should call VEVAK," she said, indicating the window and the Peugeot. "Tell them to arrest you, you *harum zadeh*!"

"You didn't answer the question," Scorpion said, going to the kitchen and wiping his face with a dish towel. "How do you know Ghanbari?"

"I don't know anybody or anything," she said angrily from the living room. "I'm supposed to keep an eye on you. That's all."

"But you know him?" he said, taking another glass and refilling it with wine. As he did so, he opened the gelcap and stirred the tasteless powder into the wine with his finger. He brought the wineglass with him back into the living room.

"What does this have to do with the missile program? And what bloody business is it of yours?" she said, taking the wineglass from him as he continued to wipe himself off. She put the glass down on a side table.

"Personally, I don't give a damn. Moscow, however, has concerns. If the Americans attack Iran—and if they find out that the Russians would even consider selling SS-27s . . ." He left it unfinished so the implication would sink in. "I'm a middleman, that's all. I wouldn't be asking the question if the Russians didn't want to know. General Vahidi suggested Ghanbari is with al Quds and Asaib al-Haq. Is it true?"

"I don't know," she said, coming close again. Be careful, he told himself. She was changing tactics. "These are not things one should meddle with. I ruined your suit," she said, brushing his jacket lapel with her fingers. She moistened her lips with her tongue. "Maybe you should take it off."

He pulled her close and kissed her on the lips. They were soft, yielding, and he knew she was somewhere between wanting him and playing him. Was she just trying to dodge the question? Or was she afraid? The tip of her tongue darted between his lips as if searching for something.

"Just tell me. Do you know him? Where can I find him?"

She looked at him, her face a mask. Beautiful. Unreadable.

"I can't tell you. Don't ask," she whispered, taking off his suit jacket, then his tie, then his shirt. He let her. As she started to fumble with his zipper, he stopped her.

"Wait," he said. "Let's finish our drink," getting the wineglasses.

A minute later she was on the carpet, unconscious. He picked her up and carried her to the bedroom, setting her on top of the bedspread. The good thing about Ketamine, he thought, was that it worked quickly, was virtually untraceable, and when she woke she would have no memory of what had happened.

He checked the pulse in her neck to make sure she wasn't faking it, went back to the window to check that the Peugeot was still parked there, then got to work. He planted an electronic listening bug/ transmitter under the base of the lamp by her bedroom telephone, a second one behind a plastic electric outlet plate in the living room, and replaced the SIM in her cell phone with an NSA SIM that would forward her location and all her conversations to his computer tablet. Then he went on to the laptop computer she kept on a desk in her bedroom, glancing over at her to make sure she was still out cold.

Her e-mails and files were in Farsi, but that wasn't a problem for him, especially since Farsi and Arabic lettering were similar, except for additional Perso-Arabic letters for *p*, *t*, *zh*, *g*, and a few other changes. A lot of the e-mails were the usual junk. The only personal ones were between her and her brother, Amjud. He scanned through them quickly while plugging in an NSA flash drive that copied all her files and e-mails.

He was about to close her e-mail when he spotted one from Amjud complaining that his wife's brother, Muhammad, had gone over the deep end. Muhammad had told them to let him know if they noticed anything unusual. Muhammad exaggerates everything, including his own importance, Amjud said, and that he was involved in a dispute within the Pasdaran—the Revolutionary Guards—claiming that a rival, whose name he didn't mention, was out to destroy him.

Was it possible? Scorpion wondered. Is that what General Vahidi meant when he said "You should ask"? Muhammad was a common enough name. The most common in the Middle East. But was it possible that Zahra's brother-in-law's brother, Muhammad, was Muhammad Ghanbari?

The flash drive finished copying the files. Using her computer, he went online to the *Tehran Times* website. The headline read: IRAN NAVAL FORCES WILL FIRE ON U.S. SHIPS IN IRANIAN WATERS. According to the article, after discussions with the Supreme Leader, the president of Iran had authorized all

Iranian and Revolutionary Guard naval vessels and planes to attack any U.S. ships that ventured into Iranian waters in the Persian Gulf. Any attempt by American naval or air forces to impose a blockade on Iran would be met with force. If there were any further provocations by the Americans, Iran would mine the Straits of Hormuz, blocking all oil shipments from the Middle East that passed through the Gulf.

Iran's president declared: "The Iranian people will not be intimidated by the bullying attacks of the American imperialists and their Zionist puppet masters, pulling the strings behind the curtain. Iran will fight to the death to preserve its freedom and the freedom of peace-loving people everywhere."

He switched to nytimes.com. That he was able to get to it meant the Iranian government hadn't yet blocked access to websites outside the country. The headline read: WHITE HOUSE IMPOSES NEWS BLACK-OUT. It cited sources that said it was in response to the action in the Persian Gulf and the Iranian government's announcement. Scorpion knew what the blackout meant. It was a long-established protocol to stop all news and the possibility of leaks when the Pentagon went to DEFCON 2. Damn, he thought. That was higher than the DEFCON level they had gone to after the 9/11 attack in 2001. At DEFCON 2 the news blackout would last seventy-two hours, after which military action could occur.

There was only one solution: he would have to make something happen.

He turned off her computer, put his shirt and jacket back on, checked to see if Zahra was still sleeping soundly, and pulled a bedcover over her. Then he went over to the window. The Peugeot was still parked in the same spot. Making sure everything in the apartment was the way it had been before he came in, he left, closing the door silently behind him.

CHAPTER TWENTY-THREE

Laleh Park,
Tehran, Iran

The park was a few blocks from Scorpion's hotel. Traffic was light this time of night, but he had taken no chances and had gone out of the hotel using the back entrance, around the block in one direction and another block in the opposite direction, to make sure he wasn't followed.

It was still raining. He walked down Keshavarz Boulevard under an umbrella, shielded from view by plane trees on either side of the center pedestrian island. A water canal shrouded by foliage ran through the center of the pedestrian walkway for the length of the wide boulevard to Laleh Park. The city was crisscrossed by such water channels.

The streets were nearly empty in the rain. The cafés were closed, their plastic chairs folded and stacked, leaning against the sides of buildings; the only sound was the splash of a passing car and the gurgle of water flowing in the canal. He stopped for a moment as if to tie his shoe and glanced behind him. The boulevard was empty. Either he wasn't being followed or they were giving him plenty of rope to hang himself, he thought, straightening and walking into Laleh Park.

Except for the occasional streetlight beside a paved walkway, the park was dark and still and wet. There were broad green spaces, fountains and trees and the patter of raindrops on the leaves.

"A dead-drop. That's the best we can do," Shaefer had said in Dubai. "As it is, someone will have to risk their life to get anything to you."

"If I find Ghanbari, how do I get something to you?" he had asked.

"There'll be something in the dead drop. Just use it once and get rid of it because the VEVAK'll be on you like white on rice," Shaefer had drawled in response.

He made his way past a fountain with a statue in the middle and down a lane so overhung with trees they formed a tunnel over benches where, in evenings when the weather was good, couples who had nowhere else to go for privacy would hang out and kiss. The lane opened to a broad green, a children's playground, and two concrete structures for men's and women's public restrooms. He went into the men's restroom. The first stall was empty. In the second stall he found a black Tumi messenger bag identical to the one he was carrying.

He closed the stall door and put his bag down, leaving it where the other bag had been. Inside the new bag there were two cell phones, a plug-in flash drive, and a PC-9 ZOAF—an Iranian copycat version of the SIG Sauer P226 9mm pistol. There was also a sound suppressor and four magazines of ammunition, wrapped with rubber bands . He loaded the ZOAF with a fifteen-round magazine and put it and the cell phones into his raincoat pocket, zipping up the new messenger bag and slinging it over his shoulder as he left the restroom.

The area was still empty. He didn't bother to scan the trees. The contact who had left the bag was either watching, waiting for him to leave to retrieve the empty messenger bag he'd left in the stall, or would be back in a half hour; certainly before dawn, he thought.

Before leaving the park Scorpion stopped in a stand of trees, and after making sure there were no eyes on him, turned on both cell phones, one at a time. The second phone had a text message. It was a jumble of letters that didn't seem to represent anything but changed daily based on a random-number algorithm on his flash drive, which could be plugged into any USB port or cell phone. The letters represented multiple alphabet values, to avoid frequency analysis, and were synchronized with identical results on drives held by Rabinowich and Shaefer; a key that could only be used by the three of them. Once translated, it read: *tangoershadfinal-wmzexpectedarlingtonfullcourtpress*. Pure Rabinowich, he thought.

They had topped it off with a simple reversal code he'd worked out with Rabinowich and Shaefer in Dubai just in case. The reversal wasn't serious encryption, just meant to slow someone down a few crucial minutes in case they broke the random number code. They were acting on the assumption that any communication was bound to be picked up by the COMINT monitoring by VEVAK and the Revolutionary Guards that blanketed the city.

"Tango" was military-speak for the letter T, the seventh letter from the end of the alphabet, so Scorpion knew that Rabinowich was referring to the seventh letter from the beginning of the alphabet, G, obviously meaning either Ghanbari or the Gardener. He assumed it stood for Ghanbari or there would have been more. ERSHAD was a Farsi acronym. It stood for the Ministry of Culture and Islamic Guidance, the Iranian ministry in charge of government censorship of media and the Internet. Combing through reams of data, Rabinowich had somehow uncovered that Ghanbari worked there as a cover for his al Quds activities; either that or someone at that particular ministry knew how to get to him.

Scorpion knew that going through the ministry would be difficult. He had appointments with General Vahidi's people in the IRGCAF, the Islamic Revolutionary Guard Corps Aerospace Force. It would be next to impossible to explain to VEVAK what business he had with the Islamic Guidance ministry, and in any case it didn't matter. He was counting on Zahra, he thought, looking around at the stand of trees in the darkness.

The silence was complete; no bird or animal stirrings, not even the faint patter of rain on the leaves. The rain was tapering off.

Final wmz, when the three letters were numerically reversed alphabetically, stood for "final DNA." Combining that with "expected" meant that the final DNA tests on the bodies of the terrorists in

Bern had yielded the expected results they first talked about in Zug and that had since been broadcast all over the world. Except for the Kurdish girl, the dead terrorists in Bern had been Iranians.

It was starting to look like that was enough for Washington. Arlington meant the Pentagon plus full-court press. It meant the generals were pressuring the pols, telling them that they couldn't hold at this DEFCON level for too long without a security breach or losing mission readiness. He could feel the pressure coming from Harris, who was obviously trying to hold his finger in the dike. Unless they heard otherwise from him soon, the U.S. was seriously considering attacking Iran, even without the proof they needed. Except neither he nor anyone in Washington understood what was going on. Especially in this internal battle within Iran's Revolutionary Guards. It could be a huge potential fiasco, he thought. And Harris was all he had. The DCIA, the head of the CIA, was a political appointee. He couldn't stand up to the generals and the politicos forever.

Message received, Bob, he thought, taking the SIM out of the cell phone, burying it in dirt at the base of a tree and covering the ground over it with sodden leaves. As he walked back on the path, he dropped the rest of the cell phone into a plastic trash can. Coming out of the park onto Keshavarz Boulevard, he saw that the rain had stopped. He closed the umbrella and kept walking. Ahead of him, to the east, a gray predawn light was visible behind the buildings. To his left loomed the Alborz mountain range, white with snow from the foothills to the peaks. The rain must have fallen as snow at the higher elevations, he thought.

On the empty boulevard's center island he listened for cars and footsteps and thought about the timing. They were closing the window. He had to find Ghanbari soon or leave Iran. Behind him, he heard a car. It had turned onto the boulevard from a side street.

He ducked behind a shrub next to the water channel and watched as a white Saipa sedan completed the turn and crawled slowly along the boulevard. Through the leaves, he could see two policemen in the sedan scanning the empty sidewalks and center island. If they spotted him, he was blown. As he watched the car the alarm on the personal cell phone he'd used to swipe the data and eavesdrop on Zahra's cell phone vibrated. He took it out and put it to his ear, never taking his eyes off the sedan.

It was Zahra's voice. She must have just woken up.

"Someone's been asking about you," she said in Farsi. He checked the screen. The number she was calling wasn't the number they had for Ghanbari. One of the policemen in the car ran his eyes over the shrubbery and for an instant Scorpion thought he had been seen. His hand slid to the gun in his pocket, but the policeman's eyes didn't react and continued scanning the trees and walkway. He let out his breath as the car drove slowly past, the sound of an Iranian pop song floating from its radio.

"Who is it?" a man's voice replied in Farsi on the cell phone. He was whispering and it was hard to hear him.

"A foreigner. A Swiss," she said.

"Who is he? Where is this coming from?"

"Are you crazy?!" she said. "We can't talk like this."

"I know. If Sadeghi were to hear . . ."

Scorpion's mind raced. Who the hell was Sadeghi? Was he the Gardener? Is that what Ghanbari was afraid of? According to Shaefer and the CIA, the U.S. was about to go to war and pin the attack in Bern on Ghanbari. What if they got it wrong? What was going on?

"You don't think—" she started, then stopped.

"*Khodaye man!*" he said. My God! "Don't even say it."

"Where can we meet?"

"Tonight. The ski cabin," he said, ending the call.

Scorpion's mind raced as he stood and began walking rapidly back to the hotel. Two things were clear. Zahra knew Ghanbari well. Were they really related? Could they be lovers? She was embedded with General Vahidi, while Ghanbari was in al Quds and tied to the saw-scaled snake. Maybe one of them was running the other. But who ran whom?

More importantly, they were both afraid of someone else. This Sadeghi. So which one was the Gardener? Ghanbari or Sadeghi? Or someone else? And what was behind it? He had to find out and then get it to Shaefer and Rabinowich. And he had less than seventy-two hours to do it.

As he approached the hotel, people and cars began to appear on the street, the city beginning to wake up. A black BMW SUV was parked in front of the hotel, two men in suits sitting inside. VEVAK, he thought, taking a deep breath and pretending to ignore them as he walked by and up the front steps into the hotel. If they questioned him about where he had been so early in the morning, he would have to tell them about Zahra and make it about sex— possibly telling them that in some torture cell in Evin Prison.

The gleaming marble lobby was nearly empty except for a man in a suit sitting on a sofa, reading a copy of *Abrar*, a pro-government newspaper. The headline in Farsi read: PRESIDENT SAYS IRAN WILL FIGHT. As he walked to the elevator, he glanced at the front desk. The clerk behind the counter caught his glance and quickly looked away.

Shit, he thought, continuing to the elevator. He couldn't go back to his room. VEVAK or al Quds or Kta'eb Hezbollah would be waiting for him there. He stepped into the elevator and pressed the button, not for his floor but two floors below it. As the elevator door closed, the man with the newspaper lowered it and looked directly at him.

CHAPTER TWENTY-FOUR

Route 425,
Tehran, Iran

He turned from Lashgarak Road onto Route 425, a paved two-lane road into the mountains, bordered by a guardrail and trees. A place of incredible beauty, with waterfalls tumbling from rocks to a gorge beside the road. About five kilometers up and above the tree line, the snow got deep enough that he had to stop at a turnoff to put on chains even with the rented Toyota RAV4's all-wheel drive. He looked around at the mountains, stark and covered with snow. No one was following him on the road and only the occasional car or truck came the other way, down the mountain from Shemshak. He didn't expect a lot of traffic heading up. It was late afternoon and there was no night skiing at the resort; not to mention the crisis. He didn't need to check his iPad again to see where Zahra was. She had left her cell phone on, and his tracking software on the iPad showed she was about ten kilometers ahead of him up toward the Dizin ski resort.

He had gotten away from the hotel that morning through the service entrance, after opening a locker in the employees' room in the basement. Waiting till the room was empty, he had folded up his Burberry raincoat and packed it into his messenger bag, then pulled a hotel workman's white coverall on over his clothes and simply walked out the service door. Only one person, a bearded young man in a windbreaker smoking a cigarette, had been watching the service exit from across the street, and with Scorpion changing his appearance with the coveralls, the man hadn't given him a second look.

As soon as he had gone a few blocks, he stepped into an alley, pulled off the coveralls, and put the Burberry back on. He kept walking. What had changed, he thought, that the VEVAK or Kta'eb Hezbollah was now on to him? Was it just that he had slipped their leash? They had followed him in the Peugeot, so they knew he was with Zahra last night.

He'd thought to get in touch with Vahidi, if that door was still open to him, but he knew it was too early, and rubbing his unshaven cheek, that he had to clean up. An early morning café on Felestin Avenue was just opening. He went in and ordered breakfast: *lavash* bread, feta cheese, walnuts, jam, and tea served in a glass, Iranian-style. While he was eating, his cell phone rang.

"What happened last night?" Zahra had asked.

"Don't you know?"

"I don't understand. I remember leaving the party. Beyond that, my memory's a complete blank."

Ketamine, he thought, looking around to see if anyone in the café could overhear him. A waiter was sweeping the floor near the front door, too far away to hear.

"Too much Grey Goose," he said. She had been drinking cosmos.

"Did we— " she started, then stopped, obviously about to ask whether they'd had sex.

"No," he said. "I put you to bed."

"You left my clothes on. Don't you like me?" she asked.

"It was tempting, but it wouldn't have been . . ." He hesitated. " . . . *ta'arof*."

"You're a good person," she said. "At first I didn't think so, but you are."

"No, I'm not," he said seriously. "But I don't take advantage of helpless people, especially women."

"Never?" she whispered.

Just how kinky was she? he'd wondered. She was sexy, all right. But she wasn't doing any of this for him. It was for Vahidi. Or Ghanbari. It wasn't clear who she was working for.

"Only if they really want it," he teased. "Maybe I should take you over my knee. Tonight?" Testing to see what she'd say. He knew she was meeting Ghanbari that night in the mountains.

"Not tonight," she said. Of course not, he thought. "But tomorrow perhaps?" She left it hanging.

"That's fine. I've got plenty to do," he told her, then whispered into the cell, "We need to talk. The VEVAK were waiting for me at the hotel."

"You're an important man. They're there to protect you."

"No, they're there to watch me—and that means watch us. Call General Vahidi. Tell him to make them go away."

"I'm not sure he can do that," she had said, and he could hear the fear in her voice. It wasn't the VEVAK she was afraid of. But she was afraid of someone. Of course, that could be said of almost everyone in Iran. There were two Irans, Vahidi had said. On the surface it was a normal modern society, but underneath you could feel the fear. It permeated everything, like the smog.

"If he can't, I'll go away. That means Glenco-Deladier and Rosoboronexport go away. Iran will have to deal with the Americans without us," he said sharply, and hung up. He took a sip of hot sweet tea and for the first time began to eat with a relish. He was hungry.

After that, the rest of the day had been a blur. Renting the SUV, having his suit cleaned and pressed while he waited and getting new clothes, including ski clothes, at the Tandis Center shopping mall, all glass and gleaming brass and indoor palm trees. Later, a meeting with senior missile engineers in General Vahidi's Revolutionary Guards AFAGIR missile command offices. They went over SS-27 specifications. Fortunately, Rabinowich had prepared his materials well. Authentic documents with Russian RVSN and Rosoboronexport letterheads and watermarks, plus a summary of facts he had memorized on the flight in from Dubai.

General Vahidi came in during the meeting and pulled him aside into a small private office off the conference room. Through the window he could see the dense traffic below; the nearby buildings vaguely indistinct in the hazy yellow-brown smog.

"You went back to the hotel early this morning, but left without ever going to your room," Vahidi said. "For a person new to Tehran, you do get around, Westermann *agha*."

So Vahidi knew. Were they his men in the Peugeot and at the hotel or was he just that well informed? Scorpion wondered.

"I don't like all these people watching me," he said. "It makes me nervous. This isn't how I do business, General. Who were they?"

"What you are really asking is, are they VEVAK?"

"Are they?"

Vahidi looked at him, an eyebrow raised.

"Something new: a direct question. I'll answer with one of my own. Are you a spy, Westermann *agha*?"

"If I were, would I tell you? You've checked my credentials. You know who I am—and you know where I spent last night," he said.

"A beautiful woman, Zahra," Vahidi said. "But you shouldn't go wandering around Tehran on your own. Not on the eve of a war. Or any other time, come to that." He stepped closer to Scorpion. "Did you find what you were looking for?" Meaning information on Ghanbari.

"She wouldn't tell me. She passed out. I fell asleep, then left." Scorpion shrugged. "Ask her yourself." He assumed she had already reported all of that to Vahidi.

"They weren't VEVAK," Vahidi said. "The men at the hotel."

VEVAK was bad; not VEVAK was even worse, Scorpion thought. At least VEVAK was answerable to the government. In the Iranian Revolutionary Guards structure, secret units like Asaib al-Haq and Kta'eb Hezbollah were answerable only to themselves.

"Who are they?"

"I don't know. But if I were you, Westermann *agha*, honored guest though you are, I would be very careful." He motioned Scorpion closer. "It hasn't been made public yet, but there's been another incident in the Gulf," he whispered. "One of our patrol planes, a MiG-29, was shot down by an American F/A-18 off a carrier. The Expediency Council is holding a secret meeting right now. If we're going to do this deal, we don't have much time."

"You sound like you'd like to avoid this war."

"Only an idiot would take on the Americans head upon head. There's an old Persian saying: 'If fortune turns against you, even jelly breaks your tooth.'" He looked sharply at Scorpion. "Where is the Kremlin in all this?"

"I wouldn't know. We Swiss are neutrals. Boring businessmen. Nothing more."

"*Khob*, my friend. I don't believe you, but *khob*," Vahidi said, nodding. Okay. "But I would conclude my business quickly if I were you. It's funny," glancing out the window at the traffic in Fatimi Square. "It's March, almost Nowruz, our Persian New Year. This is supposed to be a good time for us; a funny time."

"Well, it's a funny world," Scorpion said.

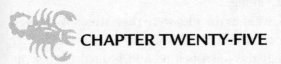

CHAPTER TWENTY-FIVE

Dizin Ski Resort,
Shemshak, Iran

It was getting dark. The sunset formed a rim of golden light along the tops of the snow-covered peaks. The air was cold and thin. The resort's ski lifts were at 3,600 meters, higher than any ski resort in Europe, and he zipped up his ski jacket against the chill. The road grew steeper and full of curves and he had to follow the truck ruts in the snow to get through. Ahead were the lights of Shemshak village, a cluster of houses and a few buildings six or seven stories high. Like Dizin, Shemshak was a ski resort, and from the road he could see the chair lifts going up the mountain; one of them was still going. He was tempted to stop and get some tea and a bite to eat, but something pushed him on.

Ghanbari or the other person, Sadeghi? Which one was the Gardener? And why had they risked war with the United States to attack the embassy? In a sense, the answer might have been staring them in the face all along, he thought. The CIA files. What if the attackers didn't get lucky grabbing the CIA files? What if the files had been the object of the attack all along?

If so, what in the files were they after? What was so important that it was worth risking a war?

He left the town behind and headed farther up the winding mountain road, his headlights shining against the white snow. He turned the heater up; it was getting colder. Stopping in the middle of the road, he checked his iPad. The tracking software showed Zahra had stopped moving. She had gotten to her destination. He put the RAV4 in gear and moved on.

Coming around a curve, he saw the lights of the ski resort, the hotel at the base of the slope outlined by lights on the ski lifts. There were a number of chairlifts and several gondolas that could be seen from the road, but none of them were moving. There were only a few cars parked in the snow by the hotel. One of them was Zahra's Mercedes.

Two rows of wooden cabins, more than a dozen of them, stretched up the slope behind the hotel. The cabins had pitched roofs, vaguely suggesting ultra-utilitarian Alpine chalets. Only two of them had lights on, one in the middle and the last cabin at the end of the row. The last cabin would be where she was meeting Ghanbari, he thought, parking the Toyota around the side of the hotel, next to another SUV.

He checked the windows of the hotel and the other structures before getting out of the Toyota but could see no one watching. It was a shame he didn't have his night vision goggles, he thought, but bringing them through Iranian customs would have been a dead give-away. The Iranians were all over him as it was. He took out the ZOAF pistol, attached the sound suppressor, put it in his ski jacket pocket and got out of the SUV. The night was cloudy. He couldn't see the stars. A cold wind filled with tiny snow particles blew down from the peak. He walked through the snow behind the first cabin, then higher up and across the slope behind the cabins so he could approach the last cabin from the rear.

It was harder going through the deeper snow on the slope. He was leaving deep footprint tracks. Hopefully, no one would spot them till morning. The middle cabin had lights on downstairs but not upstairs, where presumably the bedroom was. Maybe they were at the hotel restaurant having dinner, or maybe downstairs watching TV. As he crunched through the snow above the last cabin, he spotted two sets of footprints in the snow leading to the front of the cabin. First Zahra, then Ghanbari, he thought, taking the pistol out of his pocket.

The last cabin's lights were on both upstairs and down. There were no trees and no place where anyone might be hiding, unless someone was watching from one of the darkened windows in the resort hotel.

There were no back doors and he didn't see the point of breaking a window. The minute he entered the cabin, his cover would be blown. There was a back window covered by a curtain; it showed there was a light on, but because of the curtain he couldn't see anyone. He went around to the front of the cabin and pressed his ear against the door. Someone was talking but he couldn't make out what they were saying. He knocked on the door.

The voices inside stopped.

"Taksi takhir darad, jenab," he called out, holding the gun behind his thigh. The taxi is delayed, sir. He knocked again, harder. Someone whispered and then the door opened. A thin man with glasses and a trim beard, wearing a shirt and sweater, stood in the doorway. He looked like an academic. Someone good in his field. Although, if he was head of al Quds in charge of Asaib al Haq, his field was killing people. Zahra, in slacks and a *rusari* on her head, was behind him.

"I didn't order a—" the man started to say in Farsi and stopped as Scorpion pressed the muzzle of the pistol's sound suppressor against the center of his forehead. Backing him into the cabin, Scorpion stepped inside and closed the door behind him. Zahra's eyes were wide with shock.

"You!" she said in English.

"Good evening," Scorpion said, frisking Ghanbari for a weapon with his free hand, then gesturing for them to go back into the living room. It was furnished simply, Ikea-style, with a plain couch and a couple of chairs. He motioned them onto the couch with the pistol.

"You're Muhammad Ghanbari?" he asked, sitting in one of the chairs, resting the pistol on his crossed leg so it was pointed at Ghanbari, who nodded.

"What is this about? What do you want?" Ghanbari asked in Farsi.

"The attack on Bern—and be careful how you

answer. I don't have to leave you alive," Scorpion replied in Farsi. Zahra's eyes devoured him.

"You speak Farsi," she said accusingly. "You lied."

"Makes two of us," Scorpion replied. He looked at Ghanbari. "Are you Baghban?" he asked. The Gardener?

"Who are you?" Ghanbari said, looking around. "Are you Israeli? CIA?"

"No," Scorpion said, getting up and kicking Ghanbari hard in the side of the knee. Ghanbari cried out. "Next time, I'll put a bullet in it and it'll really hurt."

Ghanbari clasped his knee, his face screwed up in pain.

"Why did you order the hit on the American embassy?" Scorpion demanded, touching the sound suppressor muzzle of the ZOAF to Ghanbari's knee.

"Are you crazy?" Ghanbari gasped. "I had nothing to do with it!"

"He didn't," Zahra said. "*Vay Khoda!* He had nothing to do with it."

"Why? What do you know?" Scorpion said to her.

"I know he didn't do it, you fool. Why do you think we're meeting?"

"What makes you think it was me?" Ghanbari asked.

"You're al Quds? Liaison with Asaib al Haq, *bale*?" Yes?

Ghanbari's eyes narrowed. "How do you know that?"

Scorpion tapped his knee with the sound suppressor.

"Bale ya na?" Yes or no? "I won't ask again."

"Why are you doing this?" Zahra said to him, tears in her eyes. "I thought you were a good man."

"Please. Don't insult either of us with nonsense," Scorpion said. "Well?" to Ghanbari.

"Why do you think I'm the Gardener?" he asked.

"Because a call was made from Begur, Spain, most likely by an agent code-named 'Saw-Scaled Snake' to your phone."

Ghanbari paled. "That's impossible."

"Forty-eight dead in Switzerland and a war about to start. Don't tell me what's *kiram* impossible," Scorpion cursed, standing up.

"It wasn't me. I'm not the Gardener," Ghanbari said as Scorpion aimed at his knee, holding up his hand as if to stop the bullet. "Wait! You said they called me. What's the number?"

Scorpion took out his cell phone and showed him the number he'd gotten from Shaefer.

"That's not one of my numbers," Ghanbari said.

"And I'm supposed to believe you?" Scorpion said.

"Look, here's my phone," he said, taking his cell phone out of his pocket and handing it to Scorpion. "See for yourself."

Scorpion checked the numbers for calls and texts made, received, and contacts. The number wasn't there.

"Doesn't prove anything," tossing the phone back to Ghanbari.

"Sadeghi," Zahra said. *"Vay Khoda,* my God, tell him," to Ghanbari.

"What about Sadeghi? Is he the Gardener?" Scorpion said. For a moment he thought he heard something from outside the cabin. Time to get the hell out of there, he thought, motioning them to be quiet. They listened. Nothing, then the sound of creaking snow.

Suddenly the cabin door burst open, the silence shattered by a burst of automatic gunfire.

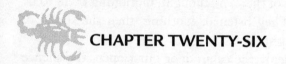

CHAPTER TWENTY-SIX

Darband-e Sar,
Shemshak, Iran

Eight men in camouflage fatigues and green baseball-type caps with the insignia of the Iranian Revolutionary Guards charged into the cabin, shouting and pointing automatic weapons at the three of them. Scorpion dropped the pistol and raised his hands over his head. Within seconds they had knocked him, Ghanbari, and Zahra to the floor and bound their hands behind them with plastic ties.

Their leader was a small thin man with unusually large hands, so big they looked like they belonged to another man. Scorpion recognized him at once from the photograph Yuval had shown him in Barcelona. The photograph taken on a street in Beirut. It was Saw-Scaled Snake of Kta'eb Hezbollah. The man who had almost certainly led the attack on the embassy in Bern and probably in Begur as well. As two men hauled him to his feet, he faced the small man. When in doubt, CIA protocol was to play the cover to the hilt.

"I'm a Swiss national in Iran on important classified business with AFAGIR and the Defense Ministry," he said in English. "By what right are you doing this?"

"Swiss," the small man said, picking up Scorpion's ZOAF pistol from the floor. "And yet you bring a pistol to a ski resort? Do you shoot people when you ski?"

"This is a dangerous country. People were just shooting at me," Scorpion said. Although it had been dark in Begur and he only saw them for a second from the back, he was almost certain the small man had been one of the two who escaped over the railing at the villa in Begur. Looking at him now, Scorpion vowed that if he survived this, he would kill him.

"What a distinguished group," the small man said, looking at the three of them. "*Jenab* Muhammad Ghanbari *agha*, *Sarkar khanom* Zahra Ravanipour, and Mr. Switzerland *agha*."

"What are you going to do with us, Scale?" Ghanbari said in Farsi. "If Farzan Sadeghi *jenab* thinks he's going to get away with this . . ."

His code name is Scale, not Saw-Scaled Snake, Scorpion thought as the small man slapped Ghanbari hard across the face, staggering him.

"*Khafe sho*, traitor!" Shut up, Scale snapped. "This man," pointing at Scorpion, "is a CIA spy. You were meeting with him. This proves you're a CIA spy and a traitor."

"Liar! It's Sadeghi who's the traitor, not me!" Ghanbari shouted. "This is a ploy to take over the Pasdaran," the Revolutionary Guard. "You fools will destroy the Islamic Republic!"

"Who's the fool?" Scale said icily. "My orders come from Baghban." The Gardener. Ghanbari stared at him, wide-eyed. Scale motioned to his men to take them outside.

"What about me? I had nothing to do with this. I came to warn him about the Swiss," Zahra said, indicating Scorpion as they were led out into the cold night, their breath visible in the headlights. There were three vehicles parked in the snow, a white police panel van and two sedans. A half-dozen people stood under the lights outside the hotel entrance down the slope, watching.

"They're waiting at Evin Prison," Scale told her. "You'll have a long time to tell them about it. A long time." He looked at Scorpion. "I'll see you again, Westermann *agha*."

Scorpion didn't answer. He looked down at the snow so his eyes wouldn't reveal what he was thinking.

One thing was clear. Ghanbari wasn't the Gardener. And he didn't have anything to do with the Bern attack. Sadeghi—and it seemed he might or might not be the Gardener—had gotten a cell phone in Ghanbari's name and ID and used it to coordinate the attack with Scale. Part of the plot was that if it came back on Iran, it would throw suspicion on Ghanbari instead of Sadeghi. Meanwhile, back in Washington, Rabinowich, Harris, and the National Security Council were acting on the assumption that Ghanbari had ordered the attack. That's what they were telling the President. Scorpion could see how it would unfold. The Iranians would do a show trial in front of the whole world using the

Americans' own evidence to prove Ghanbari was a CIA spy. And they would drag him in front of the cameras to prove it. They would claim that the CIA had ordered the attack on Bern to falsely justify a war against an innocent Iran. He had to get this to Langley.

The guards bundled them into the police truck. Two of them, armed with what looked like MPT-9s, Iranian clones of the H & K MP-5 submachine gun, climbed in with them. The rear cargo door was shut, and they heard it locked and barred from the outside. Scorpion sat on a bench on the side of the truck, sandwiched between Ghanbari and Zahra. One guard sat opposite them, the other near the rear door, their submachine guns cradled across their knees.

A window at the back of the truck cab showed another guard and a driver getting in and starting up the truck. Scorpion assumed that Scale and one of his men got into one of the sedans and two of the other Revolutionary Guards got into the other. They would box the truck in, front and back, down the mountain. It wasn't that far; seventy kilometers. In little more than an hour he'd be in an interrogation cell in Evin Prison and no way out.

The truck started. They moved slowly, crunching through the snow to the road, and began a slow descent down the curving mountain road in the darkness. Scorpion glanced at the cab window. He could see the taillights of the sedan ahead of them. Scale and one of his men, he assumed. Although he couldn't see out the back, he knew the other sedan would be in place following them, perhaps five or ten meters behind.

He glanced around the interior of the truck. If he was going to make an escape, it would have to be now from the truck, before they got into Tehran. Once inside Evin Prison, escape would be near impossible. He leaned against Ghanbari, who appeared in shock, making it seem he'd been jostled by the ride, and whispered in English.

"Suppose I said I believe you. You had nothing to do with Bern."

"It's true. It's Sadeghi. Kta'eb Hezbollah. It must be," Ghanbari whispered back.

"*Khafe sho,*" the Revolutionary Guard opposite them snapped. Shut up.

"Listen to me," Scorpion whispered back. "In a minute all hell's going to break loose. I need you to rip off my right shoe and sock. Can you do that?"

"I don't understand," Ghanbari whispered.

"I said, shut up!" the guard growled.

"It has to be fast. Pull off my shoe and sock. There's a scalpel taped to the bottom of my foot. Use it to cut my hands free," Scorpion whispered. "Can you do it?"

"I said 'shut up'!" the guard shouted, pointing his weapon at Scorpion.

"*S'il vous plaît, monsieur, je suis suisse. Je ne comprends pas,*" Scorpion said in French, trying to look meek and frightened. Please sir, I'm Swiss. I don't understand.

The guard looked at him with contempt. "*Harum zadeh,*" he muttered. Asshole.

Ghanbari looked stunned. Scorpion wasn't sure he was going to do it.

"If you don't, they'll kill us all," Scorpion whispered, and leaned against Zahra. "I need you to distract the guard," he told her.

"How?" she whispered.

"You're a woman. Think of something," he whispered, and smiled meekly at the guard, who snorted with contempt at him. Scorpion looked away, toward the back door and the other guard and at the truck floor.

"*Khahesh mikonam,*" please, Zahra said. "My ties are too tight. They're hurting me."

She twisted to show the guard her hands tied behind her. He just looked at her.

"Please," she repeated, tears in her eyes, standing and nearly falling. "I'm just a woman. It hurts!" she whimpered, backing to the guard, holding out her tied hands behind her, arching her back and in the process presenting her gorgeous rounded posterior to him. The guard stared mesmerized at her buttocks in tight jeans. This was something unimaginable for an Iranian woman to do.

"Get ready," Scorpion whispered to Ghanbari, crossing his leg so his right shoe was touching Ghanbari's leg. As the truck lurched, Zahra fell on the guard's lap. For an instant his view of Scorpion and Ghanbari was blocked as she sprawled on him.

Ghanbari turned his back to Scorpion and pulled off his shoe and sock in a few seconds with his tied hands. Zahra was tangled wriggling on the guard's lap. The other guard tried to move toward them, holding on as the truck swayed on the road. Scorpion felt Ghanbari's fingernails digging at the sole of his foot, clawing at the flesh-colored adhesive tape then ripping it off. Swaying with the truck, Ghanbari hacked at the plastic tie handcuffing Scorpion's wrists with the scalpel that had been attached to the tape. Scorpion pulled hard but the plastic tie held taut. Zahra tumbled to the floor of the moving truck. It wasn't going to work, he thought, and then suddenly he felt his hands free.

As the second guard reached for Zahra, to pull her up, Scorpion moved. He used the Krav Maga submachine gun disarm, wrapping his right arm around the guard's arm, trapping the hand on the MPT-9. With his left arm he did a downward elbow smash to the guard's jaw, then an upward elbow smash while twisting the submachine gun out of the man's grasp with his right hand. Then, with both hands stroking up with the MPT-9's butt, he smashed the guard's jaw. Before the guard crashed to the floor of the truck, Scorpion fired a single shot into the other guard's head, killing him. Zahra screamed as the guard's blood splattered the side of the truck.

From the floor, the guard whose gun he had taken grabbed at his leg to pull him off-balance. As the guard he'd shot toppled over, Scorpion raised the MPT-9 by its muzzle and smashed the butt down hard on the other guard's head, cracking his skull. The man collapsed, unconscious. Scorpion glanced at the cab window. The guard next to the driver stared wide-eyed through the glass, swinging his weapon into position.

"Hold on!" Scorpion shouted to Zahra and Ghanbari in English as he sent a burst through the cab window and a second burst lower down, through the metal partition, to shoot the two guards sitting in the cab in the back. The face of the guard in the cab window was gone, and the driver was slumped over the wheel. The truck swerved almost ninety degrees and careened off the road, bouncing wildly out of control down the steep mountain slope. Scorpion was tossed off balance onto the bodies of the two Revolutionary Guards, all of them tumbling around as if inside a washing machine.

"Grab on!" he shouted, grabbing the bench bracket and holding on for dear life as the truck bounced and rocketed out of control down the slope for what seemed like forever, though it could only have been a half minute or so. All at once, with a sharp jolt that almost turned them over and smashed them against the cab partition, the truck came to a sudden jarring stop.

For a moment, nothing. Then they stirred.

"Everyone all right?" Scorpion asked, pulling himself up. The truck was on an angle but still upright.

"You killed them!" Zahra said. *"Vay Khoda!"* My God!

Scorpion knelt and felt for a pulse in the neck of the guard whose skull he had cracked.

"No, this one's still alive," he said.

"Now what? We're still locked in," Ghanbari shouted in Farsi, getting up and turning his back for Scorpion to free his hands. Scorpion took the adhesive tape with the scalpel still stuck to it from Ghanbari's hand and cut the plastic hand-tie, then did Zahra's.

"Scale and the others will be here any second," Zahra said. "What'll we do?"

"Get out," Scorpion said, handing Ghanbari the second MPT-9, then searching the pockets of both guards for extra magazines. "I'll need that tape with the scalpel."

"You're going to shoot the lock?" Ghanbari asked, straightening his glasses, which had gotten knocked sideways as they moved to the van's locked cargo door.

"Impossible. That only works in movies," Scorpion said, positioning the muzzle about five inches below the door lock, mindful of the sight offset. At extreme close range you had to aim low because the gun's sights were higher than the bore; also, he wanted to be clear of the lock. "Ninety-nine times out of a hundred, shooting makes a lock harder to open, not easier," he added, then fired a burst into the truck door. The bullets ripped a dozen holes through the metal below the lock. He fired another burst, trying to connect the bullet holes in a circle and punch a single hole in the door big enough for a hand to slip through.

He had made a small hole, about three, four centimeters. Not big enough. He slipped in another magazine and fired the entire magazine to widen the hole, then pulled the lock pick with a flat polymer hook, away from the adhesive tape and handed it to Zahra.

"My hand's too big," he told her. "See if you can get your hand through and open the lock with this."

"I don't know how to pick a lock," she said.

"A car or truck door lock only has five tumblers. It's easy," he said, giving her the pick. "Just stick your hand through the hole and up till you feel the lock. Then stick the pick with the hook end down into the lock and turn. As you stick it in it'll rake across the tumblers. That's half the battle."

"I don't know how to do this," she said.

"Would you rather die? That's the choice. Scale will be here any minute," he said.

"This is crazy," she said, shaking her head as she stuck her hand through the rough hole made by the bullets, pressing the side of her body against the door. Her face was strained as she twisted her hand up on the outside of the door. "I feel the lock," she said.

"Good. Now stick it in," he said, loading a new magazine into his MPT-9.

They waited; only seconds, but it seemed an hour. Every second, Scorpion knew, Scale was getting closer. Unless they got out quickly, there was a good chance they would walk out into a hail of bullets.

"It's in," she announced.

"Turn it," he told her.

"It's not turning," she said.

"Jiggle it."

"How?"

"Not side to side. Up and down. Just a little. Jiggle twice then turn."

They heard the door lock click.

"Now what?" she said.

"Leave the pick in the lock. Turn your hand down and pull in and up on the bar," he said.

"I'm trying," she said, then looked at him. "I can't. It's too hard."

"Scale's coming any second, damn it! Pull in and up," he said.

She looked terrified, and a moment later she grunted.

"It moved," she said, pressing her weight against the back door, her face white with the strain. They heard something move and then the door swung open.

Zahra freed her hand and the three of them jumped out onto a steep rocky slope below the snow line. Scorpion hit the ground laying flat and motioned them down as he looked up the slope.

In the dark it was almost impossible to see. There were shadows, not moving, at the edge of the road high above them. Probably the two sedans, he thought. They had been very lucky their van had come so far down the slope, he thought. If they were close to the road, Scale would have been waiting for them as they exited.

He could hear something moving, the sound far above them, although it was too dark to see clearly. But if he couldn't see them, they couldn't see him either. It had to be Scale and the other three Revolutionary Guards making their way down the slope toward them.

"What do we do?" Zahra asked. She was crouched beside him. Ghanbari, next to her, cradled the second MPT-9. Scorpion looked around. About four hundred meters below he saw the lights of houses. Probably Darband, a tiny village adjoining the Shemshak ski resort, a little farther down the mountain. He had come through it on his way up. There would be cars there; he could steal one. They had to get into Tehran before a roadblock could be set up.

Options. To stay and fight it out. They were outnumbered and outgunned and had limited ammo. The odds were lousy. Plus, in Begur he had learned not to underestimate Scale.

Or they could go up. Go around Scale and his men coming down in the dark, steal one of the sedans and hightail it for Tehran. On the plus side, it would be unexpected. They would catch Scale by surprise. On the minus side, the slightest sound and they would be caught out in the open in the snow. Sitting ducks for Scale and his trained Revolutionary Guards. And if they did make it to the cars, they would have a lot farther to go down the mountain to reach Shemshak and the road back to Tehran. If Scale made a cell phone call to set up a roadblock before they got into the city, they'd be in Evin Prison within the hour.

Or they could go down the rest of the slope on foot to Darband, grab a car and try to outrun the roadblock. It was the shortest way, but on the minus side, he didn't know how fast the others could move and at some point they'd be in the open, easy targets if Scale and his men got close enough before they reached the winding village road below.

All the options were bad. Find another one, he told himself, and a thought occurred.

"What stopped us?" he asked out loud and walked around the van. The right front of the vehicle was smashed against a rock outcrop. The hood was buckled in as though hit by a battering ram. He didn't have to look inside to know the engine had been damaged. He glanced down the slope to the road and the village below. The angle was steep. At least fifty degrees. Still, it might just be possible, he thought, looking up to see moving shadows barely visible near the edge of the snow line. In a minute or less Scale and his men would be within shooting range.

Scorpion opened the cab door and pulled the driver's body out onto the ground. The key was still in the ignition. He got in behind the wheel and, just to make sure, tried to start the van, but the engine was dead, as he'd suspected. Motioning to the others, he went around and pulled the other body out of the cab.

"Scale's coming. We have less than a minute to live," he told them.

"What do you suggest?" Ghanbari asked, swallowing hard.

"Help me push the van back up off this rock outcropping, just maybe ten centimeters. Then you two jump into the back of the van. As far back as you can go for the weight, to keep us from flipping over."

"You're not thinking . . ." Zahra started, staring down at the distant lights below in horror.

"What's to stop us from rolling down before we can get in the back?" Ghanbari asked.

"The brakes—and that," Scorpion said, pointing to a roughly flat rock the size of a basketball. "Come on," he said, putting his hands and chest against the front of the van. "And when you jump in, hang on for your life."

He pushed as hard as he could with his entire body against the van to move it uphill. After a second Zahra and Ghanbari, slinging the MPT-9 over his shoulder, joined him.

At first the van didn't budge. They heard the

rattle of automatic gunfire from above. Scale. They heaved together and the van budged an inch. Legs and muscles straining, they moved the van moved another inch, then another, till they'd managed to push it almost a foot back up the slope.

"Hold it!" Scorpion shouted, grabbing the rock to wedge it just in front of the side of the right tire, about two centimeters of it acting as a stop, while Ghanbari and Zahra strained with every fiber to hold it till he got the rock in place. A bullet cracked through one of the cab windows. A second bullet tore through the side of the van.

"Now! Go! Go!" Scorpion shouted as he ran around and dived into the driver's seat. "And hang on!"

As Ghanbari and Zahra ran around to the back and jumped into the van, Scorpion put on the seat belt, pulling it so tight he could scarcely breathe while stomping with all his weight on the brake. More automatic gunfire sounded. They were getting closer.

"Ready!" Ghanbari shouted from the back.

A bullet pinged off a corner of the windshield post.

Scorpion took his foot off the brake, put the transmission into Neutral, and turned the wheel sharply to the left, away from the outcropping and the rock wedged under the tire. For the briefest instant the van started to roll slowly, then quickly gathered momentum as it headed down the steep rocky slope. Multiple bursts of automatic fire sounded behind them as Scale and his men began to realize what was happening.

The van bounced and lurched over the rocky, uneven ground, going faster and faster. He was already over fifty kilometers per hour and the slope looked unbelievably steep. He pumped the brakes to try and control the descent without burning them out as the van went faster and faster down the slope. The automatic gunfire sounded fainter behind them. The lights of the village and the road were getting closer, but he was losing control as the van slewed and bounced over the rocky terrain. Over sixty-five kilometers per hour and it felt like he was driving blindly in the darkness almost straight down. He heard Zahra cry out in back, but there was no stopping now.

Eighty kilometers per hour, more than fifty mph down a mountain and still gathering speed, Scorpion hanging on for dear life. The force of bouncing around and the momentum pressed his body forward, straining against the seat belt. He had to use all of his strength to keep himself from slamming into the steering wheel.

Ninety kilometers per hour. Ghanbari shouting and Zahra screaming. Bouncing around like being trapped inside a washing machine. The force almost ripping the steering wheel from his hands and Scorpion standing almost upright on the brake to try to slow it.

One hundred kilometers per hour; sixty mph. He could see the road now and the houses in the village. He was hanging onto the wheel and pumping the brake like a jackhammer when suddenly he felt it slip and it was like pressing on air all the way to the floorboard. He pumped it a couple of times. Nothing.

The brakes were gone.

At 110 kilometers per hour the road came up fast. Scorpion hit a bump and the van flew into the air, crashing down and bouncing wildly He fought to regain control. They were nearly at the road, bordered by trees. If he tried to turn onto it at this speed they would flip over. There would be bodies from the back flying everywhere. The road was empty this time of night; at least he wouldn't be killing anyone. He saw a single gap in the trees and across the road a two-story house in a stand of trees, and next to it a car.

Pick one, he told himself. The lights in the house were on. If he hit it he might kill someone. He aimed for the car—it looked like an Iranian Khodro—and braced himself straight-armed on the steering wheel, hoping the impact wouldn't impale him on the steering column. Here it came.

They crashed head first into the car with a jarring smash that nearly tore his arms from his shoulder sockets. The seat belt dug deep into him. The van drove the car six or seven meters along the ground before coming to rest against a tree. From somewhere, a dog started frantically barking. Lights in the nearby houses came on.

Scorpion unclipped the seat belt, looking at it for a second. It had saved his life. Then he grabbed the MPT-9 from the floor and jumped out of the van. He ran around to the back and opened the rear cargo door. Zahra was trying to get up, her face bruised and bleeding from a cut on her forehead. Ghanbari, on the van floor, looked dazed.

"Come," Scorpion said, helping Zahra out of the

van. He half lifted Ghanbari to his feet and helped him out. A man came out of the house he had almost crashed into.

"*Va'isin!*" Scorpion shouted sharply in Farsi. Stop! Showing him the MPT-9. "Go back inside and don't call anyone."

The man hurriedly went back inside. Scorpion could hear him talking to someone. He looked around. A dark-colored Renault compact was parked in front of the next house. Motioning to Ghanbari and Zahra, he went over to it.

He was about to use the pick when he decided to try the door. It was unlocked. Before getting in, he glanced back up at the mountain. High up he could see headlights from two vehicles moving on the mountain road. Scale and his men had climbed back up to the road and were in pursuit. Ghanbari and Zahra came up beside him.

"That was the scariest thing that's ever happened to me," she gasped.

"We have to go," Scorpion said. "They're after us."

"You saved us," she said, coming so close the tip of her breast brushed his arm. He could smell her perfume. Behind her, Ghanbari nodded his agreement.

"Get in," Scorpion said, motioning at her with the MPT-9. "On the way, you can tell us why you set us up."

CHAPTER TWENTY-SEVEN

Ozgol,
Tehran, Iran

Racing 125 kilometers per hour down the Lashgarak Road; trying to get into the city before Scale could order a roadblock. Zahra beside him in the front passenger seat, Ghanbari in back, leaning forward to hear. Lonely highway lights and a metal barrier along the side of the road, and in the distance, a haze of lights from the city.

"I don't know what you're talking about," she said. "What are you saying?"

"We don't have time for these games," Scorpion said through clenched teeth. "They knew who I was. They knew Ghanbari *agha* would be there. They knew how many men they'd need and exactly where and when to go in. The only way they could have done that is if you told them."

"How could I? I didn't know you were following me!" She turned on him. "How did you find me?"

"They probably followed you the same way I did—GPS-tracking your cell phone. Speaking of which," he held out one hand as he drove, "give it to me."

She hesitated a moment, then handed her phone to him. He put it in his pocket.

"You're right," he said. "They didn't know I would be there. But Scale sure knew all about me. I was the icing on the cake. But they knew he'd be there," indicating Ghanbari. "Why'd you do it?"

"Why me? Maybe you did it," she insisted sullenly. "Or Muhammad *jan*," meaning Ghanbari.

"Liar!" Ghanbari shouted. "You betrayed your own family, you *jendeh* whore!"

"We don't have time for this!" Scorpion exclaimed, highway lights flashing by. "First of all, it couldn't have been me. I didn't even know Sadeghi existed till tonight. As for Ghanbari *agha*, he didn't call to meet you. You called him. It was your idea. I like you Zahra," glancing at her, looking small, scrunched up in the passenger seat. "But this is business. Who are you working for?"

"You know who I work for," she snapped. "General Vahidi. AFAGIR." The Iranian missile command.

He slapped her hard across her face with the back of his hand.

"Who else?" he demanded. "VEVAK?"

"No one else," she gasped.

"Not good," Ghanbari muttered from the backseat. "I trusted you, Zahra *khahar*." Implying she was like a sister to him.

"I'm doing this with one hand," Scorpion said. "If I lose control of the car, we all die. Who'd you tell about the meeting at the cabin tonight? Sadeghi?"

"I had no choice!" she cried out. They were coming up fast on the red taillights of a car ahead of them in the darkness. Checking the rearview mirror to make sure there were no headlights behind him yet, he whipped the Renault around the car and sped on. Another couple of minutes and they'd be in the city and it would be harder for Scale or VEVAK to know where to put a roadblock.

"We've got to get rid of this car. Where's the nearest Metro?" he asked Ghanbari.

"The Tajrish station. I'll show you," Ghanbari said.

"What do you mean, no choice?" Scorpion asked her. They reached the outskirts of the city. He could see oil storage tanks and multistory apartment buildings. They slowed for traffic as he cloverleafed onto Babaei Highway, heading west across North Tehran.

"He threatened me. Not just me, my brother and your sister," she said accusingly, darting an angry glance over her shoulder at Ghanbari. "This is your war you got me caught up in, Muhammad *jan*, not mine."

"Is Sadeghi the Gardener?" Scorpion asked.

"Are you CIA, Westermann *agha*? Or maybe Mossad?" Ghanbari asked, his eyes flashing.

"Neither, not that it matters," Scorpion said. "We're all in the same jam. So, Sadeghi, is he the Gardener?"

Neither of them answered. The traffic grew heavier. In the distance ahead Scorpion could see lanes of red taillights bunching up. Accident or roadblock? he wondered. They couldn't afford to find out.

"We've got to get off the highway," he told them.

He crept through bunched-up traffic to get off the next exit, then drove through a darkened area with wide streets. He had no sense of where he was, except for the darkness of the mountains looming over them.

"Where are we?" he asked.

"Ozgol," Ghanbari said. "Not far from Niavaran Palace, where the Shah used to live. It's a museum now."

"And the Metro?"

"If we want to avoid highways, we can take Ozgoli Avenue. I'll show you."

"And you didn't answer my question about Sadeghi. Is he the Gardener?"

Ghanbari shook his head.

"I don't know."

"What do you mean you don't know? Makes no sense."

"You don't understand. No one knows who the Gardener is. No one knows his name or anything about him. It is said you only meet him once. And the encounter is usually fatal."

"Why is everyone so afraid of him? What organization is he a part of?" Scorpion asked.

"No organization. He works directly for the Supreme Leader, Grand Ayatollah Ali Khamenei, and is answerable only to him. No one knows his cover, his office, even his real name. He handles matters for the leader that cannot be spoken about."

"The Ayatollah's hatchet man," Scorpion suggested.

"It's all rumors," Zahra said. "No one knows anything. Some people just disappear. Some even in

VEVAK—all right, I do work for VEVAK—claim he's a myth. No one speaks about him, and if anyone does, people stop talking. But there have been stories. Horrible stories," she whispered.

"Like what?"

"A special section of Evin Prison," she said. "No one—not even the commander of the prison—can go there. Special guards that don't belong to the prison, they come from the Ayatollah's personal bodyguard. People who go in there and somehow survive are changed forever. They will inform on their friends, their family, their own children even."

"Could Sadeghi be the Gardener?"

"Who else would have dared challenge me and al Quds? If so, Kta'eb Hezbollah is trying to take over not just al Quds, but the Pasdaran, the entire Revolutionary Guards," Ghanbari said.

"Which means the entire government," Zahra said. "The Pasdaran are the source of the Supreme Leader's power. They are his instrument."

"I have to call my wife," Ghanbari said, tapping the keys on his cell phone. "She—my family—are in danger."

"Make it quick," Scorpion said. "They're tracking us by yours and Zahra's cell phones right now."

"Should we throw them away?"

"Not yet," Scorpion said. "You understand, we can't go home, any of us?"

"*Vay Khoda*, what can we do?" Zahra asked. Behind them Ghanbari murmured urgently into his phone. It sounded like he was pleading with his wife. The conversation ended abruptly.

"How is it?" Scorpion asked.

Ghanbari looked away. "Not good," he said. "Now what?"

"First we have to evade Scale," Scorpion said. "Where are we?" They were on a wide well-tended street with tall apartment buildings and brightly lit still-crowded stores, illuminated billboards advertising chic new clothing for the upcoming Nowruz holiday, the Persian New Year. It was like a different world, as if what they'd just gone through hadn't happened.

"Farmanieh," Ghanbari said. "Lavasani Boulevard. We're almost there."

"We should check the radio," Scorpion said. "See if they mention us on the news."

Zahra turned the radio on. A man's voice came on, soft, slightly hoarse, speaking in Farsi. They didn't even have to change the station.

"Shhh!" she said. "It's the Supreme Leader."

They listened intently.

" . . . cannot be threatened," the Ayatollah said. "These unprovoked attacks by American air and naval forces against the peace-loving people of the Islamic Republic will not be tolerated. Acting with the unanimous consent of the Expediency Council and the Guardian Council, I have today instructed President Ahmadinejad and General Hassan Majizadeh *jenab* that any forces of the United States, their allies, or their Zionist dogs venturing into the Persian Gulf will be detained or destroyed by the military forces of the Islamic Republic of Iran.

"To enforce this strict ban against Satan America, I have further instructed General Majizadeh *jenab* to close the Straits of Hormuz to all non-Iranian shipping with mines and naval ships until such time as the Americans and their Zionist puppets cease their violent provocations and admit their accusations that Iran had anything to do with the supposed attack in Switzerland are lies manufactured in Tel Aviv. If the world wants its oil, it must stand with us against the aggression of the American demons.

"We further declare that the Zionist entity called Israel will be destroyed if there are any further provocations. *Allahu akhbar,* God is great and God is with us. *Salam,* my brothers and sisters, my sons and daughters."

Zahra looked at them, the boulevard lights reflected on the car window next to her head.

"Does it mean what I think it means?" she asked.

"It means war," Ghanbari said.

CHAPTER TWENTY-EIGHT

Haft-e Tir Square,
Tehran, Iran

They bought new prepaid cell phones for each of them at an electronics shop next to the bus station in Tajrish Square. They went down the stairs to the Metro platform and waited for the Line 1 train. Scorpion and Ghanbari boarded a middle car; Zahra rode in the front car, reserved for women. As they rode, Scorpion captured Zahra's and Ghanbari's contacts from their phones and enslaved their new phones to his with the NSA software from his flash drive.

"What will we do with the old phones?" Ghanbari asked.

"They're GPS tracking yours and Zahra's," Scorpion said. "That's why I wanted the Metro."

"Clever. We leave them on the train," Ghanbari nodded approvingly. "You're an interesting man, Westermann *agha.*"

Scorpion nodded. "Call me Laurent, Muhammad *jan.* By the time they find the old phones, we'll have gone to ground."

"But then what? We'll be wanted men. Everyone, the police, the Basiji, the VEVAK, Kta'eb Hezbollah, will be after us. And then there's the crisis. And in the middle of Nowruz!"

Scorpion's mind was already at warp speed. He had to get the intel to Langley about Sadeghi possibly being the Gardener and that the call from Begur hadn't been made to Ghanbari. All hell would break loose if they went public using such misinformation as a basis for war.

Langley would ask for his assessment. Best guess: Sadeghi and Kta'eb Hezbollah were behind the hit on Bern. As to why, maybe Rabinowich could figure it out. Clearly, it was, as Vahidi had suggested, part of a power struggle for control of the Iranian Revolutionary Guards.

Another problem: he wasn't sure if he could even get the intel out. One of the first things the Iranians would likely do would be to quarantine access to the Internet outside Iran, if they hadn't done it already.

As the train pulled into the Haft-e Tir station, Scorpion let his arm hang down and quietly deposited Zahra's and Ghanbari's old cell phones on the floor beside the bench, as out of sight as possible. With any luck, they wouldn't be noticed. And if someone did take them, all the better. It would take that much longer for Scale and his men to track down the old cell phones.

When they got off the train, Zahra joined them on the platform. They came up out of the Metro into a wide well-lit square. This was an older, poorer part of town. Even at night, the smog was thicker here. It smelled of trash and diesel fumes. Many of the women in the streets were dressed in head-to-foot chadors like black-robed ghosts, instead of Western clothes. People were shopping at market stalls in the square. Vendors called out, hawking flowers, goldfish in bowls, and green plants in clay containers shaped like animals.

"Why the goldfish?" Scorpion asked.

"*Vay Khoda!*" Zahra slapped her forehead. "It's Monday."

"Goldfish Monday?" he asked.

"No, *beshoor*." Idiot. Then he understood. "Tomorrow is Tuesday; tomorrow night's the eve of Red Wednesday."

"The last Wednesday before Nowruz, the Persian New Year," Ghanbari explained.

"They don't seem very festive," Scorpion said.

"No, they don't. It's the crisis," she said thoughtfully, walking with them out of the square down Karimkhan Zand, a wide boulevard with plane trees on both sides, crowded with cars and yellow buses. Despite the crisis, people were out with their families, shopping for the holiday.

"I've never seen it like this. It's not like any Nowruz ever." She looked around. "Where are we going?" she asked.

"We keep an apartment. I'll show you," Ghanbari said.

"We being al Quds?" Scorpion asked.

"We have many of these," Ghanbari nodded. "But this is one only I and two of my closest people know about."

"Except in a very short time they're going to be told you're a traitor," Scorpion said.

"They won't believe it," Ghanbari said. "I'm not the only one who will realize what's happening, that Sadeghi and the Kta'eb Hezbollah are trying to take over."

"So Scale works for Sadeghi?"

Ghanbari shook his head.

"Scale works for the Gardener. In this case, he seems to be acting for Sadeghi. That would suggest . . ." He stopped, leaving Scorpion to draw his own conclusions.

"Sadeghi's the Gardener. It must be," Zahra said. "It all makes sense."

"How long do you think before Sadeghi gets to your people?"

"We should be all right for tonight. They can't check everywhere and there's a lot going on," Ghanbari said, turning off the boulevard. He led them to an apartment building on Second Street. "This is an interesting neighborhood. Lots of Armenians and Assyrians."

"Stop talking nonsense," Zahra snapped as they went in and began walking up the four floors to the apartment. "What are we going to do?"

"We counterattack," Scorpion said. "It's our only chance."

"Just the three of us? And the entire country mobilizing for war. How do we do that?"

"Wait!" Scorpion said when they reached the door, stopping Ghanbari before he unlocked it. He checked for any signs of intruders, electronic monitoring or explosives, getting down and peeking at the crack between the door and the doorstep, then signaling Ghanbari to open the door. They went inside.

The apartment was Scorpion's kind of place. Half a dozen bunk beds, tables for desks, floor-to-ceiling shelves stocked with computers and electronics and weapons, black curtains over the windows. It could have come from a CIA catalogue labeled "Safe house." Zahra stood in the middle of the living room.

"How?" she insisted. "What are we going to do?"

"Not we," Scorpion said. "You."

For weapons, he chose a Nakhir sniper rifle, an Iranian version of the Russian Dragunov, chambered for 7.62x54mm rounds. Effective range eight hundred meters, but with a 4x scope, the maximum range was 1,300 meters; eight-tenths of a mile. Plus a handful of ten-round mags. For a handgun he took another PC9 ZOAF. Ghanbari selected an MPT-9 submachine gun.

"They might let you go. It might just be Muhammad *jan*," Scorpion said to Zahra, indicating Ghanbari, "and me they're after. If they do take you somewhere, try to stay visible. In public, or near a window. It's the best way I can protect you."

"Maybe I don't want protecting," she said, looking in a mirror to put on lipstick and mascara, her weaponry. "Maybe they just want you and Muhammad *jan*."

"You'd give us up?" Ghanbari asked.

"In a heartbeat. I want to be safe. I want to go home," she said. Turning to Scorpion: "You've been in this country one day and you've already ruined my life. I knew you were trouble." Going back to the mirror: "All men are trouble, but you're something extra special, Westermann *agha*. You should come with a warning label."

Scorpion smiled ironically.

"What's so funny?" she asked.

"You're not the first person to say that," he said.

"It must be true," she said. "What do I tell them when they take me?"

"You're giving us up. You alerted Sadeghi to the meeting. You're working for him but we forced you to come with us on the assumption you're on our side. Tell him where we're hiding out, this apartment. Hopefully, he'll believe you."

She lit a cigarette and exhaled thoughtfully.

"And if he doesn't?"

"Stay visible," he said again.

CHAPTER TWENTY-NINE

Zafaraniyeh,
Tehran, Iran

They picked Zahra up from a street stall in the square, crowded with Red Wednesday shoppers. One minute she was standing there, holding a handful of red tulips she had just purchased, and the next, three men had hustled her into a black Mercedes sedan and she was gone.

Scorpion, on a Kavir motorbike arranged by Ghanbari, weapons and backpack bundled on the seat behind him, didn't hurry after them. He waited and checked the laptop on which he had installed his NSA and tracking software to follow her. In addition to tracking her cell phone via GPS, he had glued a GPS transmitter to the back strap of her bra, just in case. The bugs showed as an intersecting double dot moving toward Modares Highway. They were going north, back to North Tehran.

Alerting Langley had been a problem. He had been right that the Internet would be blocked for transmission outside Iran. As an emergency stopgap he and Shaefer had arranged to send e-mail via an encrypted Virtual Private Network, for his Swiss firm, Glenco-Deladier, to his supposed superior, a mythical Monsieur Henri von Bergen, which would be immediately rerouted to Shaefer. The problem was how to get to a server outside Iran that would allow him to complete the routing.

Fortunately, Ghanbari had been able to provide a workaround—a server at the military base at Lavizan. Because Ghanbari's group needed outside Internet access to communicate with Asaib al-Haq in Iraq, the server on the Lavizan base provided Internet access outside Iran, even when all other external communications were shut down. Scorpion used it to bounce a VPN connection from Lavizan to an Asaib al-Haq server in Kirkuk in Kurdish Iraq, and from there to Glenco-Deladier in Switzerland using IP routing addresses from an NSA database.

He prefaced the message with *uozthgzuu*, Flagstaff, in the simple reverse alphabet code they were using, even though the VPN already provided encryption security. In less than a minute Shaefer got back to him with "Mendelssohn" for himself and "Capablanca," the famous chess champion from the 1920s, which Scorpion immediately understood meant that Rabinowich, a chess fanatic, was on the e-mail thread.

Scorpion responded: *Tango*—reverse code for Golf, or Ghanbari—*not the Gardener*. That ought to set the fox among the chickens, he thought. When Shaefer and Rabinowich reported that, it would leave the whole DEFCON preparation hanging in midair. Washington would go berserk.

Rabinowich wrote back, *???!*, meaning, "Who

is?" The exclamation point was recognition that he had just tossed them a bombshell.

Scorpion typed in the reverse code: *uziamazmhzwvtsr.* Farzan Sadeghi.

Head of ZJU? from Rabinowich, reversing the acronym standing for AQF. Al Quds Force. Good man, Scorpion thought. Rabinowich knew who Sadeghi was and understood the implications.

Kta'eb Hezbollah, Scorpion responded.

Power struggle within IRG? Shaefer asked. Iranian Revolutionary Guards. So Shaefer understood now why the Iranians had attacked the embassy in Bern. Kta'eb Hezbollah was taking over the Revolutionary Guards, doing it by forcing the issue.

Scorpion typed back: *yrmtl.* Bingo. Then added: *instructions?*

There was a three minute delay, Scorpion getting more anxious as the clock ticked. Every second that went by made it more likely that the Revolutionary Guards and Scale would track his location. Shaefer and Rabinowich were probably connecting with Harris, he thought. He wasn't sure how long he could afford to wait. What time was it in Washington? He glanced at his watch: 11:30 P.M. in Tehran; 3:00 P.M. Washington time. Harris would be in the middle of a meeting, probably somewhere on the Hill, he imagined, stepping outside into the hall, saying, "Excuse me, Senator." Harris had it down to an art form.

Ghanbari came over and glanced at the laptop screen.

"I was right. You are CIA," he said. "I should kill you," fingering his pistol.

"For the last time, I'm not. Not that it matters."

"So you say," Ghanbari said, then hesitated. "What does matter?"

"I can help," Scorpion said. "Sadeghi won't leave you alive to talk. Do you want to leave?"

Ghanbari straightened.

"You mean asylum?"

"I mean whatever. Do you want out?"

"This is my country. I have a family. Let that *madar sag* leave."

Just then Shaefer's response came.

It took Scorpion a couple of seconds to translate *gvinrmzgv*. It meant terminate.

So that was how the NSC and CIA wanted to end the crisis. Identify and eliminate the attackers, put it out to the world what had happened and that U.S. intelligence had eliminated the threat and punished the guilty inside Iran itself, letting the Iranians and the rest of the world know the CIA could strike anywhere, anytime. U.S. Navy ships and minesweepers would open the Straits of Hormuz. Net result: Iran loses face and the White House manages to avoid a nasty war while at the same time coming out of it looking like a hero, like the Bin Laden killing. There'd be a photo of the President and the NSC in the Situation Room looking determined on the cover of *Time* magazine and prime-time network news. Worth a few million votes come election time. Scorpion turned to Ghanbari.

"Last chance, Muhammad *jan*," he offered. "They want me to do something and then I'm gone. Are you coming?"

"You're going to kill Sadeghi, aren't you?" Ghanbari said. You had to give it to the Iranian; he may have looked like an academic, but he caught on fast, Scorpion thought.

"Whatever I do, they'll call you a traitor. They'll hang you for a Mossad or CIA spy," he said.

"You know that's not true."

"What has truth got to do with anything in our business?" Scorpion said. "Last chance?"

"I'll tell you after tonight," Ghanbari said.

Scorpion nodded and typed: *vcrg?* Meaning what's the exit strategy?

The answer was: *xszofh.* Scorpion translated: Chalus. A small Iranian port city on the southern coast of the Caspian Sea, not far from either the Azerbaijan or Turkmenistan borders. A pickup by boat or seaplane, he thought, and in a short time out of Iranian jurisdiction. Perfect.

He took a deep breath. Shaefer and Rabinowich hadn't been idle. They'd realized the only way to secure the operation was to handle the tactical issues so the Iranians didn't get their hands on him for a show trial.

May be more than one coming, he typed, thinking of Ghanbari and Zahra, and after a few more details ended the session.

"What was that about?" Ghanbari asked.

"It's not just the Gardener," Scorpion said. "Who's behind all this and why? If Sadeghi goes, who comes after him?"

Ghanbari stared at him, his eyes round behind his glasses.

"Zahra was right," he said. "You are a very dangerous man, Laurent *jan.*"

They brought Zahra to a four-story stone house on Baghestan 5 Street in the Zafaraniyeh district, an exclusive neighborhood in the foothills of the Alborz, west of Vali Asr, North Tehran's main street.

Three men in suit jackets hustled her out of the Mercedes and up to an office on the top floor of the building. A window faced out to the tree-shaded street, a curtain partially but not completely covering it. The room was luxuriously decorated with custom Italian furniture, a red Varamin carpet on the floor, and on the wall, portraits of the Ayatollah Khomeini, founder of the Iranian Islamic Republic and Grand Ayatollah Ali Khamenei, the Supreme Leader.

Sadeghi was a tall man, almost skeletally thin, in his fifties, in a dark shirt, no tie. He had first made his reputation, Zahra recalled, as one of the militant Islamist students who took over the U.S. embassy in Tehran in 1979. Sadeghi gestured for her to sit facing a marble table he used as a desk. One of his men, young, with a sparse, young man's mustache, stood against the wall behind her, a ZOAF pistol in his belt.

"*Salam.* Are you all right, *Sarkar khanom* Ravanipour?" Sadeghi said sympathetically, not taking his dark eyes off her. "We were concerned about you."

Zahra bit her lip. "*Mersi, mersi. Khayli mamnun, jenab Sardar* Sadeghi *agha*," she whispered. Thank you. Thank you so much, General Sadeghi, sir, a tear glistening in the corner of her eye. "I was so frightened."

"They forced you to go with them?" Sadeghi asked, lighting a cigarette. "Would you like *chai*?"

gesturing for the young man to bring them tea, not waiting for her response.

"*Mersi*," she said. "It was terrible. One minute we were prisoners being taken in the police van, and suddenly the Swiss, Westermann, somehow managed to get free and kill the two guards. I don't know how. He is a demon, that one."

"More than you know. You pretended to go along?" Sadeghi said, gesturing for her to go on.

"What choice did I have? Besides, I never thought we'd get away. He almost killed us!"

"How did you get away?"

"He stole a car and we came into the city and got on the Metro. I was alone with them. What was I to do? I thought you would follow us. I expected to be arrested again any second," she said. She held her hands out. They were trembling. "Look at me. I thought I was going to die."

"We followed your cell phone with GPS on the Metro. Some *beshoor* idiots had taken it and we had to waste time arresting them." He grimaced. "They'll never take anything again."

The young man came back into the room with a tray of tea with a dish of *nabat*, candied sugar on a stick, with fried *zoolbia* pastries, which he placed on the table. Sadeghi took a glass of tea and poured one for her from a small silver samovar. Zahra bit into a sweet *zoolbia* and glanced at the window between the parted curtains, seeing only the light from the room reflected back at her.

"You know where they are now?" Sadeghi asked, stirring his tea with a *nabat* sugar stick.

"Of course," she said, and gave him the address of

the safe house apartment on Second Street. Sadeghi gestured to the young man, who immediately left. The safe house would be stormed within minutes, she assumed.

"Are you taking over the al Quds Force?" she asked, sipping her tea, not looking at him. "I can't believe Muhammad *jan* is a traitor," referring to Ghanbari. "Is he?"

"How is it they let you go out on your own, Zahra *jan*?" Sadeghi said, putting a black rubber truncheon on the table.

"What are you saying?" she asked, panicked. "I did everything you told me. I called you and set it up so you could capture him. I'm working for you, Farzan Sadeghi *jan*. Not VEVAK, not Ghanbari, not General Vahidi *jenab*. You! You know it!"

"Do you imagine I'm a child that you can deceive me, you *jendeh*?" Sadeghi snapped, coming around the table, grabbing her by her hair. "You were working with the Swiss, Westermann. He is CIA. Do you think we don't know this? And then he just lets you walk out on your own so you can call us? What do you take me for?"

"Why wouldn't they trust me?" she cried. "I was arrested with them. Handcuffed. Taken to Evin Prison with them. They sent me out to shop for food, that's all. They're probably wondering where I am this second."

"Because this Westermann *madar sag* is not stupid like you, you *gav*," he said. Cow. He picked up a rubber truncheon and pulled her by her hair so she was bent over. "Do you think he hasn't asked himself how we caught him and Ghanbari in the cabin in Dizin? Do you?" he shouted, smashing the truncheon on the peroneal nerve on the back of her thigh, above the knee. "Do you?" hitting her again.

She screamed. Her leg collapsed under her and she fell to the floor. She clutched the back of her thigh, unable to move.

"Please!" she sobbed. "I did what you told me. I'll do anything. Don't hurt me anymore, *ghorban*."

"*Khob*," he said, okay, pulling her up and putting her, curled in agony, back in the chair. "This time you'll tell me everything, won't you?"

"Yes, *ghorban*," she muttered, looking desperately past him toward the slice of window between the parted curtains. "Anything."

From his perch on the roof of a ten-story apartment building two blocks away, Scorpion listened intently through ear buds. This was what he had wanted to find out, beyond flushing Sadeghi out, why he wanted her to see Sadeghi. To find out what Sadeghi knew and how he knew it. And to confirm that he was the Gardener.

He checked the range finder again. It showed he was 450 meters from the office where Zahra and Sadeghi were on Baghestan 5. The length of about five football fields. Through the sniper scope he could make out the lighted interior of the room in the space between the parted curtains. He had only a glimpse of Zahra and only part of the back of a tall man in a dark shirt. He could take the shot now, he thought, settling the Nakhir rifle on top of his backpack, making sure it was secure for stability. He looked around. From this distance at night and wearing a dark jacket, he was virtually invisible, though that wasn't why he had selected this building for the hit.

The key to any lethal operation, he knew, wasn't the setup, but the exit. Finding a spot, say in an empty apartment across the street from the target, would make the shot trivially easy. Lee Harvey Oswald killed President Kennedy with an old 6.5mm Mannlicher-Carcano rifle with a 4x scope at a maximum distance of eighty-eight yards—as a Marine sharpshooter, Oswald had routinely received high scores on head-sized targets at two hundred yards— with Kennedy's car a slow-moving target heading away from the shooter at a steady rate of approximately eleven miles per hour. Great shooting wasn't the issue. Getting away was.

On a single residential street in a neighborhood with plenty of local security, given the opposition's ability to seal the street and nearby streets almost immediately, it would make escape next to impossible. Odds were, within 120 seconds of firing the shot he'd be dead or on his way to the torture cells in Evin Prison.

Firing from the roof of a tall building two blocks away meant there would be no direct visual by anyone or any security camera of the shot or its trajectory or the muzzle flash. Anyone on the scene would have a much more difficult time calculating the trajectory and source of the shot. There would be a half dozen or more full city blocks facing the target house that would have to be shut down and searched. Scorpion had timed the elevator and stairs in the building he was in and determined he could be down from the roof, out of the building, and on Pesyan Avenue in less than seventy seconds. And from there by foot to Vali Asr, one of the busiest streets in the city, in another two minutes or less.

At 450 meters, the shot wasn't especially difficult. The real issue was calculating the elevation and windage correctly for the mil-dot scope. Elevation, because a bullet starts slowing and dropping the instant it leaves the barrel; windage, because a single mil in diameter off at a distance of 450 meters would result in a gap of about eighteen inches at the target. The sniper scope had a dial with 0.1 mil increments. After checking and calculating twice, he set it for fourteen clicks elevation. As for windage, he could feel just the barest touch of wind on his face at about a forty-five degree angle coming toward him. There were no flags or clothes on lines to check, but holding a strip of cloth in front of him, it barely stirred. He estimated a three mph wind, which at forty-five degrees gave a value of seventy percent on a 4.5 MOA, or Minute of Angle. It wasn't worth a horizontal adjustment in the scope. At 450 meters the shot would be off by two inches at most to the right. He would simply aim a hair to the left to compensate.

At this point, when he aimed, he should be dead on.

The only other concern was the sound of the shot, which might alert the target in the event of a miss about a second after he fired. But the urban setting would make the sound reverberate, and thus harder to alert the target or identify the shooting source. Also, he didn't intend to miss.

The downside was that from his location, if Zahra got into trouble, he would be too far away to help her. And then he heard one of Sadeghi's men come in and say something.

"Hold her," he heard Sadeghi respond, followed by a slap. "You *jendeh*!" Sadeghi shouted. "The safe house! They weren't there!"

"Of course they weren't there," Zahra said. "Did you think they would wait around for you? They're probably halfway out of the country."

"No. Ghanbari wouldn't just leave. He'd fight me. But it won't work."

"Why not?"

"Let's just say his closest associates are no longer in a position to help him," Sadeghi said.

"Dead?"

"Forget about them. It's the Swiss, Westermann, that concerns me."

"You keep saying he's CIA. What makes you so sure?" she asked.

What Sadeghi said next riveted Scorpion, sending a chill down his spine.

"I'm going to ask you something," Sadeghi said. "It's the most important question you have ever been asked. I'm only going to ask it once. Have you ever heard of 'Scorpion'?" He used the Farsi word, *aqrab*. It was unmistakable. Scorpion.

He took his prone shooting position and sighted in, taking deep breaths to calm the sudden rapid beating of his heart. My God, what was this about? Through the scope he could see Sadeghi's back. It blocked his view of Zahra, but he could just make out part of the face of one of Sadeghi's men behind her, holding her arms.

But it confirmed that Sadeghi was the Gardener.

Only the Gardener would know about Scorpion from the Bern CIA files.

"I don't understand. Scorpion. No. Never," she stammered. "Why?"

"Are you protecting him, *jendeh*?" Sadeghi demanded. "Did you sleep with him?" using the vulgarity.

"No!" she cried. "I would have. It's what VEVAK and General Vahidi *jenab* wanted, but I fell asleep. I think he put something in my drink."

"Too late," Sadeghi said. Through the scope, Scorpion saw him holding a pistol. "You're tainted. And you haven't told us where you are supposed to meet him."

"I don't know!" she pleaded. "Please, I don't know where he is. I'd tell you if I did. I swear."

"Don't blaspheme, you *jendeh* whore. No one can trust you now. And the war coming," Sadeghi said, aiming his pistol.

Scorpion aimed as well, held his breath and tightening his finger on the trigger.

"I don't understand . . ." she wailed. She knelt before him, grabbing at his knees. "I'll find out. I'll get him for you. I will."

"We need to know who this Westermann is. This is his visa photo. This is him, correct?" He showed her something.

"Yes," she said.

"Is it possible he's American, not Swiss?"

"I don't know. He speaks French and English. And Farsi. I'll find out for you," she whispered.

"You're wasting my time! You either know or you don't," Sadeghi said.

Scorpion took a long deep breath and held it; all his focus in the scope was on top of Sadeghi's back. Sadeghi was going to kill her. He couldn't hold off any longer.

"But why?" Zahra wailed. "Who is this Scorpion? Why is he so important?"

"You little fool! What do you think this is all about?" Sadeghi said, aiming at her head.

Scorpion fired.

The crack of the shot echoed over the buildings. A squadron of pigeons flew up from a distant roof. Through the scope, he saw Sadeghi jerk up for an instant and then he was gone. There was the briefest glimpse of Zahra's terrified blood-splattered face looking up toward the window, the young man next to her moving forward, and then nothing, because Scorpion was already moving.

Even as he cleaned the gun with an antiseptic wipe and left it there, grabbing his pack and already running for the roof door, he felt his stomach heave. Zahra was on her own. He hoped she'd run and get away, but there was nothing he could do to help her. Worse, the entire universe had just shifted, and as he got into the elevator and rode down to the building lobby, Sadeghi's statement blotted everything else out of his mind.

What do you think this is all about?

CHAPTER THIRTY

Bakaara Market,
Mogadishu, Somalia

"Will you come?" Ghedi asked her, tucking a *belawa* knife in the waist of his *ma'awis*.

"How do you know it's her?" Sandrine asked. She was in her tent, getting ready for what had to be the most dangerous thing she had ever done. Shadows from passersby flickered past on the canvas siding from the blazing sunlight outside. "What do you know of this boy?"

"This boy. He is Labaan. Of Buur Hakuba. I know this place. It is not far from Baidoa."

"But he is not of your clan. Turn around," she ordered.

He complied. She fished inside a pair of Bensimon sneakers she kept inside her carry-on next to the cot and pulled out a thick wad of five hundred shilling bills. About 100,000 Somali shillings; sixty U.S. dollars. Plus three fifty-dollar bills. Total $210 U.S. It would have to be enough. It was all she had. She turned Ghedi back around and sat on the bunk so she could look levelly into his eyes.

"What makes him think it's your sister? Did he know her?"

"He says her name. Amina. Six years old. This is right name, age. He say Al-Shabaab is bringing her to Mogadishu from Baidoa to be in the House of Flowers," using the name for the children's brothel. "Right time when she disappear. It must be Amina."

"And how does this boy know of the House of Flowers? Does he work there?" she asked, going outside the tent. The camp was crowded, dusty and trash strewn. The heat was intense and she could smell the open ditch used as a public toilet. The South African, Van Zyl, was waiting near the road with a white Toyota SUV with the UNHCR decal painted on the side.

"His brother is *oday*," Ghedi said, using the Somali word for elder or boss.

"You mean his brother is a *maquereau* for children," she said, a pimp, covering her head with a *hijab*, both for the sun and to appear less threatening to Somali men. "How can you trust this boy?"

"I don't trust," Ghedi said, touching the handle of his *belawa* knife. "I trust you, *isuroon*."

"If it is your sister, Amina, there's no guarantee we can get her out. All I can offer is money—not very much. If they say no, we might have to leave her."

"If Amina is in this place, I will not leave her. Better to die," he said, looking up at her.

She nodded. His mind was made up. If she didn't come, it was almost certain they would kill him. As they reached the road, she stopped for a moment at a roadside stall, where two women were selling *kashaato*, squares of white coconut candy, one of them waving her hand to brush away the flies.

"For the children," she said, paying the women, who counted out forty pieces of candy into a big plastic bag.

"This is a bloody stupid idea," Van Zyl growled, getting into the SUV. She noticed he was wearing a pistol in a holster on his hip. "Have you any idea how dangerous this is?"

"You don't need come, *mzungu*," Ghedi said to Van Zyl, climbing in. "*Isuroon* and I, we can do this."

"Don't get your *broekies* in a knot, kid," Van Zyl said, starting the SUV. And to Sandrine: "He's worse than you, this one." He looked back over his shoulder. "Which way?"

"Bakaara Market. Then I show," Ghedi said.

"Christ," Van Zyl breathed. "Bakaara's the worst shit hole in this whole godforsaken arsehole of the universe."

Sandrine looked at him.

"So I should leave his sister there to be a whore, where the best she can hope for is to get AIDS and die? Is that the best idea you've got, Monsieur Van Zyl?" she said.

"I said I'd take you," he mumbled, shaking his head. "It's all going to hell here anyway. We're losing what little funding we have. Bloody Americans. This thing with Iran. And now the Israelis."

"What are you talking about?"

"The news on the BBC world service, luv. Looks like the Americans and the Iranians are about to have at it. Now it seems the Israelis have ordered a partial mobilization too. The whole bloody Middle

East is about to explode. No one's paying piss-all attention to Africa."

For some reason, she and Ghedi looked at each other as if they had both thought of the American at the same instant. Nick, his real name was. Not David. He'd told her that in Nairobi like it was a gift. She didn't know why she thought he was involved in whatever was happening with the Americans and Iran, but there it was. The boy Ghedi sensed it too. He took her hand.

They sat there as Van Zyl drove through the hot dusty streets packed with battered trucks and cars, cinder-block houses pockmarked with bullet holes and jagged tears in the concrete from earlier fighting. Traffic slowed as they approached the Bakaara Market, a giant space under plastic tarps filled with men armed to the teeth, women in candy-colored *direhs*, vendors in stalls selling AK-47s, M-4 carbines, large piles of ammunition and RPGs stacked like fruit, bundles of *qat* leaves, and prostitutes, women, girls, teenage boys, tugging at male passersby under the watchful eyes of tribesmen with guns.

"Go right," Ghedi said, pointing toward a street off the square. The street was narrow, full of potholes a foot deep, with laundry hanging on lines strung between the houses and half-naked children playing on the trash-strewn asphalt, broiling in the sun. "Here is the house," pointing at a three-story concrete house in the middle of the block.

Two bearded men in *koofiyud* caps holding AK-47s kept guard under ragged umbrellas in front, the door painted sky blue. A line of tin-roofed sheds nestled against the building's walls. The bearded men chewed *qat*, cheeks bulging like chipmunks, and watched the street. They paid little attention as Sandrine, Van Zyl, and the boy got out and went inside.

They entered a dark hallway, cooler than outside, and almost immediately a crowd of children, perhaps two dozen, nearly all girls in *direhs*, ages from six or seven to about fourteen, clustered around them. Two young boys, naked except for drooping underpants, hung back and watched.

"*Odkhol, odkhol,*" the children cried, tugging at them. Come in, come in.

One of the girls—she couldn't have been more than eight years old—put her hands on the front of Van Zyl's trousers, rubbing his crotch and tugging at his zipper, calling something to him.

Van Zyl squirmed and held her off.

"What's she saying?" he asked Ghedi.

"She saying, 'Choose me. Come with me,'" Ghedi said.

"Do you see her?" Sandrine asked Ghedi.

A Somali man in jeans holding a camel whip came in then, a pistol tucked in his waist. He was young, thin, his hair dyed orange like the color of a soft drink, and cross-eyed in a way that made him look stupid. His other hand was draped around a pretty young girl, about eleven years old, her dark eyes unreadable. He pulled her along with him. There were also two boys with him, about thirteen years old, both carrying AK-47s decorated with seashells and feathers. They were chewing *qat*, their teeth green. The young girls immediately fell silent.

Then another little girl wandered out and stood there, sucking on her thumb. About six years old with dark almond eyes, wavy hair, and an exquisite, almost perfect café au lait face. She was the most beautiful child Sandrine had ever seen.

"It's her," Ghedi whispered to Sandrine. He ran up to the girl and looked directly into her eyes. At first she seemed not to recognize him. All of a sudden, she collapsed on the stone floor, put her hands on top of her head and started to scream.

"*Eskoot!*" the Somali man shouted at the girl. Shut up. She stopped and looked fearfully at the Somali man. Ghedi took the girl's hand. She held back but didn't resist. He led her over to Sandrine.

"I have come to—" Sandrine began.

"Stop," the Somali man said in Arabic, looking at her in his cross-eyed way. Ghedi translated in a whisper. "I know who you are, doctor woman. You must not be here. This is not your place."

"I'm taking these children with me," she said.

The Somali man took out his pistol, pointing first at one little girl, then another, then another, ending by pointing at Sandrine. He raised his arm higher and fired a bullet into the wall over her head. Sandrine flinched. The children stood there, watching the two of them, the man and Sandrine.

"These are my property. My *sharmutat*." My whores. "I will kill them first," he said, motioning to the two boys, who flipped the safety levers and pointed the AK-47s at Sandrine and the girls.

Sandrine's heart pounded. The eyes of the *qat*-chewing boys were vacant. They've killed before, she thought, even at their age, suddenly realizing she might be about to die. She looked desperately at Van Zyl, who just stood there.

"And how if I take them?" she said, scarcely breathing. Ghedi translated. Van Zyl glanced around uneasily, his hand on his holster.

The Somali man blinked rapidly. Somewhere, that *qat*-addled brain was trying to think, Sandrine thought.

"These are Al-Shabaab property, doctor woman," the man said. "Al Qaeda's whores. Understand? Even if I gave them to you, men would come and kill them. They would kill them and you and me before you even get back to Badbaada Camp."

"Is this so?" Sandrine whispered to Ghedi, leaning her head close to his. He stood there, holding his sister's hand. It was terrifying to think they knew exactly where she lived and worked. If al Qaeda or Al-Shabaab came shooting in the camp, the havoc would be unbelievable.

"This is true, *isuroon*," he whispered.

"And if I take only one . . ." she said. The Somali man followed her gaze and understood immediately.

"That one, impossible. Her *batuliya* is worth much," he said, making the sign for money. Sandrine understood. He planned to auction her virginity.

The two boys with the AK-47s looked restless. She had to do something, and quickly.

"I have an idea," she said, and sat down on the stone floor, motioning for the girls to gather around her.

"*Ecoutez, mes enfants . . .*" she began.

None of them moved. She opened the plastic bag of coconut candy and indicated they should pass it around. A few of the older girls looked over at the Somali man, who nodded.

One by one the children gathered around her. As they were doing so, she passed the wad of money to Ghedi and whispered: "Give him the money. Then take your sister and go to the camp. Don't wait for me and don't look back."

She looked around at the girls gathered around her. A few of them started to giggle and eat the candy. She smiled, took a deep breath and started to speak in English.

"I'm going to tell you a story about a little girl named Cinderella. Once there was a man who married, for his second wife, the proudest woman you ever saw. She had two nasty daughters of her own, who were just like her. The good man also had a beautiful young daughter from his first wife, a good sweet girl. Her name was Cinderella."

As she recited, she saw Ghedi give the Somali man the money. Then she watched as Ghedi and the girl left with Van Zyl, a shiver going up her spine when they were gone and she was there alone with the child prostitutes and the Somalis with guns, all of them listening rapt to her story, though they could barely understand a word.

If she ever got back to camp, they would have to leave Mogadishu, she thought. Al-Shabaab and al Qaeda weren't going to let this go. They would get back to Dadaab somehow. She and Ghedi and the little girl, Amina. And then what? What was she to do with them? They couldn't live forever in Dadaab.

An odd thought. The American, Nick, would find her there, if he survived his war, she thought.

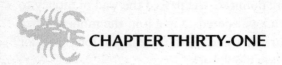# CHAPTER THIRTY-ONE

Mellat Park,
Tehran, Iran

"**Y**ou heard? We're wanted by the police, VEVAK, everyone," Ghanbari said. "Our faces are everywhere."

"I know," Scorpion said, leaning on the rail of the yellow metal footbridge over the lake in Mellat Park. His and Ghanbari's faces were on the front pages of *Abrar* and the *Tehran Times* and all the major TV channels; wanted for murder in the killing of Farzan Sadeghi, an officer and a hero of the Revolutionary Guards, and Zahra Ravanipour, an employee with the AFAGIR missile command.

He had watched the news on the television at a chain restaurant, Nayeb Kebab, in Kaj Square. For a disguise, he was dressed in a floppy red outfit and a tall floppy red hat, his face covered with blackface, like something from a late nineteenth century minstrel show. He had bought the outfit from a costume shop near the Grand Bazaar, and thought he looked ludicrous. He was supposed to be Haji Firuz, the traditional Persian minstrel of the Red Wednesday festivities. While playing peekaboo with two small children who were with their parents at the next table, and shaking his tambourine, he kept one eye on the door and on the TV. He was tired. It had been a killer night and he needed to go to ground, but there would be no sleep anymore. Not till he left Iran.

The news announcer on the restaurant TV cut back to talk about the American forces in the Persian Gulf and rumors about Israel, then the scene shifted to a reporter interviewing a burly Iranian man in his fifties in an expensive suit, wearing glasses and a white *dulband* turban, his tie at half-mast. They were in a government office; the TV screen caption read: ABOUZAR BEIKZADEH, SECRETARY OF THE EXPEDIENCY COUNCIL.

Beikzadeh, stared into the camera and declared: "These innocent Iranians were good people. Patriots. Murdered by CIA agents and Zionist terrorists who wish to destroy Iran. They will be found out and justice will be done. We expect to have these criminals in custody by tonight and then we will seek out and destroy those who sent them. I call upon all citizens to be vigilant. I call upon the Basiji to go out into the streets to help us find these CIA criminals."

Scorpion had already seen Basiji militiamen out in force on every street corner. Besides the police, VEVAK, Revolutionary Guards, and ordinary citizens, it meant at least 100,000 Basiji vigilantes looking for Ghanbari and him. He could feel a prickling at the back of his neck. The noose was growing tighter.

"Further," Beikzadeh continued, "because of the actions of the traitor, Muhammad Ghanbari, acting with the unanimous consent of the Expediency Council and the Supreme Leader, I have this morning assumed personal command of the Revolutionary Guards." He stared into the TV camera. "All traitors everywhere will be rooted out. The criminals will not escape," adding that anyone seeing the foreigner, Laurent Westermann, or the fugitive CIA spy, Muhammad Ghanbari, was to contact the nearest Naja police office or Basiji militiamen at once. There was no mention of the incident at Dizin or any other casualties.

Although Scorpion had known from the instant he fired the shot that he couldn't save her, seeing Zahra's face on the TV, confirmation that she was dead, was like a kick in the gut. How many casualties had there been on this mission? Harandi in Hamburg. Glenn. Chrissie; all of the Gnomes in Zurich. Rutledge and Mini Me on the Costa Brava. Now Zahra. She had been right about him. Just knowing him was lethal, he thought. He'd been right to stay away from Sandrine. All he could bring her was grief.

He had spent the night into the morning moving, riding buses and the Metro, not keeping still or holing up anywhere they might try to track him. After midnight he went back to the dead drop in Laleh Park to see if there was anything for him in the public men's room.

There wasn't.

He had torn his Laurent Westermann passport and papers into tiny pieces and flushed them down the toilet, pulling his last available ID from his backpack. A red Republic of Ireland passport in the name Sean O'Donnell, a documentary filmmaker from Dublin. It wasn't deep cover, but better than nothing. He hoped he wouldn't have to use it.

He'd slept fitfully on the stone floor of the public men's room, curled next to the wall, the stink in his nostrils, ZOAF pistol in his hand. He kept waking in the dim light of a single bulb at every sound outside. In the morning, he washed and shaved with cold water and tried to clean up as best he could. Looking at himself in the mirror, he understood that without a disguise he would be caught before the morning was out. That was when he thought of Haji Firuz. The one and only piece of luck he'd had in this whole operation was that it happened at Nowruz, the Persian New Year. He wondered whether Rabinowich had taken that into account when planning the op. Which reminded him, he had to find a way to let Langley know about Sadeghi.

When he walked out in the early morning, sunlight had been filtering through the trees. The park was green, the pathways empty and beautiful. He heard a bird singing and it felt unworldly. It seemed insane that everyone in Iran was hunting him and that he would in all probability die today or that they were about to go to war.

He'd caught a bus in Vali Asr Square. Watching the city traffic and smog getting denser by the second, he calculated that he could risk up to five minutes online before the Revolutionary Guards could track him, got off and went into an Internet café. There, using the VPN, he bounced a Chattanooga message to Shaefer via the server at the Revolutionary Guards military base at Lavizan, through Iraq, Syria, and Turkey. "Chattanooga" was the agreed-upon signal that meant he had terminated the Gardener. He could only imagine the cheers and big smiles, handshakes all around, when Harris—or the DCIA himself—presented it to the President. Except he couldn't stop thinking about Zahra and didn't feel much like cheering.

Shaefer had responded with coded instructions for the escape. A dead drop under the fourth seat, seventh row, in a cinema on Shahrivar Avenue in Chalus. At midnight a seaplane would taxi close to the beach, and as soon as he and whomever he was bringing were aboard, they would take off for Baku in Azerbaijan. Plus one more piece of information. A coded addendum from Shaefer that translated to: "Baylor full mob." Baylor was the code word he, Rabinowich, and Shaefer had agreed to use for Israel. "Full mob" meant total mobilization.

He'd thought of Yuval then. The Israelis were using the crisis as an excuse to launch the attack they had long wanted on the Iranian nuclear facilities. They wanted to do it with U.S. forces still in place in the Persian Gulf to give them cover, whether the Americans wanted to or not. All hell was about to break out across the Middle East. He had to get out of Iran now.

He would get to Chalus under cover of the Red Wednesday celebrations that night, he decided, signed off the computer and cleaned any trace of having been there with his NSA software. He checked his watch, saw he'd been online four minutes fifteen seconds, and looked around uneasily. Just the usual crop of students online and teenagers playing video games; nothing out of the ordinary. But he couldn't shake the feeling that he was pushing it. He left the café and was less than a block away when he spotted plainclothes VEVAK agents barging into the Internet café.

They had been faster than he thought. He hadn't had much of a margin at all.

And now Scorpion knew he had to leave the restaurant. Despite his Haji Firuz disguise, a waiter near the kitchen kept looking at him, then away. When the waiter disappeared into the kitchen, no doubt to make a phone call, he left a stack of *tomans* on the table and walked out, not looking back for two blocks before heading down an alley and doubling back on the next street. He was waiting at a bus stop when he got the text message from Ghanbari to meet him on the bridge in Mellat Park.

Ghanbari had shaved his beard. Sporting sunglasses and a fake Tom Selleck–like mustache, he looked more like a sports car salesman than an academic.

"What about your colleagues?" Scorpion asked, eyes restlessly running over the families and young people, students mostly, playing or walking near the lake. Apart, it was dangerous enough. The two of them together was like a neon sign saying, *Call the police.*

"Under arrest or disappeared. My two closest friends, Koosha and Nader, are disappeared. I'm sure they're dead. Beikzadeh and Kta'eb Hezbollah have taken over the al Quds Force, which means the Revolutionary Guards. The tail is wagging the dog. If they find me, I'm dead," Ghanbani said, rubbing his hands over and over, as if they were cold.

"What about your wife and children?"

Ghanbari looked at him, his eyes stricken.

"We talked. She's going to divorce me, denounce me. She'll testify I'm a CIA spy, whatever they want. It's the only way to protect her and the children. Later, when it's safe, she'll go back to her family in Isfahan. *Inshallah*—" God willing "—someday we'll see each other again. But my parents!" he exclaimed. "They will think I'm a traitor. They will live with shame," shaking his head. "I can't do this."

"I'm leaving Iran tonight," Scorpion said. "Are you coming?"

"What are you offering?"

"Me? I'm not offering anything. I'll get you out. Someone else will take it from there."

"The CIA?"

Scorpion didn't say anything. Ghanbari's face knotted up.

"They force me to be a traitor. My own people." He grabbed at Scorpion's arm. "What will they offer me?"

"The Americans?" He shrugged. "I don't know. Depends on the value of the information you give them. Asylum, some money probably."

"For a spy, you've been honest with me," Ghanbari said, his face twisting. "Tell me the truth. They'll use me up and throw me away, yes?"

Scorpion looked at him and at the sun sparkling on the lake. From the shore came the sounds of families and children's voices. It's like their last moments of peace and innocence, he thought. Not for the first time, he wished he were in another line of work.

"Yes," he said.

"It's hopeless. I should kill myself," Ghanbari said, taking his ZOAF pistol out of his pocket and looking down at it.

"Then Beikzadeh and his kind win. Is that what you want?" Scorpion asked.

"What else is there for me?"

"Things change. I've seen things I never would have believed," he said. "Besides, you can't commit suicide on Red Wednesday."

"Why not?" Ghanbari said.

"Bad luck," Scorpion said, and smiled.

As the sun set at last, a smoggy orange glow like a fire burning over the skyline, Red Wednesday exploded. There were fireworks, bonfires, rockets, and firecrackers all over the city. Children dressed in costumes or black shrouds ran through the streets, banging spoons on pots and pans and going door-to-door. They banged their pans loudly and were greeted by beaming adults offering scoops of *ajeel*, mixed nuts and berries, and clear water to refresh them.

People wore new clothes and broke earthen jars shaped like animals that supposedly held last year's bad luck, so only good luck would come in the New Year. Others went up to total strangers in the street asking them to untie a knot in their handkerchiefs as a way of taking away any bad luck. Young single women, practicing *fal gosh*, would eavesdrop on conversations of passersby in the street. It was said that one could tell one's future, including the romantic future, from a scrap of conversation from the first passerby you overheard.

In every street, square, and park across the country there were bonfires where people of all ages, adults and children who were old enough, would jump over the fire, singing: *"Zardi-ye man az to, Sorkhi-ye to az man."* My sickly yellow paleness is yours; your fiery red color is mine.

"You understand, this is early Zoroastrianism, thousands of years older than Islam," Ghanbari said. "Rebirth of life after winter. That sort of thing. What are we waiting for?" he asked as Scorpion, still dressed as Haji Firuz, jumped and capered around him like a clown.

"That," Scorpion said, watching a family with three children, parents, and grandparents parking their white Peugeot 4008 SUV in a lot on Sadaqat next to Mellat Park. He also kept an eye on two Basiji militia-men who were watching the parking lot and the street. There was a sudden crackling from a string of firecrackers as the family entered the park to join the festivities.

Scorpion draped an arm over Ghanbari, who wore a spooky Guy Fawkes type mask, as if they were drunken buddies, and making gestures like a fool, he pulled Ghanbari with him as they followed the family toward the park entrance. There were more *Basiji* militiamen at the entrance, but they ignored him and Ghanbari, focusing on a group of teenagers, one of whom tossed a firecracker into the park. Two of the Basiji grabbed the teenager. For tonight at least, being Haji Firuz was saving his life, he thought. But what about tomorrow?

They followed the family from the Peugeot down the path to an open area with illuminated water fountains and dozens of bonfires surrounded by crowds, singing and talking and taking turns making a running leap over the fire. People were clapping and laughing as if the crisis didn't exist. There was a high whistling sound and a vertical stream of sparks as someone fired a rocket into the sky.

As the family from the Peugeot approached one of the bonfires, Scorpion accidentally bumped into the father, knocking a messenger-type bag off his shoulder.

"*Bebakhshid, ghorban,*" Scorpion apologized. "*Khahesh mikonam,*" please, picking the bag up off the ground and handing it to the father with a bow.

"*Bashe, mersi,* Haji Firuz," the father laughed with a shrug. It's okay, thanks.

"*Mersi, mersi,*" Scorpion said, shook his tambourine and danced a little jig for the children who giggled. He gestured for them to jump over the fire.

The father took one of his sons, a boy of about seven, and stood him about six or seven feet from the fire, then gave him a nudge. The boy ran at the fire, his tongue sticking out and jumped over and everyone cheered.

"*Barikallah! Barikallah!*" Bravo! Bravo! Scorpion joined in cheering. As the others in the family started their jumps over the fire, Scorpion nudged Ghanbari and they began to edge away in the crowd.

They made their way on the crowded walkways, shadows from the flames dancing on faces as they headed across an open area toward a hedge near the edge of the park.

"What just happened?"

"We got ourselves a ride," Scorpion said, nodding and shaking his tambourine at a group of preteens. On top of the tambourine he showed Ghanbari he was holding a car key he'd stolen from the Iranian man. "They'll be busy here for a couple of hours at least."

"Where did you learn to do something like that?"

"Remy le Panthère. Remy the Panther. He was from Côte d'Ivoire. Black, handsome devil; best pickpocket in Paris. He could strip your pockets clean in three seconds and you'd never know he'd been there. No gangs of Roma kids, no man and woman front-and-back team. Didn't even need the kind of crude bump and grab I just did."

"You spent time in Paris?"

"At the Sorbonne," Scorpion nodded, glancing around before stepping through the hedge and out to the street. A moment later Ghanbari followed.

"You didn't learn that at the Sorbonne."

"No. The useful stuff I learned on the streets."

They headed for the parking lot where the Peugeot was parked. Another minute and they were inside the Peugeot. Scorpion took off his Haji Firuz hat and put his ZOAF pistol with its sound suppressor next to him. As they headed for the parking lot exit, two Basiji militiamen stepped out of the shadows and waved them down. Scorpion's eyes darted around. There were no other police or militia around. Ghanbari, next to him, looked terrified.

One of the Basiji motioned for him to roll down the window.

"Your papers, Haji Firuz?" the Basiji said.

Scorpion reached into his pocket and handed him some crumpled-up handful of rials.

"What's this?" the Basiji said, his eyes suspicious. "Get out of the *mashin*."

"Bashe," okay, Scorpion said, and shot him in the forehead. He shot the second Basiji in the head a second later and drove out of the parking lot. From the park came the sound of firecrackers. Anyone who might have heard the shots probably assumed they were firecrackers too, he thought, driving carefully down the street and onto Niayesh Highway heading west.

"You killed them," Ghanbari said, wide-eyed, looking at Scorpion as if he had just seen him for the first time.

"Yes."

"Just like that. You just killed them and drove off like it's nothing," he said, breathing hard, like he had just been running.

"Would you rather be on your way to Evin Prison? I killed your enemy, Sadeghi, too."

They drove on the highway, crowded with traffic. They had to get out of town and on the road to Chalus before there were roadblocks, which the police might be reluctant to do, he thought, causing massive traffic jams on the night of Red Wednesday.

For a time, Ghanbari didn't say anything, then: "How do you live with yourself?"

"Look who's talking? What did you think Asaib al Haq was doing in Iraq? Kissing Sunnis and Kurds—and American soldiers too? You probably have more blood on your hands than I do."

The traffic eased as they took the cloverleaf south onto Yadegar-e Emam Highway past a big market, lit up at night for the holiday. There were fireworks in the night sky over Pardisan Park.

"Doesn't it bother you?" Ghanbari asked finally.

"No."

"I don't believe you."

"Look, I never talk about this," Scorpion said, eyes flicking up to the rearview mirror to make sure there were no tails. "But just this once. Because we're on the run together. Did you see those people tonight in the park? All happy, enjoying the holiday, hoping for the best for the New Year? Just people."

"Yes," Ghanbari nodded.

"They're closer to war than they can imagine. Thousands, maybe hundreds of thousands, might die. Not just in Iran, but America, Israel, Europe, the entire Middle East. Mostly innocent people who just want to live their lives. The Gardener put all that at risk. Last night we brought justice and maybe a chance to prevent the war. If you don't think that's worth the lives of a few Basiji, then your moral calculus is very different from mine."

They drove on through the night. Scorpion headed west toward Karaj, a suburb in the extreme northwestern corner of Tehran, then turned north on Route 59, the only road through the Alborz Mountains to the northern coast of Iran on the

Caspian Sea. He drove at a good pace, taking the curves of the winding two-lane road through the mountains at speed. With any luck, in another hour or so they'd be in Chalus, and another hour or two after that out of Iran.

"It's a shame we couldn't drive this road during the day," Ghanbari said. "This is the most beautiful road in the world. Steep green mountain slopes, clear rushing streams, waterfalls, rainbows. It can take your breath away."

They drove for a while. Ghanbari tried to get news on the radio but everything was about Red Wednesday. Then Scorpion began to slow. They were in a deep narrow canyon. There was a glow of light coming somewhere from around the bend of the road ahead. He pulled to the side of the road, stopped and got out, taking the pistol.

"What's wrong?" Ghanbari asked, getting out too.

"Not sure," Scorpion said, walking on the edge of the road, barely the width of his shoulders. Below him was a drop of at least a hundred feet where a clear rushing stream ran tumbling over rocks. The air was clean—the first clean air he'd breathed since he'd been in Tehran—and the sky above the canyon was full of stars. He walked a hundred yards, then crossed to the other side of the road and began climbing the face of a rocky cliff. It was mossy green, and smelled of vegetation, and was wet with water trickling down the rock face. When he was up about twenty feet or so, he leaned out and was able to peer around the bend into the serpentine winding of the road through the canyon. The light was coming from a massing of vehicles a kilometer up the road. It looked like there were at least twenty of them.

"What is it?" Ghanbari called in a whisper from below.

"Roadblock," Scorpion said.

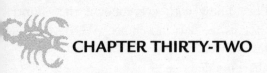

CHAPTER THIRTY-TWO

Zanjan,
Iran

They ran out of gas four kilometers outside Zanjan. It was an hour before dawn and the sky behind them had a violet predawn light just outlining the tops of the mountains. Scorpion told Ghanbari to wait in the Peugeot and began walking alone toward the city on the empty road.

The roadblock on the road to Chalus was like a cork in a bottle. For a second Scorpion had briefly flirted with the idea of using the gasoline in the Peugeot's fuel tank as part of the explosive for a car bomb, but the narrowness of the canyon road and the number of vehicles and the amount of force at the roadblock made it impassable. They would never reach the Caspian Sea.

"How did they know we were coming on Route 59?" Ghanbari had asked as Scorpion made a careful U-turn on the narrow road and headed as fast as he could back toward Karaj.

"It's logical," Scorpion said, darting a glance at Ghanbari, his face shadowed by the light from the dashboard. "It's the only road through the mountains. They know with everyone in the country looking for us we have no choice. We have to get out of the country."

Ghanbari nodded.

"So now what?"

"Plan B."

"Which is?"

"Iraq," Scorpion said, driving faster as the road became straighter coming down out of the mountains. When he reached Karaj, he got off the highway to avoid the highway interchange where there might be another roadblock. Instead, he used dark back streets on the outskirts of Karaj, the bonfires all burned out and nearly everyone gone to bed by now, to zigzag his way to the Karaj-Qazvin Freeway. He drove onto the freeway and headed west toward the Iraqi border.

"That border is very heavily guarded," Ghanbari said. "It'll be even worse now that they're looking for us. It'll be impossible to get through."

"We'll see. Turn on the radio; maybe we can catch some news now," Scorpion said. Ghanbari fiddled with the radio, then found a late night news broadcast on Iranian twenty-four-hour IRIB radio.

" . . . according to Fars News Agency, Foreign Minister Hamid Gayeghrani *jenab* reiterated to reporters that the Islamic Republic of Iran will regard any attack by the illegitimate Zionist regime called Israel as an attack also by the United States. The foreign minister stated 'Iran has the means to retaliate against American bases and interests anywhere in the world.'

"In other news, authorities suspect that the wanted criminals, the foreign spy Laurent Westermann and the traitor Muhammad Ghanbari, added to their crimes by killing two heroic Basiji militiamen in Mellat Park. The murderers are believed to have fled in a stolen white Peugeot 4008 SUV . . ."

Ghanbari turned the radio off.

"How did they know it was us?"

"They know we're on the run. We can't use a bus or a train or get on a plane. We'd be spotted in a second. They know we can't rent a car or buy one. They assume we have to steal one. The Peugeot was stolen; the Basiji are dead. It had to be us—and even if it wasn't, they'd say it was us," Scorpion said. He didn't say what he really thought: Scale is running this. It would be a mistake to underestimate him. In fact, Scorpion was counting on it.

"We have to get rid of the Peugeot," Ghanbari said.

"We will. A few more hours and we'll either be out of Iran or we'll be dead."

Now, walking on the shoulder of the freeway near Zanjan, Scorpion watched the sky lighten with the dawn. He had no illusions about what was about to happen. It would all depend on Shaefer and Dave Rabinowich, because he was out at the end of a very shaky limb. And even though the countryside as he approached Zanjan looked peaceful, there was no question but that the Revolutionary Guards would catch any communications he tried to make, regardless of the mechanism. It was going to be unbelievably close, he thought, hiking over fields to a side road roughly paralleling the freeway, spotting a gas station at the edge of the city.

The cell phone in his pocket vibrated. Looking at it for a minute in the gray early morning light, he thought it was the final piece of the puzzle, then put the phone back in his pocket. He walked over to the gas station. It was too early. He sat down on the pavement to wait for them to open.

Almost an hour later a middle-aged Azeri man dressed in a sweater and a traditional *papaq* lamb's wool hat, came yawning to open the gas station. He smiled broadly when he saw Scorpion, still in blackface and red costume.

"*Sobh be khayr*, Haji Firuz," the Azeri man said. Good morning, Haji Firuz.

"*Salam*, brother. We ran out of petrol."

"On Red Wednesday? We must correct your luck for the New Year, brother," the Azeri said. "How far is your machine?" unlocking the office.

"Only four kilometers back on the freeway. And if it's possible, I need to make a phone call."

"Of course, brother. I will drive you to your machine with enough petrol for you to come back and fill up. And please, make your call at no charge."

Ta'arof, of course, Scorpion thought. Only it might cost the Azeri his life.

"Please, brother, you must let me pay. My honor demands it and I am already too greatly in your debt. Your generosity overwhelms this poor brother."

"For your honor only," the Azeri said, touching his hand to his chest, and went outside to fill a fuel can with gasoline. Meanwhile, Scorpion used the office phone and dialed the emergency number in Mosul, in northern Iraq. He spoke briefly to someone, who only repeated "*Bale, bale*," yes, yes,

mentioned PJAK, and described a remote farmhouse on Kohneh Khaneh Road on the outskirts
of Piranshahr, a town close to the Iran-Iraq border.
The voice at the other end of the line didn't have to
elaborate. Scorpion understood immediately what
Rabinowich and Shaefer had in mind.

PJAK, the Free Life Party of Kurdistan, was a
paramilitary organization that operated in the
border region between Kurdish Iraq and Iran. They
were affiliated with the Kurdish PKK party, and
although officially designated a terrorist organization by the U.S. government, there were neverthe-
less links between PJAK and both the CIA and the
Israeli Mossad, which sometimes used them for targeted actions against the Iranian regime. The PJAK
group would come for them at the farmhouse and
smuggle them over the mountains into the Kurdish
region of Iraq. Plan B.

Later, the Peugeot fully gassed up, the morning
bright and sunny, he and Ghanbari were speeding
on the Zanjan-Tabriz Freeway toward the border. If
their luck held and there were no roadblocks till later
in the day—even VEVAK and the Basiji would be
getting up late Red Wednesday morning—they had
a chance. More and more traffic began to appear on
the road, which made Scorpion more comfortable.
They would be harder to spot from the air.

Ghanbari found a map in the glove compartment.
They tried to decide the route.

"Where do you think they'll put a roadblock?"
Scorpion asked.

"Tabriz is the biggest city in this region. If I were
them, I'd put it on the freeway outside Tabriz. I'd

go here," Ghanbari said, pointing at a smaller road, Highway 26, that would take them around Lake Urmia, the largest salt lake in the Middle East.

"Sounds right," Scorpion said.

When he saw the road sign for Mahabad, he turned off the freeway and south onto Highway 26. Driving around the southern curve of the lake, he had to squint against the glare of the sun on the white salt fringe and sparkling blue of the water. Just another two or three more hours, he thought. That's all he needed. He glanced over at Ghanbari. He looked like he had fallen asleep, his head against the car window. Maybe he was, Scorpion thought. Not that it mattered. The only question now was whether they'd be dead before the afternoon was over.

The farmhouse was at the end of a road at the edge of the town. Scorpion parked the Peugeot behind the house, out of sight from the road. Beyond the fields were the mountains, the slopes green and only the peaks still snow-covered. He estimated they were about four miles from the border. He had expected the farmhouse to be unoccupied, but there were three generations of a family living there. Kurds, of course. This whole area was Kurdish on both sides of the border, and Kurdish was the language the farmhouse family spoke among themselves, though they used Farsi with guests. The house was carpeted throughout, but with no furniture; typical for this part of Iran, Ghanbari whispered.

Scorpion placed all his Iranian money on the carpet on the floor, a stack of rials thick as a man's

high, and told the family they would have to leave.
The farmer's wife, a heavy-set woman, was having
none of it.

"It's PJAK, you understand? PJAK," Scorpion
told her. She said something in rapid-fire Kurdish
that he didn't understand. "Tell your woman," he
told the farmer. "You have to go. It's too dangerous
now."

The farmer took the money but didn't go. The
wife shouted at him, gesturing that the strangers should leave. The farmer looked at the money,
clearly reluctant to give it up, and at Scorpion and
Ghanbari.

"Maybe you should leave, honored guests," the
farmer said awkwardly.

"PJAK is on their way. If you are still here, it will
be very dangerous for you. Tell your wife to think of
her parents," Scorpion gestured at the older couple,
"and her children."

The farmer spoke to his wife. She shouted at him.
As she was shouting, Scorpion took out his pistol
and fired three shots straight up through the roof.
The woman stopped shouting.

"*Berid!*" Go away! Scorpion shouted, motioning
with his head for Ghanbari to help him get them out
of the house. "Get out! Now!"

The farmer and his wife glared at them, but gathered up the children.

"Come back in twenty-four hours. Not sooner,"
Scorpion said, shoving them out of the house. They
piled into an old Nissan pickup truck, the entire
family, muttering and throwing him the evil eye,
two of the children clinging to their mother's skirts.

Ghanbari spoke to them for a moment and then they were bouncing away down the road in the truck, leaving behind a cloud of dust and diesel fumes.

Ghanbari came back into the house.

"Was that necessary?" he asked, coming over to Scorpion.

"You probably just saved their lives," Scorpion said.

"What if they call the police?"

"They won't."

Ghanbari shook his head.

"How can you be so sure?"

"They'd have to give the money to the police and it would mysteriously disappear. Then, three months, six months, a year from now, PJAK would deal with the husband. No Kurd will help them. They'll end up begging in the streets. They know that. They'll argue, they'll hate me, but they won't go to the Persian police. Not Kurds."

"I'll make some *chai*. You know, I'm not sure I like you any—" Ghanbari started to say. Before he could finish, Scorpion smashed his pistol against the side of Ghanbari's head. As Ghanbari staggered, Scorpion grabbed Ghanbari's pistol out of his holster and kicked his legs out from under him. Ghanbari crashed to the floor. He started to crawl on his hands and knees, then stopped as Scorpion cocked and aimed his pistol at him.

"Let's talk about the Gardener," Scorpion said.

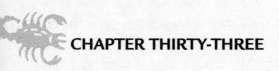 **CHAPTER THIRTY-THREE**

Dagmada Yaaqshid,
Mogadishu, Somalia

The car bomb exploded just after one in the afternoon outside a hotel on Jidka Sodonka Road favored by foreign aid workers and freelance journalists working on the cheap. Somali government troops first on the scene brought the wounded—there were scores of wounded and dead—to Medina Hospital. Government troops surrounded the warren of narrow twisting alleys of the nearby Dagmada Yaaqshid neighborhood, but as soon as they tried to move in, they were fired upon and forced to pull back. No way to avoid ambushes and heavy casualties in those cramped narrow streets. As the hospitals filled up, they began bringing some of the wounded to the makeshift hospital tent at the Badbaada refugee camp.

Sandrine was directing her cadre of helpers, a half-dozen Somali women refugees and one male, to make cots ready for the wounded when Ghedi pulled her outside. A boy she had never seen before, about Gheli's age, was standing there, hatless in the blazing sun.

"This is Labaan, *isuroon*," Ghedi said. "He has news."

"*Salaam aleikem*," Sandrine said to the boy, who didn't respond, only looked at her. She turned to Ghedi. "We have wounded coming. I don't have time."

The boy said something to Ghedi in Somali.

"Labaan say al Qaeda is coming. He says they want my sister back. He says we must run away now," Ghedi said.

"How soon?" she asked, squinting at the boy in the sun. Ghedi translated.

The boy showed her his arm and pants. There was blood on his sleeve and pants but no wound.

"*Achi*," Labaan said.

"His brother," Ghedi said. "They killed him. We must go now."

"The one in the House of Flowers? With the orange hair? He's dead?"

Ghedi nodded.

"What about the children, the little girls, in the house?"

Ghedi asked Labaan, who answered.

"He says al Qaeda will be here in ten minutes. He doesn't know about the girls, but he wants to come with us. He says they will kill him. Where do we go, *isuroon*?" Ghedi asked.

"The airport," she said. "Get Van Zyl and your sister. Bring everything you can carry, especially your papers, and meet me back here in one minute. Run!"

She ran to her tent, grabbed her passport, wallet and money, Médecins Pour le Monde paperwork and the papers she'd arranged for Ghedi, though she had nothing for his sister, and ran back to the hospital tent, her heart pounding. People were coming in, carrying wounded men, women, and children on doors, blankets, and other makeshift stretchers. Some were missing limbs; nearly all were bleeding and in various stages of shock. The tent began to fill, everyone shouting, the wounded groaning and a woman in a purple *direh* screaming. Ghedi, carrying a sack in one hand and holding his sister, Amina, with the other hand, rushed in, followed by Van Zyl and Labaan.

"I bloody warned you, didn't I?" Van Zyl said. He was going to say more but there was shouting outside, screams, and then at least twenty armed Somali men rushed in carrying a wounded Somali. Van Zyl started to step in front of Sandrine and one of the Somali men clubbed him to the ground with an M4 carbine. Another Somali, a tall bearded man with one eye milky-white, wearing a *ma'awis* and an *imaamad* shawl over his left shoulder, fired a burst from a submachine up into the air.

The tent fell silent, except for the groans of the wounded. The man with the white eye—cataract, she thought automatically—and the submachine gun looked at Sandrine. His face was hard, set. She tried to swallow and couldn't.

"You are the one they call 'doctor woman'?" he said in English.

"I'm Dr. Delange, yes," her throat so dry the words barely came.

"My brother," gesturing at the wounded man

they'd brought in with them and put on a cot. "The car bomb. You fix him."

She tried to take a deep breath and couldn't. She couldn't breathe or move. He stared at her with his good eye.

"What are you waiting for? You're a doctor. He's dying. Fix him!"

"Yes," she said, and ran over to the cot. The man on the cot was in his twenties. There was blood on his chest and sleeve and he was gasping for air. Bleeding, possible pneumothorax, she thought, rubbing her hands with Purell, because there was precious little running water, and pulling on latex gloves. One of her assistants, Nadifa, handed her shears and turned away. It was not fitting for a Somali woman to see a grown man undressed. The man with the white eye, who appeared to be the leader, and several more of his men crowded around as Sandrine began to cut off the wounded man's shirt.

"Have you come to kill us?" she asked.

"What are you talking about, doctor woman?" the leader said.

"Al Qaeda is coming to kill us."

"I *hooyadaa was* the mothers of al Qaeda," the leader growled. "Let them come. We'll see who kills who. Why do they want to kill you?"

She motioned with her head at Ghedi and Amina.

"I took the girl from the House of Flowers so she would not be a whore. She is still innocent."

"Give the girl back," the man said, making the twisting gesture with his hand that in Somalia meant no or get rid of it. "No one dies."

The man on the cot gasped, his breathing rapid,

shallow, fighting for air. She could see the wound in the chest. About three centimeters. A metal fragment had probably punctured the lung, blood bubbling pink out of the wound. The big gash in his arm was rhythmically spurting blood. An artery. She straightened up.

"Another minute or two, your brother will die. But I won't help him unless you help me first."

"Fix him now, doctor woman," the leader said, putting the muzzle of the submachine gun against her head. "Or I kill you and give the children and anyone else they want to al Qaeda."

"Kill me, your brother dies," she said, looking straight into his eyes, trying to keep a quaver out of her voice. "Kill me now or help me get the children away from al Qaeda, away from Mogadishu," her heart beating a mile a minute. She wondered if she was about to die.

"Where do you want to go?" he asked, glancing down at his brother.

"Kenya."

"You crazy, doctor woman? A thousand kilometers. Better I shoot you," aiming at her head. She closed her eyes and heard a wheezing strangling sound coming from the patient, who moved his arms, the blood spurting out in an arc.

"I mean it. I'll let him die," she said.

"What kind of doctor are you?" he demanded angrily, his finger tightening on the trigger.

"The only one you've got," she said, surprised she could get the words out.

He let the submachine gun hang down and scratched his beard.

"You crazy, doctor woman. But for a female, you're braver than most men. You save him, I'll get rid of al Qaeda and take you to Mombasa."

"The children too. All of them," she demanded.

"The children too," he made a face. "Even the girls."

She was already moving, giving orders to Nadifa, Ghedi, and Van Zyl, whom she told to get his bottle of vodka, since they had no boiling water or steam ready to sterilize instruments. The two most critical things to stabilize the patient were to deal with the pneumothorax so he could breathe and to stop the bleeding. She heard shooting outside the tent and looked at the man with the cataract, who was already herding his men outside, but from the sides, crawling under the tent flaps. Suddenly there were the sounds of explosions and a storm of firing. Inside the tent people screamed and nearly everyone hit the floor. Sandrine continued to work on the patient.

This is insane, she thought, working furiously and trying to ignore the bullets ripping holes in the sides of the tent. She wasn't a surgeon or an E.R. doctor. She had almost nothing to work with and the patient was showing early signs of hypoxia, the skin starting to tinge blue. In France she'd already have him on pure oxygen, be typing him for transfusion and preparing an occlusive dressing and intercostal chest drain.

She checked his vitals. Heartbeat erratic. Blood pressure too low. He's in trouble, she thought. And he needed fluids. Ghedi came with a couple of plastic sandwich bags and an IV. Nadifa brought adhesive tape, syringes, antibiotics, a surgical dressing, and a couple of hemostats. Van Zyl brought the vodka, which she had him pour into a bowl to use to sterilize the plastic bag and the hemostats. *Dieu*, she thought, feeling inside the chest wound for bleeding blood vessels. The wound wasn't bleeding too excessively, though the blood made it hard to see. She couldn't feel blood spurting; there was a chance no major blood vessel had been hit. The main thing was to seal the wound. The patient could survive on one lung, and with any luck, if no vessels were hit, the bleeding would coagulate on its own and the collapsed lung might partially reinflate.

She flushed the wound with saline, then put the plastic Baggie over it and taped it tightly on all sides to seal the wound, hopefully relieving the collapsed lung and minimizing infection. To make sure it was sealed, she secured the heavy dressing on top of it. Almost immediately the patient began to breathe more normally. She found the torn artery in the arm, put a hemostat on it, and started a saline IV in the other arm.

While she worked, the man with the cataract came back with a number of his men.

"He's breathing better," he said. "Will he live?"

"There's a good chance, but there's still a lot to do."

"You're not from Mogadishu, are you, mate?" Van Zyl said to him.

The man looked at Van Zyl and then at Sandrine. "Who is this?" he asked her.

"God knows," she said. "A South African. With the UN. Name's Van Zyl."

"I *khara* in the milk of the mothers of the UN,"

the man said. And to her: "I am Abdirahman Ali Abdullahi. From Puntland."

"What do you do?" she asked, working.

"I am commander," he said, grinning broadly.

"Of what?"

"The Puntland Coast Guard," Ali said.

Van Zyl leaned close and whispered in her ear.

"Coast Guard, my bum. He's a bloody pirate."

"What about al Qaeda?" she asked the pirate, Ali. At some point she would have to deal with infection. She needed a tissue culture and there was no lab. She had no way of knowing what kind of infection she might be dealing with and therefore no way to know which antibiotic to use. She only had two anyway: gentamicin and penicillin. The former would deal with most gram negative bacteria. Penicillin would handle staph and anaerobic bacteria, the more likely infections in this environment. She decided on penicillin, thinking it was as good as it was going to get.

"We chased them away." He grinned, showing yellowed, broken teeth and gums green from *qat*. "My men went to the House of Flowers, but it's better if we leave. They will be back."

"When?" she asked.

He looked at his watch, a Rolex, and she had a sudden absolute conviction it had been stolen.

"Now," he said.

An hour later they were driving in a convoy of Land Rovers to the Old Port, some of them mounted with big .50 caliber machine guns on the roofs, manned by men sitting there, scanning the streets. Ali had kept his word. The Land Rovers were crammed with the children from the

House of Flowers, Ali and his men, and as many of the wounded from the hospital tent as they could manage, bandaged arms and legs sticking out of the open windows.

"It's like the bloody Exodus from bloody Egypt," Van Zyl said.

They boarded a rusty small coastal merchant ship with motorized skiffs tied to its sides and stern. As they went up the gangplank, she noticed men carrying RPGs and machine guns and a small cannon mounted near the bow of the ship.

"Pirate mothership," Van Zyl muttered.

They might have been barefoot pirates, but they were efficient, she thought. Within minutes they cast off. She stood on the bridge with Ali and two of his men, Ghedi, Amina, and Van Zyl, watching the city recede as they headed out into the blue waters of the Indian Ocean.

"I'll go below. I need to take care of your brother," she told Ali. "Thank you."

He shoved a few *qat* leaves into his mouth and started chewing.

"Listen, doctor woman," moving the wad to his cheek, "maybe when we get to Mombasa, I sell the children. Sell you too. Mombasa is a good market for human traffic. Good prices."

"You won't," she said, heading toward the ladder, trying to balance against the sway of the ship.

"How do you know?" he said.

"Because Allah is watching," she said, pointing a finger at the sky. "You keep your word."

"She's a lioness, this one," Ali said to Van Zyl. "Maybe I take her for my fifth wife."

"You can't," she said, pausing on the ladder.

"Why not?"

"I'm already taken," she said, the thought of the American, Nick, suddenly flashing in her mind. She wondered where in the name of God he was and suddenly realized that what she had just said was true.

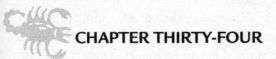

CHAPTER THIRTY-FOUR

Piranshahr,
Iran

"I think you broke my jaw," Ghanbari said, holding the reddened side of his face. They were sitting on the carpet facing each other, Scorpion holding the pistol on his thigh.

"No, but I might if I don't get the answers I want," Scorpion said.

"I don't understand," Ghanbari said, looking bewildered. "You told me yourself you killed Sadeghi. What's this about?"

"I didn't say Sadeghi. I said the Gardener."

Ghanbari's eyes narrowed.

"Sadeghi is the Gardener. You said so yourself."

"No, actually you did," Scorpion said. "You and Zahra."

"If you weren't sure he was the Gardener, why'd you kill him?" Ghanbari said, wincing as he spoke.

"Because I wasn't sure. But now I am."

"What are you saying?"

"Sadeghi wasn't the Gardener. But you already knew that, didn't you, Muhammad *jan*?"

"I have no idea what you're talking about. What are you saying?"

"*Bashe*," Scorpion exhaled. All right. "We'll do it by the numbers. You sent Zahra to Sadeghi."

"You wanted her to go too," Ghanbari said hotly. He was breathing hard, and although the temperature was a little cool, he was sweating. The air in the farmhouse was still, particles of dust visible in a shaft of sunlight from a window.

"Yes, but for different reasons. When we were on the run, you brought us to the safe house. You equipped me. You gave me the motorbike and the Nakhir rifle. You sent Zahra to him knowing he wouldn't trust a word she said. You wanted to get rid of Sadeghi and you used Zahra and me to do it for you. She flushed him out; I did the killing."

"And what did I get for it? Look at me! My life is ruined. I'm on the run. I'm probably going to die, and even if I don't, I'll be cut off from my family, my country. You've ruined me, you *madar ghahbeh*!"

"Or maybe not."

"What are you saying?"

"I'm saying, maybe your life isn't ruined after all."

"How can you say that? Look at me! Look at where we are!" Gesturing at the farmhouse. "We're being hunted like animals. They're looking for us everywhere."

"I doubt that, Muhammad *jan*. I think they know exactly where we are."

"Are you insane?" Staring at him, wide-eyed. "How could they know?"

"Because you told them."

"What? What are you saying?"

"*Bashe.*" Scorpion gestured. "Not you. Your cell phone. They've been GPS-tracking you all along. That was no ordinary roadblock on the road to Chalus. There must have been thirty Revolutionary Guards military vehicles. They knew we were coming."

"But you said yourself it was logical. The only road to Chalus and the Caspian coast," Ghanbari sputtered.

"I lied. A sea or air-sea operation is the most complex thing possible and requires full communications and setup; something they assumed we didn't have because they've got every piece of COMINT—communications intelligence—blanketed over the country, especially Tehran. Besides, there are easier ways to get out of Iran. Like I said, they knew we were coming."

"All right, so they figured out how to track my phone. How can you blame me?"

"No good. We bought the new cell phones together, remember? I programmed yours myself. You've had it less than twenty-four hours. There's no way they could've gotten the number to GPS-track unless you gave it to them."

Ghanbari straightened.

"I don't know what you're talking about," he said.

"Sure you do. Scale made a cell phone call from Begur, Spain, to you. Zahra thought she was helping you, her sister-in-law's brother, by deflecting the identity of the Gardener to Sadeghi, which was what you had planned all along because the rivalry between you two had gotten so intense only one of you could survive." Scorpion took a deep breath.

"You know, I think it's the hypocrisy that gets to me the most. All that moral outrage when I killed those two Basiji. But you," he said accusingly. "Knowing what Sadeghi would do, you sent her to her death without turning a hair, you *lashy* piece of shit."

The two men glared at each other in silence.

"What makes you say Sadeghi wasn't the Gardener?" Ghanbari said, never taking his eyes off Scorpion.

"Sherlock Holmes."

"What?"

"In one of the Sherlock Holmes stories, the key clue was a dog that didn't bark."

"A dog? What are you talking about?"

"The clue was that the dog didn't bark but should have. It's the negative; a thing that should have happened, but didn't. Sadeghi said a number of things. But what was curious was not what he knew, but what he didn't know."

"This is absurd," Ghanbari said, looking around as if for a way out.

"Don't even think about it," Scorpion said. "And hand me your cell phone. Carefully," aiming the pistol at Ghanbari's face. Ghanbari reached into his pocket and after a second's hesitation tossed his cell phone on the carpet in front of Scorpion. "Where were we?" Scorpion continued. "Right. The dog that didn't bark. Or in this case, the curious fact of *Scorpion*."

Ghanbari's eyes behind his glasses revealed nothing. Scorpion couldn't tell if he'd ever heard of Scorpion before.

"What's that?"

"You've never heard the term 'Scorpion,' *aqrab*, before?"

"I told you. I don't know what you're talking about," Ghanbari said, rubbing the side of his face where he'd been hit. It was turning red and beginning to swell on that side like the mumps.

"Just before he died, Sadeghi seemed to be suggesting that everything that happened, the attack on Bern, the crisis, everything, had to do with this Scorpion. You wouldn't know anything about that either, Muhammad *jan*?"

Ghanbari threw up his hands.

"I don't know anything about this 'Scorpion.' I think you're making it all up."

"But that's not the dog that didn't bark."

"Will you please either explain or shut up!" Ghanbari snapped.

"He didn't know what Scorpion looked like."

"Who? Sadeghi? Why should he?"

"Because the Gardener would have," Scorpion said, thinking he should have realized it at the time. The Olympic Torch software had changed it for everyone else, but the Gardener had seen the original Kilbane file photo from Bern. The real Gardener would have known that Laurent Westermann was Scorpion. But Sadeghi didn't.

"This is a total fantasy. You can't prove anything," Ghanbari said. He started to get up. "I'm leaving."

"I don't have to prove anything," Scorpion said, aiming. "And move another centimeter and I will shoot you."

Ghanbari sat back on his heels. "Maybe you're Scorpion," he said. "We already know you're CIA."

"Maybe I am," Scorpion said, a little tingle of electricity going through him at hearing it actually said. "In any case, this is all beside the point. Why do you suppose I left you alone and went for petrol on my own this morning?"

"So you could make your own arrangements on the escape," Ghanbari said.

Scorpion smiled. "True, but that's not why. It was to give you a chance to make a call without me being there."

For the first time Ghanbari looked disconcerted.

"You mean it was a trap?"

Scorpion stood up.

"I think we should have that *chai* now. We'll know very soon, one way or the other. If PJAK shows up, I'm delusional and I'll apologize to you and do everything I can to make it up to you. If the Kta'eb Hezbollah or the Revolutionary Guards show up, you're the Gardener."

Keeping the gun on Ghanbari, they made tea and sat down again on the carpet in the main room. He watched Ghanbari sip the tea, his hands trembling. While they waited, Scorpion decided that if it went bad, he wouldn't be taken alive. If necessary, he would use the gun on himself. He caught himself straining to hear sounds outside. From nearby, perhaps under the eaves of the roof, he heard the sound of a bird and thought about the bird in Laleh Park. Then the bird went silent. They waited.

He could hear Ghanbari breathe. The sound of his own heartbeat. Then there was a rumble. An undefined noise, far off, a sudden rush of sound.

The house began to tremble. The liquid in the

tea glasses rippled and danced. The glasses began to rattle and fell over, spilling on the carpet. The house started shaking as if in an earthquake. Then the unmistakable *whop-whop* of a helicopter over-head, then multiple helicopters and the house began to shake even more. Through the windows they could see military vehicles racing on the road toward them, one after the other, kicking up storms of dust. Outside the window they saw one helicopter, then two, landing in the fields. The minute they touched down, Revolutionary Guards in camouflage uniforms piled out and began running toward the farmhouse, assault rifles ready to fire. There was so much noise and dust it was getting hard to see outside the windows.

With his free hand Scorpion tossed the cell phone to Ghanbari.

"If you want to live another minute, call Scale," he shouted over the noise.

 **CHAPTER THIRTY-FIVE**

Haj Omran,
Iran

Scorpion hauled Ghanbari to his feet and over by the side of the front window as Revolutionary Guards deployed, weapons aimed. Keeping the pistol pressed against Ghanbari's head just behind his ear, Scorpion watched as Ghanbari called.

"*Salam.* This is Muhammad Ghanbari," he said, shouting over the noise, and listened for a second.

"Is it Scale?" Scorpion whispered in his ear.

Ghanbari nodded.

"Give me the phone," Scorpion said, pressing the muzzle of the ZOAF hard against Ghanbari's ear. "Scale?" he said in English into the phone.

"Scorpion?" he heard a not unpleasant voice on the phone say. Peering through the window, he tried to see if he could spot Scale, but there were too many men and vehicles and too much dust.

"This is Scorpion. I believe we met in Begur. I want you to hear something," Scorpion said, and fired.

The bullet exploded a gob of blood and matter

from Ghanbari's head, splattering the window and wall.

"Scale? That was Ghanbari. He's dead," Scorpion said into the phone.

"In a second, so will you be, you *madar sag*," Scale said.

"Oh no! Wait one second. Please. I'll call you right back," Scorpion said.

He peeked out the window one last time. A small man in camouflage BDUs, barely visible behind one of the vehicles, was holding a cell phone to his ear. It might be Scale, he thought. He had gambled everything that Scale's normal human curiosity would have him wait the extra second or two. If he was wrong, he would die. He dived to the floor next to Ghanbari's body. Using his own personal cell phone, he redialed Scale's cell phone number. Scale answered immediately.

"Scorpion?" Scale said. "I have something I want *you* to hear. *At—*" he started to shout, and Scorpion didn't have even enough time to complete the thought about what Scale was shouting. "*—esh*! Fire!"

The world exploded.

The ground shook, the walls of the farmhouse rattling and buckling in a hurricane of sound and force. There were multiple explosions coming one on top of another so hard and fast they were impossible to tell apart. An almost continuous roar, punctuated by the unearthly hum of vehicles and screams of men being obliterated by big 25mm depleted uranium rounds at a staggering thirty rounds a second. The explosions, some bigger every few seconds—those are the 105s, Scorpion thought—

and the explosions of smaller shells at a rate of two per second from the Bofors 40mm autocannon, went on for what seemed like an hour, but by Scorpion's watch lasted a little more than a minute. The firing was continuous and with pinpoint accuracy as the unseen U.S. Air Force gunship, too high and far away to be seen or heard, made its pylon turn so its weapons were kept precision-trained on the target.

He heard another massive explosion coming from the field behind the farmhouse. One of the helicopters blowing up, a rain of debris and shrapnel battering the farmhouse roof, a chunk of red hot metal tearing a jagged hole in the roof the size of a basketball and ripping through the floor less than a meter from Scorpion. There was a clatter as the second Revolutionary Guards helicopter tried to lift off. It got about ten meters into the air before exploding in a giant orange fireball that sent a wave of force and heat toward the farmhouse, washing over Scorpion on the floor. He crawled on the carpet to the other window, raised himself up and peeked out.

The AC-130U Spooky gunship had done its work from many miles away, and he couldn't believe what he was seeing. The force of some twenty-plus Revolutionary Guards military vehicles, trucks, and APCs, and more than a hundred armed men, were gone. All that was left were bits and pieces of smoking metal wreckage and parts of human bodies. There not only wasn't anyone left, there wasn't even a part of anything left, not even a portion of a human torso intact. The Air Force's big gunship had been so high and so far away—no doubt still over the border in Iraq when it first fired—that none of the men killed had ever seen or heard it before they died. Yet the combination of the GPS-located cell phone Scale was using, targeted by Scorpion's call, combined with the pinpoint accuracy of the Spooky's AN/APQ-180 radar, meant that the enemy had been completely obliterated without a single round hitting the farmhouse where he was hiding.

Scorpion's ears were ringing as he staggered out the farmhouse's back door and into the field, covered with the still burning debris from the two downed helicopters. He walked past one Revolutionary Guard who was somehow still alive, although the bottom half of his body was missing. The two men looked at each other, the Revolutionary Guard's eyes confused, and then Scorpion remembered he was in blackface and still wearing the floppy red costume of Haji Firuz. *Maybe he thinks he's hallucinating,* Scorpion thought, suddenly realizing his cell phone was ringing.

"Flagstaff," he said.

"Where are you?" Shaefer's voice shouting over the sound of something very loud; probably a helicopter rotor, Scorpion thought.

"I'm in the field behind the farmhouse on the side toward the mountains," he said.

"We'll be there in five."

"I won't be hard to spot. I'm wearing red," Scorpion said, walking past the smoldering rubble of the second Iranian helicopter, burning fragments starting small brush fires, and into the open fields.

A few minutes later he spotted the helicopter flying in from the direction of the Haj Omran border station. It was an Apache AH-64. He watched as it swooped down from the blue sky over the green slopes of the mountains. His cell phone rang again.

"Mendelssohn. We're dropping you a harness."

"The LZ's cold, Top. You can pick me up," Scorpion said.

"We want to stay high, in case any Bravo Golfs," Bad Guys, "are coming down the road," Shaefer said. He said something else but Scorpion couldn't hear it because the Apache was almost directly over him. He could feel the push of the rotor wind flattening the grass as they lowered a harness on a line. When the line reached him, he pulled it over, got into the harness, and snapped the buckles closed.

He signaled a thumbs-up to the crew and immediately felt himself being hoisted high into the air, the sound from the chopper growing louder, and, as he rose up, the wind pressing against him, he could see the spread of burning debris like a scorched wasteland around the farmhouse. Rising higher, the rest of the town and the surrounding countryside was spread out below, untouched all the way to the highway. He looked up and saw Shaefer in BDUs and a crewman in the open hatchway waiting to bring him in.

This is how the crisis ends, he thought. A successful JSOC mission that killed all the Bravo Golfs responsible for the attack on the embassy in Bern. Medals all around and the U.S. administration gets a political plus on their report card, looking macho without having to go to war.

They hauled him into the helicopter, the sound of the rotor and the wash of wind so loud, he could barely hear.

"You *are* wearing red," Shaefer said, shaking his head as they unhooked him and sat him down. "And blackface too." Scorpion was suddenly conscious of Shaefer being African-American. "What's that about?" Shaefer continued.

"I've been playing the fool," Scorpion said.

CHAPTER THIRTY-SIX

Galata Bridge,
Istanbul, Turkey

The three men met on the Galata Bridge shortly after midnight. Scorpion, in a leather jacket against the cool evening wind, came from the Beyoglu side. Lights from buildings and ships on both sides of the Golden Horn reflected on the dark water. He walked toward the other two men, leaning on the pedestrian rail near the middle of the bridge. A quartet of men in the shadows a hundred meters in either direction, Soames was one of them, secured the area and kept watch. There was little traffic on the bridge at this hour; just the occasional car or taxi. Scorpion came over and leaned on the rail next to Bob Harris.

"For the record, this meeting never happened," said Yuval, head of the Israeli Mossad. "No recordings, no notes, nothing. I will never tell anyone. Bob Harris and you, Scorpion, will not reveal anything no matter what. Not to the director of the CIA, the DCI, or the President of the United States. Not one of us will ever mention this again, not even among ourselves."

They looked out over the water and the city, landmarks like the mosques on the hills and the Galata Tower lit up at night. Scorpion could smell the roast kabobs from the restaurants below that crammed the bridge's lower deck and the apple-tobacco smoke from the *nargileh* cafés.

"Pretty," Harris said. "Can you imagine what it must have been like for some officer on some Roman, what-do-you-call-'em, quinqueremes, warship, a couple of thousand years ago? Byzantium. A major posting; at anchor in the Golden Horn. Probably thought he was in the big-time, on his way up."

"Or missing his wife or thinking it was a shit hole and the whores in Rome were prettier," Scorpion said.

"We Jews had our own share of troubles with the Romans," Yuval said, lighting a cigarette.

"You Jews have trouble with everyone. With you, it's never easy," Harris said.

"It's true. We argue even with God." Yuval looked at Scorpion. "So you know, we had somebody watching your Dr. Sandrine Delange. A South African Jew before he made *aliyah* to Israel. She knows him as Van Zyl, an official from UNHCR. She's in the refugee camp in Dadaab. Apparently she's acquired two Somali children, a boy and a girl, along the way. Anyway, she's safe."

"Good to know," Scorpion said, feeling something lift inside, a weight he didn't know he was carrying.

"The least we can do," Yuval said, exhaling a stream of smoke. He glanced at Harris next to him. "You could have told us what you were planning. An AC-130U Spooky gunship. Impressive."

"Why the hell should we tell you?"

"We're supposed to be allies."

"Never stopped us from stabbing each other in the back before," Harris said. "This is about the strike on the nuclear facilities and missile sites in Iran, right?"

Yuval smiled. "Ah, that. You know, I'm almost tempted to let you believe you're going to find out something you don't think we know you know." He flicked the ash from his cigarette, the tip glowing orange in the darkness. "No, this is something more . . ." He groped for the word. "What I'm about to tell you is the most critical, most highly classified secret in the state of Israel. I can't even begin to tell you how many rules and laws I'm violating, not to mention an oath I took on Masada when I was eighteen years old."

"I'm listening," Harris said. "And I've agreed to the terms, even though it might be breaking a few oaths of my own. As for Scorpion . . ." He gestured.

"In a curious way, we trust Scorpion," Yuval said. "He belongs to no one, certainly not to us, but what I'm about to tell, he needs to know. Also it's in his interest to keep this to himself."

"I know part of it," Scorpion said. "The other piece is why I'm here."

Harris looked at him curiously.

"Like what?"

"Just before I terminated Farzan Sadeghi of Kta'eb Hezbollah, he said something that stuck in my brain. He implied that the Bern attack was because of me. It made no sense. I'm not that important in the scheme of things."

"What were his exact words?" Yuval asked.

"He mentioned my code name. Scorpion. *Aqrab* in Farsi. The woman, Zahra, asked him why this Scorpion was so important, and he said, 'What do you think this is all about?'"

"Is that why you terminated him?" Harris asked.

Scorpion shook his head.

"There were only two possible candidates for the Gardener: Sadeghi and Ghanbari. The only way to be sure the Gardener was eliminated was to eliminate them both. Plus, he was about to kill Zahra." He turned to Yuval. "But that doesn't explain why they were after me in particular or why they attacked the embassy. That's why I'm here."

Yuval nodded. He took a drag from his cigarette and flipped it over the rail. They watched the glow of its burning tip as it fell down to the dark water. He leaned on his side to face them.

"He was the most extraordinary person I've ever met," he began. "You have to understand, I've—let's just say I've been around. I've known prime ministers, kings—eight U.S. Presidents—all kinds, mass murderers, some people who will live in history, but never anyone like him. And certainly never anyone who did what he did."

Harris looked irritably at his watch.

"Come on, Yuval," he said. "Skip the commercial. I'm impressed, all right? Who the hell is he?"

Yuval smiled. "You're such an ass, Bob. Aren't you the one who looked at the Golden Horn," gesturing vaguely at the lights on the Eminönü side of the bridge, "and talked about the Romans? What I'm talking about," he tapped the metal rail. "This is history. This is what's about to happen."

"All right." Harris frowned. "I'm listening."

"I first met him when he was seven years old. This was in the 1980s. Reagan was the U.S. President. The boy had come from Isfahan in Iran, where he had seen his parents murdered before his own eyes. His father had literally been torn apart by chains attached to trucks pulling in opposite directions. They made him watch. They raped his mother. Many times. They cut off her arms and legs, then poured gasoline over her and his little brother and set them on fire right in front of him. A child. Can you imagine?

"They sent him to the Iraqi front to die. He was about to be executed by a firing squad when an unknown Iranian woman helped him get away and some of the few Jews left in Iran smuggled him to Israel. We called him David.

"I was his trainer. His first and only case officer. In a way, he was my creation. You must understand," he said, biting his lip, and to Scorpion it seemed he was trying to defend himself to an invisible jury, "we don't train children. Ever. It was hard enough for him, dealing with what he had just gone through, being in a new country with a new language, customs, new everything, but it was his idea. He insisted.

"Do you understand?" Yuval said, his face in shadow, only the lights from the bridge reflected in his eyes. "He knew what he was going to do. He knew what his revenge would be. He had formulated it, all of it. At age seven!

"That first time we walked on Gordon Beach in Tel Aviv, just the two of us, me and this child walking on the sand, I told him it was impossible, and he told me, 'Today, Saddam Hussein is the Ayatollah's enemy. Tomorrow, they will come for all the Jews.' Seven years old—and this is how he talked!" he said, shaking his head.

"For two years I trained him. The Mossad became his school, his parents, his family. It wasn't like training a child. He was brilliant. More than brilliant. Imagine you were the music teacher of Mozart or Mendelssohn. Your pupil not just more brilliant than you, but someone born to it in a way that you couldn't even imagine. It didn't just come naturally to him, it was as if compared to him you were a caveman, banging one stone against another. Mozart. Even while we trained and prepared, I tried to talk him out of it, not only because he was a child, but because what he was going to do, no one had ever done before."

"He was a mole?" Harris said.

"More than a mole. Much more," Yuval said.

"What more?"

"A weapon," Yuval said. "But not for us. Not for Israel." He looked at them. "For his parents. His life, his entire life, would be an act of revenge. Can you imagine what it must have been like to live your entire life as a lie? On guard every second of every day; even when he slept. Never dropping your guard for an instant. Never trusting a single human being, ever. Becoming with every fiber of his being the very thing he hated and despised most in the entire world. He would marry, have children, and none of them would ever know for a second who or what he really was, that what they thought was love was actually hate. All for a single purpose. Can you imagine? The psychic cost," he said, shaking his head. "In the end, he would pay."

"How'd you infiltrate him?" Scorpion asked. "Must have been something."

"You have no idea. We had to create the most bulletproof cover ever created for any agent. We had to create perfect forged records in dozens of places and destroy others in a way so natural that no one would ever suspect; all in a country where a single mistake was death.

"He was an orphan from parents who were *shahidan*—martyrs of the Iranian Revolution. It took an entire year and cost the life of one of our top agents in Iran to make sure there wasn't a single record, a single shred of evidence or a single human being anywhere, who could refute or even suspect that this child was not exactly who he was supposed to be.

"This was during the First Intifada of the Palestinians, when all our resources were strained. No one, not one single person in the government or the cabinet, knew anything about this operation except me and the prime minister. At the time, it was Yitzhak Shamir. In a way, out of all the prime ministers of Israel, it could have only been Shamir who would have approved such an operation. His entire family was wiped out in the Holocaust. Shamir himself once told me that when his father, who was in Poland, was facing execution, he said, 'I will die. But I have a son in the land of Israel; he will take my revenge.'

"And he did. In 1948, during the War of Independence, Shamir was in Lehi. The most extreme of the radical groups. The British considered him the most dangerous terrorist in Palestine. Shamir never met the boy, David. But I always thought that in a way, he understood him better than anyone.

"Mostly I remember the boy, David's last day in Israel, before we infiltrated him back into Iran. We walked on the beach. It was late afternoon; the sun casting long shadows. Young men with their rackets playing *matkot* on the sand, girls in bikinis, mothers with children in the playgrounds, some of the children not much younger than he was. Everyone watchful because of the Intifada. Can you see how insane it was? I felt like a father to him. I think he knew how I felt, but I don't think it mattered to him. We were using him—and he was using us. And he knew it.

"'Even now, I can stop it. You can have a life, David,' I told him. 'You don't have to do this.'

"'Yes, I do.' That was all he said."

Yuval stopped and lit another cigarette, cupping the match flame against a faint breeze coming from the Bosphorus.

"From the beginning," he continued, "he was positioned to be a leader in the Revolutionary Guards. The cover was critical. An orphan child, the only survivor of an Iranian *shahid* and his wife, martyrs of the Revolution. He distinguished himself in the *madrasa*. By age twelve he knew the Quran by heart, and by fourteen he could quote chapter and verse of the Shiite *hadith*, al-Kulayni, al-Qummi, all that. Even among the most extreme, the most radical of the Revolutionary Guards candidates, he was extreme."

"The perfect Jesuit," Harris murmured.

"The perfect spy," Scorpion said.

"By the time he graduated with top grades from Tehran University, he was already a rising star," Yuval continued. "And of course, he married well. The daughter of a very powerful man within the Supreme Leader's inner circle. "

"The intel he gave was good?" Harris asked.

"Beyond good," Yuval said. "Essential—and pure platinum."

Harris frowned. "You could've shared the wealth."

"Once in a while we did. Including the most precise data about the Iranian nuclear and missile programs. You didn't always believe us."

"That's the trouble with our profession—we're a distrustful lot." Harris grimaced, pulling up the collar of his suit jacket against the wind.

"There's distrustful and there's politics," Yuval said. "The uranium enrichment memo, from Fordow. 89.5 kilos at ninety-two percent purity. The smoking gun. Proof positive the Iranians were close to a bomb. You did nothing."

Harris turned on Yuval.

"We *did* put it in the President's Daily Brief. But we had to mark it 'Unconfirmed.' What choice did we have?" he snapped. "You wouldn't reveal the source."

"How could we without blowing Absalom—that was his internal Mossad code name—the most important asset we ever had? So the President and his National Security team assumed it was just us pressuring America to act against Iran." Yuval sighed. "On such stupidities, wars are lost."

Harris turned to Yuval. "You asked us to contact Scorpion for you a while back. Was that why?"

Yuval nodded. "For us, that's when the crisis really intensified. Four months ago Absalom suddenly went silent. First weeks, then months went by—and nothing. We had no word from him. And no way of getting in touch with him either. His identity had been buried deep inside Iran's inner circle. Here he was, Israel's most essential asset, the key to Iran, and all we had was silence. For all we knew, he was dead, or blown, or worse. We had no idea."

"You panicked?" Scorpion put in.

"Worse than panicked. We started to secretly prepare for full-scale war. Only war with our eyes blindfolded and our hands tied behind our back. At that point, without Absalom, we believed the very existence of Israel, of the Jewish people, was at stake. That's when we contacted Rabinowich to try to recruit you," he said to Scorpion.

"Did you ever hear from him?" Harris asked.

"In a way," Yuval said, ducking his head into his shoulders as if about to receive a blow. "This is the hard part. This is why we had to meet here, the three of us, in person."

"Jesus Christ!" Scorpion said. Suddenly all the pieces came together. He looked out at the city and the water; a single ferry, a row of windows lit along its side, was plying its way along the Beyoglu shore. The world was suddenly different. "Bern. It was a message," he said, and looked at Yuval. "You miserable son of a bitch. You bastard!"

Yuval exhaled a thin stream of smoke and looked away.

"No," he said. "It wasn't us. On my grandchildren's lives, it wasn't us. It was him. Absalom. What he had become. What we made him." He stared out over the rail. "What I made him."

"Son of a bitch," Harris growled. "So Absalom aka the Gardener aka Ghanbari orders the hit on the embassy in Bern to send us a message. Why couldn't he use an e-mail or a dead drop or whatever the fuck other mechanism you guys had set up? Why did people have to die? What was he trying to say?"

"Because the message wasn't for the Israelis," Scorpion put in. "He wanted to force America's hand."

"Meaning what?" Harris demanded.

"The Iranians crossed the line," Scorpion said. "They have a nuclear bomb and they were going to use it. Probably give it to Kta'eb Hezbollah."

"He did it to force the United States to stop them?" Harris asked.

"No," Yuval said, shaking his head. "He did it because he wanted the United States to attack. To bring them down. Samson in the temple."

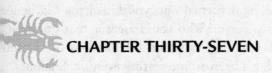

CHAPTER THIRTY-SEVEN

esilköy,
tanbul, Turkey

"**W**hat will the President do?" Yuval asked Harris.

"Nothing." Harris shrugged. "Take credit for omething they didn't do. It's what Washington's est at."

Yuval grimaced. "You leave us no choice."

"No. Given your history, Jewish history, probably ot," Harris said, turning his collar back down and etting ready to go. "I'm sorry. This kind of thing above my pay grade. Yours too, probably. Are we one?"

"Just one thing," Scorpion said. "After Bern, the ardener focused on me. They found me in Paris— nd I'm not that easy to spot—which means they used ton of manpower just on me. Sadeghi used my code ame, Scorpion, and told Zahra it was all about me. o I need to know, what was that about? Why me?"

Yuval shrugged. "I don't know. It's a mystery."

He's lying, Scorpion thought. Holding some- ing back. But what? He turned to Harris.

"Bob?" he asked.

"Unfortunately, or actually fortunately for everyone, as it turned out, you killed the Gardener the only person who could answer that question," Harris said. He extended his hand to the Israeli "Yuval, it's been an interesting evening. Shalom."

The two men shook hands.

"Shalom," Yuval said. His eyes searched Harris's face. "You'll discuss just the part about the nuclear bomb with the President? Nothing about Absalom."

"I will, but I'll have to tell him it's just a surmise We don't have definitive proof. Scorpion terminated the proof," Harris said. He turned to Scorpion "Give you a lift to the airport?"

"No thanks," Scorpion said.

Harris paused. "That wasn't a request."

"Yes it was, because I'm not coming," Scorpion said. And to Yuval: "Thanks for this," gesturing vaguely. "I needed to know."

Yuval stepped on his cigarette butt and nodded.

"I'm told she's very beautiful, your Dr. Delange Good luck." He turned and started to walk away Two men, Mossad agents with Yuval, detached themselves from the shadows.

"To a hundred and twenty," Scorpion called afte him. Yuval raised his hand to show he heard. Scorpion turned and started back toward the Beyoglu side. Harris put a hand on his arm, and Scorpion stopped and looked at him. Harris let his hand drop

"You can't let this go. It's urgent," Harris said. " have a car."

"Do you?"

"We have to talk," Harris said, signaling Soame and another agent.

Before they got to the end of the bridge, a black
adillac sedan pulled over and stopped. Scorpion
nd Harris climbed into the backseat. Soames
arted to get into the front passenger seat.

"If he gets in, I get out," Scorpion said.

"Why?" Soames said. "What did I do?"

"I don't like you. Also, the grown-ups are going
• talk about things the children shouldn't hear,"
corpion said. "As a matter of fact, nobody likes
ou."

"You're a prima donna, you know that? That's
hat everyone says. A goddamn prima donna,"
oames said.

"Were the Gnomes prima donnas too?" Scorpion
id quietly, his hand on the door handle.

"Get in the other car," Harris said to Soames,
ho darted one last venomous look at Scorpion and
ot out. He walked back and got into a second black
dan, a Mercedes, that had stopped behind the Ca-
llac. Harris motioned to his Turkish driver and
ey drove off.

"He's right," Harris said. "You are a prima donna.
nfortunately, a very necessary one."

"Where are we going?" Scorpion asked.

"Ekrem?" Harris said to the driver.

"The E-5 to the airport, sir," the driver, Ekrem,
id.

They drove past the so-called New Mosque,
uilt in the 1600s, and into the Old City. Scorpion
ecked the side mirror; the Mercedes was behind
em.

"That was quite a story," Harris said.

"Yes it was," Scorpion said, thinking about the

code name Absalom and the Bible story. King David, *O Absalom, my son, my son*. Was it guilt? Was that why Yuval told them? Or was it just that the American relationship was the oxygen that Israel needed in order to live, and Yuval was afraid that if it ever came out that would be the end of it? He turned to Harris.

"This better be important," he said.

"I need to show you something," Harris said, taking out his iPhone. He tapped it a couple of times and held it up for Scorpion to see.

It was a video from an airport security camera. People walking or sitting near a gate waiting for a flight. At first he couldn't tell which airport it was. Then he understood. He watched himself walk over and sit down next to a man. Now he knew which airport and when. Fiumicino, Rome. About seven weeks ago. Before he had gone to Africa. Before he met Sandrine and any of this had happened.

"All right, it's me," Scorpion said, handing the iPhone back.

"The man is Ahmad Harandi—or at least that was his cover name—the Mossad agent killed in Hamburg."

"What about him?"

"You want to tell me about it?"

"Not really."

"Don't fuck with me, Scorpion," Harris snapped. "Not on this. How long have you been working with the Israelis?"

"Never."

"So what is this?" holding up the iPhone. "Seven weeks ago. Before this all started."

"That was Harandi aka Avi Benayoun trying to recruit me in Rome. For the record, I turned him down. Just like I turned down your pet monkey, Soames, in Nairobi. And for the same reason. I was done with it. Finished. I wanted out."

Harris shook his head.

"I don't believe you. Why do I get the feeling that this was some giant chess game between you and the Gardener, and the rest of us only pawns? There's something you're holding back. With every fiber of experience after way too many years in this business, I'm sure of it. If you're lying, you better tell me now. You don't want the CIA for an enemy."

"Works both ways, Bob old buddy," Scorpion said quietly.

They didn't speak. They were driving on Ataturk Boulevard and passed under one of the towering arches of the ancient Roman aqueduct that spanned the road, lit up at night. You couldn't look anywhere in this city without being reminded of how old it was, he thought.

"Deception isn't always the best policy . . ." Harris began.

"Funny, I thought it was our stock in trade," Scorpion said. "Anything else?"

"This Frenchwoman, Sandrine Delange. She'll have to be vetted."

"No one comes within a million miles of her. If she so much as chips a fingernail in her own bathroom, I'm going to hold you personally responsible. I mean it."

"I know," Harris said softly. "I can see it. Love."

He made a face. "To feel that way. Did you mean what you said about quitting?"

"Depends on her. I tried to quit and found out it's not so simple. I endanger the very people I care about. We'll see," Scorpion said. "You owe me money."

Harris nodded. They were on the E-5 motorway. Scorpion saw a sign ahead for Ataturk International Airport, Yesilköy.

"You'll get it—plus your bonus. We've gone from egg on our face after Bern to heroes, in no small part thanks to you. The White House has asked for time from all the networks. The President will announce that the perpetrators of the Bern massacre, including the man behind the attack, the 'Gardener,' have been killed in a joint CIA-JSOC-Air Force operation. They'll be busy pinning medals on each other for months. I have a request from the President. He wants you to come to the Oval Office. He wants to thank you in person."

"Negative," Scorpion said. "Besides, it'll blow my cover."

"We'll keep it secure. Scouts' honor," Harris said holding up three fingers.

"Right. Because nobody in Washington ever leaked anything. Tell him no thanks."

"I can't. It's the President. What'll I say?"

"Tell him I have a previous engagement," Scorpion said.

CHAPTER THIRTY-EIGHT

ngita Sabora,
erengeti, Tanzania

hey had dinner under an acacia tree near their
r-conditioned tent, the table set with white linen,
ne crystal and china, and good French wine. Their
eward, Godfrey, and his assistant, Samwel, had
ung the tree with lanterns, and it was magical,
e lights seeming to float in the darkness over the
erengeti Plain. A zebra grazed nearby, and while
ey were eating, a baby elephant came within a
ozen feet of the table, studying them curiously till
s mother, a large female, nudged it away with her
unk.

"They say they're as intelligent as we are," San-
rine said. She was wearing a sky-blue cocktail
ress, and he thought he had never seen anything so
eautiful in his life.

"I don't know about as intelligent. Certainly
etter, kinder than we are," Scorpion said.

Afterward, Godfrey brought them Spring-
ank scotch on the rocks as they sat on the raised
ooden deck in front of their tent, looking out at

the Serengeti under a sky filled with stars. From th
lounge tent came music from an old hand-woun
gramophone—all the furnishings were African Co
lonial, antiques dating from the turn of the century
it was as if they had stepped into another time—
someone playing songs from the 1920s, like th
Charleston and "Yes Sir, that's My Baby" and "I
Had to Be You." Zebras and wildebeests wandere
by and then scampered off, and they saw why, spo
ting the female leopard that came by every nigh
at that time, eyes glowing like yellow disks in th
darkness.

They made love in the big four-poster bed in th
tent, open to the night except for the mosquito ne
ting. They took their time, slow and soft and swee
and strong, exploring every part of each other. Le
ting it grow and grow until he couldn't tell where h
left off and she began, only a single intensity, fillin
to bursting through them, and as she cried out, pa
of it was the low rumbling roar of a lion.

They slept, and in the middle of the night sh
reached for him and they started again. They wer
like addicts, unable to get enough of each other unt
finally, sometime near dawn, they slept again. Th
sun came up over the horizon, and Godfrey brough
them coffee and breakfast on their deck, and the
sat and ate, never taking their eyes off each othe
except to breathe in the gold and green grasses an
the herds on the Serengeti and to laugh at a giraff
lowering himself splayed-footed to graze on th
grass next to the tennis court.

"*Dieu*, I love Africa," she said.

"So do I," he said.

She bit her lip.

"I'm almost afraid to say it. I don't want to break the spell," she said.

"I know."

"What do we do about the children?" she asked. Ghedi and Amina. She wanted to take them back to Paris to live, despite the massive bureaucratic mess it would entail with the Kenyan, Somali, and French governments. They also talked about bringing them to America.

"Are you sure it's the right thing?" Scorpion said. "To turn them into little French people or little Americans. They have their own culture, their own language, their own world. Not necessarily inferior to ours, just different. They have to have a say in their lives too. I told Ghedi that."

"What did he say?"

Scorpion smiled. "He said his sister was too little to understand such a big thing. I told him he would have to be the man and decide. He said, 'I will,' and showed me his *belawa* knife."

"I know," she smiled. "He's ready to kill anyone who touches me."

"I know how he feels," he said.

"You think they should stay in Africa? They'll never have opportunities like we could give them in France."

"They're African. Let's not pretend the other kids in *collège* will accept them like French kids or that they'll be able to get into one of the *grande écoles*. America is more accepting."

"And you, Nick. What do you want?"

"Whatever part of you you'll let me have."

"Do I have that much power?"

"Look!" he said, standing up and pointing at a herd of wildebeests, thousands of them, crossing the plain in the distance; a lioness prowled on the edge of the herd. Godfrey and Samwel brought them binoculars and they watched for a while.

"It's like the Garden of Eden," she said, reaching her arm around him and pulling him close. She whispered: "And what about the people who tried to kill us? Is that over?"

"For now," he said.

Later, after a day with the two of them on horseback, tracking the herds, the zebras, wildebeests, elands, giraffes, and elephants, they took turns in the thatched outdoor shower and he thought about the conversation he'd had with Dave Rabinowich during a middle-of-the-night layover in Doha, Qatar, on the flight from Istanbul to Nairobi. He was using a new SME PED Harris had given him, sitting in the airport, nearly empty at that hour, well away from the few Arabs in white *thawbs* and keffiyehs and bleary-eyed Western businessmen in traveling clothes, so as not to be overheard.

"Hawkeye," Scorpion said. The Avenger character was the latest Flagstaff code word.

"Albuquerque. I'm having dinner. The Knicks are on," Rabinowich complained, using the new countersign.

"Like interrupting frozen dinner is a hardship. You know why I'm calling?"

"I was wondering when you'd knock on my door. There's a loose end. Knowing you, you can't let it go, can you?"

"You shouldn't be so clever. They'll demote you."

"No chance. They're too busy patting each other's backs about how brilliant they all were on Iran. You figure it out yet?"

"Partly. You won't pass this on."

"And upset everyone's apple cart, especially after POTUS went on national TV acting like John Wayne? Uh-uh. I plan to collect my pension."

"I'm the loose end. First the way they came after me in Paris. Then Sadeghi's comment to Zahra that the whole thing was about me. What was so important about me?"

"Come on. You know why. You're just fishing for confirmation," Rabinowich said, sounding like he was talking while eating.

"You shouldn't talk with your mouth full. You might choke."

"Wouldn't give Harris and Soames the satisfaction. Come on, give," Rabinowich said, with a strange grunt that was his version of a laugh.

"First they nailed Harandi in Hamburg. Then Paris, coming after me with a ton of resource. Harandi had given me a key lead in the Palestinian business. It all ties back to Bassam Hassani, the Palestinian in Rome, which was ultimately an Iranian operation. Correction, the Gardener's operation."

"Finally! Somebody besides me knows how to actually use a few brain cells," Rabinowich said. "Keep going."

"A power struggle over control of the Revolutionary Guards."

"Exactly. You eliminate Sadeghi and Ghanbari and who wins?"

"Beikzadeh. Now he's head of both the Expediency Council and the Revolutionary Guards."

"So now he owns the brain *and* the muscle. Makes him the most powerful man in the country; more powerful even than the Supreme Leader," Rabinowich said.

"Now comes the loose end," Scorpion said. "Sadeghi didn't know who I was when he saw my photo. Meanwhile, Ghanbari set up Zahra instead of me till he tried to have Scale take me out at the end. What does that tell you?"

"You're warm. Hot even. You know, you might actually make it as an intelligence analyst here in McLean."

"Can't stand the CIA cafeteria food."

"Come on, say it. Nobody here but us girls," Rabinowich said.

"What if neither of them was the real Gardener? What if he's still alive?"

"Indeed. What if? Think about it," Rabinowich said. "The beauty of it. The sheer symmetry. The Gardener provokes an action that forces you out from wherever you're hiding and into the game. If he takes you out, he eliminates the key person who spiked the Palestinian op and killed one of his key operatives. He's a hero and he's eliminated a big threat. If he doesn't take you out, he's set it up so you eliminate not just one, but both his rivals for him, which he then uses to justify him taking over. No matter what happens, he wins. It's so elegant. Like a perfect equation."

Mozart, Scorpion thought. That's what Yuval called him. Mozart. They'd all been doing arithmetic; he'd been doing calculus.

"So—and this is purely hypothetical . . ."

"Totally."

"Just a wild-ass theory, mind you; the question is, who's the Gardener?"

"Think about it," Rabinowich said. "Who wins?"

"Beikzadeh."

"Head of the class, pal. Gold star."

Except Rabinowich was wrong, Scorpion thought. Beikzadeh wasn't the Gardener. Wrong age. Beikzadeh, the man he'd seen on TV, was in his fifties. Based on what Yuval had told them, Absalom would have to be in his late thirties, early forties.

"So what do you think? Is he still after me?"

"Doubt it," Rabinowich said. "Everybody in the Pickle Factory thinks the Gardener is dead. This totally theoretical person we're talking about loves that. But if you get hit, especially given that I'm around, suddenly everyone on Planet CIA knows he's alive. Why risk it? Besides, they've got their hands full with the Israelis who might attack any second. Can I go back to my dinner now?"

"One more thing. Who's Beikzadeh's hatchet man? Who does his shovel work? I need a name. Somebody connected with him." Whoever ran Beikzadeh's dirty work was the real Gardener, Scorpion thought. Someone, like Absalom, in his thirties.

"Give me some time. Whoever it is, is really buried."

"Come on, Dave. Give me something. A wild-ass guess, anything."

There was a moment of silence. Scorpion could hear the sound of a basketball game on TV in the background over the phone.

"There was this one thing I came across a few years ago," Rabinowich said. "A wedding announcement in Fars, the Iranian news agency. Something about Beikzadeh's daughter getting married."

That's it, Scorpion thought. What was it Yuval had said about Absalom? "Of course, he married well. The daughter of a very powerful man within the Supreme Leader's inner circle."

"The article mentioned something about him working in one of Beikzadeh's departments. Now I remember. It was odd."

"Why?"

"Because there was no other mention of him anywhere. Not even university. Nothing. It's as if he never existed except to marry Beikzadeh's daughter."

"What was his name?" Scorpion asked, excitement building. It was the Gardener. That was exactly how he'd do it.

"That was even odder," Rabinowich said. "They didn't say. Can you imagine writing an article about a prominent wedding and not mentioning the name of the groom?"

"They must have said something. Anything. What department was he in?"

"Let me think," Rabinowich muttered. "It was years ago."

Come on, Scorpion thought. Rabinowich was stalling. A genius with a near photographic memory, Rabinowich was taking his time because he hadn't decided whether to tell him.

"Ministry of Islamic Guidance," Rabinowich said finally. "I think that was it. Shit!"

"What's the matter?"

"Soames, on the other line."

"Tell him your poem," Scorpion said, and ended he call.

That night, after dinner, they made love on the our-poster bed. Afterward, she lay with her head on he pillow, looking out at the night.

"How does this work?" she said.

"I don't know. If you had any sense, you should un as fast and as far as you can in the opposite di-ection."

She raised herself on an arm to look at him, her yes reflecting the light from the half-moon risen ver the plain.

"Is that what you want?"

He pulled her close, inhaling the smell of her, the eel of her.

"What do you think?" he whispered.

"Hypothetically, where would we live? What vould we do?" she asked.

"Whatever you want. I have a house on the Costa meralda in Sardinia. A sailing ketch. We could go here. We could stay in Africa, America, Paris," he aid. He'd already told her everything. His real name, Nick Curry. That he was born in Santa Monica, California, and his father took him to Saudi Arabia s a child after his mother died and then his father vas killed and his strange childhood, raised by the Bedouin in the desert. All of it. Tehran University, he Sorbonne, Harvard. U.S. Special Forces, JSOC, he CIA, and how he left and became an indepen-ent agent. Whatever she wanted to know.

"And from time to time, you go away and kill eople. I don't know if I can live with that," she said, raising her head and looking at him with those luminous eyes.

"Except if I didn't, many innocent people—sometimes thousands, tens of thousands, millions even—will die. What's the moral calculus on that?"

He got up and walked out onto the deck in his jockey shorts. A zebra yawned and trotted away, and the sky was so bright with the moon and stars he thought he could almost read by it. Godfrey had left out clean glasses, the bottle of Springbank scotch, Evian water, and an ice bucket on the off chance they'd want a late nightcap. He poured himself a drink and took a sip. In the distance, he heard the sound of an elephant's trumpeting.

There was something else, he thought. Because Harris was right. He'd lied about his meeting with Harandi in Rome before any of this had happened. He had deceived them. Yes, he'd turned the Israelis down about Absalom, but before they parted, Harandi had said to him, "Promise me. If anything happens to me, you'll go to Iran." He'd promised because in his world, until Sandrine, it was the only thing he had to hang onto. When you lose someone, you can't just let it go. Things have to be made right. Oddly, he sensed he shared that with his enemy. Absalom. The Gardener. The man who had run the Palestinian. The man behind the embassy attack in Bern.

He wondered if the Israelis had attacked Iran. He and Sandrine had avoided cell phones, the Internet, anything to do with the outside world. Oddly enough, at that moment he didn't want to know.

He felt her come up beside him, her lithe body

naked under a sheer nightgown. It was all he could do not to grab her as tightly as he could. Instead, he handed her the glass and she drank.

"Where'd you go just now?" she asked.

"Just a drink," he said.

"No. I mean in your mind."

He didn't answer.

"It isn't simple, is it?" she said.

"No, it isn't."

"It's beautiful," she said, gazing out at the acacia tree and the endless African plain under the moon and the stars. She slipped her arm around him and leaned against him. "What are we going to do?"

"We'll think of something," he said.

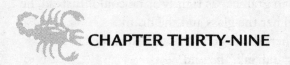

CHAPTER THIRTY-NINE

Baharestan Square,
Tehran, Iran

It was late, well past midnight. He got up from his desk in his office on the secure third floor of the Ministry of Islamic Guidance and went over to the window. His was the only window still lit in any of the office buildings around Baharestan Square. He looked down at the grassy oval and trees under the street lamps, nearly empty of traffic at this hour. It looked lonely, deserted. It was hard to believe that massive public demonstrations in this square had threatened to topple the regime. His role in the brutal suppression and elimination of the opposition leadership during the demonstrations had been key in advancing his position with both Expediency Council chairman Beikzadeh and the Supreme Leader. Of course, that was before he married the chairman's daughter, Afareen, thereby cementing his position in the leadership's inner circle.

He went over the voice mail from Colonel Jamshid Moharami, the commandant of Evin Prison, confirming that the witnesses were being held in

omplete isolation in the sealed-off section of the
rison reserved for special activities. A farmer, his
ife, and another villager from Piranshahr. Kurds,
f course. They each independently confirmed that
ney had seen a foreign helicopter over the site of
ne battle where the Revolutionary Guards force
ad been wiped out and that a man dressed like Haji
iruz was raised by a rescue line into the helicopter.

Scorpion, he thought.

The Americans had found a way out of the crisis
ithout having to go to war. At first, after learning
om the Bern CIA files that it was Scorpion who
rminated his protégé, Bassam Hassani, the Pal-
stinian, the best recruit he'd ever trained, in the
ome operation, he wanted to eliminate him. But
hen Scorpion survived in Paris and again on the
osta Brava, it confirmed how good the American
eally was and gave him a better idea. He used Spain
lure Scorpion to Tehran, where those fools, Sa-
eghi and Ghanbari, might think they had the ad-
antage of the Swiss, Westermann, on their home
rrain, never imagining who they were dealing
ith.

Especially Ghanbari, who had been quietly inves-
gating around Mashhad, going into his—Qassen
fari's—childhood school records. That's why he
ad cut off communication with the Mossad; with
hanbari sniffing around, it was getting too danger-
us. But with Scorpion, he had managed to get rid
f both Ghanbari and Sadeghi, his only other rival,
ithout any possibility of suspicion falling on him.

It was just a matter of cleaning up loose ends.

He went back to his desk and picked up the hard

copy Scorpion file. It had the original photograph
of Scorpion as Michael Kilbane from the CIA file in
Bern, then the phony photograph in all the Iranian
computer files, MOIS, VEVAK, al Quds, border
security, that had been modified by some virus
software—no doubt from the Americans or the
Israelis—that made Kilbane's face unrecognizable,
and the visa photograph of the Swiss businessman
Laurent Westermann, which clearly matched the
original Kilbane photograph.

He studied the Kilbane and Westermann photographs. In a way, they were alike, this Scorpion and
him. They were like World War One flying aces,
enemies who tried to kill each other but who would
afterwards salute, one airman to another, in their
open cockpits.

Scorpion had stopped the American war, for the
moment. *Barikallah!* Bravo! Even better, thanks to
Scorpion, the CIA now believed that he, the Gardener, was dead. Perhaps we'll meet again someday,
he thought, getting up and putting the file in his
high security office safe, with multiple locks and
fingerprint recognition pad, hidden in the floor beneath his desk.

He went back to his computer and sent a Highest Expediency Level Secret e-mail to Shahab
Dejagadeh, head of his IT special attack team, to
permanently delete all the files and photographs of
Kilbane and Westermann from all Iranian databases
and computer networks. It would leave his hardcopy
photographs as the only recognizable image of Scorpion. When he was done, the Gardener picked up
his secure phone and called Moharami at the prison

"Have the villagers confessed?" he asked.

"To what, *baradar*? We only questioned them about the helicopter and the Swiss," Moharami said.

"They're Kurdish spies. Members of PJAK," the Gardener said.

Moharami didn't hesitate for a second.

"Of course, *baradar*. Give us a day or two. We'll get them to confess to everything."

"You have twenty-four hours. Then execute them. No public announcement. Nothing. I want their confessions on my desk by noon tomorrow."

"It's not much time, *baradar*," Moharami said. The Gardener could sense his hesitation. "They're simple villagers."

"Do you have any idea who this is coming from, Jamshid *jan*?" the Gardener said quietly, suggesting the orders came from the Supreme Leader himself. "This is a matter of state security in a time of national crisis. They are spies."

"Of course, *baradar*," Moharami said.

"*Ta farda.*" Till tomorrow, the Gardener said, and ended the call.

He leaned back in his chair. For the moment, his position was unassailable. As for those Pasdaran who had killed his parents and brother, he had arranged their deaths years earlier, making sure he was there in person to watch every second of their execution.

To complete his revenge would take more waiting. That's all right, he thought. He was good at it.

ACKNOWLEDGMENTS

My sincerest thanks to Dr. Luciano Del Guzzo of New York for reviewing the medical descriptions in his book. My thanks are also due to Andrew Peerson, author of *First to Kill* and a nationally recognized championship shooter and holder of the classification of Master in the NRA's High Power Rifle ranking system, for his invaluable feedback on the sniper sequence. As always, my first reviewers, my wife, Anne, my son, Justin, my agent, Dominick Abel, and my editor at HarperCollins, David Highfill, provided feedback that helped make this book better. The convention regarding errors is in this case absolutely true. Any errors that might have somehow slipped through, despite best efforts, are mine alone.